A
Garland Series

VICTORIAN
FICTION

NOVELS OF FAITH
AND DOUBT

A collection of 121 novels
in 92 volumes, selected by
Professor Robert Lee Wolff,
Harvard University,
with a separate introductory volume
written by him
especially for this series.

THE NEW
ABELARD

Robert Buchanan

Three volumes in one

Garland Publishing, Inc., New York & London

1976

———

Bibliographical note:

Vol. I. is a facsimile of a copy at the
British Museum (12636.n.10)
Vols. 2 and 3 are facsimiles of copies at
Yale University Library
(Ip.B851.884)

———

Library of Congress Cataloging in Publication Data

Buchanan, Robert Williams, 1841-1901.
   The new Abelard.

   (Victorian fiction : Novels of faith and doubt)
   Reprint of the 1884 ed. published by Chatto &
Windus, London.
   I.   Title.   II.   Series.
PZ3.B852N15   [PR4262]   823'.8   75-1531
ISBN 0-8240-1603-3

82-1254

THE NEW ABELARD

VOL. I.

THE NEW ABELARD

𝔄 𝔕omance

BY

ROBERT BUCHANAN

AUTHOR OF 'THE SHADOW OF THE SWORD' 'GOD AND THE MAN' ETC.

IN THREE VOLUMES—VOL. I.

London

CHATTO & WINDUS, PICCADILLY

1884

LONDON : PRINTED BY
SPOTTISWOODE AND CO., NEW-STREET SQUARE
AND PARLIAMENT STREET

THE NEW ABELARD.

PROEM.

Shipwreck . . . What succour ?—

On the gnawing rocks
The ship grinds to and fro with thunder-shocks,
And thro' her riven sides with ceaseless rush
The foam-fleck'd waters gush :
Above, the soot-black sky ; around, the roar
Of surges smiting on some unseen shore ;
Beneath, the burial-place of rolling waves—
Flowerless, for ever shifting, wind-dug graves !

A moment on the riven deck he stands,
Praying to Heaven with wild uplifted hands,
Then sees across the liquid wall afar
A glimmer like a star ;
The lighthouse gleam !   Upon the headland black
The beacon burns and fronts the stormy wrack—
Sole speck of light on gulfs of darkness, where
Thunder the sullen breakers of despair . . .

The ship is gone . . . Now in that gulf of death
He swims and struggles on with failing breath :
He grasps a plank—it sinks—too frail to upbear
His leaden load of care ;
Another and another—straws !—they are gone !
He cries aloud, stifles, and struggles on ;
For still thro' voids of gloom his straining sight
Sees the sad glimmer of a steadfast light !

He gains the rocks . . . What shining hands are these,
Reached out to pluck him from the cruel seas ?
What shape is this, that clad in raiment blest
Now draws him to its breast ? . . .
Ah, Blessèd One, still keeping, day and night,
The lamp well trimm'd, the heavenly beacon bright,
He knows Thee now !—he feels the sheltering gleam—
And lo ! the night of storm dissolves in dream !

CHAPTER I.

THE TWO.

Miriam. But whither goest thou?
Walter.   On the highest peak,
        Among the snows, there grows a pale blue flower—
        The village maidens call it *Life-in-Death*,
        The old men *Sleep-no-more*; I have sworn to pluck it;
        Many have failed upon the same wild quest,
        And left their bleaching bones among the crags.
        If I should fail——
Miriam.   Let me go with thee, Walter !
        Let me not here i' the valley—let us find
        The blessed flower together, dear, or die !
                              The Sorrowful Shepherdess.

ON a windy night in the month of May, the
full moon was flashing from cloud to cloud,
each so small that it began to melt instanta-
neously beneath her hurried breath; and, in

the fulness of the troubled light that she was shedding, the bright tongues of the sea were creeping up closer and closer through the creeks of the surrounding land, till they quivered like quicksilver under the walls of Mossleigh Abbey, standing dark and lonely amongst the Fens.

It was a night when, even in that solitude, everything seemed mysteriously and troublously alive. The wind cried as with a living voice, and the croaks of herons answered from the sands. The light of the moon went and came as to a rhythmic respiration; and when it flashed, the bats were seen flitting with thin z-like cry high up over the waterside, and when it was dimmed the owl moaned from the ivied walls. At intervals, from the distant lagoons, came the faint 'quack, quack' of flocks of ducks at feed. The night was still, but enchanted ; subdued, yet quivering with sinister life. Over and above all was the heavy breath of the ocean, crawling nearer and nearer, eager yet fearful, with deep tremors, to the electric wand of that heavenly light.

Presently, from inland, came another sound—the quick tramp of a horse's feet coming along the narrow road which wound up to, and past, the abbey ruins. As it grew louder, it seemed that every other sound was hushed, and everything listened to its coming ; till at last, out of the moonbeams and the shadows, flashed a tall white horse, ridden by a shape in black.

Arrived opposite the ruins, the horse paused, and its rider, a woman, looked eagerly up and

down the road, whereupon, as if at a signal, all
the faint sounds of the night became audible
again.　The woman sat still, listening ; and her
face looked like marble.　After pausing thus
motionless for some minutes, she turned from
the road, and walked her horse through. the
broken wall, across a stone-strewn field, and in
through the gloomy arch of the silent abbey,
till she reached the roofless space within,
where the grass grew rank and deep, mingled
with monstrous weeds, and running green and
slimy over long neglected graves.

How dark and solemn it seemed between
those crumbling walls, which only the dark ivy
seemed to hold together with its clutching
sinewy fingers ! yet, through each of the
broken windows, and through every archway,
the moonlight beamed, making streaks of lumi-

nous whiteness on the grassy floor. The horse moved slowly, at his own will, picking his way carefully among fragments of fallen masonry, and stopping short at times to inspect curiously some object in his path. All was bright and luminous overhead ; all dim and ominous there below. At last, reaching the centre of the place, the horse paused, and its rider again became motionless, looking upward.

The moonlight pouring through one of the arched windows suffused her face and form.

She was a fair woman, fair and tall, clad in a tight-fitting riding dress of black, with black hat and backward-drooping veil. Her hair was golden, almost a golden red, and smoothed down in waves over a low broad forehead. Her eyes were grey and very large, her features exquisitely cut, her mouth alone being, perhaps, though beautifully moulded, a little too full and ripe ; but let it be said in passing, this mouth was the soul of her face— large, mobile, warm, passionate, yet strangely firm and sweet. Looking into the grave eyes of this woman, you would have said she was some saint, some beautiful madonna ; looking at her mouth and lips, you would have said it was the mouth of Cytherea, alive with the very fire of love.

She sat motionless, still gazing upward on the dim milky azure, flecked with the softest foam of clouds. Her face was bright and happy, patient yet expectant ; and when the low sounds of the night were wafted to her ears, she sighed softly in unison, as if the sweetness of silence could be borne no longer.

Suddenly she started, listening, and at the same moment her horse, with dilated eyes and nostrils, trembled and pricked up his delicate ears. Clear and distinct, from the distance, came the sound of another horse's feet. It came nearer and nearer, then it ceased close to the abbey wall; and, almost simultaneously, the white steed threw forth his head and neighed aloud.

The woman smiled happily, and patted his neck with her gloved hand.

A minute passed. Then through the great archway slowly came another rider, a man. On seeing the first comer, he rose in the saddle and waved his hand; then leaping down, he threw his reins over an iron hook fixed in the wall, and came swiftly through the long grass.

A tall man of about thirty, wrapt in a
dark riding cloak and wearing a broadbrimmed clerical hat. He was clean shaven,
but his black hair fell about his shoulders.
His eyes were black and piercing, his eyebrows
thick and dark. The head, with its square
firm jaw and fine aquiline features, was set
firm upon a powerful neck and shoulders. His
cloak, falling back from the throat, showed the
white neckcloth worn by English clergymen.

The white horse did not stir as he approached, but, turning his head, surveyed him
calmly with an air of recognition. He came
up, took the rein and patted the horse's neck,
while the woman, with a cry of welcome, leapt
from her seat.

'Shall I fasten your horse with mine?' he
asked, still holding the rein.

'No ; let him ramble among the grass. He will come at my call.'

Released and riderless, the horse moved slowly through the grass, approaching the other in a leisurely way, with a view to a little equine conversation. Meantime the man and woman had sprung into each other's arms, and were kissing each other like lovers—as indeed they were.

'You are late, dearest,' said the woman presently, when the first delight of meeting was over. 'I thought perhaps you could not come to-night.'

Her voice was deep and musical—a soft contralto—with vibrations of infinite tenderness. As she stood with him, fixing her eyes fondly upon him, it almost seemed as if she, not he, were the masculine, the pre-

dominant spirit; he the feminine, the possessed. Strong and passionate as he seemed,
he was weak and cold compared to her;
and whenever they clung together and kissed,
it seemed as if her kisses were given in the
eagerness of mastery, his in the sweetness of self-surrender. This, seeing her
delicate beauty, and the powerful determined
face and form of the man, was strange
enough.

'I could not come earlier,' he replied
gently. 'I had a call to a dying man
which detained me. I left his bedside and
came straight hither.'

'That is why you look so sad,' she said,
smiling and kissing him. 'Ah, yes—death
is terrible!'

And she clung to him fondly, as if

fearful that the cold cruel shadow even then and there might come between them.

' Not always, Alma. The poor man whose eyes I have just closed—he was only a poor fenman—died with a faith so absolute, a peace so perfect, that all the terrors of his position departed, leaving only an infinite pathos. In the presence of such resignation I felt like an unholy intruder. He went away as calmly as if Our Lord came to him in the very flesh, holding out two loving hands—and, indeed, who knows? His eyes were fixed at last as if he *saw* something, and then . . . he smiled and passed away.'

They moved along side by side through the deep shadows. She held his hand in hers, drawing life and joy from the very touch.

'What a beautiful night!' he said at last, gazing upwards thoughtfully. 'Surely, surely, the old argument is true, and that sky refutes the cry of unbelief. And yet men perish, generations come and go, and still that patient light shines on. This very place is a tomb, and we walk on the graves of those who once lived and loved as we do now.'

'Their souls are with God,' she murmured; 'yes, with God, up yonder!'

'Amen to that. But when they lived, dearest, belief was so easy. They were not thrust into a time of doubt and change. It was enough to close the eyes and walk blindly on in assurance of a Saviour. Now we must stare with naked eyes at the Skeleton of what was a living Truth.'

'Do not say that. The truth lives, though its face has changed.'

'*Does* it live? God knows. Look at this deserted place, these ruined walls. Just as this is to habitable places, is our old faith to the modern world. Roofless, deserted, naked to heaven, stands the Church of Christ. Soon it must perish altogether, leaving not a trace behind; unless . . .'

'Unless? . . .'

'Unless, with God's aid, it can be *restored*,' he replied. 'Even then, perhaps, it would never be quite the same as it once was in the childhood of the world; but it would at least be a Temple, not a ruin.'

'That is always your dream, Ambrose.'

'It is my dream—and my belief. Meanwhile, I am still like a man adrift. O Alma, if I could only *believe*, like that poor dying man!'

'You do believe,' she murmured; 'only your belief is not blind and foolish. Why should you reproach yourself because you have rejected so much of the old superstition?'

'Because I am a minister of the Church, round which, like that dark devouring ivy, the old superstitions still cling. Before you could make this place what it once was, a prosperous abbey, with happy creatures dwelling within it, you have to strip the old walls bare; and it is the same with our religion. I am not strong enough for such a task. The very falsehoods I would up-root have a certain fantastic holiness and beauty; when I lay my hands upon them, as I have sometimes dared to do, I seem to hear a heavenly voice rebuking me. Then I say to myself that perhaps, after all, I am committing an act of desecration; and so—my life is wasted.'

She watched him earnestly during a long pause which followed. At last she said :—

'Is it not, perhaps, that you *think* of these things too much? Perhaps it was not meant that we should always fix our eyes on what is so mysterious. God hid himself away in the beginning, and it is not his will that we should comprehend him.'

The clergyman shook his head in deprecation of that gentle suggestion.

'Then why did He plant in our souls such a cruel longing? Why did He tempt our wild inquiry, with those shining

C

lights above us, with this wondrous world, with every picture that surrounds the soul of man? No, Alma, He does not hide himself away—it is we who turn our eyes from him to make idols of stone or flesh, and to worship these. Where, then, shall we find him? Not among the follies and superstitions of the ruined Church at the altar of which I have ministered to my shame!'

His words had become so reckless, his manner so agitated, that she was startled. Struck by a sudden thought, she cried—

'Something new has happened? O Ambrose, what is it?'

'Nothing,' he replied; 'that is, little or nothing. The Inquisition has begun, that is all.'

'What do you mean?'

He gave a curious laugh.

'The clodhoppers of Fensea have, in their small way, the instinct of Torquemada. The weasel is akin to the royal tiger. My Christian congregation wish to deliver me over to the moral stake and faggot; as a preliminary they have written to my Bishop.'

' Of what do they complain *now*? '

'That I am a heretic,' he answered with the same cold laugh. 'Conceive the ridiculousness of the situation! There was some dignity about heresy in the old days, when it meant short shrift, a white shirt, and the *auto-da-fé*. But an inquisition composed of Summerhayes the grocer, Hayes the saddler, and Miss Rayleigh the schoolmistress; and, instead of Torquemada, the mild old Bishop of Darkdale and Dells!'

She laughed too, but somewhat anxiously. Then she said tenderly, with a certain worship—

'You are too good for such a place. They do not understand you.'

His manner became serious in a moment.

'I have flattered my pride with such a thought, but, after all, have they not right on their side? They at least have a definite belief; they at least are satisfied to worship *in a ruin*, and all they need is an automaton to lead their prayers. When they have stripped me bare, and driven me from the church——'

'O Ambrose, will they do that?'

'Certainly. It must come, sooner or later; perhaps the sooner the better. I am tired of my own hypocrisy—of frightening the poor fools with half-truths when the whole of the truth of unbelief is in my heart.'

' But you *do* believe,' she pleaded ; ' in God, and in our Saviour ! '

' Not in the letter, dearest. In the spirit, certainly ! '

' The spirit is everything. Can you not defend yourself ? '

' I shall not try. To attempt to do so would be another hypocrisy. I shall resign.'

' And then ? You will go away ? '

' Yes.'

' But you will take *me* with you ? '

He drew her gently to him ; he kissed her on the forehead.

' Why should you share my degradation ? ' he said. ' A minister who rejects or is rejected by his Church is a broken man, broken and despised. In these days martyrdom has no glory, no honour. You yourself would be the first to feel the ignominy of my situation, the wretchedness of a petty persecution. It would be better, perhaps, for us to part.'

But with a look of ineffable sweetness and devotion she crept closer to him, and laid her head upon his breast.

'We shall not part,' she said. 'Where you go I shall follow, as Rachel followed her beloved. Your country shall be my country, dearest, and—your God my God!'

All the troubled voices of the night responded to that loving murmur. The moon rose up luminous into the open heaven above the abbey ruins, and flashed upon the two clinging frames, in answer to the earth's incantation.

CHAPTER II.

OLD LETTERS.

What's an old letter but a rocket dark—
Once fired i' the air and left without a spark
Of that which once, a fiery life within it,
Shot up to heaven, and faded in a minute?
But by the powdery smell and stick corroded,
You guess—how noisily it once exploded!

Cupid's Postbag.

I.

*To the Right Reverend the Bishop of Darkdale
and Dells.*

RIGHT REVEREND SIR,—We, the under-
signed, churchwardens and parishioners of the
Church of St. Mary Flagellant, in the parish
of Fensea and diocese of Dells, feel it our duty

to call your lordship's attention to the conduct of the Rev. Ambrose Bradley, vicar of Fensea aforesaid. It is not without great hesitation that we have come to the conclusion that some sort of an inquiry is necessary. For many months past the parish pulpit has been scandalised by opinions which, coming from the pulpit of a Christian church, have caused the greatest astonishment and horror; but the affair reached its culmination last Ascension Day, when the Vicar actually expressed his scepticism as to many of the Christian miracles, and particularly as to the Resurrection of our Lord Jesus Christ *in the flesh*. It is also reported, we believe on good authority, that Mr. Bradley is the author of an obnoxious article in an infidel publication, calling in question such facts as the miraculous conversion of the Apostle Paul, treating other portions of the gospel narrative as merely ' Symbolical,' and classing the Bible as only one of many Holy Books with equal pretensions to Divine inspiration. Privately we believe the Vicar of Fensea upholds opinions even more extraordinary than these. It is for your lordship to decide, therefore, whether he is a fit person to fill the sacred office of a Christian minister, especially in these times, when Antichrist is busy at work and the seeds of unbelief find such ready acceptance, especially in the bosom of the young. Personally, we have no complaint against the Vicar, who is well liked by many of his congregation, and is very zealous in works of charity and almsgiving. But the pride of carnal knowledge and the vanity of secular approbation have turned him from that narrow path which leads to righteousness, into the howling wilderness of heterodoxy, wherein, having wandered too far, no man may again find his soul alive. We beseech your lordship to investigate this matter without delay; and, with the assurance of our deepest respect and reverence, we beg to subscribe ourselves, your lordship's humble and obedient servants,

HENRY SUMMERHAYES,

EZEKIEL MARVEL,

WALTER ROCHFORD,

SIMPSON PEPPERBACK,

JOHN DOVE,

TABITHA RAYLEIGH, *spinster*,

all of the parish of Fensea.

II.

From the Bishop of Darkdale and Dells to the Rev. Ambrose Bradley, Vicar of Fensea.

Darkdale, May 28.

DEAR MR. BRADLEY,—I have just received from some of the leading members of your congregation a communication of an extraordinary nature, calling in question, I regret to say, not merely your manner of conducting the sacred service in the church of Fensea, but your very personal orthodoxy in those matters which are the pillars of the Christian faith. I cannot but think that there is some mistake, for I know by early experience how ready churchgoers are, especially in the rural districts, to distort the significance of a preacher's verbal expressions on difficult points of doctrine.

When you were first promoted to the living of Fensea, you were named to me as a young man of unusual faith and zeal—perfervid, indeed, to a fault; and I need not say that I had heard of you otherwise as one from whom your university expected great things. That is only a few years ago. What then has occurred to cause this sad misconception (I take it for granted that it *is* a misconception) on the part of your parishioners? Perhaps, like many other young preachers of undoubted attainments but limited experience, you have been trying your oratorical wings too much in flights of a mystic philosophy and a poetical rhetoric ; and in the course of these flights have, as rhetoricians will, alarmed your hearers unnecessarily. Assuming this for a moment, will you pardon me for saying that there are two ways of preaching the gospel: one subtle and mystical, which appeals only to those spirits who have penetrated into the adytum of Christian theology; one cardinal and rational, which deals only with the simple truths of Christian teaching, and can be understood by the veriest child. Perhaps, indeed, of these two ways, the latter one most commends itself to God. 'For except a man be born again,' &c. Be that as it may, and certainly I have no wish to undervalue the subtleties of Christian philosophy, let me impress upon you that, where a congregation is childlike, unprepared, and as it were uninstructed, no teaching can be too direct and simple. Such a congregation asks for bread, not for precious stones of oratory; for kindly promise, not for mystical speculation. That you have seriously questioned, even in your own mind, any of the Divine truths of our creed, as expressed in that Book which is a light and a law unto men, I will not for a moment believe ; but I shall be glad to receive forthwith, over your own signature, an assurance that my surmise is a correct one, and that you will be careful in the future to give no further occasion for misconception.—I am, my dear Mr. Bradley, yours,

W. H. DARKDALE AND DELLS.

III.

From the Rev. Ambrose Bradley to the Right Reverend the Bishop of Darkdale and Dells.

Vicarage, May 31, 1880.

MY DEAR BISHOP,—I am obliged to you for your kind though categorical letter, to which I hasten to give you a reply. That certain members of my congregation should have forwarded complaints concerning me does not surprise me, seeing that they have already taken me to task on many occasions and made my progress here difficult, if not disagreeable. But I think you will agree with me that there is only one light by which a Christian man, even a Christian clergyman, can consent to be directed—the light of his own conscience and intellect, Divinely implanted within him for his spiritual guidance.

I will be quite candid with you. You ask what has changed me since the day when, zealous, and, as you say, 'perfervid,' I was promoted to this ministry. The answer is simple. A deep and conscientious study of the wonderful truths of Science, an eager and

impassioned study of the beautiful truths of
Art.

I seem to see you raise your hands in
horror.   But if you will bear with me a little
while, perhaps I may convince you that what
I have said is not so horrible after all—nay,
that it expresses a conviction which exists at
the present moment in the bosom of many
Christian men.

The great question before the world just
now, when the foundations of a particular faith
are fatally shaken, when Science denies that
Christ as we conceive Him ever was, and when
Art bewails wildly that He should ever have
been, is whether the Christian religion can
continue to exist at all ; whether, when a few
more years have passed away, it will not present to a modern mind the spectacle that

paganism once presented to a mediæval mind.
Now, of our leading Churchmen, not even you,
my Lord Bishop, I feel sure, deny that the
Church is in danger, both through attacks from
without and through a kind of dry-rot within.
Lyell and others have demolished and made
ridiculous the Mosaic cosmogony   Strauss and
others have demolished, with more or less
success, the Biblical and Christian miracles.
No sane man now seriously believes that the
sun ever stood still, or that an ass spoke in
human speech, or that a multitude of people
were ever fed with a few loaves and fishes, or
that any solid human form ever walked on the
liquid sea.   With the old supernaturalism has
gone the old asceticism or other-worldliness.   It
is now pretty well agreed that there are sub-
stantially beautiful things in this world which

have precedence over fancifully beautiful things in the other. The poets have taught us the loveliness of Nature, the painters have shown us the loveliness of Art. Meantime, what does the Church do? Instead of accepting the new knowledge and the new beauty, instead of building herself up anew on the débris of her shattered superstitions, she buries her face in her own ashes, and utters a senile wail of protestation. Instead of calling upon her children to face the storm, and to build up new bulwarks against the rising wave of secularism, she commands them to wail with her, or *to be silent*. Instead of perceiving that the priests of Baal and Antichrist might readily be overthrown with the weapons forged by their own hands, she cowers before them powerless, in all the paralysis of superstition, in all the blind fatuity of prayer.

But let us look the facts in the face.

The teachers of the new knowledge have unroofed our Temple to the heavens, but have not destroyed its foundations; they have over- thrown its brazen images, but have not touched its solid walls. Put the case in other and stronger words. The God who thundered upon Sinai has vanished into air and cloud, but the God of man's heavenly aspiration is wonderfully quickened and alive. The Bible of wrath and prophecy is cast contemptuously aside, but the Bible of eternal poetry is im- perishable, its wild dreams and aspirations being crystallised in such literature as cannot die. The historic personality of the gentle Founder of Christianity becomes fainter and

fainter as the ages advance ; but, on the other
hand, brighter and fairer grows the Divine
Ideal which rose from the ashes of that godlike man. Men reject the old miracles, but
they at last accept a miracle of human idealism.
In one word, though Christianity has perished
as a dogmatic faith, it survives as the philosophic religion of the world.

This being so, how does it behove a
Christian minister, eating the Church's bread,
but fully alive to her mortal danger, to steer
his course ?

Shall he, as so many do, continue to act
in the nineteenth century as he would have
acted in the fifteenth, or indeed in any century
up to the Revolution ? Shall he base his
teaching on the certainty of miracles, on the
existence of supernaturalism, on the evil of the

human heart, the vanity of this world, and the certainty of rewards and punishments in another? Shall he brandish the old hell fire, or scatter the old heavenly manna?

I do not think so!

Knowing in his heart that these things are merely the cast-off epidermis of a living and growing creed, he may, in perfect consciousness of God's approval, put aside the miraculous as unproven if not irrelevant ; warn the people against mere supernaturalism ; proclaim with the apostles of the Renaissance the glory and loveliness of *this* world—its wondrous scenes, its marvellous story as written on the rocks and in the stars, its divine science, its literature, its poetry, and its art ; and treading all the fire of Hell beneath his feet, and denouncing the threat of eternal wrath as a chimera, base his hope of immortality on the moral aspirations that, irrespective of dogma, are common to all mankind.

This I think he may do, and must do, if the Church is to endure.

Let him do this, and let only a tithe of his brethren imitate him in so doing, and out of this nucleus of simple believers, as out of the little Galilean band, may be renewed a faith that will redeem the world. Questioned of such a faith, Science will reply—'I have measured the heavens and the earth, I have traced back the book of the universe page by page and letter by letter, but I have found neither here nor yonder any proof that God is *not*; nay, beyond and behind and within all phenomena, there abides one unknown quantity which you are quite free to call—God.'

Similarly questioned, Art will answer—' Since you have rejected what was so hideous, tested by the beauty of this world, and since you hold even my work necessary and holy, I too will confess with you that I hunger for something fairer and less perishable; and in token of that hunger, of that restless dream, I will be your Church's handmaid, and try to renew her Temple and make it fair.'

The keystone of the Church is Jesus Christ. Not the Jesus of the miracles, not Jesus the son of Joseph and Mary, but Jesus Christ, the Divine Ideal, the dream and glory of the human race. Not God who made himself a man, but man who, by God's inspiration, has been fashioned unto the likeness of a God.

And what, as we behold him now, is this Divine Ideal—this man made God ?

He is simply, as I conceive, the accumulated testimony of human experience—of history, poetry, philosophy, science, and art—in favour of a rational religion, the religion of earthly peace and heavenly love. Built upon the groundwork of what, shorn of its miraculous pretensions, was a gentle and perfect life, the Divine Ideal, or Ideal Person, began. At first shadowy and almost sinister, then clearer and more beautiful; then, descending through the ages, acquiring at every step some new splendour of self-sacrifice, some new consecration of love or suffering, from every heart that suffered patiently, from every soul that fed the lamp of a celestial dream with the oil of sweet human love. And now, far removed as is man himself from the archetypal ape, is the Christ of modern Christendom, this spiritual

Saviour of the world, from the ghostly skeleton of the early martyrs, from the Crucified One of early Christian art. The life of generations has gone to fashion him—all our human experience has served to nourish him — gradually from age to age He has drunk in the blood of suffering and the milk of knowledge, till He stands supreme as we see him— not God, but man made God.

Does it matter so much, after all, whether we worship a person or an idea, since, as I suggest, the Idea has become a Person, with all the powers and privileges of divinity? Nay, who in this world is able, even with the help of philosophy, to distinguish what *is* from what seems—the phenomenal from the real? So long as Our Lord exists as a moral phenomenon, so long in other words as we can apprehend him as an ideal of human life, Christ is not dead, and his resurrection is not a dream. He walks the world. He remembers Greece and Rome, as well as Galilee ; He blesses the painter and the poet, as well as the preacher in the Temple. He rejects nothing ; He reads the rocks and the stars, and He adds their gospel to his own ; He cries to men of all creeds, as his prototype cried to his disciples of yore, ' Come unto me, all ye that are heavy laden, and ye shall rest.'

Pardon me, my Lord Bishop, the desultory thoughts noted down in this long letter. They perhaps give you some clue as to the sentiments with which I pursue the Christian mission. You will doubtless think me somewhat heterodox, but I have at least the courage of my opinions; and on some such heterodoxy as mine—though on one, I hope, much broader and wiser—it will soon be found necessary to reconstruct the Christian Church. I am, my Lord Bishop, yours,

AMBROSE BRADLEY.

IV.

From the Bishop of Darkdale and Dells to the Rev. Ambrose Bradley, Vicar of Fensea.

MY DEAR SIR,—I cannot express to you with what feelings of sorrow and amazement I have read your terrible letter! I must see you personally at once. My only hope now is that your communication represents a passing aberration, rather than the normal condition of your mind. I shall be at Darkdale on Saturday next, the 2nd. Will you make it convenient to be in the town on that day, and to call upon me at about eleven in the fore-noon? I am,

W. M. DARKDALE AND DELLS.

CHAPTER III.

THE BISHOP.

A priest he was, not over-merry,
Who loved sound doctrine and good sherry;
Who wound his mind up every morning
At the sedate cathedral's warning,
And found it soberly keep time,
In 's pocket, to each hourly chime;
Who, church's clock-face dwelling under,
Knew 'twas impossible to blunder,
If Peter's self at 's door should knock,
And roundly ask him— *What 's o'clock?*

The Hermitage.

ON the morning of June 2 the Rev. Ambrose
Bradley left Fensea by the early market train,
and arrived at Darkdale just in time for his
interview with the Bishop of his diocese.

Seen in broad daylight, as he quickly made

his way through the narrow streets to the episcopal residence, Bradley looked pale and troubled, yet determined. He was plainly drest, in a dark cloth suit, with broad felt hat; and there was nothing in his attire, with the exception of his white clerical necktie, to show that he held a sacred office. His dress, indeed, was careless almost to slovenliness, and he carried a formidable walking-stick of common wood. With his erect and powerful frame and his closely shaven cheeks he resembled an athlete rather than a clergyman, for he had been one of the foremost rowers and swimmers of his time. He wore no gloves, and his hands, though small and well formed, were slightly reddened by the sun.

Arrived at his destination, an old-fashioned residence, surrounded by a large garden, he rang the gate bell, and was shown by a foot-man into the house, where his card was taken by a solemn-looking person clerically attired. After waiting a few moments in the hall, he was ushered into a luxuriously furnished study, where he found the Bishop, with his nether limbs wrapt in rugs, seated close to a blazing fire.

Bishop —— was a little spare man of about sixty, with an aquiline nose, a slightly receding forehead, a mild blue eye, and very white hands. He was said to bear some facial likeness to Cardinal Newman, and he secretly prided himself upon the resemblance. He spoke slowly and with a certain precision, never hurrying himself in his utterance, and giving full force to the periods of what was generally considered a beautiful and silvery voice.

'Good morning, Mr. Bradley,' he said, without noticing the other's extended hand. 'You will excuse my rising? The rheumatism in my knees has been greatly increased by this wretched weather. Pray take a chair by the fire.'

Bradley, however, found a seat as far from the fire as possible; for the weather was far from cold, and the room itself was like a vapour bath.

There was a pause. The Bishop, shading his face with one white hand, on which sparkled a valuable diamond ring, was furtively inspecting his visitor.

'You sent for me?' said Bradley, somewhat awkwardly.

'Yes—about that letter. I cannot tell you how distressed I was when I received it;

indeed, if I may express myself frankly, I never was so shocked in my life. I had always thought you so different, so very different. But there! I trust you have come to tell me that the hope I expressed was right, and that it was under some temporary aberration that you expressed sentiments so extraordinary, so peculiarly perverted, and—hem!—unchristian.'

The clergyman's dark eye flashed, and his brow was knitted.

' Surely not unchristian,' he returned.

' Not merely that, sir, but positively atheistic!' cried the Bishop, wheeling round in his chair and looking his visitor full in the face.

' Then I expressed myself miserably. I am not an atheist; God forbid!'

' But as far as I can gather from your

expressions, you absolutely dare to question the sacred character of the Scriptures, and the Divine nature and miraculous life and death of Our Lord and Saviour Jesus Christ!'

'Not at all,' replied Bradley, quietly.

'Not at all!' echoed the Bishop.

'Permit me to explain. I expressed my humble opinion that there are many things in the Scriptures which are contradicted by modern evidence, so that the sacred writings must be accepted not as history but as poetry; and I said that, although the miraculous narrative of Christ's life and death might have to be revised, the beautiful Ideal it had set before us was sufficient for all our needs. In other words, whether Our Lord was a Divine personage or not, He had become a Divine Influence—which, after all, is the same thing.'

'It is *not* the same thing, sir!' exclaimed the Bishop, horrified. 'It is very far from being the same thing. Why, any Unitarian would admit as much as you do! — and pardon me for reminding you, you are not a Unitarian—you are a clergyman of the Church of England. You have subscribed the Articles —you—God bless my soul! what is the world coming to, when a Christian minister uses language worthy of the atheist Bradlaugh?'

'You remind me that I subscribed the Articles,' said Bradley, still preserving his calmness. 'I did so without thought, as so many do, when I was a very young man.'

'What are you now, sir? A young man, a very young man; and in the audacious spirit of youth and inexperience you touch on subjects which the wisest minds of the world have been content to approach with reverence, with awe and trembling. I see your position clearly enough. The horrible infidelity which fills the air at the present day has penetrated your mind, and with the pride of intellectual impiety—that very pride for which Satan was cast from heaven—you profane the mysteries of your religion. After what you have said, I am almost prepared to hear you tell me that you actually *did* write that article on Miracles, which your parishioners impute to you, in the " Bi-monthly Review ! " '

'It is quite true. I did write that article.'

'And you have contributed to other infidel publications ; for instance, to the " Charing Cross Chronicle," which is edited by an infidel and written for infidels? '

' Excuse me ; the " Chronicle " is not generally considered an infidel publication.'

' Have you contributed to it—yes or no, sir ? '

' Not on religious subjects ; on literary topics only.'

' But you have written for it ; that is enough. All this being granted, I think I may safely gather whence you receive your inspirations. From that portion of the press which is attempting to destroy our most sacred institutions, and which is endeavouring, in one way or another, to undermine the whole foundations of the Christian Church.'

Bradley rose to his feet and stood on the hearthrug, facing his superior, who looked up at him with ill-concealed horror and amazement. By this time he was not a little agitated ;

but he still preserved a certain outward composure, and his manner was full of the greatest humility and respect.

'Will you permit me to explain?' he said in a low voice. 'The hope and dream of my life is to upraise the Church, not to destroy it.'

'Humph! to upraise *a* church, perhaps, but not the Church of Christ.'

'The Church of Christ—a church wherein all men may worship, irrespective of points of dogma, which have been the curse of every religion, and of ours most of all. For such a communion only two articles of faith would be necessary—a belief in an all-loving and all-wise Creator, or First Unknown Cause, and a belief in a Divine Character, created and evolved we need not ask how, but bearing the name of the Founder of Christianity.'

' And the Bible, sir, the Bible!' cried the Bishop, impatiently. 'What would you do with that?'

' I would use it in its proper place as— literature.'

' Literature!' said the Bishop with uplifted hands. 'You would then class that Blessed Book, from which the world has drawn the milk of immortal life, in the same category as Homer's Iliad, the profane poems of Horace and Catullus, and—save the mark!—Lord Byron's poems, and the miserable novels of the period?'

' You do not quite understand me!'

' Sir, I understand you only too well.'

I do not call all printed matter literature; but I hold that all literature of the higher kind is, like the Bible, divinely inspired. Dante,

Milton, and Shakespeare were as assuredly sent by God as Moses and Elijah. Shall we call the Book of Job a divine piece of moral teaching, and deny that title to "Hamlet" and "King Lear"? Is not the "Faust" of Goethe as spiritual a product as the Song of Solomon? Ezekiel was a prophet; prophets also are Emerson and Thoreau. Spinoza has been called God-intoxicated; and it is true. There might be some question as to the mission of Byron (though I myself believe there is none); but surely no thinking person can reject the pretensions of that divine poet and martyred man who wrote the "Prometheus Unbound"!'

'Shelley!' ejaculated the other, as if a bomb had exploded under his feet. 'Are you actually speaking of *him*, sir?—the atheist Shelley?'

' He was no atheist. More than most men he believed in God—a god of love.'

This was too much. Quite forgetting his rheumatism, the Bishop threw off his rugs and rose tremulously to his feet.

' Mr. Bradley,' he said, ' let there be an end to this. I have heard you patiently and respectfully, thinking perhaps you might have something to say in your own defence; but every word you utter is an outrage—yes, sir, an outrage. Such opinions as you have expressed here to-day, and the other day in your letter, might be conceivable in a boy fresh from college ; but coming from one who has been actually ordained, and has held more than one office in the Church, they savour of blasphemy. In any case, I shall have to take the matter into consideration, with a view to your immediate suspension. But if you wish it I will give you time—a little time—to reflect. I would do anything to avoid a scandal.'

The clergyman lifted his hat and stick, with a slight involuntary shrug of the shoulder.

'It is, then, as I expected,' he said. 'I am to be denounced and unfrocked. The days of persecution are not yet quite over, I perceive.'

The Bishop flushed angrily.

'It is absurd to talk of persecution in such a case, Mr. Bradley. Do you yourself conceive it possible that you, bearing such opinions, can remain in the Church?'

'I do not conceive it possible. Shall I resign at once?'

'Permit me to think it over, and perhaps to consult with those who in such matters are wiser than myself. I shall do nothing hasty, or harsher than the occasion warrants, be sure of that.'

'Thank you,' returned Bradley, with a peculiar smile.

'You shall hear from me. In the meantime, let me entreat you to be careful. Good morning.'

And with a cold bow the Bishop dismissed his visitor.

On leaving the episcopal residence Bradley went straight to the railway station, had a slight and hasty lunch at the buffet, and then took the midday express to London. Entering a second-class carriage, the only other occupants of which were a burly personage going up for a Cattle Show and a spruce

individual with ' bagman ' written on every
lineament of his countenance, he resigned himself to reflections on his peculiar position.

Throughout these reflections I have no
intention of following him, but they seemed
less gloomy and miserable than might be
conceived possible under the circumstances.
His eye was clear and determined, his mouth
set firmly, and now and then he smiled sadly
to himself—just as he had smiled in the
presence of the Bishop.

The express reached London in about six
hours, so that it was evening when Bradley
arrived at King's Cross, carrying with him
only a small hand-bag. Instead of hailing a
cab, he walked right on along the streets—
through Taviton Street to Russell Square,
thence into Holborn, and thence, across Lin-

coln's Inn Fields, into the Strand. He then turned off towards the Temple, which he entered with the air of one who knew its quiet recesses well.

He was turning into Pump Court when he suddenly came face to face with a man of about thirty, elegantly dressed, with faultless gloves and boots, and carrying a light cane. He was very fresh and fair-complexioned, with sandy whiskers and moustaches ; and to complete his rather dandified appearance he sported an eyeglass.

' Cholmondeley ! ' cried the clergyman, pronouncing it ' Chumley ' according to the approven mode.

' Ambrose Bradley ! ' returned the other. ' Is it possible? Why, I thought you were hundreds of miles away.'

'I came up here by the express, and was just coming to see you.'

'Then come along with me and dine at the " Reform."'

They looked a strange contrast as they walked on side by side—the powerful, grave-looking man, shabbily attired in his semi-clerical dress, and the elegant exquisite attired in the height of London fashion, with his mild blue eye and his eyeglass in position. Yet John Cholmondeley was something more than the mere ornamental young person he appeared; and as for his mildness, who that had read his savage articles on foreign politics in the 'Bi-monthly Review' would have taken him for a harmless person? He was a Positivist of Positivists, an M.A. of Oxford, and the acting-editor of the 'Charing Cross Chronicle.'

His literary style was hysterical and almost feminine in its ferocity. Personally he was an elegant young man, with a taste for good wines and good cigars, and a tendency in external matters to follow the prevailing fashion.

They drove to the ' Reform ' in a hansom, and dined together. At the table adjoining theirs on one side two Cabinet Ministers were seated in company with Jack Bustle, of the 'Chimes,' and Sir Topaz Cromwell, the young general just returned from South Africa ; at the table on the other side an Under-Secretary of State was giving a little feast to Joseph Moody, the miners' agent and delegate, who had been a miner himself, and who was just then making some stir in political circles by his propaganda.

After dinner they adjourned to the smoking-room, which they found almost empty; and then, in a few eager sentences, Bradley explained his position and solicited his friend's advice. For that advice was well worth having, Cholmondeley being not only a clever thinker but a shrewd man of the world.

CHAPTER IV.

WORLDLY COUNSEL.

A pebble, not a pearl !—worn smooth and round
With lying in the currents of the world
Where they run swiftliest—polished if you please,
As such things may and must be, yet indeed
No shining agate and no precious stone ;
Nay, pebble, merely pebble, one of many
Thrown in the busy shallows of the stream
To break its flow and make it garrulous.
The City Dame ; or, a Match for Mammon.

' I AM not at all surprised at what you have
told me,' said Cholmondeley, sipping his coffee
and smoking his cigar. ' I knew that it *must*
come sooner or later. Your position in the
Church has always been an anomalous one,
and, egad ! if you have been going on as you

tell me, I don't wonder they want to get rid of you. Well, what do you intend to do?'

'That is just the point I came to consult you upon,' returned the clergyman.

'I know what I should do in your place. I should stand to my colours, and give them a last broadside. The ' Chronicle ' is open to you, you know. The old ship of the Church is no longer seaworthy, and if you helped to sink it you would be doing a service to humanity.'

'God forbid!' cried Bradley, fervently. 'I would rather cut off my right hand than do anything to injure the Establishment. After all, it is the only refuge in times of doubt and fear.'

'It strikes me you are rather inconsistent,' said Cholmondeley with cool astonishment.

'Not at all. It is precisely because I love

the Church, because I believe in its spiritual mission, that I would wish to see it re-organised on a scientific and rational basis. When all is said and done, I am a Christian —that is, a believer in the Divine Idea of self-sacrifice and the enthusiasm of humanity. All that is beautiful and holy, all that may redeem man and lead him to an everlasting righteousness, is, in my opinion, summed up in the one word, Christianity.'

'But, my dear Bradley, you have rejected the *thing*! Why not dispense with the *name* as well?'

'I believe the name to be indispensable. I believe, moreover, that the world would waste away of its own carnality and atheism without a Christian priesthood. In the flesh or in the spirit Christ lives, to redeem the world.'

'Since you believe so much,' said Cholmondeley drily, 'it is a pity you don't believe a
little more. For my own part, you know my
opinion—which is, that Christ gets a great
deal more credit for what is good in civil-
isation than He deserves. Science has done
more in one hundred years to redeem the
race than Christianity has done in eighteen
hundred. *Verb. sap.*'

'Science is one of his handmaids,' returned
Bradley, 'and Art is another; that is why I
would admit both of these into the service
of the Temple. But bereft of his influence,
separated from the Divine Idea, and oblivious
of the Divine Character, both Science and Art
go stumbling in the dark—and blaspheme.
When Science gives the lie to any deathless
human instinct—when, for example, she nega-

tives the dream of personal immortality—she simply stultifies herself ; for she knows nothing and can tell us nothing on that subject, whereas Christ, answering the impulse of the human heart, tells us *all*. When Art says that she labours for her own sake, and that the mere reproduction of beautiful earthly forms is soul-satisfying, she also is stultified ; for there is no true art apart from the religious spirit. In one word, Science and Art, rightly read, are an integral part of the world's religion, which is Christianity.'

'I confess I don't follow you,' said the journalist, laughing ; ' but there, you were always a dreamer. Frankly, I think this bolstering up of an old creed with the truths of the new is a little dishonest. Christianity is based upon certain miraculous events, which have been proved to be untrue; man's foolish belief in their truth has led to an unlimited amount of misery; and having disposed of your creed's miraculous pretensions——'

'Are you quite sure you have disposed of them?' interrupted Bradley. 'In any case, is not the personal and posthumous influence of Our Saviour, as seen in the world's history, quite as miraculous as any of the events recorded of Him during His lifetime?'

'On the contrary! But upon my life, Bradley, I don't know where to have you! You seem to have taken a brief on both sides. Beware of indecision—it won't do in religion. You are stumbling between two stools.'

'Then I say with Mercutio, "a plague on both your houses!"' cried Bradley, laughing.

' But don't you see I want to reconcile them ? '

' You won't do it. It's too old a feud—a vendetta, in fact. Remember what Mercutio himself got by trying to be a peacemaker. The world can understand your Tybalts and your Parises—that is to say, your fire-eating Voltaires and your determined Tom Paines— but it distrusts the men who, like Matt Arnold *et hoc genus omne*, believe simply nothing, and yet try to whitewash the old idols.'

There was a silence. The two men looked at each other in friendly antagonism, Cholmondeley puffing his cigar leisurely with the air of a man who had solved the great problem, and Bradley smoking with a certain suppressed excitement.

Presently the clergyman spoke again.

'I don't think we shall agree—so let us cease to argue. What I want you to understand is, that I do love the Church, and cannot part from her without deep pain—without, in fact, rupturing all my most cherished associations. But there is another complication which makes this affair unusually distressing to me. You know I am engaged to be married?'

'Ah, yes! I heard something about it. I begin to see your difficulty. You are afraid——'

He hesitated, as if not liking to complete the sentence.

'Afraid of what, pray?'

'Well, that, when you are pronounced heretical, she will throw you over!'

The clergyman smiled curiously and shook his head.

' If that were all,' he replied, ' I should be able very easily to resign myself to the consequences of my heresy ; but, fortunately or unfortunately, the lady to whom I am engaged (our engagement, by the way, is only private) is not likely to throw me over, however much I may seem to deserve it.'

' Then why distress yourself ? '

' Simply because I doubt my right to entail upon her the consequences of my heterodoxy. She herself is liberal-minded, but she does not perceive that any connection with a heretic must mean, for a sensitive woman, misery and martyrdom. When I leave the Church I shall be practically ruined—not exactly in pocket, for, as you know, I have some money of my own—but intellectually and socially. The Church never pardons, and seldom spares.'

' But there are other careers open to you—literature, for example ! We all know your talents—you would soon win an eminence from which you might laugh at your persecutors.'

' Literature, my dear Cholmondeley, is simply empiricism—I see nothing in it to attract an earnest man.'

' You are complimentary ! ' cried Cholmondeley, with a laugh.

' Oh !—you are different ! You carry into journalism an amount of secular conviction which I could never emulate ; and, moreover, you are one of those who, like Harry the Smith, always fight " for your own hand." Now, I do not fight for my own hand ; I repeat emphatically, all my care is for the Church. She may persecute me, she may despise me, but still I love her and believe in her, and shall pray till my last breath for the time when she will become reorganised.'

'I see how all this will end,' said the journalist, half seriously. 'Some of these days you will go over to Rome!'

'Do you think so? Well, I might do worse even than *that*, for in Rome, now as ever, I should find excellent company. But no, I don't fancy that I shall go even halfway thither, unless—which is scarcely possible— I discover signs that the doting mother of Christianity accepts the new scientific miracle and puts Darwin out of the *Index*. Frankly, my difficulty is a social, or rather a personal, one. Ought I, a social outcast, to accept the devotion of one who would follow me, not merely out of the Church, but down into the very Hell of atheism, if I gave her the requisite encouragement ? '

Cholmondeley did not reply, but after reflecting quietly for some moments he said :—

' You have not told me the name of the lady.'

' Miss Alma Craik.'

' *Not* the heiress ? '

' Yes, the heiress.'

' I know her cousin, George Craik—we were at school together. I thought they were engaged.'

' They were once, but she broke it off long ago.'

' And she has accepted *you*? '

' Unconditionally.' He added with strange fervour : ' She is the noblest, the sweetest, and most beautiful woman in the world.'

'Then why on earth do you hesitate?' asked Cholmondeley. 'You are a lucky fellow.'

'I hesitate for the reason I have told you. She had placed her love, her life, her fortune at my feet, devotedly and unreservedly. As a clergyman of the Church, as one who might have devoted his lifetime to the re-establishment of his religion and the regeneration of his order, one, moreover, whom the world would have honoured and approved as a good and faithful servant, I might have accepted the sacrifice; indeed, after some hesitation, I did accept it. But now it is altogether different. I cannot consent to her martyrdom, even though it would glorify mine.'

Although Bradley exercised the strongest control over his emotions, and endeavoured to

discuss the subject as dispassionately and calmly
as possible, it was clear to his listener that he
was deeply and strangely moved. Cholmondeley was touched, for he well knew the secret
tenderness of his friend's nature. Under that
coldly cut, almost stern face, with its firm eyebrows and finely chiselled lips—within that
powerful frame which, so far at least as the
torso was concerned, might have been used as
a model for Hercules—there throbbed a heart
of almost feminine sensitiveness and sweetness ;
of feminine passion too, if the truth must be
told, for Bradley possessed the sensuousness of
most powerful men. Bradley was turned thirty
years of age, but he was as capable of a *grande
passion* as a boy of twenty—as romantic, as
high-flown, as full of the fervour of youth and
the brightness of dream. With him, to love a
woman was to love her with all his faith and

all his life ; he was far too earnest to trifle for a moment with the most sacred of all human sentiments. Cholmondeley was aware of this, and gauged the situation accordingly.

'If my advice is worth anything,' he said, 'you will dismiss from your mind all ideas of martyrdom. You are really exaggerating the horrors of the situation ; and, for the rest, where a woman loves a man as I am sure Miss Craik loves you, sacrifice of the kind you mention becomes easy, even delightful. Marry her, my dear Bradley, and from the very altar of pagan Hymen smile at the thunderbolts of the Church.'

Bradley seemed plunged in deep thought, and sat silent, leaning back and covering his face with one hand. At last he looked up, and exclaimed with unconcealed emotion—

'No, I am not worthy of her! Even if

my present record were clean, what could I say of my past? Such a woman should have a stainless husband! I have touched pitch, and been defiled.'

'Come, come!' said the journalist, not a little astonished. 'Of all the men I ever knew —and I have known many—you are about the most irreproachable.'

The clergyman bent over the table, and said in a low voice, 'Do you remember Mary Goodwin?'

'Of course,' replied the other with a laugh. 'What! is it possible that you are reproaching yourself on *that* account? Absurd! You acted by her like a man of honour; but little Mary was too knowing for you, that was all.'

'You knew I married her?'

' I suspected it, knowing your high-flown notions of duty. We all pitied you—we all——'

' Hush !' said the clergyman, still in the same low, agitated voice. ' Not a word against her. She is asleep and at peace ; and if there was any sin I shared it—I who ought to have known better. Perhaps, had I been a better man, I might have made her truly happy ; but she didn't love me—I did not deserve her love —and so, as you know, we parted.'

' I know she used you shamefully,' returned Cholmondeley, with some impatience. ' Come, I *must* speak ! You picked her from the gutter, and made her what Mrs. Grundy calls an honest woman. How did she reward you? By bolting away with the first rascal who offered her the run of his purse and a flash set of diamonds. By-the-by, I heard of her last in India, where she was a member of a strolling company. Did she die out there? '

' Yes,' answered the clergyman, very sadly. ' Nine years ago.'

' You were only a boy,' continued Cholmondeley, with an air of infinite age and experience, 'and Mr. Verdant Green was nothing to you. You thought all women angels, at an age when most youngsters know them to be devils. Well, that's all over, and you have nothing to reproach yourself with. I wish *I* could show as clean a book, old fellow.'

' I do reproach myself, nevertheless,' was the reply. ' That boyish episode has left its taint on my whole life ; yes, it is like the mark of a brand burned into the very flesh. I had no right to woo another woman; yet I have done so, to my shame, and now Heaven is about to punish me by stripping me bare in her sight and making me a social outlaw. I have deserved it all.'

The two remained together for some time longer, but Bradley, though he listened gently to his friend's remonstrances, could not be persuaded to take a less gloomy view of the situation. He was relieved unconsciously, nevertheless, by the other's cheery and worldly counsel. It was something, at least, to have eased his heart, to have poured the secret of his sorrow and fear into a sympathetic bosom.

They had dined very early, and when they rose to separate it was only half-past eight o'clock.

'Will you go on to my chambers?' asked

Cholmondeley. ' I can give you a bed, and I will join you after I have done my duties at the office.'

' No ; I shall sleep at Morley's Hotel, and take the early morning express down home.'

They strolled together along Pall Mall and across Leicester Square, where they separated, Cholmondeley sauntering airily, with that sense of superhuman insight which sits so lightly on the daily journalist, towards the newspaper office in Cumberland Street, and the clergyman turning into Morley's, where he was well known, to arrange for his room.

As it was still so early, however, Bradley did not stay in the hotel, but lighted his pipe and strolled thoughtfully along the busy Strand.

At a little after nine o'clock he found him-

self close to the Parthenon Theatre, where
' Hamlet ' was then being performed for over
the hundredth night.   He had always been a
lover of the theatre, and he now remembered
that Mr. Aram's performance of the Danish
prince was the talk of London.   Glad to discover any means of distracting his dreary
thoughts, he paid his two shillings, and found
a place at the back of the pit.

   The third act was just beginning as he
entered, and it was not until its conclusion that
he began to look around the crowded house.
The assemblage was a fashionable one, and
every box as well as every stall was occupied.
Many of the intelligent spectators held in their
hands books of the play, with which they
might be supposed to be acquainting themselves for the first time ; and all wore upon

their faces more or less of that bored expression characteristic of audiences which take their pleasures sadly, not to say stupidly. In all the broad earth there is nothing which can quite equal the sedate unintelligence of an English theatrical audience.

Suddenly, as he gazed, his eyes became attracted by a face in one of the private boxes —he started, went pale, and looked again—as he did so, the head was turned away towards the back of the box. Trembling like one that had seen an apparition, he waited for it to incline again his way—and when it did so he watched it in positive horror. As if to convince himself of its identity, he borrowed an opera-glass from a respectable-looking man seated near him, and fixed it on the face in the box.

The face of a woman, splendidly attired,

with diamonds sparkling on her naked throat and arms, and other diamonds in her hair. The hair was jet-black, and worn very low down on the forehead, almost reaching to the thick black eyebrows, beneath which shone a pair of eyes as black and bold as those of Circe herself. Her complexion had the olive clearness of a perfect brunette, and her mouth, which was ripe and full, was crimson red as some poisonous flower—not with blood, but paint. She was certainly very handsome, though somewhat *petite* and over-plump. Her only visible companion was a plainly dressed elderly woman, with whom she seldom exchanged a word, and a little boy of seven, elegantly dressed.

Bradley looked again and again, and the more he looked the more his wonder and horror grew. During all the rest of the performance he scarcely withdrew his eyes, but just before the curtain fell he slipped out of the pit, and passed round to the portico in front of the theatre.

There he waited, in the shadow of one of the pillars, till the throng began to flow forth, and the linkmen began summoning the carriages and cabs to take up their elegant burthens. The vestibule of the theatre was full of gentlemen in full dress and ladies in opera-cloaks, laughing and chatting over the evening's performance. He drew close to the glass doors and looked in, pale as death.

At last he saw the lady he sought, standing with the woman and the child, and talking gaily with an elderly gentleman who sported an eyeglass. How bold and beautiful she looked! He watched her in fascination, always taking care to keep out of the range of her vision.

At last she shook hands with the gentleman, and moved towards the door. He drew back into the shadow.

She stood on the threshold, looking out into the night, and the linkman ran up to her, touching his cap.

' Mrs. Montmorency's carriage,' she said in a clear silvery voice; and the man ran off to seek the vehicle.

Presently a smart brougham came up, and, accompanied by her elderly companion and the child, she stepped in. Almost simultaneously, Bradley crossed the pavement and leapt into a hansom.

' Keep that carriage in view,' he said to the

driver, pointing to the brougham, ' and I will give you a sovereign.'

The man laughed and nodded, and immediately the pursuit began.

CHAPTER V.

' MRS. MONTMORENCY.'

Ay me, I sowed a seed in youth,
Nor knew that 'twas a dragon's tooth,
Whereof has sprung to bring me shame
Legions of woe without a name.—*Fausticulus*.

THE brougham passed rapidly up Wellington Street into Long Acre, thence into Oxford Street, passing westward till it came to Regent Circus, then it was driven up Portland Place to the gates of Regent's Park. It entered, and the hansom followed about fifty yards behind. Passing to the left around the park, it reached Cranwell Terrace, and drew up before one of the large houses fronting the artificial water.

The hansom paused too, but Bradley kept his seat until he saw the lady and her companion alight, knock at the door, and enter in ; while the brougham drove round to the stables at the rear. Then he sprang out, paid the man his sovereign, and prepared to follow.

For a moment he hesitated on the steps of the house, as if undecided whether to knock or fly ; but recovering his determination he knocked loudly. The sound had scarcely died away when the door was opened by the same elderly woman he had noticed at the theatre.

' Mrs. Montmorency ? ' he said, for he had got the name by heart.

The woman looked at him in surprise, and answered with a strong French accent.

' Madame has only just come in, and you cannot see her to-night.'

' I *must* see her,' returned the clergyman, entering the hall. ' It is a matter of very important business.'

' But it is so late. To-morrow, monsieur ? '

' To-morrow I am leaving London. I must see her at once.'

Seeing his persistence, and observing that he had the manners of a gentleman, the woman yielded.

' If you will step this way, I will tell madame, but I am afraid she will not see you.'

So saying she led the way into a room on the ground floor, furnished splendidly as a kind of study, and communicating with a small dining-room, which in its turn led to a large conservatory.

' Your name, monsieur, if you please ? ' said the woman.

' My name is of no consequence—perhaps your mistress would not remember it. Tell her simply that a gentleman wishes to see her on very important business.'

With another look of wonder, the woman withdrew.

Still dreadfully pale and agitated, Bradley surveyed the apartment. It was furnished oddly, but with a perfect disregard of expense. A gorgeous Turkey carpet covered the floor; the curtains were of black-and-gold tapestry, the chairs of gold and crimson. In a recess, close to the window, was an elegant ormolu writing-desk, surmounted by a small marble statue, representing a young maid just emerging from the bath. Copies of well-known pictures covered the walls, but one picture was a genuine Etty, representing Diana and her

virgins surprised by Actæon. Over the mantelpiece, which was strewn with golden and
silver ornaments, and several photographs in
frames, was a copy of Titian's Venus, very
admirably coloured.

To the inexperienced mind of the clergyman, ill acquainted with a certain phase of
society, the pictures seemed sinister, almost
diabolic. The room, moreover, was full of a
certain sickly scent like *patchouli*, as if some
perfumed creature had just passed through it
leaving the scent behind.

He drew near the mantelpiece and looked
at the photographs. Several of them he failed
to recognise, though they represented women
well known in the theatrical world ; but in one
he recognised the elderly gentleman with the
eyeglass whom he had seen at the theatre, in

another the little boy, and in two the mistress of the house herself. In one of the two last she was represented semi-nude, in the spangled trunks, flesh-coloured tights, and high-heeled boots of some fairy prince.

He was gazing at this photograph in horror, when he heard the rustle of a dress behind him. Turning quickly, he found himself face to face with the woman he sought.

The moment their eyes met, she uttered a sharp cry and went even more pale than usual, if that were possible. As she recoiled before him, he thought she did so in fear, but he was mistaken. All she did was to move to the door, peep out into the lobby, then, closing the door rapidly, she faced him again.

The expression of her face was curious to behold. It was a strange mixture of devilry and effrontery. She wore the dress she had worn in the theatre—her arms, neck, and bosom were still naked and covered with diamonds; and her eyes flashed with a beautiful but forbidding light.

'So it is *you!*' she said in a low voice. 'At last!'

He stood before her like a man of marble, livid, ghastly, unable to speak, but surveying her with eyes of infinite despair. The sickly scent he had noticed in the room clung about her, and filled the air he was breathing.

There was a long silence. At last, unable any longer to bear his steadfast gaze, she laughed sharply, and, tripping across the room, threw herself in a chair.

'Well?' she said, looking up at him with a wicked smile.

His predominant thought then found a broken utterance.

'It is true, then!—and I believed you *dead!*'

'No doubt,' she answered, showing her white teeth maliciously, ' and you are doubtless very sorry to find yourself mistaken. No, I am very much alive, as you see. I would gladly have died to oblige you, but it was impossible, *mon cher.* But won't you take a seat? We can talk as well sitting as standing, and I am very tired.'

Almost involuntarily, he obeyed her, and taking a chair sat down, still with his wild eyes fixed upon her face.

' My God!' he murmured. ' And you are still the same, after all these years.'

She leant back in her chair, surveying him

critically. It was obvious that her light manner concealed a certain dread of him ; for her bare bosom rose and fell quickly, and her breath came in short sharp pants.

' And you, my dear Ambrose, are not much changed—a little older, of course, for you were only a foolish boy then, but still very much the same. I suppose, by your clerical necktie, that you have gone into the Church ? Have you got on well? I am sure I hope so, with all my heart ; and I always said you were cut out for that kind of life.'

He listened to her like one listening to some evil spirit in a dream. It was difficult for him to believe the evidence of his own senses. He had been so certain that the woman was dead and buried past recall !

' How did you find me out ? ' she asked.

' I saw you at the theatre, and followed you home.'

' *Eh bien !* ' she exclaimed, with a very doubtful French pronunciation. ' What do you want with me ? '

' Want with you ? ' he repeated. '**My God !** Nothing ! '

She laughed again, flashing her teeth and eyes. Then springing up, she approached a small table, and took up a large box of cigarettes. Her white hand trembled vio-lently.

' Can I offer you a cigarette ? ' she said, glancing at him over her naked shoulder.

' No, no ! '

' With your permission I will light one myself ! ' she said, striking a wax match and suiting the action to the word. Then holding the cigarette daintily between her white teeth, she again sat down facing him. 'Well, I am glad you have not come to make a scene. It is too late for that. We agreed to part long ago, and it was all for the best.'

'You *left* me,' he answered in a hollow voice.

'Just so,' she replied, watching the thin cloud of smoke as it wreathed from her lips. 'I left you because I saw we could never get along together. It was a stupid thing of us to marry, but it would have been a still stupider thing to remain tied together like two galley-slaves. I was not the little innocent fool you supposed me, and you were not the swell I at first imagined ; so we were both taken in. I went to India with young St. Clare, and after he left me I was very ill, and a report, which I did not contradict, got into the papers that I had died. I went on the stage out there under an assumed name, and some years ago returned to England.'

'And. now,' he asked with more decision than he had yet shown, 'how are you living?'

She smiled maliciously.

'Why do you want to know?'

He rose and stood frowning over her, and despite her assumed *sang-froid* she looked a little alarmed.

'Because, when all is said and done, I am your *husband!* Whatever you now call yourself, you are the same Mary Goodwin whom I married at Oxford ten years ago, and the tie which links us together has never been legally broken. Yet I find you here, living in luxury, and I suppose in infamy. Who pays for it all? Who is your present victim?'

With an impatient gesture and a flash of her white teeth she threw her cigarette into the fire, and rose up before him trembling, with fear, or anger.

'So you have found your tongue at last!' she said. 'Do you think I am afraid of you? No, I defy you! This is my house, and if you are not civil I will have you turned out of it. Bah! it is like you to come threatening me, at the eleventh hour.'

Her petulant rage did not deceive him; it was only a mask hastily assumed to conceal her growing alarm.

'Answer my question, Mary!—how are you living?'

'Sit down quietly, and I will tell you.'

He obeyed her, covering his eyes with his hand. She watched him for a moment ; then, reassured by his subdued manner, she proceeded.

' I am not sure that I ought to tell you, but I dare say you would find out. Lord Ombermere——'

' Lord Ombermere ! ' echoed the clergyman. ' Why, to my knowledge, he has a wife—and children.'

She shrugged her white shoulders, with a little grimace.

' That is his affair, not mine,' she said. ' For the rest, I know the fact, and never trouble myself about it. He is very good to me, and awfully rich. I have all I want. He sent me to France and had me taught French and music ; and he has settled a competence upon our boy. That is how the matter stands. I do pretty much as I like, but if Eustace knew I had a husband actually living he would make a scene, and perhaps we should have to part.'

' Is it possible ? — and — and are you happy ? '

' Perfectly,' was the cool reply.

Bradley paced up and down the chamber in agitation.

' Such a life is an infamy,' he at last exclaimed. ' It is an offence against man and God.'

' I know all that cant, and I suppose you speak as a clergyman ; but I do my duty by the man who keeps me, and never—like some I could name—have intrigues with other men. It wouldn't be fair, and it wouldn't pay. I hope,' she added, as if struck suddenly by the thought, ' you have not come here to-night imagining I shall return to *you?* '

He recoiled as if from a blow.

' Return to me? God forbid ! '

' So say *I,* though you might put it a little more politely. By the way, I forgot to ask you,—but perhaps you yourself have married again? '

The question came suddenly like a stab. Bradley started in fresh horror, holding his hand upon his heart. She exclaimed :—

' You might have done so, you know, thinking me food for worms, and if such were the case you may be sure I should never have betrayed you. No ; " live and let live " is my motto. I am not such a fool as to suppose you have never looked at another woman ; and if you had consoled yourself, taking some nice,

pretty, quiet, homely creature, fit to be a
clergyman's wife, to mend his stockings, and to
visit the sick with rolls of flannel and bottles of
beef-tea, I should have thought you had acted
like a sensible man.'

It was too horrible. He felt stifled, as-
phyxiated. He had never before encountered
such a woman, though their name is legion in
all the Babylons, and he could not understand
her. With a deep frown he rose to his feet.

'Are you going?' she cried. 'Pray don't,
till we understand each other!'

He turned and fixed his eyes despairingly
upon her, looking so worn, so miserable, that
even her hard heart was touched.

'Try to think I am really dead,' she said,
'and it will be all right. I have changed both
my life and my name, and no one of my old

friends knows me. I don't act. Eustace
wanted to take a theatre for me, but, after all,
I prefer idleness to work, and I am not likely
to reappear. I have no acquaintances out of
theatrical circles, where I am known only as
Mrs. Montmorency. So you see there is no
danger, *mon cher.* Let me alone, and I shall
let you alone. You can marry again whenever
you like.'

Again she touched that cruel chord, and
again he seemed like a man stabbed.

' Marry ? ' he echoed. ' But I am not free !
You are still my wife.'

'I deny it,' was the answer. ' We are
divorced ; I divorced myself. It is just the same
as if we had gone before the judge : a course
you will surely never adopt, for it would disgrace you terribly and ruin *me*, perhaps.

Eustace is horribly proud, and if it should all come out about his keeping me, he would never forgive me.   No, no, you'll never be such a fool!'

Yet she watched him eagerly, as if anxious for some assurance that he would not draw her into the open daylight of a legal prosecution.

He answered her, as if following her own wild thoughts—

'Why should I spare you?   Why should I drag on my lifetime, tied by the law to a shameless woman?   Why should I keep your secret and countenance your infamy?   Do you take me for one of those men who have no souls, no consciences, no honour?   Do you think that I will bear the horror of a guilty secret, now I know that you live, and that God has not been merciful enough to rid me of such a curse? '

It was the first time he had seemed really violent. In his pain he almost touched her with his clenched hand.

' You had better not strike me ! ' she said viciously.

At this moment the door opened, and a little boy (the same Bradley had seen at the theatre) ran eagerly in. He was dressed in a suit of black velvet, with bows of coloured ribbon, and, though he was pale and evidently delicate, he looked charmingly innocent and pretty.

' *Maman ! maman !* ' he cried in French.

She returned angrily, answering him in the same tongue—

' *Que cherchez-vous, Bébé?   Allez-vous-en !* '

'*Maman, je viens vous souhaiter la bonne nuit.*'

'*Allez, allez,*' she replied impatiently, '*je viendrai vous baiser quand vous serez couché.*'

With a wondering look at the stranger the child ran from the room.

The interruption seemed to have calmed them both. There was a brief silence, during which Bradley gazed drearily at the door through which the child had vanished, and his companion seemed lost in thought.

The time has perhaps come to explain that, if this worldly and sin-stained woman had one redeeming virtue, it was love for her little boy. True, she showed it strangely, being subject to curious aberrations of mood. The child was secretly afraid of her. Sometimes she would turn upon him, for some trivial fault, with violent passion ; the next moment she would cover him with kisses and load him with toys. In her heart she adored him ; indeed, he was the only thing in the world that she felt to be her own.   She knew how terribly his birth, when he grew up, would tell against his chances in life, and she had so managed matters that Lord Ombermere had settled a large sum of money unconditionally upon the child ; which money was already invested for him, in his mother's name, in substantial Government securities.   Her own relation with Ombermere, I may remark in passing, was a curious one.   Whenever he was in London, his lordship dropped in every afternoon at about four, as ' Mr. Montmorency ' ; he took a cup of tea in company with mother and child; at a quarter to six precisely he looked at his watch and rose to go ; and at seven he was dining in Bentinck Square, surrounded by his legal children, and faced by his lady. Personally, he was a mild, pale man, without intelligence or conversational powers of any kind, and 'Mrs. Montmorency' found his company exceedingly tedious and tame.

'You see my position,' said Mrs. Montmorency at last. 'If you have no consideration for me, perhaps you will have some for my boy.'

The clergyman sighed, and looked at her as if dazed.

'I must think it over,' he said. 'All this has come as a terrible shock upon me.'

'Shall I see you again ? '

'God knows ! '

'If you should call, never do so between

four and six ; those are Eustace's hours. I am generally in during the evening, unless I go to the theatre. Good night ! '

And with the ghost of a smile she extended her hand. He took it vacantly, and held it limply for a moment. Then he dropped it with another sigh, and went to the door, which he opened. Turning on the threshold, he saw her standing in the centre of the room, pale, beautiful, and baleful. She smiled again, flashing her eyes and showing her white teeth. With a shudder that went through all his frame, he passed out into the silent street.

It was now very late, and the Park lay still and sleeping under the dim light of the moon. From time to time a carriage passed by, but the pavement was quite deserted. Full of what he had seen, with the eyes of his soul turned inward to the horrible reflection, he wandered slowly along, his footfalls sounding hollow and ominous on the footpath, as he went.

Instinctively, but almost unreflectingly, he took the direction of his hotel; passed out of the park and into Harley Street, thence across Cavendish Square to Regent Circus.

It seemed now to him as if his fate was sealed. God, in indignation at his revolt, meant to deal him full measure. Attacked on one side by the thunders of the Church, and tormented on the other by the ghost of his own youthful folly, where was he to find firm foothold for his feet? His one comfort in the strenuousness of his intellectual strife had been the sympathy and devotion of a woman who was now surely lost to him for ever; a woman

who, compared to this frightful apparition of a
dead past, was a very spirit of heaven. Yes,
he loved an angel—an angel who would have
redeemed him ; and lo ! in the very hour of
his hope, his life was to be possessed by an
incarnate devil.

His thoughts travelled back to the past.

He thought of the time when he had first
known Mary Goodwin. He was a youth at
Oxford, and she was the daughter of a small
tradesman. She was very pretty and modest-
looking in those days ; though she knew the
world well, and the worst side of it, she seemed
to know it very little. His boy's heart went
out to her beauty, and he became entangled in
an amour which he thought a seduction ; she
played her part prettily, with no lack of
tears, so that, although he already knew that

his first wild fancy was not love, he married her.

Afterwards his eyes were opened. The tender looking, mildspoken, black-eyed little beauty showed that she had been only acting a part. As their marriage was a secret one, and they could not live together, she resided in the town, and was left a good deal to herself. Once or twice whispers came to his ears that he did not like, and he remonstrated with her; she answered violently, in such terms as opened his eyes still wider to her character. She was exorbitant in her demands for money, and she dressed gorgeously, in execrable taste. When his supplies fell short, as was inevitable, she was still well provided; and he accepted her statement that the supplementary sums came from her father. Once, coming upon her one evening unexpectedly, he found her hysterical and much the worse for liquor: empty champagne bottles and glasses were lying on the table, and the room was full of the scent of tobacco smoke. He discovered that two men of his own college had been calling upon her. A scene ensued, which was only one of many. I have no intention, however, of going into all the wretched details of what is a very common story ; but it is sufficient to say that Bradley discovered himself tied miserably to a creature without honour, without education, without virtue, sometimes without decency. Nevertheless he did not cast her off or expose her, but during the Vacation took her with him to London, trying hard to reclaim her. It was while they were stopping there that she relieved him of all further suspense by walking off one day with all his ready cash, and joining an officer whose acquaintance she had made by accident in the open street. Bradley searched for her everywhere without success. It was not for many weeks afterwards that he received a line from her, addressed from Gibraltar, telling him that she was *en route* for India, and that she had no wish either to see him or to hear from him again.

So she disappeared from his life, and when the report of her death reached him he was touched, but secretly relieved. Few even of his own personal friends knew much of this chapter of his experience: he had been wise enough to keep his actual marriage to the woman as dark as possible. So he entered the Church a free man, and purer than most men in having only one unfortunate record, throughout which he had acted honourably, on his conscience.

And now, after all those years, she had arisen from the grave! At the very moment when he was most threatened with other perils, of body and of soul, and when his place in the world of work and duty was most insecure, she had appeared, to drive him to despair! He had been so certain that she had passed away, with all her sins, that she had become in time almost a sad sweet memory, of one more sinned against than sinning. And all the time she had been roaming up and down the earth, painted and dissolute, cruel and predatory—no longer a reckless girl, but a cold, calculating woman, with all the audacity of her experience.

But she was worse, he thought; she, in her

splendour of wealth and mature beauty, was infinitely fouler. How calmly she wore her infamy! how lightly she trafficked with him for his silence, for his complicity! Unconscious of her own monstrosity, she dared to bargain with *him*—her husband—a priest of Christ!

Let those who sympathise with Bradley in his despair beware of sharing his revengeful thoughts. In simple fact, the woman was rising, not falling; her life, bad as it was from certain points of view, was still a certain advance upon what it once had been— was certainly a purer and an honester life than that of many men; than that, for example, of the honoured member of the aristocracy who paid her bills. She was faithful to this man, and her one dream was to secure comfort and security for her child. She had never loved Bradley, and had never pretended to love him. She did not wish to bring him any unhappiness. She had, as she expressed it, divorced herself, and, according to her conceptions of morality, she owed him no obligation.

But the more he thought of her and of the fatality of her resurrection, the more his whole soul arose in hate against her.

Of course there was one way which led to liberty, the one which she had implored him not to take. The law could doubtless at once grant him a formal divorce from the woman; but this could not be done without publicity, from which his soul shrank in horror. He pictured to himself how his adversaries would exult on seeing his name dragged through the mud! No; come what might, he would never think of that!

I cannot follow either his spiritual or his bodily wanderings any further at present. He walked the night away, not returning to his hotel until early dawn, when, pale, dishevelled, and wild, like a man after a night's dissipation (as, indeed, he seemed to the waiter, whose experience of clergymen on town visits was not small), he called for his hand-bag, had a hasty wash, and crept away to take the morning train.

CHAPTER VI.

ALMA.

Blue-buskin'd, with the softest turquoise blue,
Faint, as the speedwell's azure dim with dew ;
    As far away in hue
        As heaven the dainty shade is,
    From the dark ultra-blue
        Of literary ladies.—*The Mask.*

ON the morning that the Rev. Ambrose
Bradley, Vicar of Fensea, had his memorable
interview with the Bishop of Darkdale and
Dells, Miss Alma Craik, of the Larches,
walked on the home farm in the immediate
neighbourhood of her dwelling, accompanied
by her dear friend and companion Agatha
Combe, and attended by half a dozen dogs of

all sizes, from a melancholy old St. Bernard to
a frivolous Dandie Dinmont.

The two ladies, strolling along side by side,
presented a curious contrast, which was heightened not a little by their peculiarities of
costume. Miss Craik, bright as Eos, and tall
and graceful as a willow-wand, was clad in a
pink morning dress, with pink plush hat to
match, and carried a parasol of the same
colour. She walked lightly, with a carriage
which her detractors called proud, but which
her admirers thought infinitely easy and
charming ; conveying to the most casual observer that she was a young lady with a will
of her own, perfectly mistress of herself, and
at home among her possessions. Miss Combe,
on the other hand, was very short, scant of
breath, and dressed in a costume which looked

like widow's weeds, but which was nothing of the sort, for at five-and-fifty she was still a virgin. Her face was round and sunny, her eyes were bright and cheerful, and few could have recognised, in so homely and kindly looking a person, the champion of Woman's Rights, the leader-writer of the 'Morning News,' and the champion Agnostic of the controversial reviews.

Yet Miss Combe, though mild enough as a woman, was terribly fierce as a writer. She had inherited her style and opinions from her father, a friend and playfellow (if such an expression may be applied to persons who *never* played) of John Mill. She had been crammed very early with Greek, Latin, moral science, and philosophy; and she would certainly have developed into a female of the

genus Griffin, had it not been for a pious aunt
who invited her once a year into the country,
and there managed to fill her lungs with fresh
air and her mind with a certain kind of natural
religion. When Agnosticism was first invented
she clutched at the word, and enrolled herself
as an amazon militant under the banner of the
creed. She hated two things about equally—
Materialism and dogmatic Christianity. She
was, in fact, a busy little woman, with a kind
heart, and a brain not quite big enough to
grasp all the issues she was so fond of discussing.

Miss Craik had met her in London, and
had taken to her immediately—chiefly, if the
truth must be told, on account of her opinions;
for though Miss Craik herself was nominally
a Christian, she was already a sufficiently lax

one to enjoy all forms of heterodoxy. They had come together first on one great *quæstio vexata*, that of vivisection, for they both adored dogs, and Miss Combe was their most uncompromising champion against the users of the scalpel. So it happened in the course of time that they spent a part of the year together. The Larches was Miss Combe's house whenever she chose to come to it, which was very often, and she became, in a certain sense, the companion of her rich young friend.

Their way lay along green uplands with a distant sight of the sea, and they followed the footpath which led from field to field.

Presently Miss Combe, somewhat out of breath, seated herself on the foot-rest of a stile,

'Won't you take a rest, dear?' she said;
'there's room for two.'

The young lady shook her head. As she
fixed her eyes upon her companion, one
peculiarity of hers became manifest. She
was rather short-sighted, and, whenever ex·
amining anything or anybody, slightly closed
her eyelashes.

'If I were as rich as you,' continued Miss
Combe after a pause, 'I know what I should
do with my money.'

'Indeed! pray tell me.'

'I should build a church to the New
Faith!'

'Are you serious?' said Alma merrily.
'Unfortunately, I don't know what the new
faith is.'

'The faith of Humanity; not Comte's,

which is Frenchified rubbish, but the beautiful
faith in human perfection and the divine future
of the race. Just think what a Church it
would make! In the centre an altar "to the
Unknown God"; painted windows all round,
with the figures of all the great teachers, from
Socrates to Herbert Spencer, and signs of the
zodiac and figures of the planets, if you like,
on the celestial roof.'

'I don't quite see, Agatha, in what respect
the new Church would be an improvement on
the old one,' returned Alma; and as she spoke
her eyes travelled over the still landscape, and
saw far away, between her and the sea, the
glittering spire of the church of Fensea.

'It would be different in every particular,'
said Miss Combe good-humouredly. 'In the
first place, the architecture would be, of course,

pure Greek, and there would be none of the paraphernalia of superstition.'

'And Jesus Christ?—would He have any place there at all? or would you banish Him with the rest of the gods?'

'Heaven forbid! He should be pictured in the very central window, over the altar—not bleeding, horrible, and crucified, but as the happy painters represented Him in the early centuries, a beautiful young Shepherd—yes, beautiful as Apollo—carrying under His arm a stray lamb.'

Alma sighed, and shook her head again. She was amused with her friend's opinions, and they never seemed to shock her, but her own attitude of mind with regard to Christianity was very different.

'I don't think we have got so far as that

yet,' she said, still watching the distant spire. 'If you abolish Christ crucified you abolish Christ the Saviour altogether; for sorrow, suffering, and death were the signs of His heavenly mission. Besides, I am of Mr. Bradley's opinion, and think we have too many churches already.'

'Does *he* think so?' exclaimed Miss Combe with some surprise.

'Yes, I have often heard him say that God's temple is the best — the open fields for a floor and the vaulted heavens for a roof.'

Miss Combe rose, and they strolled on together.

'Is he as heterodox as ever?' asked Miss Combe.

'Mr. Bradley? I don't know what you

mean by heterodox, but he has his own opinions on the articles of his religion.'

'Just so. He doesn't believe in the miracles, for example.'

'Have you heard him say so?'

'Not explicitly, but I have heard——'

'You mustn't believe all the nonsense you hear,' cried Alma eagerly. 'He is too intellectual for the people, and they don't understand him. You shall go to church next Sunday, and hear him preach.'

'But I'm not a church-goer,' said the elder lady, smiling. 'On Sundays I always read Herbert Spencer. Sermons are always so stupid.'

'Not always. Wait till you hear Mr. Bradley. When I listen to him, I always think of the great Abelard, whom they called

" the angel of bright discourse." He says such wonderful things, and his voice is so beautiful. As he speaks, the church seems indeed a narrow place—too small for such words, for such a speaker; and you long to hear him on some mountain top, preaching to a multitude under the open sky.'

Miss Combe did not answer, but peeping sideways at her companion she saw that her face was warmly flushed, and her eyes were strangely bright and sparkling. She knew something, but not much, of Alma's relations with the vicar, and she hoped with all her heart that they would never lead to matrimony. Alma was too wise a vestal, too precious to the cause of causes, to be thrown away on a mere country clergyman. In fact, Miss Combe had an errant brother of her own who, though an objectionable person, was a freethinker, and in her eyes just the sort of husband for her friend. He was rather poor, not particularly handsome, and somewhat averse to soap and water; but he had held his own in platform argument with divers clergymen, and was generally accounted a ticklish subject for the Christians. So she presently remarked :—

'The finest speaker I ever heard is my brother Tom. I wish you could hear *him*.'

Alma had never done so, and, indeed, had never encountered the worthy in question.

'Is he a clergyman?' she asked innocently.

'Heaven forbid!' cried Miss Combe. 'No; he speaks at the Hall of Science.'

'Oh!'

'We don't quite agree philosophically, for he is too thick with Bradlaugh's party, but I know he's coming round to Agnosticism. Poor Tom! He is so clever, and has been so unfortunate. He married miserably, you know.'

'Indeed,' said Alma, not much interested.

'There was a black-eyed sibyl of a woman who admired one of the Socialist lecturers, and when he died actually went to his lodgings, cut off his head, and carried it home under her cloak in the omnibus.'

'Horrible!' said Alma with a shudder. 'But what for?'

'To *boil*, my dear, so that she might keep the skull as a sacred relic! When Tom was introduced to her she had it under a glass case on her mantelpiece. Well, she was a very intellectual creature, wonderfully "advanced," as they call it, and Tom was infatuated enough to make her his wife. They lived together for

a year or so; after which she took to
Spiritualism, and finally died in a madhouse.
So poor Tom's free, and I hope when he
marries again he'll be more lucky.'

Of course Miss Combe did not for a moment
believe that her brother would have ever had
any attraction in the eyes of her rich friend;
for Tom Combe was the reverse of winsome,
even to humbler maidens—few of whom felt
drawn to a man who never brushed his hair,
had a beard like a Communist refugee, and
smelt strongly of beer and tobacco. But blood
is thicker than water, and Miss Combe could
not forbear putting in a word in season.

The word made little or no impression.
The stately beauty walked silently on full of
her own thoughts and dreams.

CHAPTER VII.

A SIDE CURRENT.

That bore of bores—a tedious male cousin !—*Old Play*.

LOITERING slowly onward from stile to stile, from field to field, and from pasture to pasture, the two ladies at last reached a country road leading right through the heart of the parish, and commanding from time to time a view of the distant sea. They found Fensea, as usual, fast asleep, basking in the midst of its own breath; the red-tiled houses dormant, the population invisible, save in the square or market-place opposite the tavern, where a drowsy cart-horse was blinking into a water trough, and a somnambulistic ostler was vacantly looking on. Even in the open shops such as Radford the linendraper's and Summer-hayes the grocer's, nothing seemed doing. But just as they left the village behind them, and saw in front of them the spire of the village church peeping through the trees, they suddenly came face to face with a human being who was walking towards them in great haste and with some indications of ill-temper.

'Ah, here you are!' ejaculated this individual. 'I have been hunting for you up and down.'

He was a man under thirty, and looking very little over twenty, though his face showed little of the brightness and candour of early manhood. His hair was cropped close and he was clean-shaven; his eyes were yellowish and

large, of an expression so fixed and peculiar as
to have been compared by irreverent friends to
' hard-boiled eggs '; his forehead was low, his
jaw coarse and determined. With regard to
his dress, it was of the description known as
horsey ; short coat and tight-fitting trousers of
light tweed, a low-crowned hat of the same
material, white neckcloth fastened by a horse-
shoe pin.

This was George Craik, son of Sir George
Craik, Bart., of Craik Castle, in the neighbourhood, and Alma's cousin on her father's side.

Alma greeted him with a nod, while he
shook hands with her companion.

' Did you ride over, George ? ' she inquired.

' Yes ; I put my nag up at the George,
and walked up to the Larches. Not finding
you at home, I strolled down to the vicarage,

thinking to find you *there.* But old Bradley is not at home; so I suppose there was no attraction to take you.'

The young lady's cheek flushed, and she looked at her relation, not too amicably.

' Old Bradley, as you call him (though he is about your own age, I suppose), is away in London. Did you want to see him ? '

George shrugged his shoulders, and struck at his boots irritably with his riding-whip.

' I wanted to see *you,* as I told you. By the way, though, what's this they're telling me about Bradley and the Bishop? He's come to the length of his tether at last, I suppose? Well, I always said he was no better than an atheist, and a confounded radical into the bargain.'

' An atheist, I presume,' returned the

young lady superciliously, 'is a person who does not believe in a Supreme Being. When you describe Mr. Bradley as one, you forget he is a minister of the Church of Christ.'

George Craik scowled, and then laughed contemptuously.

'Of course *you* defend him!' he cried. 'You will tell me next, I dare say, that you share his opinions.'

'When you explain to me what they are, I will inform you,' responded Alma, moving slowly on, while George lounged after her, and Miss Combe listened in amused amazement.

'It's a scandal,' proceeded the young man, 'that a fellow like that should retain a living in the Church. Cripps tells me that his sermon last Sunday went slap in the face of the Bible. I myself have heard him say that some German fellow had proved the Gospels to be a tissue of falsehoods.'

Without directly answering this invective, Alma looked coldly round at her cousin over her shoulder. Her expression was not encouraging, and her manner showed a very natural irritation.

'How amiable we are this morning!' she exclaimed. 'Pray, do you come all the way from Craik to give me a discussion on the whole duty of a Christian clergyman? Really, George, such attempts at edification have a curious effect, coming from *you*.'

The young man flushed scarlet, and winced nervously under his cousin's too ardent contempt.

'I don't pretend to be a saint,' he said, 'but I know what I'm talking about. I call

Bradley a renegade! It's a mean thing, in my opinion, to take money for preaching opinions in which a man does not believe.'

' Only just now you said that he preached heresy—or atheism—whatever you like to call it.'

' Yes ; and is paid for preaching the very reverse.'

Alma could no longer conceal her irritation.

' Why should we discuss a topic you do not understand ? Mr. Bradley is a gentleman whose aims are too high for the ordinary comprehension, that is all.'

' Of course you think me a fool, and are polite enough to say so !' persisted George. ' Well, I should not mind so much if Bradley had not succeeded in infecting *you* with his pernicious opinions. He *has* done so, though you may deny it! Since he came to the neighbourhood, you have not been like the same girl. The fellow ought to be horse-whipped if he had his deserts.'

Alma stopped short, and looked the speaker in the face.

' Be good enough to leave me,—and come back when you are in a better temper.'

George gave a disagreeable laugh.

' No ; I'm coming to lunch with you.'

' That you shall not, unless you promise to conduct yourself like a gentleman.'

' Well, hang the parson,—since you can't bear him to be discussed. I didn't come over to quarrel.'

' You generally succeed in doing so, how-ever.'

'No fault of mine; you snap a fellow's head off, when he wants to give you a bit of good advice. There, there,' he added, laughing again, but not cordially, 'let us drop the subject. I want something to eat.'

Alma echoed the laugh, with about an equal amount of cordiality.

'Now you are talking of what you do understand. Lunch will be served at two.'

As she spoke they were passing by the church gate, and saw, across the churchyard, with its long rank grass and tombstones stained with mossy slime, the old parish church of Fensea :—a quaint timeworn structure, with an arched and gargoyled entrance, Gothic windows, and a belfry of strange device. High up in the belfry, and on the boughs of the great ash-trees surrounding the burial acre, jackdaws were gathered, sleepily discussing the weather and their family affairs. A footpath, much overgrown with grass, crossed from the church porch to a door in the weather-beaten wall communicating with the adjacent vicar age—a large, dismal, old-fashioned residence, buried in gloomy foliage.

Miss Combe glanced at church and church-yard with the air of superior enlightenment which a Christian missionary might assume on approaching some temple of Buddha or Brahma. George, glancing over the wall, uttered an exclamation.

'What's the matter now?' demanded Alma.

'Brown's blind mare grazing among the graves,' said young Craik with righteous in-dignation. He was about to enlarge further on the delinquencies of the vicar, and the shameful condition of the parish, of which he had just discovered a fresh illustration, but, remembering his recent experience, he controlled himself and contented himself with throwing a stone at the animal, which was leisurely cropping the grass surrounding an ancient headstone. They walked on, and passed the front of the vicarage, which looked out through sombre ash-trees on the road. The place seemed dreary and desolate enough, despite a few flower-beds and a green lawn. The windows were mantled in dark ivy, which drooped in heavy clusters over the gloomy door.

Leaving the vicarage behind them, the three followed the country road for about a mile, when, passing through the gate of a pretty lodge, they entered an avenue of larch-trees leading up to the mansion to which they gave their name. Here all was bright and well kept, the grass swards cleanly swept and variegated with flower-beds, and leading on to shrubberies full of flowering trees. The house itself, an elegant modern structure, stood upon a slight eminence, and was reached by two marble terraces commanding a sunny view of the open fields and distant sea.

It may be well to explain here that the Larches, with a large extent of the surrounding property, belonged to Miss Alma Craik in her own right, the lady being an orphan and an only child. Her father, a rich railway contractor, had bought the property and built the house just before she was born. During her infancy her mother had died, and before she was of age her father too had joined the great majority; so that she found herself, at a very early age, the heiress to a large property, and with no relations in the world save her uncle, Sir George Craik, and his son. Sir George, who had been knighted on the completion of a great railway bridge considered a triumph of engineering skill, had bought an adjacent property at about the time when his brother purchased the lands of Fensea.

The same contrast which was noticeable between the cousins had existed between the brothers, Thomas and George Craik. They were both Scotchmen, and had begun life as common working engineers, but there the resemblance ceased. Thomas had been a comparative recluse, thoughtful, melancholy, of advanced opinions, fond of books and abstruse speculation; and his daughter's liberal education had been the consequence of his culture, and in a measure of his radicalism. George was a man of the world, quick, fond of money, a Conservative in politics, and a courtier by disposition, whose ambition was to found a ' family,' and who disapproved of all social changes unconnected with the spread of the railway system and the success of his own commercial speculations. Young George was his only son, and had acquired, at a very early age, all the instincts (not to speak of many of the vices) of the born aristocrat. He was particularly sensitive on the score of his lowly origin, and his great grudge against society was that it had not provided him with an old-fashioned ancestry. Failing the fact, he assumed all the fiction, of an hereditary heir

of the soil, but would have given half his heir-
loom to any one who could have produced for
him an authentic 'family tree,' and convinced
him that, despite his father's beginnings, his
blood had in it a dash of 'blue.'

George Craik lunched with his cousin
and her companion in a spacious chamber,
communicating with the terrace by French
windows opening to the ground. He was
not a conversationalist, and the meal passed
in comparative silence. Alma could not fail
to perceive that the young man was unusually
preoccupied and taciturn.

At last he rose without ceremony, strolled
out on the terrace, and lit a cigar. He paced
up and down for some minutes, then, with the
air of one whose mind is made up, he looked
in and beckoned to his cousin.

' Come out here,' he said. ' Never mind your hat—there is no sun to speak of.'

After a moment's hesitation, she stepped out and joined him.

' Do you want me?' she asked carelessly. ' I would rather leave you to your smoke, and go to the library with Miss Combe. We're studying Herbert Spencer's " First Principles " together, and she reads a portion aloud every afternoon.'

She knew that something was coming by the fixed gaze with which he regarded her, and the peculiar expression in his eyes. His manner was far less like that of a lover than that of a somewhat sulky and tyrannical elder brother,—and indeed they had been so much together from childhood upward that she felt the relation between them to be quite a fraternal one.   Nevertheless, his mind just then was occupied with a warmer sentiment—the one, indeed, which often leads the way to wedlock.

He began abruptly enough.

'I say, Alma, how long is this to last?' he demanded not without asperity.

'What, pray?'

'Our perpetual misunderstandings.   I declare if I did not know what a queer girl you are, I should think you detested me!'

'I like you well enough, George,—when you are agreeable, which is not so often as I could wish.'

Thus she answered, with a somewhat weary laugh.

'But you know I like *you* better than anything in the world!' he cried eagerly. 'You know I have set my heart on making you my wife.'

'Don't talk nonsense, George!' replied Alma. 'Love between cousins is an absurdity.'

She would have added an 'enormity,' having during her vagrant studies imbibed strong views on the subject of consanguinity, but, advanced as she was, she was not quite advanced enough to discuss a physiological and social problem with the man who wanted to marry her. In simple truth, she had the strongest personal objection to her cousin, in his present character of lover.

'I don't see the absurdity of it,' answered the young man, 'nor does my father. His heart is set upon this match, as you know;

and besides, he does not at all approve of your living the life you do—alone, without a protector, and all that sort of thing.'

By this time Alma had quite recovered herself, and was able to reassume the air of sweet superiority which is at once so bewitching in a pretty woman, or so irritating. It did not bewitch George Craik; it irritated him beyond measure. A not inconsiderable experience of vulgar amours in the country, not to speak of the business known as ' sowing wild oats' in Paris and London, had familiarised him with a different type of woman. In his cousin's presence he felt, not abashed, but at a disadvantage. She had a manner, too, of talking down to him, as to a younger brother, which he disliked exceedingly; and more than once, when he had talked to her in the language of love, he had smarted under her ridicule.

So now, instead of taking the matter too seriously, she smiled frankly in his face, and quietly took his arm.

'You must not talk like that, George,' she said, walking up and down with him. 'When you do, I feel as if you were a very little boy, and I quite an old woman. Even if I cared for you in that way—and I don't, and never shall—we are not at all suited to each other. Our thoughts and aims in life are altogether different. I like you very much as a cousin, of course, and that is just the reason why I can never think of you as a husband. Don't talk of it again, please!—and forgive me for being quite frank—I should not like you to have any misconception on the subject.'

'I know what it is,' he cried angrily. 'It is that clergyman fellow! He has come between us.'

'Nothing of the sort,' answered Alma with heightened colour. 'If there was not another man in the world, it would be all the same so far as you and I are concerned.'

'I don't believe a word of it. Bradley is your choice. A pretty choice! A fellow who is almost a beggar, and in a very short time will be kicked out of the Church as a heretic.'

She released his arm, and drew away from him in deep exasperation ; but her feeling towards him was still that of an elder sister annoyed at the *gaucherie* of a privileged brother.

'If you continue to talk like that of Mr.

Bradley, we shall quarrel, George. I think you had better go home now, and think it over. In any case, you will do no good by abusing an innocent man who is vastly your superior.'

All the bad blood of George Craik's heart now mounted to his face, and his frame shook with rage.

'Bradley will have to reckon with me,' he exclaimed furiously. 'What right has he to raise his eyes towards you ? Until he came down here, we were the best of friends ; but he has poisoned your heart against me, and against all your friends. Never mind ! I'll have it out with him, before many days are done ! '

Without deigning to reply, Alma walked from him into the house.

An hour later, George Craik mounted his horse at the inn, and rode furiously homeward. An observer of human nature, noticing the expression of his countenance, and taking count of his square-set jaw and savage mouth, would have concluded perhaps that Alma estimated his opposition, and perhaps his whole character, somewhat too lightly. He had a bull-dog's tenacity, when he had once made up his mind to a course of action.

But when he was gone, the high-spirited lady of his affections dismissed him completely from her thoughts. She joined Miss Combe in the library, and was soon busy with the problem of the Unknowable, as presented in the pages of the clearest-headed philosopher of our time.

CHAPTER VIII.

MYSTIFICATIONS.

'What God hath joined, no man shall put asunder,'
Even so I heard the preacher cry—and blunder !
Alas, the sweet old text applied could be
Only in Eden, or in Arcady.
This text, methinks, is apter, more in season—
'What man joins, God shall sunder—when there's reason !'
Mayfair : a Satire.

AMBROSE BRADLEY came back from London
a miserable man. Alighting late in the evening at the nearest railway station, nearly ten
miles distant, he left his bag to be sent on by
the carrier, and walked home through the
darkness on foot. It was late when he knocked
at the vicarage door, and was admitted by his
housekeeper, a melancholy village woman,

M

whose husband combined the offices of gardener and sexton. The house was dark and desolate, like his thoughts. He shut himself up in his study, and at once occupied himself in writing his sermon for the next day, which was Sunday. This task occupied him until the early summer dawn crept coldly into the room.

The Sunday came, dull and rainy; and Bradley went forth to face his congregation with a deepening sense of guilt and shame. A glance showed him that Alma occupied her usual place, close under the pulpit, but he was careful not to meet her eyes. Not far from her sat Sir George Craik and his son, both looking the very reverse of pious minded.

It was a very old church, with low Gothic arches and narrow painted windows, through which little sunlight ever came. In the centre of the nave was the tomb of the old knight of Fensea, who had once owned the surrounding lands, but whose race had been extinct for nearly a century ; he was depicted, life-size, in crusader's costume, with long two-handed sword by his side, and hands crossed lying on his breast. On the time-stained walls around were other tombstones, with quaint Latin inscriptions, some almost illegible ; but one of brand-new marble recorded the virtues of Thomas Craik, deceased, the civil engineer.

Alma noticed in a moment that Bradley was ghastly pale, and that he faced his congregation with scarcely a remnant of his old assurance, or rather enthusiasm. His voice, however, was clear and resonant as ever, and under perfect command.

He preached a dreary sermon, orthodox enough to please the most exacting, and on an old familiar text referring to those sins which are said, sooner or later, to ' find us out.' All those members of the flock who had signed the letter to the Bishop were there in force, eager to detect new heresy, or confirmation of the old backsliding. They were disappointed, and exchanged puzzled looks with one another. Sir George Craik, who had been warned by his son to expect something scandalous, listened with a puzzled scowl.

The service over, Alma lingered in the graveyard, expecting the clergyman to come and seek her, as he was accustomed to do. He did not appear; but in his stead came her uncle and cousin, the former affectionately effusive, the latter with an air of respectful injury. They went home with her and spent the afternoon. When they had driven away, she announced her intention, in spite of showery weather and slushy roads, of going to evening service. Miss Combe expressed her desire of accompanying her, but meeting with no encouragement, decided to remain at home.

There were very few people at the church that evening, and the service was very short. Again Alma noticed the vicar's death-pale face and always averted eyes, and she instinctively felt that something terrible had wrought a change in him. When the service was done, she waited for him, but he did not come.

Half an hour afterwards, when it was

quite dark, she knocked at the vicarage door. It was answered by the melancholy housekeeper.

'Is Mr. Bradley at home? I wish to speak to him.'

The woman looked confused and uncomfortable.

'He be in, miss, but I think he be gone to bed wi' a headache. He said he were not to be disturbed, unless it were a sick call.'

Utterly amazed and deeply troubled, Alma turned from the door.

'Tell him that I asked for him,' she said coldly.

'I will, miss,' was the reply; and the door was closed.

With a heavy heart, Alma walked away Had she yielded to her first impulse, she would have returned and insisted on an interview; but she was too ashamed. Knowing as she did the closeness of the relationship between them, knowing that the man was her accepted lover, she was utterly at a loss to account for his extraordinary conduct. Could anything have turned his heart against her, or have aroused his displeasure? He had always been so different; so eager to meet her gaze and to seek her company. *Now*, it was clear, he was completely changed, and had carefully avoided her; nay, she had no doubt whatever, from the housekeeper's manner, that he had instructed her to deny him.

She walked on, half pained, half indignant. The night was dark, the road desolate.

All at once she heard footsteps behind

her, as of one rapidly running. Presently someone came up breathless, and she heard a voice calling her name.

'Is it *you*, Alma?' called the voice, which she recognised at once as that of Bradley.

'Yes, it is I,' she answered coldly.

The next moment he was by her side.

'I came after you. I could not let you go home without speaking a word to you.'

The voice was strangely agitated, and its agitation communicated itself to the hearer. She turned to him trembling violently, with an impulsive cry.

'O Ambrose, what has happened?'

'Do not ask me to-night,' was the reply. 'When I have thought it all over, I shall be able to explain, but not *now*. My darling, you must forgive me if I seem unkind and rude, but I have been in great, great trouble, and even now I can scarcely realise it all.'

'You have seen the Bishop?' she asked, thinking to touch the quick of his trouble, and lead him to confession.

'I have seen him, and, as I expected, I shall have to resign or suffer a long persecution. Do not ask me to tell you more yet! Only forgive me for having seemed cold and unkind—I would cut off my right hand rather than cause you pain.'

They were walking on side by side in the direction of the 'Larches.' Not once did Bradley attempt to embrace the woman he loved, or even to take her hand. For a time she retained her self-possession, but at last, yielding to the sharp strain upon her heart, she stopped short, and with a sob, threw her arms around his neck.

'Ambrose, why are you so strange? Have we not sworn to be all in all to one another? Have I not said that your people shall be my people, your God my God? Do not speak as if there was any change. Whatever persecution you suffer I have a right to share.'

He seemed to shrink from her in terror, and tried to disengage himself from her embrace.

'Don't, my darling! I can't bear it! I need all my strength, and you make me weak as a child. All *that* is over now. I have no right to love you.'

'No right?'

'None. I thought it might have been,

but now I know it is impossible. And I am not worthy of you ; I was never worthy.'

'Ambrose ! has your heart then changed ? '

'It will never change. I shall love you till I die. But now you must see that all is different, that our love is without hope and without blessing. There, there; don't weep ! '

'You will always be the same to me,' she cried. 'Whatever happens, or has happened, nothing can part you and me, if your heart is still the same.'

'You do not understand !' he returned, and as he spoke he gently put her aside. 'All must be as if we had never met. God help me, I am not so lost, so selfish, as to involve you in my ruin, or to preserve your love with a living lie. Have compassion on me ! I will see you again, or better still, I will write to you—and then, you will under-stand.'

Before she could say another word to him he was gone. She stood alone on the dark road, not far from the lights of the lodge. She called after him, but he gave no answer, made no sign. Terror-stricken, appalled, and ashamed, she walked on homeward, and enter-ing the house, passed up to her room, locked the door, and had her dark hour alone.

The next day Alma rose early after a sleepless night. She found awaiting her on the breakfast table a letter which had been brought by hand. She opened it and read as follows :

My Darling,—Yes, I shall call you so for the last time, though it means almost blasphemy. You would gather from my wild words last night that what has happened for ever puts out of sight and hope my dream of making you my wife. You shall not share my degradation. You shall not bear the burthen of my unfortunate opinions as a clergyman, now that my social and religious plans and aims have fallen like a house of cards. It is not that I have ceased to regard you as the one human being that could make martyrdom happy for me, or existence endurable. As long as life lasts I shall know that its only consecration would have come from you, the best and noblest woman I have ever met, or can hope to meet. But the very ground has opened under my feet. Instead of being a free agent, as I believed, I am a slave, to whom love is a forbidden thing. Even to think of it (as I have done once or twice, God help me, in my horror and despair) is an outrage upon *you*. I shall soon be far from here. I could not bear to dwell in the same place with one so dear, and to know that she was lost to me for ever. Grant me your forgiveness, and if you can, forget that I ever came to darken your life. My darling! my darling! I cry again for the last time from the depths of my broken heart, that God may bless you! For the little time that remains to me I shall have this one comfort—the memory of your goodness, and that you once loved me!

Ambrose Bradley.

Alma read this letter again and again in the solitude of her own chamber, and the more she read it the more utterly inscrutable it seemed.

That night Bradley sat alone in his study, a broken and despairing man. Before him on his desk lay a letter just written, in which he formally communicated to the Bishop his resignation of his living, and begged to be superseded as soon as possible. His eyes were red with weeping, his whole aspect was indescribably weary and forlorn. So lost was he in his own miserable thoughts, that he failed to notice a ring at the outer door, and a momentary whispering which followed the opening of the door. In another instant the chamber door opened, and a woman, cloaked and veiled, appeared upon the threshold.

'Alma!' he cried, recognising the figure in a moment, and rising to his feet in over-mastering agitation.

Without a word she closed the door, and

then, lifting her veil to show a face as white as marble, gazed at him with eyes of infinite sorrow and compassion. Meeting the gaze, and trembling before it, he sank again into his chair, and hid his face in his hands.

'Yes, I have come!' she said in a low voice; then, without another word, she crossed the room and laid her hand softly upon his shoulder.

Feeling the tender touch, he shivered and sobbed aloud.

'O, why did you come?' he cried. 'You —you—have read my letter?'

'Yes, Ambrose,' she answered in the same low, far-away, despairing voice. 'That is why I came—to comfort you if I could. Look up! speak to me! I can bear everything if I can only be still certain of your love.'

He uncovered his face, and gazed at her in astonishment.

'What! can you forgive me?'

'I have nothing to forgive,' she replied mournfully. 'Can you think that my esteem for you is so slight a thing, so light a straw, that even this cruel wind of evil fortu ie can blow it away? I know that you have been honourable in word and deed; I know that you are the noblest and the best of men. It is no fault of yours, dear, if God is so hard upon us; no, no, *you* are not to blame.'

'But you do not understand! I am a broken man. I must leave this place, and——'

'Listen to me,' she said, interrupting him with that air of gentle mastery which had ever exercised so great a spell upon him, and which gave to her passionate beauty a certain splendour of command. 'Do you think you are quite just to *me* when you speak—as you *have* spoken—of leaving Fensea, and bidding me an eternal farewell? Since this trouble in the church, you have acted as if I had no part and parcel in your life, save that which might come if we were merely married people ; you have thought of me as of a woman to whom you were betrothed, not as of a loving friend whom you might trust till death. Do you think that my faith in you is so slight a thing that it cannot survive even the loss of you as a lover, if that must be ? Do you not know that I am all yours, to the deepest fibre of my being, that your sorrow is my sorrow, your God my God —even as I said ? I am your sister still, even if I am not to be your wife, and whither you go, be sure I shall follow.'

He listened to her in wonder; for in proportion as he was troubled, she was strangely calm, and her voice had a holy fervour before which he bent in reverent humiliation. When she ceased, with her soft hand still upon his shoulder, he raised his eyes to her, and they were dim with tears.

'You are too good!' he said. 'I am the dust beneath your feet.'

'You are my hero and my master. As Heloise was to Abelard, so would I be to you. So why should you grieve? I shall be to you as before, a loving friend, perhaps a comforter, till death separates us in this world, to meet in a better and a fairer.'

He took her hands in his own, and kissed them, his tears still falling.

'Thank God you are so true! But how

shall I look you in the face after what has happened? You must despise me so much— yes, yes, you *must!*'

She would have answered him with fresh words of sweet assurance, but he continued passionately:

'Think of the world, Alma! Think of your own future, your own happiness! Your life would be blighted, your love wasted, if you continued to care for me. Better to forget me! better to say farewell!'

'Do *you* say that, Ambrose?' she replied; '*you* who first taught me that love once born is imperishable, and that those He has once united—not through the body merely, but through a sacrament of souls—can never be sundered? Nay, you have still your work to do in the world, and I—shall I not help you still? You will not go away?'

'I have written my resignation to the Bishop. I shall quit this place and the Church's ministry for ever.'

' Do not decide in haste,' she said. ' Is *this* the letter ? '

And as she spoke she went to the desk and took the letter in her hand.

' Yes.'

' Let me *burn* the letter.'

' Alma ! '

' Give yourself another week to think it over, for my sake. All this has been so strange and so sudden that you have not had time to think it out. For my sake, reflect.'

She held the letter over the lamp and looked at him for his answer; he hung down his head in silence, and, taking the attitude for acquiescence, she suffered the paper to reach

the flame, and in a few seconds it was con-
sumed.

'Good night!' she said.   'I must go now.'

'Good night! and God bless you, Alma!'

They parted without one kiss or embrace,
but, holding each other's hands, they looked
long and tenderly into each other's faces. Then
Alma went as she came, slipping quietly away
into the night.   But no sooner had she left the
vicarage than all her self-command forsook her,
and she wept hysterically under cover of the
darkness.

'Yes, his God is my God,' she murmured to herself.   'May He give me strength
to bear this sorrow, and keep us together
till the end!'

CHAPTER IX.

FAREWELL TO FENSEA.

I am sick of timeserving. I was borne in the land of
Mother-Nakedness; she who bare me was a true woman, and
my father was sworn vassal to King Candour, ere he died of a
sunstroke; but villains robbed me of my birthright, and I was
sent to serve as a mercenary in the army of old Hypocrisy,
whom all men now hail Emperor and Pope. Now my armour
is rotten, my sword is broken, and I shall never fight more.
Heigho! I would I were sleeping under a green tree, in the
land where the light shines, and there is no lying!—*The Comedy
of Counterfeits.*

AFTER that night's parting the lovers did
not meet for several days. Bradley went
gloomily about his parochial duties, and
when he was not so engaged he was shut
up in his study, engaged in correspondence
or gloomy contemplation. Alma did not

seek him out again, for the very simple reason that the nervous shock she had received had seriously affected her generally robust health, and brought on a sort of feverish hysteria complicated with sleeplessness, so that she kept her room for some days, finding a homely nurse in Miss Combe. When Sunday came she was too unwell to go to church.

In the afternoon she received the following letter :—

DEAREST ALMA,—For so I must still call you, since my spirit shrinks from addressing you under any more formal name. I have heard that you are ill, and I know the cause is not far to seek, since it must lie at the door of him whose friendship has brought you so much misery. Pray God it is only a passing shadow in your sunny life! An eternity of punishment would not adequately meet my guilt if it should seriously imperil your happiness or your health! Write to me, since I dare not, must not, come to you — just one word to tell me you are better, and that my fears on your account are without foundation. In the pulpit to-day, when I missed your dear face, I felt terror-stricken and utterly abandoned. Hell itself seemed opening under my feet, and every word I uttered seemed miserable blasphemy. I knew then, if I did not know it before, that my faith, my religion, my eternal happiness or misery, still depend on *you.* A. B.

Two hours later Bradley received this reply :—

'Do not distress yourself, dearest. I shall soon be quite well again. I have been thinking it all over in solitude, and I feel quite sure that if we are patient God will help us. Try to forget your great persecution, and think rather of what is more solemn and urgent—your position in the Church, and the justification of your faith before the world.'

Ambrose Bradley read the above, and thought it strangely cold and calm; he was himself too distracted to read between the lines and perceive the bitter anguish of the writer. He still lacked the moral courage to make a clean breast of the truth, and confess to Alma that his change had come through that sad discovery in London. He dreaded her sorrow more than her anger; for he knew, or feared, that the one unpardonable sin in her eyes would be—to have loved another woman. She had no suspicion of the truth. An entanglement of a disgraceful kind, involving the life of a person of her own sex, was the last thing to occur to her mind in connection with her lover. She attributed everything, his change of manner, his strange passion, his unreasoning despair, to the exquisite sensitiveness of a proudly intellectual nature. How deluded she was by her own idolatry of his character the reader knows. What cared he for the Church's inquisition *now?* What cared he for dogmatic niceties, or spiritual difficulties, or philosophic problems? He was sick of the whole business. The great

problem troubled him no longer, save that
he felt more and more in revolt against
any kind of authority, more and more tired
of the sins and follies and blind fatalities of
the world. Even her tender appeals to his
vanity seemed trivial and beside the question.
His ambition was dead.

Again and again he tried to summon up
courage enough to make a complete explanation; but his heart failed him, and so
he temporised. He *could* not say the word
which, in all probability, would sunder
them for ever. He would wait; perhaps
Heaven, in its mercy, might relieve him,
and justify him. In his own mind he felt
himself a martyr; yet he could escape the
sense of contamination consequent on the
possession of so guilty a secret. The pure

currents of his life seemed poisoned,—as indeed they were.

The situation was a perilous one. Behind all Alma's assumption of tender acquiescence, she was deeply wounded by her lover's want of confidence in her devotion. His manner had shocked her inexpressibly, more even than she yet knew, yet it only drew her more eagerly towards him. In her despair and anger, she turned to the topic which, from the first moment of their acquaintance, had been constantly upon his tongue, and she tried to persuade herself that her strongest feeling towards him was religious and intellectual. In reality, she was hungering towards him with all the suppressed and suffocating passion of an unusually passionate nature. Had he been

a reckless man, unrestrained by moral sanctions, she would have been at his mercy.
So implicit was her faith in the veracity of
his perception, and so strong at the same time
was his personal attraction for her, that she
might have been ready, for his sake, had he
told her the whole truth, to accept as right
any course of conduct, however questionable,
which he might sanctify as right and just.

From all this it will be gathered that Miss
Alma Craik was in a position of no inconsiderable peril. She had long been dwelling
far too much in the sphere of ideas, not to say
crotchets, for a young lady without protectors.
Her one safeguard was her natural purity of
disposition, coupled with her strength of will.
She was not the sort of woman to be seduced
into wrong-doing, as weak women are seduced,

against her conscience. Any mistake she might make in life was certain to be the result of her own intellectual acquiescence,—or of wilful deception, which indeed was imminent.

So the days passed on, in deepening gloom ; for the situation was a wretched one. Many other letters were interchanged, but the two seldom met, and when they did it was only briefly and in the presence of other people.

It was a life of torture, and could not last.

Meantime the Bishop of the diocese had not been idle. He had consulted with the powers of the Church, and all had come to one conclusion—that under any circumstances, a public scandal must be avoided. Pending any action on the part of his superiors, Bradley gave no fresh occasion for offence. His sermons became old-fashioned, not to say infantine. For the rest, he was ready to resign at a moment's notice; and he wrote to the Bishop to that effect, inviting him to choose a successor.

'After thinking the matter well over,' he wrote, 'I have concluded that your lordship is right, and that my opinions are at present out of harmony with the principles of the Establishment. A little while ago I might have been inclined to stand my ground, or at any rate not to yield without a protest; but my mind has changed, and I shall resign without a murmur. Nor shall I seek another living in the English Church as at present constituted. Even if I were likely to succeed in my search, I should not try. Let me depart in peace, and rely on my uttering no syllable which can be construed into resistance.'

The Bishop answered him eagerly, in the following words :

MY DEAR SIR,—I think you have decided wisely, and I am grateful to you for the temper in which you have accepted the situation. You have the spirit of a true Christian, though your ideas are errant from the great principles of Christianity. What I would suggest is this, and I hope it will meet with your approval :— that under the plea of ill-health, or some similar pretext, you offer your resignation, and withdraw *temporarily* from your ministry. I say temporarily, because I believe that a brief period of reflection will bring you back to us, with all your original enthusiasm, with all the fresh faith and fervour of your first days. When that time comes, the Church, I need not say, will remember your self-sacrifice, and receive you back in due season like the Prodigal Son. Until then, believe me, now as ever, your faithful friend and well-wisher,

         W. M., DARKDALE AND DELLS.

The result of this correspondence was speedily seen in a paragraph which appeared in the ' Guardian ' :—

' We understand that the Rev. Ambrose Bradley, M.A., vicar of Fensea, has resigned his living on account of continued ill-health. The living is in the gift of the Bishop of the diocese, who has not yet appointed a successor.'

This paragraph was copied into the local paper, and when they read it, the Craiks (father and son) were exultant. Alma saw it also, but as Bradley had privately intimated his decision to her, it caused her no surprise. But an affair of so much importance was not destined to be passed over so quietly. A few days later, a paragraph appeared in some of the more secular journals to the effect that the Vicar of Fensea had 'seceded' from the Christian Church, on account of his inability to accept its dogmas, more particularly the Miracles and the Incarnation. The announcement fell like a thunderbolt, and no one was more startled by it than the clergyman himself.

He at once sat down and wrote the following letter to the ' Guardian ' :—

Sir,—I have seen with much pain a paragraph in several journals to the effect that my reason for resigning the living of Fensea is because I have ceased to believe in the essential truths of Christianity. Permit me with indignation to protest against this unwarrantable imputation, both upon myself and upon a religion for which I shall always have the deepest reverence. My reasons for ceasing to hold office are known to the Church authorities alone. It is enough to say that they are partly connected with physical indisposition, and partly with private matters with which the public has nothing to do. I believe now, as I have always believed, that the Church of England possesses within herself the secret which may yet win back an errant world into the fold of Christian faith. In ceasing to hold office as a Christian clergyman, I do not cease in my allegiance to Jesus Christ or to the Church He founded; and all assertions to the contrary are quite without foundation. —I am, Sir, &c.,

AMBROSE BRADLEY.

It will be seen that this epistle **was** couched in the most ambiguous terms; it **was** perfectly true, yet thoroughly misleading, **as** indeed it was meant to be. When he had written and posted it, Bradley felt that he had reached the depth of moral humiliation. Still, he had not the heart just then to say anything which might do injury, directly or indirectly, to the Establishment in which he had been born and bred.

CHAPTER X.

FROM THE POST-BAG.

I.

Ambrose Bradley to Alma Craik.

Versailles,——, 18—.

DEAREST ALMA,—I came here from Rouen this day week, and have more than once sat down to write to you; but my heart was too full, and the words would not come, until to-day. Since we parted—since at your loving intercession I consented to wander abroad for a year, and to write you the record of my doings from time to time—I have been like a man in the Inferno, miserable, despairing, thinking only of the Paradise from which he has fallen ; in other words, my sole thought has been of the heavenly days now past, and of you.

Well, I must not talk of that ; I must conquer my passionate words and try to write coldly, dispassionately, according to promise, of the things that I have seen. That I can do so at all, will be a proof to you, my darling, that I am already much better. Another proof is that I am almost able (as you will see when you read on) to resume my old British prerogative of self-satisfied superiority over everything foreign, especially over everything French. It is extraordinary how thoroughly national even a cold-blooded cosmopolite becomes when he finds himself daily confronted by habits of thought he does not understand.

I am staying at a small hotel on the Paris side of Versailles, within easy reach of the gay city either by train or tram. I have exchanged my white neckcloth for a black necktie, and there is nothing in my dress or manner to mark me out for that most disagreeable of fishes out of water—a Parson in Paris! I see my clerical brethren sometimes, white-tied, black-coated, broad-brim'd-hatted, striding along the boulevards defiantly, or creeping down bye-streets furtively, or peeping like guilty things into the windows of the photograph shops in the Rue Rivoli. As I pass them by in my rough tourist's suit, they doubtless take me for some bagman out for a holiday; and I—I smile in my sleeve, thinking how out of place they seem, here in Lutetia of the Parisians. But my heart goes out most to those other brethren of mine, who draw their light from Rome. One pities them deeply *now*, in the time of their tribulation, as they crawl, forlorn and despised, about their weary work. The public prints are full of cruel things con cerning them, hideous lampoons, unclean caricatures ; what the Communist left surviving the journalist daily hacks and stabs. And indeed, the whole of this city presents the peculiar spectacle of a people without religion, without any sort of spiritual aspiration. Even that vague effluence of transcendental liberal-ism, which is preached by some of their leading poets and thinkers, is pretty generally despised. Talking with a leading bookseller the other day concerning your idol, Victor Hugo, and discussing his recent utterances on religious subjects, I found the good *bourgeois* to be of opinion that the great poet's brain was softening through old age and personal vanity! The true hero of the hour, now all the tinsel of the Empire is rubbed away, is a writer named Zola, originally a printer's devil, who is to modern light literature what Schopenhauer is to philosophy—a dirty, muddy, gutter-searching pessimist, who translates the ' anarchy ' of the ancients into the bestial *argot* of the Quarties Latin.

It has been very well said by a wit of this nation that if on any fine day the news arrived in Paris that ' *God was dead*,' it would not cause the slightest astonishment or interest in a single *salon*; indeed, to all political intents and purposes the Divinity is regarded as extinct. A few old-fashioned people go to church, and here and there in the streets you see little girls in white going to confirmation; but the majority of the people are entirely without the religious sentiment in any form. A loathsome publication, with hideous illustrations, called the *Bible pour Rire*, is just now being issued in penny numbers; and the character of its humour may be guessed when I tell you that one of the pictures represents the 'bon Dieu,' dressed like an old clothesman, striking a lucifer on the sole of his boot, while underneath are the words, 'And God said, Let there be Light!' The same want of good taste, to put reverence aside as out of the question, is quite as manifest in the higher literature, as where Hugo himself, in a recent poem, thus describes the Tout-Puissant, or All-Powerful :—

> Pris d'un vieux rhumatisme incurable à l'échine,
> Après avoir créé le monde, et la machine
> Des astres pêle-mêle au fond des horizons,
> La vie et l'engrenage énorme des saisons,
> La fleur, l'oiseau, la femme, et l'abîme, et la terre,
> Dieu s'est laissé tomber dans son fauteuil-Voltaire !

Is it any wonder that a few simple souls, who still cherish a certain reverence for the obsolete orthodox terminology should go over in despair to Rome?

One of the great questions of the day, discussed in a spirit of the most brutal secularity, is Divorce. I know your exalted views on this subject, your love of the beautiful old fashion which made marriage eternal, a sacrament of souls, not to be abolished even by death itself. Well, our French neighbours wish to render it a simple contract, to be dissolved at the whim of the contracting parties. Their own social life, they think, is a living satire on the old dispensation.

But I sat down to write you a letter about myself, and here I am prosing about the idle topics of the day, from religion to the matrimonial musical glasses. I am wonderfully well in body; in fact, never better. But oh, my Alma, I am still miserably sick of soul! More than ever do I perceive that the world wants a creed. When the idea of God is effaced from society, it becomes—this Paris— a death's head with a mask of pleasure :—

> The time is out of joint—ah cursed spite,
> That ever I was born to set it right !

All my foolish plans have fallen like a house of cards. I myself seem strangling in the evils of the modern snake of Pessimism. If

it were not for you, my guardian angel, my
star of comfort, I think I should try euthan-
asia. Write to me! Tell me of yourself, of
Fensea; no news that comes from my heaven
on earth will fail to interest and soothe me.
What do you think of my successor? and what
does the local Inquisition think of him? Next
to the music of your voice will be the melody
of your written words. And forgive this long
rambling letter. I write of trifles light as air,
because I *cannot* write of what is deepest in
my heart.—Yours always,

AMBROSE BRADLEY.

II.

From Alma Craik to Ambrose Bradley.

THANKS, DEAREST AMBROSE, for your long
and loving letter. It came to me in good

season, when I was weary and anxious on your account, and I am grateful for its good tidings and its tone of growing cheerfulness. You see my prescription is already working wonders, for you wrote like your old self—almost! I am so glad that you are well in health, so thankful you are beginning to forget your trouble. If such a cure is possible in a few short weeks, what will time not do in a year?

There is no news, that is, none worth telling.

Your successor (since you ask concerning him) is a mild old gentleman with the most happy faith in *all* the articles of the Athanasian creed—particularly that of eternal punishment, which he expounds with the most benevolent of smiles. I should say he will be a favourite ; indeed, he is a favourite already, though he has the disadvantage, from the spinster point of view, of being a very, very married man. He has a wife and seven children, all girls, and is far too poor in this world's goods to think much of his vested interest in those of the next world. I have heard him preach once, which has sufficed.

What you say of life in France interests me exceedingly, and my heart bleeds for those poor priests of the despised yet divine creed. If you had not taught me a purer and a better faith, I think I should be a Roman Catholic, and even as it is, I can feel nothing but sympathy for the Church which, after all, possesses more than all others the form of the Christian tradition.

Agatha Combe has returned to London. She is still full of that beautiful idea (was it yours or mine, or does it belong to both of us?) of the New Church, in which Religion, Science, and Art should all meet together in one temple, as the handmaids of God. I hope you have not dismissed it from your mind, or forgotten that, at a word from you, it may be realised. Agatha's conception of it was, I fear, a little too secular; her Temple of worship would bear too close a resemblance to her brother's dingy Hall of Science. She has just finished a treatise, or essay, to be published in one of the eclectic magazines, the subject, ' Is growth possible to a dogmatic religion ? ' Her answer is in the negative, and she is dreadfully severe on what she calls the ' tinkering ' fraternity, particularly her *bête noire*, young Mr. Mallock. Poor Agatha ! She should have been a man by rights, but cruel fate, by just a movement of the balance, made her the dearest of old maids, and a Blue! Under happier conditions, with just a little less of the intellectual leaven, she would have made a capital wife for such a parson as your successor; for in spite of her cleverness, and what they call her infidelity, she is horribly superstitious—won't pass a pin in the road without lifting it up, throws salt over her shoulder if she happens to spill a morsel, and can tell your fortune by the cards! Besides all this, she is a born humanitarian; her thoughts for ever running on the poor, and flannel, and soup-kitchens, and (not to leave the lower animals out of her large heart) the woes of the vivisected dogs and rabbits. And yet, when the pen is in her hand and her controversial vein is open, she hurls her argumentative thunderbolts about like a positive Demon!

There, I am trying to rattle on, as if I were a giddy girl of eighteen. But my heart, like yours, is very full. Sometimes I feel as if you were lost to me for ever; as if you were gone into a great darkness, and would never come back. Dearest, you think of me sometimes—nay, often?— and when your wound is healed, you will come back to me, better and stronger and happier than ever, will you not? For am I not your Rachel, who still follows you in soul wherever you go? I sit here for hours together, thinking of the happy days that are fled for ever; then I wander out to the churchyard, and look at the dear old vicarage, and wherever I go I find some traces of him

I love. Yesterday I went over to the abbey. Do you remember, dear, when we last met there, and swore our troth in the moonlight, with our ears full of the solemn murmuring of the sea?

That reminds me of what you say concerning the French agitation on the subject of Divorce. I read some time ago an abstract of M. Naquet's famous discourse—it was published in the English newspapers—and I felt ashamed and sad beyond measure. How low must a nation have fallen when one of its politicians dares to measure with a social foot-rule the holiest of human covenants! If marriage is a bond to be worn or abandoned at pleasure, if there is nothing more sacred between man and woman than the mere union of the body, God help us women, and *me* most of all! For has not God already united my soul to yours, not as yet by the sacrament of the Church, but by that sacrament of Love which is also eternal; and if we were spiritually sundered, should I not die; and if I thought that Death could break our sacrament of Love, should I not become even as those outcast ones who believe there is no God? I have never loved another man; you have never loved (how often have you not sworn it to me!) another woman. Well, then, can man ever separate what God has so joined together? Even if we were never man and wife in the conventional sense, even if we never stand together at the earthly altar, in the eyes of Heaven we are man and wife, and we have been united at the altar of God. This, at least, is my conception of Marriage.

Between those that love, Divorce (as these hucksters call it) is impossible.

Alas! I write wildly, and my Abelard will smile at his handmaid's eager words. 'Methinks the lady doth protest too much,' I hear him exclaim with Shakespeare. But I know that you hold with me that those things are holy beyond vulgar conception.

Write to me again soon. All my joy in life is hearing from you.—Ever your own,

ALMA.

III.

From Ambrose Bradley to Alma Craik.

DEAREST ALMA,—Just a few lines to say that I am going on to Germany; I will write to you again directly I come to an anchorage in that brave land. For I am sick of France and Frenchmen; sick of a people that have not been lessoned by misfortune, but still hunger for aggression and revenge; sick of the Dead Sea fruit of Parisian pleasure, poisoned and heart-eaten by the canker-worm of unbelief. Our English poetess is virtuously indignant (you remember) with those who underrate this nation.

> The English have a scornful insular way
> Of calling the French light, &c.

And it is true they are not light, but with the weight of their own blind vanity, heavy as lead. The curse of spiritual dulness is upon them. They talk rhodomontade and believe in nothing. How I burn for the pure intellectual air of that nobler people which, in the name of the God of Justice, recently taught France so terrible a lesson! Here, in France, every man is a free agent, despising everything, the government which he supports, the ideas which he fulminates, despising most his own free, frivolous, miserable self: there, in Germany, each man is a patriot and a pillar of the state, his only dream to uphold the political fabric of a great nation. To efface one's selfish interest is the first step to becoming a good citizen; to believe in the government of God, follows as a natural consequence.

What you say about our spiritual union, touches me to the soul, though it is but the echo of my own fervent belief. But I am not so sure that *all* earthly unions, even when founded in affection and good faith, are indissoluble. Surely also, there are marriages which it is righteous to shatter and destroy?

You are a pure woman, to whom even a thought of impurity is impossible; but alas! all women are not made in the same angelic mould, and we see every day the spectacle of men linked to partners in every respect unworthy. Surely you would not hold that the union of a true man with a false woman, a woman who (for example) was untrue to her husband in thought and deed, is to last for ever? I know that is the Catholic teaching, that marriage is a permanent sacrament, and that no act of the parties, however abominable, can render either of them free to marry again; and we find even such half-hearted Liberals as Gladstone upholding it (see his 'Ecclesiastical Essays'), and flinging mud in the blind face of Milton, because (out of the bitterness of his own cruel experience) he argued the contrary. Divorce is recognised in our own country and countenanced by our own religion ; and I believe it to be necessary for the guarantee of human happiness. What is most hideous in our England is the horrible institution of the civil Court, where causes that should be heard *in camerâ* are exposed shamefully to the light of day ; so that men would rather bear their life-long torture than submit to the ordeal of a degrading publicity, and only shameless men and women dare to claim their freedom at so terrible a price.

I intended to write only a few lines, and here am I arguing with you on paper, just as we used to argue in the old times *vivâ voce*, on a quite indifferent question. Forgive me ! And yet writing so seems like having one of our nice, long, cosy, serious talks. Discussions of this kind are like emptying one's pocket to find what they contain ; I never thought I had any ideas on the subject till I began, schoolboy-like, to turn them out !

God bless you, my darling ! When you hear from me next, I shall be in the land of the ' ich ' and the ' nicht ich,' of beer and philosophy, of Deutschthum and Strasbourg pies.

AMBROSE BRADLEY.

IV.

The Same to the Same.

DEAREST,—I wrote to you the other day from Berlin—merely a line to say that my movements were uncertain, and asking you to address your next letter care of Grädener the banker, here at Frankfort. I suppose there must have been some delay in the transmission, or the letter must have gone astray: at all events, here I am, and grievously disappointed to find you have not written. Darling, do not keep me in suspense; but answer this by return, and then you shall have a long prosy letter descriptive of my recent experiences. Write! write!

AMBROSE BRADLEY.

V.

Alma Craik to Ambrose Bradley.

DEAREST AMBROSE,—You are right in supposing that your letter from Berlin went astray; it has certainly never reached me, and you can imagine my impatience in consequence. However, all's well that ends well; and the sight of your dear handwriting is like spring sunshine.

Since I last wrote to you I have been reading in a French translation those wonderful letters of Héloïse to the great Abelard, and his to her ; and somehow they seemed to bring you close to me, to recall your dear face, the very sound of your beautiful voice. Dearest, what would you have said if I had addressed this letter to you in the old sweet terms used by my prototype— not for the world to see, but for your loving eyes alone? 'A son maître, ou plutôt à son père ; à son époux, ou plutôt à son frère : sa servante, ou plutôt sa fille ; son épouse, ou plutôt sa sœur ; à Ambrose, Alma.' All these and more are you to me, my master and my father, my husband and my brother ; while I am at once your servant and your daughter, your sister and your spouse. Do you believe, did you ever feel inclined to believe, in the transmigration of souls? As I read these letters, I seem to have lived before, in a stranger, stormier time; and every word *she* wrote seemed to be the very echo of my burning heart. Ah! but our lot is happier, is it not? There is no shadow of sin upon *us* to darken our loving dream: we have nothing to undo, nothing to regret; and surely our spiritual union is blest by God. For myself, I want only one thing yet to complete my happiness— to see you raised as *he* was raised to a crown of honour and glory in the world. What I think of you, all mankind must think of you, when they know you as I know you, my apostle of all that is great and good. Ah, dearest, I would gladly die, if by so doing I could win you the honour you deserve.

But I must stop now. When I begin to

write to you, I scarcely know when to cease. *Adieu, tout mon bien !*

ALMA.

VI.

Ambrose Bradley to Alma Craik

' À Alma, sa bien-aimée épouse et sœur en Jésus-Christ, Ambrose son époux et frère en Jésus-Christ ! ' Shall I begin thus, dearest, in the very words of the great man to whom, despite my undeserving, you have lovingly compared me ? You see I remember them well. But alas ! Abelard was thrown on different days, when at least faith was *possible*. What would he have become, I wonder, had he been born when the faith was shipwrecked, and when the trumpet of Euroclydon was sounding the destruction of all the creeds? Yonder, in France, one began to doubt everything, even the divinity of love; so I fled from the Parisian Sodom, trusting to find hope and comfort among the conquerors of Sedan. Alas! I begin to think that I am a sort of modern Diogenes, seeking in vain for a people with a Soul. I went first to Berlin, and found there all the vice of Paris without its beauty, all the infidelity of Frenchmen without their fitful enthusiasm in forlorn causes. The people of Germany, it appears to me, put God and Bismarck in the same category; they accept both as a solution of the political difficulty, but they truly reverence neither. The typical German is a monstrosity, a living contradiction: intellectually an atheist, he assents to the conventional uses of Deity;

politically a freethinker, he is a slave to the
idea of nationality and a staunch upholder
of the divine right of kings. Long ago,
the philosophers, armed with the jargon of
an insincere idealism, demolished Deism with
one hand and set it up with the other;
what they proved by elaborate treatises not
to exist, they established as the only order
of things worth believing; till at last the
culmination of philosophic inconsistency was
reached in Hegel, who began by the destruction of all religion and ended in the
totem-worship of second childhood. In the
course of a very short experience, I have
learned cordially to dislike the Germans, and
to perceive that, in spite of their tall talk
and their splendid organisation, they are
completely without ideas. In proportion as

they have advanced politically, they have retrograded intellectually. They have no literature now and no philosophy; in one word, no spiritual zeal. They have stuck up as their leader a man with the moral outlook of Brander in 'Faust,' a swash-buckler politician, who swaggers up and down Europe and frowns down liberalism wherever it appears. Upon my word, I even preferred the Sullen Talent which he defeated at Sedan.

I think I see you smiling at my seeming anger; but I am not angry at all—only woefully disenchanted.

This muddy nation stupefies me like its own beer. Its morality is a sham, oscillating between female slavery in the kitchen and male drunkenness in the beer-garden. The

horrible military element predominates everywhere ; every shopkeeper is a martinet, every
philosopher a dull sergeant. And just in time
to reap the fruit of the predominant materialism or realism, has arisen the new Buddha
Gautama without his beneficence, his beauty,
his tenderness, or his love for the species.

Here in Frankfort (which I came to
eagerly, thinking of its famous Judenstrasse,
and eager to find the idea of the ' one God ' at
least among the Jews), I walk in the new
Buddha's footsteps wherever I go.

His name was Arthur Schopenhauer, a
German of Germans, with the one non-national
merit, that he threw aside the mask of religion
and morality. He was a piggish, selfish, con-
ceited, *honest* scoundrel, fond of gormandising,
in love with his own shadow, miserable, and a

money-grubber like all his race. One anecdote they tell of him is worth a thousand, as expressing the character of the man. Seated at the table d'hôte here one day, and observing a stranger's astonishment at the amount he was consuming, Schopenhauer said, ' I see you are astonished, sir, that I eat twice as much as you, but the explanation is simple—*I have twice as much brains!* '

The idea of this Heliogabalus of pessimism was that life is altogether an unmixed evil; that all things are miserable of necessity, even the birds when they sing on the green boughs, and the babes when they crow upon the breast; and that the only happiness, to be secured by every man as soon as possible, and the sooner the better, was in Nirwâna, or total extinction. A cheerful creed, without a God of any kind—

nay, without a single godlike sentiment! There are pessimists and pessimists. Gautama Buddha himself, *facile princeps*, based his creed upon infinite pity ; his sense of the sorrows of his fellow-creatures was so terrible as to make existence practically unbearable. John Calvin was a Christian pessimist ; his whole nature was warped by the sense of infinite sin and overclouded by the shadow of infinite justice. But this Buddha of the Teutons is a different being ; neither love nor pity, only a predominating selfishness complicated with constitutional suspicion.

And yet, poor man, he was happy enough when his disciples hailed him as the greatest philosopher of the age, the clearest intellect on the planet ; and nothing is more touching than to witness how, as his influence grew, and he emerged from neglect, his faith in human nature brightened. Had he lived a little longer and risen still higher in esteem—had the powers that be crowned him, and the world applauded him, he too, like Hegel, would doubtless have added to his creed a corollary that, though there is no God, religion is an excellent thing ; that though there is no goodness, virtue is the only living truth !

Be that as it may, I am thoroughly convinced that there is no *via media* between Christ's christianity and Schopenhauer's pessimism ; and these two religions, like the gods of good and evil, are just now preparing for a final struggle on the battle-field of European thought. Just at present I feel almost a pessimist myself, and inclined to laugh more than ever at poor Kingsley's feeble twaddle

about this ' singularly well-constructed world.'
Every face I see, whether of Jew or Gentile, is
scribbled like the ledger with figures of addition
and subtraction ; every eye is crowsfooted with
tables of compound interest ; and the money-
bags waddle up and down the streets, and
look out of the country house windows, like
things without a soul. But across the river,
at Sachsenhausen, there are trees, in which the
birds sing, and pretty children, and lovers
talking in the summer shade. I go there in
the summer afternoons and smoke my pipe,
and think over the problem of the time.
Think you, dearest, that Schopenhauer was
right, and that there is no gladness or goodness
in the world? Is the deathblow of foolish
supernaturalism the destruction also of heavenly
love and hope? Nay, God forbid ! But this

hideous pessimism is the natural revolt of the human heart, after centuries of optimistic lies. Perhaps, when another century has fled, mankind may thank God for Schopenhauer, who proved the potency of materialistic Will, and for Strauss, who has shown the fallacy of human judgment. The Germans have given us these two men as types of their own degradation ; and when we have thoroughly digested their bitter gospel, we shall know how little hope for humanity lies *that* way. Meantime, the Divine Ideal, the spiritual Christ survives—the master of the secret of sorrow, the lord of the shadowy land of hope. He turns his back upon the temple erected in his name ; he averts his sweet eyes from those who deny He is, or ever was. He is patient, knowing that his kingdom must some day come.

More than ever now do I feel what a power the Church might be if it would only reconstruct itself by the light of the new knowledge. Without it, both France and Germany are plunged into darkness and spiritual death. As if man, constituted as he is, can exist without religion ! As if the creed of cakes and ale, or the gospel of Deutschthum and Sauer-kraut were in any true sense of the word religion at all ! No, the hope and salvation of the human race lies now, as it lay eighteen hundred years ago, in the Christian promise. If this life were all, if this world were the play and not the prelude, then the new Buddha would have conquered, and nothing be left us but Nirwâna. But the Spirit of Man, which has created Christ and imagined God, knows better. It trusts its own deathless instinct, and by the same law through which the swallow wings its way, it prepares for flight to a sunnier zone.

Pray, my Alma, that even this holy instinct is not merely a dream ! Pray that God may keep us together till the time comes to follow the summer of our love to its bright and heavenly home !—Yours till death, and after death,

AMBROSE BRADLEY.

VII.

Alma Craik to Ambrose Bradley.

YOUR last letter, dearest Ambrose, has reached me here in London, where I am staying for a short time with Agatha Combe. Everybody is out of town, and even the Grosvenor Club (where I am writing this letter) is quite deserted.

I never like London so much as when it is empty of everybody that one knows.

And so you find the Germans as shallow as the French, and as far away from the living truth it is your dream to preach? For my own part, I think they must be rather a *stupid* people, in spite of their philosophic airs. Agatha has persuaded me lately to read a book by a man called Haeckel, who is constructing the whole history of Evolution as children make drawings, out of his own head ; and when the silly man is at a loss for a link in the chain, he invents one, and calls it by a Latin name ! I suppose Evolution is true (and I know you believe in it), but if I may trust my poor woman's wit, it proves nothing whatever. The mystery of life remains just the same when all is said and done ; and I see as great a miracle in a drop of albumen passing through endless progressions till it flowers in sense and soul, as in the creation of all things at the fiat of an omnipotent personal God and Father. The poor purblind German abolishes God altogether!

Agatha has read your Schopenhauer, and thinks him a wonderful man; I believe, too, he has many disciples in this country. To me, judging from what I hear of him, and also from your description of him, he seems another *stupid* giant—a Fee-fo-fi-fum full of self-conceit and hasty pudding, and sure to fall a victim, some day, to Little Jack Horner. But every word you write (it seems always like your own dear voice speaking!) makes me think of yourself, of your quarrel with the Church, and of your justification before the world. If purblind men like these can persuade the world to listen to them, why should your ' one talent, which is death to lose,' be wasted or thrown away? When you have wandered a little longer, you must return and take your place as a teacher and a preacher in the land. You must not continue to be an exile. You are my hero, my Abelard, my teacher of all that is great and good to a perverse generation, and I shall never be happy until you reach the summit of your spiritual ambition and are recognised as a modern apostle. You *must not* leave the ministry; you must not abandon your vocation; or if you do so, it must be only to change the scene of your labours. Agatha Combe tells me that there is a great field for a man like you in London; that the cultivated people here are sick of the old dogmas, and yet equally sick of mere materialism; that what they want is a leader such as you, who would take his stand upon the laws of reason, and preach a purified and exalted Christian ideal. Well, since the English Establishment has rejected you, why not, in the greatest city of the world, form a Church of your own? I have often thought of this, but never so much as lately. There you are tongue-tied and hand-tied, at the mercy of the ignorant who could never comprehend you; *here* you could speak with a free voice, as the great Abelard did when he defied the thunders of the Vatican. Remember, I am rich. You have only to say the word, and your handmaid (am I not still *that*, and your spouse and your *sister*?) will upbuild you a Temple! Ah, how proudly!

Yes, think of *this*, think of the great work of your life, not of its trivial disappointments. Be worthy of my dream of you, my Abelard.

When I see you wear your crown of honour
with all the world worshipping the new teaching, I shall be blest indeed.

ALMA.

VIII.

Ambrose Bradley to Alma Craik.

DEAREST ALMA,—How good you are! How
tenderly do you touch the core of my own
secret thought, making my whole spirit vibrate
to the old ambition, and my memory tremble
with the enthusiasm of my first youth. Oh,
to be a modern Apostle, as you say! to sway
the multitude with words of power, to overthrow at once the tables of the money-changers
of materialism, and the dollish idols of the
Old Church.

But I know too well my own incapacity, as

compared with the magnitude of that mighty task. I believe at once too little and too much; I should shock the priests of Christ, and to the priests of Antichrist I should be a standing jest; neither Montague nor Capulet would spare me, and I should lose my spiritual life in some miserable polemical brawl.

It is so good of you, so like you, to think of it, and to offer out of your own store to build me a church; but I am not so lost, so unworthy, as to take advantage of your loving charity, and to secure my own success—or rather, my almost certain failure—on such a foundation.

And that reminds me, dearest, of what in my mad vanity I had nearly forgotten—the difference between our positions in the world. You are a rich woman; I, as you know, am very poor. It was different, perhaps, when I was an honoured member of the Church, with all its prizes and honours before me; I certainly felt it to be different, though the disparity always existed. But *now !* I am an outcast, a ruined man, without property of any kind. It would be base beyond measure to think of dragging you down to my present level; and, remember, I have now no opportunity to rise. If you linked your lot with mine, all the world would think that I loved you, not for your dear self, but for your gold ; they would despise me, and think you were insane. No, dearest, I have thought it sadly over, again and again, and I see that it is hopeless. I have lost you for ever.

When you receive this, I shall be on my way to Rome.

How the very writing of that word thrills me, as if there were still magic in the name that witched the world! Rome! the City of the Martyrs! the City of the Church! the City of the Dead! Her glory is laid low, her pride is dust and ashes, her voice is senile and old, and yet . . . the name, the mighty deathless name, one to conjure with yet. Sometimes, in my spiritual despair, I hear a voice whispering in my ear that one word 'Rome'; and I seem to hear a mighty music, and a cry of rejoicing, and to see a veiled Figure arising with the keys of all the creeds,—behind her on the right her handmaid Science, behind her on the left her handmaid Art, and over her the effulgence of the new-risen sun of Christ.

And if such a dream were real, were it not possible, my Alma, that you and I might enter the new Temple, not as man and wife, but as sister and brother? There was something after all in that old idea of the consecrated priest and the vestal virgin. I often think with St. Paul that there is too much marrying and giving in marriage. 'Brother and sister' sounds sweetly, does it not?

Forgive my wild words. I hardly know what I am writing. Your loving letter has stirred all the fountains of my spirit, your kindness has made me ashamed.

You shall hear from me again, from the very heart of the Seven Hills! Meantime, God bless you!—Ever your faithful and devoted,

AMBROSE BRADLEY.

IX.

Alma Craik to Ambrose Bradley.

BE true to your old dream, dearest Ambrose, and remember that in its fruition

R 2

lies *my* only chance of happiness. Do not talk of unworthiness or unfitness; you are cruel to me when you distrust yourself. Will you be very angry if I tell you a secret? Will you forgive me if I say to you that even now the place where you shall preach the good tidings is rising from the ground, and that in a little while, when you return, it will be ready to welcome its master? But there, I have said too much. If there is anything more you would know, you must guess it, dearest! Enough to say that you have friends who love you, and who are not idle.

If I thought you meant what you said in your last I should indeed despair; but it was the shadow of that abominable Schopenhauer who spoke, and not my Abelard. To tell me that I am rich, and you are poor—as if even a *mountain* of money, high as Ararat, could separate those whom God has joined! To talk of the world's opinion, the people's misconception—as if the poor things who crawl on the ground could alter the lives of those who soar with living thoughts to heaven! Get thee behind me, Schopenhauer! When any voice, however like his own, talks of the overthrow of the man I love, I only smile. I know better than to be deceived by a trick of the ventriloquist. You and I know, my Ambrose, that you have not been overthrown at all—that you have not fallen, but risen— how high, the world shall know in a very little while.

Meantime, gather up strength, both of the body and the mind. Drink strength from the air of the holy city, and come back to wear your priestly robes. Your dream will be realised, be sure of that !

Do you think to daunt me when you say that I must not be your wife ? Do you think your handmaid cares so long as she may serve at your feet ? Call her by what name you please, spouse or sister, is it not all the same ? Your hope is my hope, your country my country, your God my God—now and for ever. Only let us labour together earnestly, truthfully, patiently, and all will be well.— Yours always faithfully and affectionately,

ALMA.

END OF THE FIRST VOLUME.

LONDON : PRINTED BY
SPOTTISWOODE AND CO., NEW-STREET SQUARE
AND PARLIAMENT STREET

THE NEW ABELARD

VOL. II.

THE NEW ABELARD

A Romance

BY

ROBERT BUCHANAN

AUTHOR OF 'THE SHADOW OF THE SWORD' 'GOD AND THE MAN' ETC.

IN THREE VOLUMES—VOL. II.

London
CHATTO & WINDUS, PICCADILLY
1884

LONDON : PRINTED BY
SPOTTISWOODE AND CO., NEW-STREET SQUARE
AND PARLIAMENT STREET

CONTENTS

OF

THE SECOND VOLUME.

THE NEW ABELARD.

CHAPTER XI.

AN ACTRESS AT HOME.

On a certain Monday in June, little more than a year after the last letter of the correspondence quoted in the preceding chapter, two young men of the period were seated in the smoking-room of the Traveller's Club. One was young George Craik, the other was Cholmondeley, of the 'Charing Cross Chronicle.'

'I assure you, my dear fellow,' the journalist was saying, 'that if you are in want of a religion——'

'Which I am *not*,' interjected George, sullenly.

'If you are in want of a new sensation, then, you will find this new Church just the thing to suit you. It has now been opened nearly a month, and is rapidly becoming the fashion. At the service yesterday I saw, among other notabilities, both Tyndall and Huxley, Thomas Carlyle, Hermann Vezin the actor, John Mill the philosopher, Dottie Destrange of the Prince's, Labouchere, and two colonial bishops. There is an article on Bradley in this morning's " Telegraph," and his picture is going into next week's " Vanity Fair." '

'But the fellow is an atheist and a Radical ! '

'My dear Craik, so am I ! '

'Oh, you're different!' returned the other with a disagreeable laugh. 'Nobody believes you in earnest when you talk or write that kind of nonsense.'

'Whereas, you would say, Bradley is an enthusiast? Just so; and his enthusiasm is contagious. When I listen to him, I almost catch it myself, for half an hour. But you mistake altogether, by the way, when you call him atheistical, or even Radical. He is a Churchman still, though the Church has banged its door in his face, and his dream is to conserve all that is best and strongest in Christianity.'

'I don't know anything about that,' said Craik, savagely. 'All I know is that he's an infernal humbug, and ought to be lynched.'

'Pray don't abuse him! He is my friend, and a noble fellow.'

'I don't care whether he is your friend or not—he is a scoundrel.'

Cholmondeley made an angry gesture, then remembering who was speaking, shrugged his shoulders.

'Why, how has he offended *you?* Stop, though, I remember! The fair founder of his church is your cousin.'

'Yes,' answered the other with an oath, 'and she would have been my wife if he had not come in the way. It was all arranged, you know, and I should have had Alma and— and all her money; but she met him, and he filled her mind with atheism, and radicalism, and rubbish. A year ago, when he was kicked out of his living, I thought she was done with him ; but he hadn't been gone a month before she followed him to London, and all this nonsense began. The governor has almost gone down on his knees to her, but it's no use. Fancy her putting down ten thousand pounds in solid cash for this New Church business ; and not a day passes but he swindles her out of more.'

' Bradley is not a swindler,' answered the journalist quietly. ' For the rest, I suppose that they will soon marry.'

' Not if I can help it ! Marry that man ! It would be a standing disgrace to the family.'

' But they are engaged, or something of that sort. As for its being a disgrace, that is rubbish. Why, Bradley might marry a duke's daughter if he pleased. Little Lady Augusta Knowles is crazy about him.'

True to his sarcastic instinct, Cholmondeley

added, ' Of course I know the little woman has a hump, and has only just got over her *grande passion* for Montepulciano the opera singer. But a duke's daughter—think of that!'

George Craik only ground his teeth and made no reply.

Shortly afterwards the two men separated, Cholmondeley strolling to his office, Craik (whom we shall accompany) hailing a hansom and driving towards St. John's Wood.

Before seeking, in the young man's company, those doubtful regions which a modern satirist has termed

The shady groves of the Evangelist,

let us give a few explanatory words touching the subject of the above conversation. It had all come about exactly as described. Yielding to Alma's intercession, and inspired, moreover,

by the enthusiasm of a large circle in London,
Bradley had at last consented to open a religious
campaign on his own account in the very heart
of the metropolis. A large sum of money was
subscribed, Alma heading the list with a princely
donation, a site was selected in the neighbourhood of Regent's Park, and a church was built,
called by its followers the New Church, and in
every respect quite a magnificent temple. The
stained windows were designed by leading
artists of the æsthetic school, the subjects partly
religious, partly secular (St. Wordsworth, in the
guise of a good shepherd, forming one of the
subjects, and St. Shelley, rapt up into the clouds
and playing on a harp, forming another), and
the subject over the altar was an extraordinary
figure-piece by Watts, ' Christ rebuking Superstition '—the latter a straw-haired damsel with

a lunatic expression, grasping in her hands a couple of fiery snakes. Of course there was a scandal. The papers were full of it, even while the New Church was building. Public interest was thoroughly awakened ; and when it became current gossip that a young heiress, of fabulous wealth and unexampled personal beauty, had practically created the endowment, society was fluttered through and through. Savage attacks appeared on Bradley in the religious journals. Enthusiastic articles concerning him were published in the secular newspapers. He rapidly became notorious. When he began to preach, the enthusiasm was intensified ; for his striking presence and magnificent voice, not to speak of the ' fiery matter' he had to deliver, carried everything before them.

It may safely be assumed that time had at

last reconciled him to the secret trouble of his life. Before settling in London he had ascertained, to his infinite relief, that Mrs. Montmorency had gone to Paris and had remained there with her child, under the same ' protection ' as before. Finding his secret safe from the world, he began unconsciously to dismiss it from his mind, the more rapidly as Alma's relations towards him became more and more those of a devoted sister. Presently his old enthusiasm came back upon him, and with it a sense of new power and mastery. He began to feel an unspeakable sacredness in the tie which bound him to the woman he loved ; and although it had seemed at first that he could only think of her in one capacity, that of his wife and the partner of his home, her sisterhood seemed indescribably sweet and satisfying. Then, again, her extraordinary belief in him inspired him with fresh ambition, and at last, full of an almost youthful ardour, he stepped out into the full sunshine of his London ministry.

In the least amiable mood possible, even to him, George Craik drove northward, and passing the very portals of Bradley's new church, reached the shady groves he sought. Alighting in a quiet street close to the 'Eyre Arms,' he stood before a bijou villa all embowered in foliage, with a high garden wall, a gate with a wicket, and the very tiniest of green lawns. He rang the bell, and the gate was opened by a black-eyed girl in smart servant's costume; on which, without a word, he strolled in.

'Mistress up?' he asked sharply; though it was past twelve o'clock.

' She's just breakfasting,' was the reply.

Crossing the lawn, Craik found himself before a pair of French windows reaching to the ground ; they stood wide open, revealing the interior of a small sitting-room or breakfast parlour, gorgeously if not tastily furnished —a sort of green and gold cage, in which was sitting, sipping her coffee and yawning over a penny theatrical paper, a pretty lady of uncertain age. Her little figure was wrapt in a loose silk morning gown, on her tiny feet were Turkish slippers, in her lap was one pug dog, while another slept at her feet. Her eyes were very large, innocent, and blue, her natural dark hair was bleached to a lovely gold by the art of the *coiffeur*, and her cheeks had about as much colour as those of a stucco bust.

This was Miss Dottie Destrange, of the 'Frivolity' Theatre, a lady famous for her falsetto voice and her dances.

On seeing Craik she merely nodded, but did not attempt to rise.

'Good morning, Georgie!' she said—for she loved the diminutive, and was fond of using that form of address to her particular friends. 'Why didn't you come yesterday? I waited for you all day—no, not exactly all day, though—but except a couple of hours in the afternoon, when I went to church.'

Craik entered the room and threw himself into a chair.

'Went to church?' he echoed with an ugly laugh. 'I didn't know *you* ever patronised that kind of entertainment.'

'I don't as a rule, but Carrie Carruthers

called for me in her brougham, and took me off to hear the new preacher down in Regent's Park. Aram was there, and no end of theatrical people, besides all sorts of swells; and, what do you think, in one of the painted glass windows there was a figure of Shakespeare, just like the one on our drop curtain! I think it's blasphemous, Georgie. I wonder the roof didn't fall in!'

The fair doves of the theatre, we may remark in parenthesis, have seldom much respect for the temple in which they themselves flutter; they cannot shake from their minds the idea that it is a heathen structure, and that they themselves are, at the best, but pretty pagans.

Hence they are often disposed to receive in quite a humble spirit the ministrations of their mortal enemies, the officers of the Protestant Church.

George Craik scowled at the fair one as he had scowled at Cholmondeley.

'You heard that man Bradley, I suppose?'

'Yes; I think that was his name. Do you know him, George?'

'I know no good of him. I wish the roof *had* fallen in, and smashed him up. Talk about something else; and look here, don't let me catch you going there again, or we shall quarrel. I won't have any one I know going sneaking after that humbug.'

'All right, Georgie dear,' replied the damsel, smiling maliciously. 'Then it's true, I suppose, that he's going to marry your cousin? I saw her sitting right under him, and thought her awfully pretty.'

'You let her alone,' grumbled George, 'and mind your own affairs.'

'Why don't you marry her yourself, Georgie?' persisted his tormentor. 'I hope what I have heard isn't true?'

'What have you heard?'

'That she prefers the parson!'

The young man sprang up with an oath, and Miss Dottie burst into a peal of shrill laughter. He strode off into the garden, and she followed him. Coming into the full sunlight, she looked even more like plaster of Paris, or stucco, than in the subdued light of the chamber; her hair grew more strawlike, her eyes more colourless, her whole appearance more faded and jaded.

'I had a letter this morning from Kitty,' she said carelessly, to change the subject.

' Kitty who ? '

' Kitty Montmorency. She says old Ombermere is very ill, and thinks he's breaking up. By the way, that reminds me—Kitty's first husband was a man named Bradley, who was to have entered the Church. I suppose it can't be the same.'

She spoke with little thought of the consequences, and was not prepared for the change which suddenly came over her companion.

' Her *husband*, did you say ? ' he exclaimed, gripping her arm. ' Were they married ? '

' I suppose so.'

' And the man was named Bradley—Ambrose Bradley ? '

' I'm not *quite* sure about the Christian name.'

' How long was this ago ? '

' Oh, a long time—ten years,' she replied ; then with a sudden remembrance of her own claims to juvenility, which she had forgotten for a moment, she added, ' when I was quite a child.'

George Craik looked at her for a long time with a baleful expression, but he scarcely saw her, being lost in thought. He knew as well as she did that she was ten or fifteen years older than she gave herself out to be, but he was not thinking of that. He was wondering if he had, by the merest accident, discovered a means of turning the tables on the man he hated. At last he spoke.

' Tell me all you know. Let us have no humbug, but tell me everything. Did you ever see Bradley before you saw him yester-day ? '

'Never, Georgie.'

'But Kitty Montmorency was once married to, or living with, a man of that name? You are quite sure?'

'Yes. But after all, what does it signify, unless——'

She paused suddenly, for all at once the full significance of the situation flashed upon her.

'You see how it stands,' cried her companion. 'If this is the same man, and it is quite possible, it will be worth a thousand pounds to me—ah, ten thousand! What is Kitty's address?'

'Hôtel de la Grande Bretagne, Rue Caumartin, Paris.'

All right, Dottie. I shall go over to-night by the mail.'

The next morning George Craik arrived in Paris, and drove straight to the hotel in the Rue Caumartin—an old-fashioned building, with a great courtyard, round which ran open-air galleries communicating with the various suites of rooms. On inquiring for Mrs. Montmorency he ascertained that she had gone out very early, and was not expected home till midday. He left his card and drove on to the Grand Hotel.

It might be a fool's errand which had brought him over, but he was determined, with the bulldog tenacity of his nature, to see it through to the end.

Arrived at the hotel, he deposited his Gladstone-bag in the hall, and then, to pass the time, inspected the visitors' list, pre-paratory to writing down his own name.

Presently he uttered a whistle, as he came to the entry—

'Lord and Lady Ombermere and family, London.'

He turned to the clerk of the office, and said carelessly in French—

'I see Lord Ombermere's name down. Is his lordship still here?'

'Yes,' was the reply. 'He has been here all the winter. Unfortunately, since the warm weather began, milord has been very ill, and since last week he has been almost given up by the physicians.'

CHAPTER XII.

IN A SICK ROOM.

Ah blessed promise !   Shall it be fulfilled,
Tho' the eye glazes and the sense is still'd ?
Shall that fair Shape which beckon'd with bright hand
Out of the Mirage of a Heavenly Land,
Fade to a cloud that moves with blighting breath
Over the ever-troublous sea of Death ?
Ah no ; for on the crown of Zion's Hill,
Cloth'd on with peace, the fair Shape beckons still !
The New Crusade.

It was a curious sensation for Ambrose
Bradley, after bitter experience of a somewhat
ignominious persecution, to find himself all at
once—by a mere shuffle of the cards, as it were
—one of the most popular persons in all
Bohemia ; I say Bohemia advisedly, for of
course that greater world of fashion and reli-

gion, which Bohemia merely fringes, regarded the New Church and its pastor with supreme indifference.

But the worship of Bohemia is something; nay, Bradley found it much.

He could count among the occasional visitors to his temple some of the leading names in Art and Science. ˙ Fair votaries came to him by legions, led by the impassioned and enthusiastic Alma Craik. The society journals made much of him; one of them, in a series of articles called ' Celebrities in their Slippers,' gave a glowing picture of the new Apostle in his study, in which the sweetest of Raphael's Madonnas looked down wonderingly on Milo's Venus, and where Newman's ' Parochial Sermons ' stood side by side with Tyndall's Belfast address, and the original edition of the

' Vestiges of Creation.' The correspondent of the 'New York Herald' telegraphed, on more than one occasion, the whole, or nearly the whole, of one of his Sunday discourses—which, printed in large type, occupied two columns of the great Transatlantic daily ; and he received forthwith, from an enterprising Yankee caterer, an offer of any number of dollars per lecture, if he would enter into a contract to ' stump ' the States.

Surely this was fame, of a sort.

Although, if the truth must be told, even Bohemia did not take the New Church overseriously, Bradley found his intellectual forces expand with the growing sense of power.

Standing in no fear of any authority, human or superhuman, he gradually advanced more and more into the arena of spiritual controversy ; retired further and further from the old landmarks of dogmatic religion ; drew nearer and still nearer to the position of an accredited teacher of religious æstheticism. Always literary and artistic, rather than puritanical, in his sympathies, he found himself before long at that standpoint which regards the Bible merely as a poetical masterpiece, and accepts Christianity as simply one manifestation, though a central one, of the great scheme of human morals.

Thus the cloud of splendid supernaturalism, on which alone has been projected from time immemorial the mirage of a heavenly promise, gradually dissolved away before his sight,

> And like the cloudy fabric of a vision
> Left not a wrack behind.

The creed of spiritual sorrow was exchanged

for the creed of spiritual pleasure. The man, forgetful of all harsh experience, became rapt in the contemplation of ' beautiful ideas '—of an intellectual phantasmagoria in which Christ and Buddha, St. John and Shakespeare, Mary Magdalene and Mary Shelley, the angels of the church and the winged pterodactyls of the chalk, flashed and faded in everchanging kaleidoscopic dream.

The mood which welcomed all forms of belief, embraced none utterly, but contemplated all, became vague, chaotic, and transcendental ; and Ambrose Bradley found himself in a fairy world where nothing seemed real and solemn enough as a law for life.

For a time, of course, he failed to realise his own position.

He still rejoiced in the belief that he was

building the foundation of his New Church, which was essentially the Old Church, on the rock of common sense. He was still certain that the Christ of history, the accredited Saviour of mankind, was blessing and consecrating his eager endeavour. He still persuaded himself that his creed was a creed of regeneration, his mission apostolic.

He had taken a small house on the borders of Regent's Park, and not far away from the church which Alma had built for him as a voluntary offering. It was arranged plainly but comfortably, with a touch of the then predominant æstheticism ; the decorations tasteful, the furniture mediæval ; but all this was Alma's doing and, throughout, her choosing. Bradley himself remained unchanged ; a strong unpretending man of simple habits, more like an athletic curate in his dress and bearing than like a fashionable preacher.

Of course it goes without saying that he was ostracised by the preachers of his own maternal Church, the Church of England ; so that he added the consciousness of sweet and painless martyrdom to that of popular success Attacks upon him appeared from time to time in the less important religious journals ; but the great organs of the national creed treated him and his performances with silent contempt.

He was seated in his study one morning in early summer, reading one of the attacks to which I have just alluded, when Miss Craik was shown in. He sprang up to welcome her, with outstretched hands.

'I want you to come with me at once,' she

said. 'Agatha Combe is worse, and I should like you to see her.'

'Of course I will come,' answered Bradley. 'But I thought she was almost recovered?'

'She has had a relapse; not a serious one, I trust, but I am a little alarmed about her. She talks so curiously.'

'Indeed!'

'Yes; about dying. She says she has a presentiment that she won't live. Poor Agatha! When *she* talks like that, it is strange indeed.'

Leaving the house together, Bradley and Alma entered Regent's Park. Their way lay right across, towards the shady sides of Primrose Hill, where Miss Combe was then residing. The day was fair and sunny, and there was an unusual number of pleasure-seekers and pedestrians in the park. A number of boys were playing cricket on the spaces allotted for that recreation, nursemaids and children were sprinkled everywhere, and near the gate of the Zoological Gardens, which they passed, a brass band was merrily performing. Bradley's heart was light, and he looked round on the bright scene with a kindling eye, in the full pride of his physical strength and intellectual vigour.

'After all,' he said, 'those teachers are wise who proclaim that health is happiness. What a joyful world it would be if everyone were well and strong.'

'Ah yes!' said his companion. 'But when sickness comes——'

She sighed heavily, for she was thinking of her friend Agatha Combe.

'I sometimes think that the sum of human misery is trifling compared to that of human happiness,' pursued the clergyman. 'Unless one is a downright pessimist, a very Schopenhauer, surely one must see that the preponderance is in favour of enjoyment. Look at these ragged boys—how merry they are! There is not so much wretchedness in the world, perhaps, as some of us imagine.'

She glanced at him curiously, uncertain whither his thoughts were tending. He speedily made his meaning plain.

'Religion and Sorrow have hitherto gone hand in hand, vanishing through the gate of the grave. But why should not Religion and Joy be united this side the last mystery? Why should not this world be the Paradise of all our dreams?'

'It can never be so, Ambrose,' replied Alma, 'until we can abolish Death.'

'And we can do that in a measure; that is to say, we can abolish premature decay, sickness, disease. Look what Science has done in fifty years! More than other-worldliness has done in a thousand! When Death comes gently, at the natural end of life, it generally comes as a blessing—as the last sacrament of peace. I think if I could live man's allotted term, useful, happy, loving and beloved, I could be content to sleep and never wake again.'

Alma did not answer. Her thoughts were wandering, or she would have shrunk to find her idolised teacher turning so ominously towards materialism. But indeed it was not the first time that Bradley's thoughts had drifted in that direction. It is not in moments of personal happiness or success that we lean with any eagerness towards the supernatural. Glimpses of a world to come are vouchsafed chiefly to those who weep and those who fail; and in proportion as the radiance of this life brightens, fades the faint aurora of the other.

In a small cottage, not far from Chalk Farm, they found Miss Combe. She was staying, as her custom was, with friends, the friends on this occasion being the editor of an evening paper and his wife; and she had scarcely arrived on her visit—some weeks before— when she had begun to ail. She was sitting up when Alma arrived, in an armchair drawn close to the window of a little back parlour, commanding a distant view of Hampstead Hill.

Wrapt in a loose dressing-gown, and leaning back in her chair, she was just touched by the spring sunshine, the brightness of which even the smoke from the great city could not subdue. She did not seem to be in pain, but her face was pale and flaccid, her eyes were heavy and dull. Her ailment was a weakness of the heart's action, complicated with internal malady of another kind.

Tears stood in Alma's eyes as she embraced and kissed her old friend.

'I have brought Mr. Bradley to see you,' she cried. 'I am glad to see you looking so much better.'

Miss Combe smiled and held out her hand to Bradley, who took it gently.

'When you came in,' she said, 'I was half dreaming. I thought I was a little child again, playing with brother Tom in the old churchyard at Taviton. Tom has only just gone out ; he has been here all the morning.'

Said brother Tom, the unwashed apostle of the Hall of Science, had left unmistakable traces of his presence, for a strong odour of bad tobacco pervaded the room.

'It seems like old times,' proceeded the little lady, with a sad smile, 'to be sick, and to be visited by a clergyman. I shall die in the odour of sanctity after all.'

'You must not talk of dying,' cried Alma. 'You will soon be all right again.'

'I'm afraid not, dear,' answered Miss Combe. 'I saw my mother's face again last night, and it never stayed so long. I take it as a warning that I shall soon be called away.'

Strange enough it seemed to both those who listened, to hear a person of Miss Combe's advanced views talking in the vocabulary of commonplace superstition.

'Don't think I am repining,' she continued. 'If I were not ripe, do you think I should be gathered? I am going where we all must go—who knows whither? and, after all, I've had a " good time," as the Yankees say. Do you believe, Mr. Bradley,' she added, turning her keen, grave eyes on the clergyman, ' that an atheist can be a spiritualist, and hold relations with an unseen world?'

'You are no atheist, Miss Combe,' he answered. 'God forbid!'

'I don't know,' was the reply. 'I am not one in the same degree as my brother Tom, of course; but I am afraid I have no living faith beyond the region of ghosts and fairies. The idea of Deity is incomprehensible to me, save as that of the " magnified non-natural Man " my teachers have long ago discarded. I think I might still understand the anthropomorphic God of my childhood, but having lost Him 1 can comprehend no other.'

'The other is not far to seek,' responds' Bradley, bending towards her, and speaking eagerly. 'You will find him in Jesus Christ —the living, breathing godhead, whose touch and inspiration we all can feel.'

'I'm afraid *I* can't,' said Miss Combe. 'I can understand Jesus the man, but Christ the God, who walked in the flesh and was crucified, is beyond the horizon of my conception— even of my sympathy.'

'Don't say that,' cried Alma. 'I am sure you believe in our loving Saviour.'

Miss Combe did not reply, but turned her face wearily to the spring sunlight.

'If there is no other life,' she said, after a long pause, 'the idea of Jesus Christ is a mockery. Don't you think so, Mr. Bradley?'

'Not altogether,' replied Bradley, after a moment's hesitation. 'If the life we live here were all, if, after a season, we vanished like the flowers, we should still need the comfort of Christ's message—his injunction to "love one another." The central idea of Christianity is peace and good fellowship; and if our life had raised itself to that ideal of love, it would be an ideal life, and its brevity would be of little consequence.'

Miss Combe smiled. Her keen intelligence

went right into the speaker's mind, and saw the true meaning of that shallow optimism. Bradley noticed the smile, and coloured slightly under the calm, penetrating gaze of the little **woman.**

'I have always been taught to believe,' said Miss Combe, quietly, 'that the true secret of the success of Christianity was its heavenly promise—its pledge cf a future life.'

'Of course,' cried **Alma.**

'Certainly that promise was given,' said Bradley, 'and I have no doubt that, in some way or another, it will be fulfilled.'

'What do you mean by in some way or another?' asked Miss Combe.

'I mean that Christ's Heaven may not be a heaven of physical consciousness, but of painless and passive perfection ; bringing to the weary peace and forgetfulness, to the happy absolute absorption into the eternal and unconscious life of God.'

'Nirwâna, in short!' said Miss Combe, dryly. 'Well, for my own part, I should not care so much for so sleepy a Paradise. I postulate a heaven where I should meet and know my mother, and where the happy cry of living creatures would rise like a fountain into the clear azure for evermore.'

'Surely,' said Bradley, gently, 'we all hope as much!'

'But do we *believe* it?' returned Miss Combe. 'That is the question. All human experience, all physiology, all true psychology, is against it. The letter of the eternal Universe, written on the open Book of Astronomy,

speaks of eternal death and change. Shall we
survive while systems perish, while suns go
out like sparks, and the void is sown with the
wrecks of worn-out worlds?'

In this strain the conversation continued
for some little time longer. Seeing the in-
valid's tender yearning, Bradley spoke yet
more hopefully of the great Christian promise,
describing the soul as imperishable, and the
moral order of the universe as stationary and
secure ; but what he said was half-hearted,
and carried with it no conviction. He felt for
the first time the helplessness of a transcendental Christianity, like his own. Presently
he returned, almost unconsciously, to the point
from which he had set forth.

'There is something, perhaps,' he said, 'in
the Positivist conception of mankind as one

ever-changing and practically deathless Being. Though men perish, Man survives. Children spring like flowers in the dark footprints of Death, and in them the dead inherit the world.'

'That creed would possibly suit me,' re-tuned Miss Combe, smiling sadly again, 'if I were a mother, if I were to live again in my own offspring. I'm afraid it is a creed with little comfort for childless men, or for old maids like myself! No; my selfishness requires something much more tangible. If I am frankly told that I must die, that con-sciousness ceases for ever with the physical breath of life, I can understand it, and accept my doom; it is disagreeable, since I am rather fond of life and activity, but I can accept it. It is no consolation whatever to reflect that I am to exist vicariously, without consciousness of the fact, in other old maids to come! The condition of moral existence is—consciousness; without *that*, I shall be practically abolished. Such a creed, as the other you have named, is simple materialism, disguise it as you will.'

'I am not preaching Positivism,' cried Bradley; 'God forbid! I only said there was something in its central idea. Christ's promise is that we shall live again! Can we not accept that promise, without asking " how ? " '

'No, we can't; that is to say, *I* can't. It is the " how " which forms the puzzle. Besides, the Bible expressly speaks of the resurrection of the body.'

' A poetical expression,' suggested Bradley.

' Yes; but something more,' persisted the

little woman. ' I can't conceive an existence without those physical attributes with which I was born. When I think of my dead mother, it is of the very face and form I used to know ; the same eyes, the same sweet lips, the same smile, the same touch of loving hands. Either we shall exist again *as we are*, or——'

' Of course we shall so exist,' broke in Alma, more and more nervous at the turn the conversation was taking. ' Is it not all beautifully expressed in St. Paul ? We sow a physical body, we shall reap a spiritual body ; but they will be one and the same. But pray do not talk of it any more. You are not dying, dear, thank God ! '

Half an hour later Bradley and Alma left the house together.

' I am sorry dear Agatha has not more

faith,' said Alma, thoughtfully, as they wandered back towards the park.

' I think she has a great deal,' said Bradley, quickly. ' But I was shocked to see her looking so ill and worn. Is she having good medical advice?'

' The best in London. Dr. Harley sees her nearly every day. Poor Agatha! She has not had too much happiness in this world. She has worked so hard, and all alone!'

They entered the park gate, and came again among the greenness and the sunshine. Everything seemed light and happiness, and the air had that indescribable sense of resurrection in it which comes with the early shining of the primrose and the reawakening of the year. Bradley glanced at his companion. Never had she seemed so bright and beautiful!

With the flush of the rose on her cheek, and her eyes full of pensive light, she moved lightly and gracefully at his side.

A lark rose from the grass not far away, and warbled ecstatically overhead. Bradley felt his blood stir and move like sap in the bough at the magic touch of the season, and with kindling eyes he drew nearer to his companion's side.

'Well, dearest, you were a true prophet,' he said, taking her hand and drawing it softly within his arm. 'It has all come to pass, through *you*. The New Church flourishes in spite of those who hate all things new; and I have you—you only—to thank for it all.'

'I want no thanks,' replied Alma. 'It is reward enough to forward the good work, and to make you happy.'

' Happy ? Yes, I ought to be happy, should
I not ? '

' And you are, I hope, dear Ambrose ! '

' Yes, I think so.   Only sometimes——on a
day like this, for example——I cannot help
looking back with a sigh to the dear old times
at Fensea.   A benediction seems to rest upon
the quiet country life, which contented me *then*
so little.   I miss the peaceful fields, the loneliness and rest of the fens, the silence of the
encircling sea ! '

' And Goody Tilbury's red cloak ! ' cried
Alma, smiling.   ' And the scowl of Summer-
hayes the grocer, and the good Bishop's
blessing ! '

' Ah, but after all the life was a gentle one
till I destroyed it.   The poor souls loved me,
till I became too much for them.   And then,

Alma, the days with *you*! Your first coming, like a ministering angel, to make this sordid earth seem like a heavenly dream! To-day, dearest, it almost seems as if my heaven was behind, and not before, me! I should like to live those blissful moments over again—every one!'

Alma laughed outright, for she had a vivid remembrance of her friend's infinite vexations as a country clergyman.

'That's right,' he said, smiling fondly; 'laugh at me, if you please, but I am quite serious in what I say. Here, in the great world of London, though we see so much of one another, we do not seem quite so closely united as we did yonder.'

'Not so united!' she cried, all her sweet face clouded in a moment.

'Well, united as before, but differently. In the constant storm and stress of my occupation, there is not the same pastoral consecration.

> The world is too much with us; late and soon,
> Getting and spending, we lay waste our powers.

In those days, dearest,' he added, sinking his voice to a whisper, ' we used to speak oftener of love, we used to dream—did we not?—of being man and wife.'

She drooped her gentle eyes, which had been fixed upon him earnestly, and coloured softly; then, with a pretty touch of coquetry, laughed again.

' I am not jealous,' she said, ' and since you have another bride——'

' Another bride!' he repeated, with a startled look of surprise.

'I mean your Church,' she said gaily.

'Ah yes,' he said, relieved. 'But do you know I find this same bride of mine a somewhat dull companion, and a poor exchange, at any rate, for a bride of flesh and blood. Dearest, I have been thinking it all over! Why should we not realise our old dream, and live in love together?'

Alma stood silent. They were in a lonely part of the park, in a footway winding through its very centre. Close at hand was one of the wooden benches. With beating heart and heightened colour, she strolled to the seat and sat down.

Bradley followed, placed himself by her side, and gently took her hand.

'Well?' he said.

She turned her head and looked quietly

into his eyes. Her grave fond look brought the bright blood to his own cheeks, and just glancing round to see that they were un-observed, he caught her in his arms and kissed her passionately—on lips that kissed again.

'Shall it be as I wish?' he exclaimed.

'Yes, Ambrose,' she answered. 'What you wish, I wish too; now as always, your will is my law.'

'And when?'

'When you please,' she answered. 'Only before I marry you, you must promise me one thing.'

'Yes! yes!'

'To regard me *still* as only your hand-maid; to look upon your Church always as your true Bride, to whom you are most deeply bound.'

' I'll try, dear ; but will you be very angry if I sometimes forget her, when I feel your loving arms around me ? '

' Very angry,' she said, smiling radiantly upon him.

They rose up, and walked on together hand in hand.

CHAPTER XIII.

A RUNAWAY COUPLE.

AMBROSE BRADLEY returned home that day like a man in a dream ; and it was not till he had sat for a long time, thinking alone, that he completely realised what he had done. But the state of things which led to so amatory a crisis had been going on for a long time; indeed, the more his worldly prosperity increased, and the greater his social influence grew, the feebler became his spiritual resistance to the temptation against which he had fought so long.

It is the tendency of all transcendental forms

of thought, even of a transcendental Christianity,
to relax the moral fibre of their recipient, and
to render vague and indetermined his general
outlook upon life. The harshest possible
Calvinism is bracing and invigorating, compared with any kind of creed with a terminology
purely subjective.

Bradley's belief was liberal in the extreme
in its construction, or obliteration, of religious
dogmas ; it soon became equally liberal, or lax,
in its conception of moral sanctions. The man
still retained, and was destined to retain till
the end of his days, the very loftiest conception
of human duty. His conscience, in every act
of existence, was the loadstone of his deeds.
But the most rigid conscience, relying entirely
on its own insight, is liable to corruption.
Certainly Bradley's was. He had not advanced

very far along the easy path which leads to agnosticism, before he had begun to ask himself —What, after all, is the moral law? are not certain forms of self-sacrifice Quixotic and unnecessary? and, finally, why should I live a life of martyrdom, because my path was crossed in youth by an unworthy woman?

Since that nocturnal meeting after his visit to the theatre, Bradley had seen nothing of Mrs. Montmorency, but he had ascertained that she was spending the greater part of her time somewhere abroad. Further investigations, pursued through a private inquiry office, convinced him of two things: first, that there was not the faintest possibility of the lady voluntarily crossing his path again, and, second, that his secret was perfectly safe in the keeping of one whom its disclosure might possibly ruin.

Satisfied thus far of his security, he had torn that dark leaf out of his book of life, and thrown it away into the waters of forgetfulness.

Then, with his growing sense of mastery, grew Alma's fascination.

She could not conceal, she scarcely attempted to conceal, the deep passion of worship with which she regarded him. Had he been a man ten times colder and stronger, he could scarcely have resisted the spell. As it was, he did not resist it, but drew nearer and nearer to the sweet spirit who wove it, as we have seen.

One sunny morning, about a month after the occurrence of that little love scene in Regent's Park, Bradley rose early, packed a small hand valise, and drove off in a hansom to Victoria Station. He was quietly attired in clothes not at all clerical in cut, and without the white neckcloth or any other external badge of his profession.

Arriving at the station, he found himself just in time to catch the nine o'clock train to Russetdeane, a lonely railway station taking its name from a village three miles distant, lying on the direct line to Eastbourne and Newhaven. He took his ticket, and entered a first-class carriage as the train started. The carriage had no other occupant, and, leaning back in his seat, he was soon plunged in deep reflection.

At times his brow was knitted, his face darkened, showing that his thoughts were gloomy and disturbed enough; but ever and anon, his eyes brightened, and his features caught a gleam of joyful expectation. Whenever the train stopped, which it did very fre-

quently, he shrank back in his corner, as if
dreading some scrutinising eye; but no one
saw or heeded him, and no one entered the
carriage which he occupied alone.

At last, after a journey of about an hour
and a half, the train stopped at Russetdeane.

It was a very lonely station indeed, quite
primitive in its arrangements, and surrounded
on every side by green hills and white quarries
of chalk. An infirm porter and a melancholy
station-master officiated on the platform, but
when Bradley alighted, valise in hand, who
should step smilingly up to him but Alma,
prettily attired in a quiet country costume, and
rosy with the sweet country air.

The train steamed away; porter and
station-master standing stone still, and watching it till the last faint glimpse of it faded in

the distance; then they looked at each other, seemed to awake from a trance, and slowly approached the solitary passenger and his companion.

' Going to Russetdeane, measter ? ' demanded the porter, wheezily, while the station-master looked on from the lofty heights of his superior position.

Bradley nodded, and handed over his valise.

' I have a fly outside the station,' explained Alma ; and passing round the platform and over a wooden foot-bridge, to platform and offices on the other side, they found the fly in question—an antique structure of the post-chaise species, drawn by two ill-groomed horses, a white and a roan, and driven by a preter-naturally old boy of sixteen or seventeen.

'At what hour does the next down train pass to Newhaven?' asked Bradley, as he tipped the porter, and took his seat by Alma's side.

'The down-train, measter?' repeated the old man. 'There be one at three, and another at five. Be you a-going on?'

Bradley nodded, and the fly drove slowly away along the country road. The back of the boy's head was just visible over the front part of the vehicle, which was vast and deep; so Bradley's arm stole round his companion's waist, and they exchanged an affectionate kiss.

'I have the licence in my pocket, dearest,' he whispered. 'Is all arranged?'

'Yes. The clergyman of the parish is such a dear old man, and quite sympathetic. He thinks it is an elopement, and as he ran away with his own wife, who is twenty years younger than himself, he is sympathy itself!'

'Did he recognise my name, when you mentioned it?'

'Not a bit,' answered Alma, laughing. 'He lives too far out of the world to know anything or anybody, and, as I told you, he is eighty years of age. I really think he believes that Queen Victoria is still an unmarried lady, and he talks about Bonaparte just as if it were sixty years ago.'

'Alma!'

'Yes, Ambrose!'

'You don't mind this secret marriage?'

'Not at all—since it is your wish.'

'I think it is better to keep the affair private, at least for a little time. You know how I hate publicity, in a matter so sacred; and since we are all in all to each other——'

He drew her still closer and kissed her again. As he did so, he was conscious of a curious sound as of suppressed laughter, and, glancing up, he saw the eyes of the weird boy intently regarding him.

'Well, what is it?' cried Bradley, impatiently, while Alma shrank away blushing crimson.

The eyes of the weird boy did not droop, nor was he at all abashed. Still indulging in an internal chuckle, like the suppressed croak of a young raven, he pulled his horses up, and pointed with his whip towards the distant country prospect.

'There be Russetdeane church spire!' he said.

Bradley glanced impatiently in the direc
tion so indicated, and saw, peeping through a
cluster of trees, some two miles off, the spire
in question.

He nodded, and ordered the boy to drive
on. Then turning to Alma, he saw her eyes
twinkling with merry laughter.

' You see we are found out already ! ' she
whispered. ' He thinks we are a runaway
couple, and so, after all, we are.'

The carriage rumbled along for another
mile, and ever and anon they caught the eyes
of the weird boy, peeping backward ; but
being forewarned, they sat, primly enough,
upon their good behaviour.

Suddenly the carriage stopped again.

' Missis ! ' croaked the weird boy.

' Well ? ' said Alma, smiling up at him.

' Where be I a-driving to ? Back to the
" Wheatsheaf " ? '

' No ; right to the church door,' answered
Alma, laughing.

The boy did not reply, but fixing his
weather eye on Bradley, indulged in a wink of
such preternatural meaning, that Alma was
once more convulsed with laughter. Then,
after giving vent to a prolonged whistle, he
cracked his whip, and urged his horses on.

Through green lanes, sweet with hanging
honeysuckle and sprinkled with flowers of
early summer ; past sleepy ponds, covered
with emerald slime and haunted by dragon
flies glittering like gold ; along upland stretches
of broad pasture, commanding distant views
of wood-land, thorpe and river ; they passed
along that sunny summer day ; until at last,

creeping along an avenue of ashes and flowering limes, they came to the gate of an old church, where the carriage stopped.

The lovers alighted, and ordering the boy to remain in attendance, approached the church—a time-worn, rain-stained edifice half smothered in ivy, and with rooks cawing from its belfry tower.

They were evidently expected. The clerk, a little old man who walked with a stick, met them at the church door, and informed them that the clergyman was waiting for them in the vestry.

A few minutes later, the two were made man and wife—the solitary spectator of the ceremony, except the officials, being the weird boy, who had stolen from his seat, and left his horses waiting in the road, in order to see what was going on. The clergyman, ancient and time-worn as his church, mumbled a benediction, and, after subscribing their names in the register and paying the customary fees, they shook hands with him, and came again out into the sunshine.

Whatever the future might bring forth to cloud her marriage path, that bridal morning was like a dream of paradise to Alma Craik. In a private room of the old 'Wheatsheaf,' a room sweet with newly-cut flowers, and overlooking orchards stretching down to the banks of a pretty river, they breakfasted, or lunched, together—on simple fare, it is true, but with all things clean and pure. A summer shower passed over the orchards as they sat by the open window hand in hand; and then, as the sun flashed out again, the trees dript diamonds, and the long grass glittered with golden dew.

'How sweet and still it is here, my darling! I wish we could stay in such a spot for ever, and never return again to the dreary city and the busy world.'

She crept to his side as he spoke, and rested her head upon his shoulder.

'Are you happy now, dear Ambrose?'

'Quite happy,' he replied.

Presently a buxom serving maid tript in to say that the carriage was waiting ; and, descending to the door, they found the vehicle, with Alma's travelling trunk and the clergyman's valise upon the box. The weird boy was still there, jubilant. Somehow or other he had procured a large white rosette, which he had pinned to the breast of his coat. Two or three sleepy village folk, whom the news of the wedding had partially aroused from their chronic state of torpor, were clustering on the pavement; and the landlord and landlady stood at the door to wish the strange couple God speed.

Away they drove, while one of the slumberous villagers started a feeble cheer. Through the green lanes, along the grassy uplands, they passed back to the railway station, which they reached just in time to catch, as they had planned, the down train to Newhaven.

That afternoon they crossed by the tidal boat to Dieppe, where, in a brand-new hotel facing the sea, they slept that night. They were almost the only visitors, for the summer bathing season had scarcely begun, and they would have found the place cheerless enough had they been in a less happy mood of mind.

The next day found them wandering about the picturesque old town, visiting the wharves and the old churches, and strolling on the deserted esplanade which faced the sea. They thought themselves unsuspected, but somehow everyone knew their secret—that they were a married couple on their honeymoon. When they returned to the hotel to lunch, they found a bunch of orange-blossoms on the table, placed there by the hands of a sympathetic landlady.

'We must go on farther,' said Bradley, rather irritably. 'I suppose the newly-married alight here often, and being experts in that sort of commodity, they recognise it at a glance.'

So that afternoon they went on to Rouen,

where they arrived as the sun was setting on that town of charming bridges. When their train reached the station, a train arrived almost simultaneously from Paris, and as there was a ten minutes' interval for both upward and downward passengers, the platform was thronged.

Bradley passed through the crowd, with Alma hanging upon his arm. He looked neither to right nor left, but seemed bent on passing out of the station ; and he did not notice a dark-eyed lady by whom he was evidently recognised.

On seeing him, she started and drew back among the crowd, leading by the hand a little boy. But when he had passed she looked after him, and more particularly after his beautiful companion.

'It is he, sure enough!' she muttered 'But who is that stylish party in his company? I should very much like to know.'

The lady was 'Mrs. Montmorency,' clad like a widow in complete weeds, and travelling with her little boy, also dressed in funeral black, from Paris to London.

CHAPTER XIV.

A MYSTERY.

BRADLEY and his bride were only absent from London five days; no one missed them, and of course no one suspected that they had gone away in company. Before the next Sunday came round, they were living just as before— she in her own rooms, he in the residence at Regent's Park. This was the arrangement made between them, the clergyman's plea being that it was better to keep their marriage secret for a time, until the New Church was more safely established in public estimation.

Quite happy in the loving secret between them, Alma had acquiesced without a word.

Their only confidant, for the time being, was Miss Combe, who was then staying at Hastings, and to whom Alma wrote in the following terms :

'DEAREST AGATHA,—It is all over, and we are man and wife. No one in the world is to know but *you*, yet awhile. I know you will keep our secret, and rejoice in our happiness.

'It was all decided very hastily. Ambrose thought it better to marry secretly, thinking (foolish man !) that many would misunderstand his motives, and believing that, as an unmarried person, he can better pursue the good work to which we are both devoted. After all, it matters very little. For years we have been one in soul, as you know ; and what God long ago joined man could never have put asunder. Still, it is sweet to know that my hero, my apostle, my Abelard—as I call him, is entirely mine, for richer, for poorer, for better, for worse. I am very happy, dear; proud and hopeful, too, as a loving wife can be.

'Write and tell me that you are better. Surely this bright weather should complete your cure, and drive those gloomy thoughts away? In a few days I shall come and see you; perhaps we may come together. So I won't write good bye, but *au revoir !*

'Your loving friend,

'ALMA BRADLEY.

'P.S.—My cousin George is back in town. Just fancy how he would scowl if he were to read the above *signature.*'

It so happened that George Craik,

although he was not so favoured as to read his cousin's signature as a married woman, and although he had no suspicion whatever as yet that she had entered, as she imagined, into the holy estate of matrimony, was scowling in his least amiable frame of mind about the time when Alma wrote the above letter. He had returned to London from Paris a good deal mystified, for, having procured an interview with Mrs. Montmorency, whom (as the reader knows) he had gone over to see, he had elicited nothing from that lady but a flat denial of any knowledge of or connection with his rival the clergyman.

So he came back at once, baffled but not beaten, took to the old club life, attended the different race meetings, and resumed altogether he life of a young gentleman about town.

But although he saw little of his cousin, he (as he himself figuratively expressed it ' kept his eye upon her.' The more he read about Bradley and his doings—which appeared shocking indeed to his unsophisticated mind— the more indignant he felt that Alma, and her fortune, should ever be thrown away on one so unworthy. Meantime he was in the unenviable position of a man surrounded by duns and debts. He had bills out in the hands of the Jews, and he saw no prospect whatever of meeting them. Having far exceeded the very liberal allowance given him by his father, he knew that there was no hope of assistance in that direction. His only chance of social resuscitation was a wealthy marriage, and with his cousin hanging like a tempting bait before him, he felt like a very Tantalus, miserable, indignant and ill-used.

His rooms were in the Albany, and here one morning his father found him, sitting over a late breakfast.

'Well, George,' said the baronet, standing on the hearthrug and glancing round at the highly suggestive prints which adorned the walls; 'well, George, how long is this to last?'

The young man glanced up gloomily as he sipt his coffee.

'What do you mean?' he demanded.

'You know very well. But just look at this letter, which I have received, from a man called Tavistock, this morning.'

And he tossed it over the table to his son. George took it up, looked at it, and flushed crimson. It was a letter informing Sir George Craik that the writer held in his hands a dishonoured acceptance of his son's for the sum of three hundred pounds, and that unless it was taken up within a week proceedings in bankruptcy would be instituted.

'D—— the Jew!' cried George. 'I'll wring his neck! He had no right to write to you!'

'I suppose he thought it was the only way,' returned the baronet; 'but he is quite out in his calculations. If you suppose that I shall pay any more of your debts you are mistaken. I am quite tired of it all. You have played all your cards wrong and must take the consequences.'

George scowled more furiously than ever, but made no immediate reply. After a pause, however, he said in an injured way—

'I don't know what you mean by playing

my cards wrong. I have done my best. If my cousin Alma has given me the cold shoulder, because she has gone cranky on religion, it is no fault of mine.'

'I am not astonished that she has thrown you over,' cried Sir George. 'What possible interest could a young girl of her disposition find in a fellow who bets away his last shilling, and covers his room with pictures of horses and portraits of jockeys and ballet girls? If you had had any common sense, you might at least have pretended to take some interest in her pursuits.'

'I'm not a hypocrite,' retorted George, ' and I can't talk atheism.'

'Rubbish! You know as well as I do that Alma is a high-spirited girl, and only wants humouring. These new-fangled ideas of hers are absurd enough, but irritating opposition will never lead her to get rid of them.'

'She's in love with that fellow Bradley!'

'Nothing of the kind. She is in love with her own wild fancies, which he is wise enough to humour, and you are indiscreet enough to oppose. If there had been anything serious between them, a marriage would have come off long ago; but, absurd as Alma is, she is not mad enough to throw herself away on a mere adventurer like that, without a penny in the world.'

'What is a fellow to do?' pleaded George, dolefully. 'She snubs me more than ever!'

'The more she snubs you the more you ought to pursue her. Show your devotion to her—go to the church—seem to be interested in her crotchets—and take my word for it, her sympathies will soon turn in your direction.'

Father and son continued to talk for some time in the same strain, and after an hour's conversation Sir George went away in a better humour. George drest himself carefully, and when it was about midday hailed a cab and was driven down to the Gaiety Theatre, where he had an appointment with Miss Dottie Destrange. The occasion was one of those *matinées* when aspiring amateurs attempt to take critical opinion by storm, and the *débutante* this time was a certain Mrs. Temple Grainger, who was to appear as ' Juliet ' in the *Hunchback*, and afterwards as ' Juliet ' in the famous balcony scene of Shakespeare's play. Mrs. Grainger, whose husband was somewhere

in the mysterious limbo of mysterious hus-
bands, called India, was well known in a
certain section of society, and no less a person
than His Royal Highness the Prince of Wales
had promised to be present at her *début.*

George was to join Miss Destrange in the
stalls, where he duly found her, and was
greeted with a careless smile. The seats all
round were thronged with well-known
members of society; actresses, actors, critics.
The Prince was already in his box, and the
curtain was just ringing up.

It is no part of my business to chronicle
the success or failure of Mrs. Temple
Grainger; but, if cheers and floral offerings
signify anything, she was in high favour with
her audience. At the end of the second act,
George Craik rose and surveyed the house

through his opera glass. As he did so, he was conscious of a figure saluting him from one of the stage boxes, and to his surprise he recognised—Mrs. Montmorency.

She was gorgeously drest in black, and liberally painted and powdered. George bowed to her carelessly; when to his surprise she beckoned him to her.

He rose from his seat and walked over to the side of the stalls immediately underneath her box. She leant over to him, and they shook hands.

' Will you come in ? ' she said. ' I want to speak to you.'

He nodded, passed round to the back of the box, entered, and took a seat by the lady's side.

' I thought you were still in Paris,' he said.

' I came over about a fortnight ago,' she

replied. 'I suppose you have heard of his lordship's death?'

'Yes. I saw it in the papers.'

'I waited till after the funeral, then I came away. But we won't talk about that; I've hardly got over it yet. I've something else to say to you.'

'Well?'

'Do you remember a question you asked me in Paris—whether I knew anything of a clergyman of the name of Bradley who was paying his addresses to your cousin?'

'Of course I do; and you said——'

'That I only knew him very slightly.'

'Pardon me, but you said you didn't know him at all!'

'Did I? Then I made a slight mistake. I do know the person you mean by sight!'

George Craik looked at the speaker with some astonishment, for he had a good memory, and a very vivid recollection of what she had said to him during their interview.

' I dare say I was *distrait*,' she continued, with a curious smile and a flash of her dark eyes. ' I was in such trouble about poor Ombermere. What I want to tell you is that I saw Mr. Bradley the other day at Rouen, as I was returning from Paris.'

' At Rouen,' repeated George Craik.

' Yes, on the railway platform, in company with a very charming lady, who was hanging on his arm, and regarding him with very evident adoration.'

George pricked up his ears like a little terrier ; he smelt mischief of some sort.

'I fancy you must be mistaken,' he said. 'Bradley is not likely to have been travelling across the Channel.'

'I am not at all mistaken,' answered Mrs. Montmorency. 'Mr. Bradley's appearance is peculiar, his face especially, and I am sure it was himself. What I want to find out is, who was his companion?'

'I hardly see what interest that can be to you,' observed George suspiciously, 'since you only know him—by sight!'

'The lady interested me. I was wondering if it could be your charming cousin.'

George started as if he had been shot.

'My Cousin Alma! Impossible! Surely you don't know what you are saying!'

'Oh yes, I do. Tell me, what is your cousin like?'

After some slight further urging, George described Alma's personal appearance as closely as possible. Mrs. Montmorency listened quietly, taking note of all the details of the description. Then she tapped George with her fan, and laughed outright.

'Then I was right after all!' she cried. 'It was Miss Alma Craik—that's her name, isn't it?'

'Yes; but, good heavens, it is simply impossible! Alma in company with that scoundrel, over there in France? You must be mistaken!'

But Mrs. Montmorency was quite certain that she had made no mistake in the matter. In her turn she described Alma's appearance so minutely, so cleverly, that her companion became lost in astonished belief. When the act drop was rung up, he sat staring like one bewitched, seeing nothing, hearing nothing, but gazing wildly at Mrs. Montmorency.

Suddenly he rose to go.

'Don't go yet,' whispered the lady.

'I must—I can't stay!' he replied. 'I'll find out from my cousin herself if what you have told me is true.'

'*Après?*'

'*Après!*' echoed the young man, looking livid. 'Why, *après*, I'll have it out with the man!'

Mrs. Montmorency put her gloved hand upon his arm.

'Don't do anything rash, *mon cher*,' she said. 'I think you told me that you loved your cousin, and that you would give a thousand pounds to get her away from your rival?'

'A thousand! twenty thousand! anything!'

'Suppose I could help you?' said Mrs. Montmorency, smiling wickedly.

'Can you? will you? But how!'

'You must give me time to think it over. Find out, in the first place, if what I suspect is true, and then come and tell me all about it!'

George Craik promised, and hurriedly left the theatre, without even waiting to say farewell, or make any apologies, to Miss Destrange. He was determined to call upon his cousin without a moment's delay, and get, if possible, to the bottom of the mystery of her unaccountable appearance, accompanied by Bradley, at the Rouen railway station.

CHAPTER XV.

THE COUSINS.

Madam, our house's honour is in question!
I prithee, when you play at wantonness,
Remember that our blood flows clean and pure,
In one unbroken and unmuddied line,
From crystal sources. I'm your champion,
Madam, against yourself!—*The Will and the Way.*

GEORGE CRAIK was not the man to let the grass grow under his feet when he was moving with set purpose to any object.

As we have already hinted, he possessed a certain bull-dog tenacity, very dangerous to his opponents. And now all the suspicions of a nature naturally suspicious, all the spitefulness of a disposition naturally spiteful, being fully and unexpectedly aroused, his furious instinct urged him to seek, without a moment's breathing-time, the presence of his refractory cousin.

Coupled with his jealous excitement was a lofty moral indignation.

The family credit was at stake—so at least he assured himself—and he had a perfect right to demand an explanation. Had he reflected a little, he might have known that Alma was the last person in the world to give any explanation whatever if peremptorily demanded, or to admit her cousin's right to demand it; her spirit was stubborn as his own, and her attitude of intellectual superiority was, he should have known by old experience, quite invincible.

Quitting the theatre, he leapt into a

hansom, and was driven direct to Alma's rooms. It was by this time about five in the afternoon, and he made certain of finding his cousin at home.

He was mistaken. Miss Craik was out, and had been out the greater part of the day.

'Do you know where I can find her?' he asked of the domestic, a smart servant maid.

'I don't know, sir,' was the reply. 'She went out in the morning with Mr. Bradley, and has not been home to lunch.'

'Does she dine at home?'

'Yes, sir—at seven.'

'Then I will wait for her.' And so saying he walked into the drawing-room and sat down.

He had cooled a little by this time, and before Alma made her appearance he had time

to cool a good deal more. Fidgetting impatiently in his chair, he began to ask himself
how he could best approach the subject on
which he had come. He regretted now that
he had not called for his father and brought
him with him; that, no doubt, would have
been the most diplomatic course to adopt.
The more he thought over the information he
had received, the more he questioned its
authenticity; and if, after all, the actress had
made a mistake, as he began to suspect and
fear, what a fool he would be made to look in
his cousin's eyes! The prospect of being made
to appear absurd sent a thrill of horror
through his blood; for this young person, as
has already been seen, dreaded, above all
things in the world, the shaft of ridicule.

Time slipped by, and George Craik grew

more and more uneasy. At last seven o'clock struck, and Alma had not appeared.

Growling to himself like an irritable dog, the young man rose and touched the electric bell.

'My cousin is very late,' he said to the servant when she appeared.

'Yes, sir; she is very uncertain.'

'It is seven o'clock. You said she dined at seven.'

'Yes, sir. But sometimes she does not return to dinner, If she is not here at the hour we don't expect her.'

George Craik uttered an angry exclamation.

'Where the deuce can she be?' he cried, scowling ominously.

'I can't say, sir,' returned the servant

smiling. 'Miss Craik is most uncertain, as I told you. She may be dining out—with Mr. Bradley.'

The young man seized his hat, and began striding up and down the room. Then he stopped, and seeing a curious smile still lingering on the servant's face, said sharply:

'What are you laughing at? This is no laughing matter. I tell you I must see my cousin!'

'I'm very sorry, sir, but——'

George moved towards the door.

'I'll go and look for her,' he said. 'If she returns before I find her, tell her I'll come the first thing in the morning.'

And, fuming savagely, he left the house. His temper, never very amiable, was now aroused to the extreme point of irritation, and

the servant's suggestion that Alma might at
that very moment be in his rival's company
roused in him a certain frenzy. It was scandalous ; it was insufferable. If he could not
have it out that night with her, he would seek
the clergyman, and force him to some sort of
an avowal. Bent on that purpose, he hurried
away towards Bradley's house.

He passed on foot round Regent's Park,
and came to the neighbourhood of the New
Church and the adjoining house where Bradley
dwelt. It was quite dark now, and the out-
skirts of the park were quite deserted. As he
approached the house he saw the street-door
standing open, and heard the sound of voices.
He pricked up his ears and drew back into the
shadow.

A light silvery laugh rose upon the air,

followed by the low, deep tones of a man's voice. Then the door was closed, and two figures stepped out into the road, crossing to the opposite side, under the shadow of the trees.

They passed across the lamplight on the other side of the way, and he recognised his cousin's figure, arm-in-arm with that of the clergyman. They passed on, laughing and talking merrily together.

Keeping them well at a distance, he quietly followed.

They passed round the park, following the road by which he himself had come. Happy and unsuspicious, they continued to talk as they went; and though he was not near enough to follow their conversation, he heard enough to show him that they were on the tenderest and most loving terms.

More than once he felt inclined to stride forward, confront them, and have it out with his rival; but, his courage failing him, he continued to follow like a spy. At last they reached the quiet street where Alma dwelt, and paused on the doorstep of her house.

He drew back, waited, and listened.

'Will you not come in?' he heard his cousin say.

He could not hear the reply, but it was accompanied by a kiss and an embrace, which made the jealous blood boil and burn along his veins.

'Good-night, dearest!' said Alma.

'Good night, my darling!' answered the deep voice of the clergyman.

Then the two seemed to embrace and kiss

again, and the next moment the house door opened and closed.

George Craik stepped forward, and stood waiting on the pavement for Bradley to pass, right under the light of a street lamp. Almost immediately Bradley came up quietly, and they were face to face.

The clergyman started, and at first George Craik thought that he was recognised ; but the next moment Bradley passed by, without any sign of recognition, and before the other could make up his mind what to do, he was out of sight.

George Craik looked at his watch ; it was still early, and he determined at once to interview his cousin. He knocked at the door and asked for her ; she heard his voice and came out into the lobby, charmingly attired in an evening dress of the 'crushed strawberry' tint, so much favoured by ladies of æsthetic leaning. Never had she looked more bright and beautiful. Her cheeks were flushed, her eyes sparkling, and she looked radiantly happy.

'Is it you, George?' she cried. 'What brings you so late? I hope no one is ill. My uncle——'

'O, *he's* all right!' answered George, entering the drawing-room. 'No one is ill, or dead, or that kind of thing; so make your mind easy. Besides, it's only nine o'clock, and you don't call *that* late, do you?'

His manner was peculiar, and she noticed that he hardly looked her in the face. Closing the room door, she stood facing him on the hearthrug, and by his side she looked a queen. The miserable young man was immediately submerged in the sense of inferiority irksome to him, and he looked at once cowed and savage.

'Well, George, what is it?' continued Alma. 'I suppose it's some new trouble about yourself. Uncle told me the other day you were rather worried about money, and I offered to help you out of it if I could.'

George threw himself on a sofa and leant forward, sucking the end of his cane.

'It isn't that,' he replied. 'If it were, you know I shouldn't come to you.'

'Why not?'

'Because I have no right, Alma; you have never given me any right. I hope you don't think me mean enough to sponge upon you because you happen to be my cousin, and much richer than I am! But I *am* your cousin, after all, and I think I have a right to protect you, when I see you likely to get into trouble.'

This was quite a magnificent speech for George Craik ; for anger and moral indignation had made him eloquent. Alma looked down upon him in all the pleasurable pride of her beauty, half smiling ; for to her poor George was always a small boy, whose attempts to lecture her were absurd. Her arms and neck were bare, there were jewels on her neck and heaving bosom, her complexion was dazzlingly clear and bright, and altogether she looked superb. There was a large mirror opposite to her, covering half the side of the room ; and within it another Alma, her counterpart, shone dimly in the faint pink light of the lamps, with their rose-coloured shades.

George Craik was obtuse in some respects,

but he did not fail to notice that his cousin was unusually resplendent. She had never been extravagant in her toilette, and he had seldom seen her in such bright colours as on the present occasion. Everything about her betokened an abundant happiness, which she could scarcely conceal.

'What do you mean by getting into trouble?' she inquired carelessly. 'Surely I am old enough to take care of myself.'

'I don't think you are,' he answered. 'At any rate, people are talking about you, and— and I don't like it!'

Alma shrugged her white shoulders.

'Why shouldn't people talk, if it pleases them? But what are they saying?'

The ice was broken, and now was the time for George to take the plunge. He hesitated seriously for a moment, and then proceeded.

' They are saying scandalous things, and I think you ought to know.'

' About *me*, George ? '

' About you and that man Bradley.'

' Indeed ! ' exclaimed Alma, and she laughed quite joyously.

' It's no laughing matter,' cried Craik angrily. ' It's a matter that concerns our family, and our family honour. I tell you they couple your name with his in a way that makes a fellow shudder. That is why I came here to remonstrate with you. I heard this afternoon that you and this man were seen in Normandy together, at a time when everybody supposed you to be here in London.'

Alma started and flushed crimson. Was

her secret discovered? For her own part, she did not much care; indeed, she would have rejoiced greatly to publish her great happiness to all the world; but she respected Bradley's wishes, and was resolute in keeping silence.

The young man rose to his feet, and continued eagerly:

'Let me tell you, Alma, that I don't believe a word of it. I know you are indiscreet, of course; but I am sure you would never compromise yourself or us in any way. But it's all over the place that you were seen together over at Rouen, and I want you to give me the authority to say it's an infernal lie!'

Alma was rather disconcerted. She was at a loss how to reply. But she was so secure in her own sense of happy safety, that she was

more amused than annoyed by her cousin's indignation.

'Suppose it were the truth, George?
Where would be the harm?'

'Good God! you don't mean to tell me it
is true!'

'Perhaps not,' was the quiet reply. 'I
don't mean to answer such accusations, one
way or the other.'

George Craik went livid.

'But you don't deny it!'

'Certainly not. Let people talk what nonsense they please; it is quite indifferent to me.'

'Indifferent!' echoed George Craik. 'Do
you know your character is at stake? Do
you know they say that you are this man's
mistress?'

Even yet, Alma betrayed less anger and

astonishment than one might have thought possible ; for, though the infamous charge shocked her, she was too confident in her own security, in the knowledge of her happy secret, which she could at any moment publish to the world, to be greatly or deeply moved. But if the matter of her cousin's discourse failed to disconcert her, its manner irritated her not a little. She made an eager movement towards the door as if to leave the room ; but, wheeling, round suddenly, she raked him from head to foot with a broadside from her scornful eyes.

'And I suppose *you* are quite ready to accept such a calumny ! ' she cried scornfully.

'Nothing of the sort,' returned George. 'I'm sure you'd never go as far as that ! '

She gave a gesture of supreme disdain, and

repeated the sense word for word with contemptuous emphasis.

'You're sure I'd never go as far as that!
How good and kind of you to have so much
faith in me! Do you know that every syllable
you utter to me is an insult and an outrage,
and that if Mr. Bradley heard you talk as you
have done, he would give you the whipping
you so richly deserve!'

Here George Craik's self-control gave way;
his face grew black as thunder, and clenching
his fist, he gave vent to an angry oath.

'D—— him! I should like to see him try
it on. But I see what it is. He has dragged
you down to his level at last, the infernal
atheist! He thinks nothing sacred, and his
New Church, as he calls it, is as foul as himself.
O, *I* know! He preaches that marriage isn't a

sacrament at all, but only a contract to be broken by the will of either party ; and as you agree with him in everything, I suppose you agree with him in *that*, and are his mistress after all ! '

' That is enough ! ' exclaimed Alma, who was now pale as death. ' Leave this place at once, and never let me see your face again.'

' I won't go till I have spoken my mind ; and don't make any mistake ; I shall speak it to him as well as to you ! '

' If you have any sense left, you will do nothing of the kind.'

' Won't I ? Wait and see ! ' returned George, perfectly beside himself with rage. ' As for you, I wonder you have the courage to look me in the face. I followed you both to-night, and watched you ; I saw you embracing and kissing, and it turned me sick with shame. There, the secret's out! I shall speak to my father, and see what *he* has to say about your goings on.'

As he spoke, Alma approached him and looked him steadily in the face. She was still ghastly pale, and her voice trembled as she spoke, but her entire manner expressed, not fear, but lofty indignation.

'It is like you to play the spy! It is just what I should have expected! Well, I hope you are satisfied. I love Mr. Bradley; I have loved him since the day we first met. Will you go now?'

George Craik seized his hat and stick, and crossed to the door, where he turned.

'I will take care all the world knows of your shameless conduct!' he cried. 'You have brought disgrace upon us all. As for

this man, he shall be exposed ; he shall, by—!
He is a scoundrel not fit to live ! '

Without replying, Alma pointed to the
door ; and, after one last look of concentrated
rage, George Craik rushed from the house.
She heard the outer door close behind him,
but still stood like marble, holding her hand
upon her heart. Then, with a low cry, she
sank shuddering into a chair, and covered her
face with her hands.

The scene which we have described had
tortured her delicate spirit more than she at
first knew ; and her cousin's bitter taunts and
reproaches, though they missed their mark at
first, had struck home in the end. She was a
woman of infinite sensitiveness, exceeding
sweetness of disposition ; and she could not bear
harsh words, even from one she cordially

despised. Above all, she shrank, like all good women, even the most intellectual, before the evil judgment of the world. Could it be true, as George Craik had said, that people were connecting her name infamously with that of Bradley? If so, then surely it was time to let all the world know her happiness.

She drew forth from her bosom a photographic miniature of Bradley, set in a golden locket. For a long time she looked at it intently, through a mist of loving tears. Then she kissed it fondly.

'He loves me!' she murmured to herself. 'I will tell him what they are saying, and then he will know that it is time to throw away all disguise. Ah! how proud I shall be when I can stand by his side, holding his hand, and say "This is my husband!"'

CHAPTER XVI.

IN THE VESTRY.

The Nemesis of Greece wore—nothing,
A naked goddess without clothing,
Quite statue-like in form and feature;
Ours, Adam, is a different creature:
She wears neat boots of patent leather,
A hat of plush with ostrich feather,
Her lips are painted, and beneath
You see the gleam of ivory teeth.
She, though the virtuous cut her daily,
Drinks her champagne, and warbles gaily;
But at the fatal hour she faces
Her victim, folds him in embraces,
With dainty teeth in lieu of knife
Bites through the crimson thread of life!
                    Mayfair: a Medley.

THE next day was Sunday, and one of those golden days when all things seem to keep the happy Sabbath.   The chestnuts in the great avenue of Regent's Park were in full bloom, and happy throngs were wandering in their shade. On the open green spaces pale children of the great city were playing in the sunlight, and filling the air with their cries.

There was a large attendance at the temple of the New Church that morning. It had been whispered about that the Prime Minister was coming to hear the new preacher for the first time ; and sure enough he came, sitting, the observed of all observers, with his grave keen eyes on the preacher, and holding his hand to his ear to catch each syllable. Sprinkled among the ordinary congregation were well-known politicians, authors, artists, actors, journalists.

Bradley's text that day was a significant and, as it ultimately turned out, an ominous

one.   It was this—'What God has joined, let
no man put asunder.'

Not every day did the preacher take his
text from the Christian Bible ; frequently
enough, he chose a passage from the Greek
tragedians, or from Shakespeare, or from
Wordsworth ; on the previous Sunday, indeed,
he had scandalised many people by opening
with a quotation from the eccentric American,
Walt Whitman—of whose rhapsodies he was an
ardent admirer.

As he entered the pulpit, he glanced down
and met the earnest gaze of the Prime Minister.
Curiously enough, he had that very morning,
when revising his sermon, been reading the
great statesman's 'Ecclesiastical Essays,' and
more particularly the famous essay on 'Divorce ; '—wherein it is shown by numberless

illustrations, chiefly from the Christian fathers, that marriage is a permanent sacrament between man and woman, not under any circumstances to be broken, and that men like Milton, who have pleaded so eloquently for the privilege of divorce, are hopelessly committed to Antichrist. Now, as the reader doubtless guesses, Bradley ranged himself on the side of the blind Puritan and endeavoured to show that marriage, although indeed a sacrament, was one which could be performed more than once in a lifetime. He argued the matter on theological, on moral, and as far as he could on physiological, grounds ; and he illustrated his argument by glancing at the lives of Milton himself and even of Shelley. As his theme became more and more delicate, and his treatment of it more fearless, he saw the face of the great politician kindle almost angrily. For a moment, indeed, the Prime Minister seemed about to spring to his feet and begin an impassioned reply, but suddenly remembering that he was in a church, and not in the House of Commons, he relapsed into his seat and listened with a gloomy smile.

It was a curious sermon, and very characteristic of both the place and the man. People looked at one another, and wondered whether they were in a church at all. Two elderly unmarried ladies, who had come out of curiosity, got up indignantly and walked out of the building.

Bradley paused and followed them with his eyes until they had disappeared. Then suddenly, as he glanced round the congregation and resumed his discourse, he looked full into the eyes of the goddess Nemesis, who was regarding him quietly from a seat in the centre of the church.

Nemesis in widow's weeds, exquisitely cut by a Parisian *modiste*, and with a charming black bonnet set upon her classic head. Nemesis with bold black eyes, jet black hair, and a smiling mouth. In other words, Mrs. Montmorency, seated by the side of George Craik and his father the baronet.

The preacher started as if stabbed, and for a moment lost the thread of his discourse; but controlling himself with a mighty effort, he proceeded. For a few minutes his thoughts wandered, and his words were vague and incoherent; but presently his brain cleared, and his voice rose like loud thunder, as he pictured to his hearers those shameless women, from Delilah downwards, who have betrayed men, wasted their substance, and dragged them down to disgrace and death. Were unions with such women, then, eternal? Was a man to be tied in this world, perhaps in another too, to foulness and uncleanness, to a hearth where there was no sympathy, to a home where there was no love? In words of veritable fire, he pictured what some women were, their impurity, their treachery, their mental and moral degradation; and, as a contrast, he drew a glorious picture of what true conjugal love should be—the one fair thing which sanctifies the common uses of the world, and turns its sordid paths into the flower-strewn ways that lead to heaven.

Alma, who was there, seated close under the pulpit, listened in a very rapture of sympathetic idolatry; while Mrs. Montmorency heard both denunciation and peroration with unmoved complacency, though her lips were soon wreathed in a venomous and dangerous smile.

The sermon ended, a prayer was said and a hymn sung; then Bradley walked with a firm tread from the pulpit and entered the vestry. Once there his self-possession left him, and, trembling like a leaf from head to foot, he sank upon a seat.

His sin had come home to him indeed, at last. At the very moment when he was touching on that fatal theme, and justifying himself to his own conscience, Nemesis had arisen, horrible, shameless, and forbidding; had entered the very temple of his shallow creed, smiling and looking into his eyes; had come to remind him that, justify himself as he might, he could never escape the consequence of his rash contempt of the divine sanction.

He had scarcely realised the whole danger of his situation, when he heard a light foot-tread close to him, and, looking up with haggard face, saw Alma approaching. She had used her customary privilege, and entered at the outer door, which stood open.

' Ambrose ! ' she cried, seeing his distress, ' what is the matter ? '

He could not reply, but turned his head away in agony. She came close, and put her arms tenderly around him.

' I was afraid you were ill, dear—you went so pale as you were preaching.'

' No, I am not ill,' he managed to reply.

'l felt a little faint, that was all. I think I need rest; I have been overworking.'

'You must take a holiday,' she answered fondly. 'You must go right away into the country, far from here; and I—I shall go with you, shall I not?'

He drew her to him, and looked long and lovingly into her face, till the sense of her infinite tenderness and devotion overcame him, and he almost wept.

'If I could only go away for ever!' he cried. 'If I could put the world behind me, and see no face but yours, my darling, till my last hour came, and I died in your faithful arms. Here in London, my life seems a mockery, a daily weariness, an air too close and black to breathe in freedom. I hate it, Alma! I hate everything in the world but *you!*'

Alma smiled, and, smoothing back his hair with her white hand, kissed his forehead.

'My Abelard must not talk like that! Every day you continue to fulfil your ministry, your fame and influence grow greater. How eloquent you were to-day! I heard the Prime Minister say that you were the most wonderful preacher he had ever heard, and that though he disagreed with your opinions ——'

'Do not speak of it!' he cried, interrupting her eagerly. 'I care for no one's praise but yours. Oh! Alma what would it all be to me, if I were to lose your love, your good esteem!'

And he held her to him passionately, as if fearing some violent hand might snatch her away. At that moment he heard the sound of a door opening, and looking up saw, standing on the threshold of the vestry, Mrs. Montmorency.

He started up wildly, while Alma, turning quickly, saw the cause of his alarm.

'I beg your pardon,' said the newcomer with a curious smile. 'I knocked at the door, but you did not hear me; so I took the liberty to enter.'

As she spoke, she advanced into the room, and stood complacently looking at the pair. The sickly smell of her favourite scent filled the air, and clung about her like incense around some Cytherean altar.

'Do you—do you—wish to speak to me?' murmured Bradley with a shudder.

'Yes, if you please,' was the quiet reply. 'I wish to ask your advice as a clergyman, in a matter which concerns me very closely. It is a private matter, but, if you *wish* it, this lady may remain until I have finished.'

And she smiled significantly, fixing her black eyes on the clergyman's face.

' Can you not come some other time ? ' he asked nervously. ' To-day I am very busy, and not very well.'

' I shall not detain you many minutes,' was the reply.

Bradley turned in despair to Alma, who was looking on in no little surprise.

' Will you leave us ? I will see you later on in the day.'

Alma nodded, and then looked again at the intruder, surveying her from head to foot with instinctive dislike and dread. She belonged to a type with which Alma was little familiar. Her eyebrows were blackened, her lips painted, and her whole style of dress was *prononcé* and extraordinary.

The eyes of the two women met. Then Alma left the vestry, unconsciously shrinking away from the stranger as she passed her by.

Bradley followed her to the door, closed it quietly, and turning, faced his tormentor.

'What brings you here?' he demanded sternly. 'What do you want with me?'

'I'm not quite sure,' replied Mrs. Montmorency, shrugging her shoulders. 'Before I try to tell you, let me apologise for interrupting your *tête-à-tête* with that charming lady.'

'Do not speak of her! She is too good and pure even to be mentioned by such as you.'

Mrs. Montmorency's eyes flashed viciously, and she showed her teeth, as animals, wild or only half tame, do when they are dangerous.

'You are very polite,' she returned. 'As to her goodness and her purity, you know more about them than I do. She seems fond of you, at any rate; even fonder than when I saw you travelling together the other day, over in France.'

This was a home-thrust, and Bradley at once showed that he was disconcerted.

'In France! travelling together!' he repeated. 'What do you mean?'

'What I saw. You don't mean to deny that I saw you in Normandy some weeks ago, in company with Miss Craik?'

He took an angry turn across the room,

and then, wheeling suddenly, faced her again.

'I mean to deny nothing,' he cried with unexpected passion. 'I wish to have no communication whatever with you, by word or deed. I wish never to see your face again. As to Miss Craik, I tell you again that I will not discuss her with you, that I hold her name too sacred for you even to name. What has brought you back, to shadow my life with your infamous presence? Our paths divided long ago; they should never have crossed again in this world. Live your life; I mean to live mine; and now leave this sacred place, which you profane.'

But though her first impulse was to shrink before him, she remembered her position, and stood her ground.

'If I go, I shall go straight to her, and tell her that I am your wife.'

'It is a falsehood—you are no wife of mine.'

'Pardon me,' she answered with a sneer, 'I can show her my marriage lines.'

As she spoke, he advanced upon her threateningly, with clenched hands.

'Do so, and I will kill you. Yes, kill you! And it would be just. You have been my curse and bane; you are no more fit to live than a reptile or a venomous snake, and before God I would take your wicked life.'

His passion was so terrible, so overmaster-ing, that she shrank before it, and cowered. He seized her by the wrist, and continued in the same tone of menace:

'From the first, you were infamous. In

an evil hour we met; I tried to lift you from the mud, but you were too base. I thought you were dead. I thought that you might have died penitent, and I forgave you. Then, after long years, you rose again, like a ghost from the grave. The shock of your resurrection nearly killed me, but I survived. Then, I remembered your promise—never willingly to molest me; and hearing you had left England, I breathed again. And now you have returned! — Woman, take care! As surely as we are now standing in the Temple of God, so surely will I free myself from you for ever, if you torment me any more.'

He was mad, and scarcely knew what he was saying. Never before in his whole life had he been so carried away by passion. But the woman with whom he had to deal was no

coward, and his taunts awoke all the **angry**
resentment in her heart.   She tore herself **free**
from his hold, and moved towards the **vestry**
door.

'You are a brave man,' she said, '**to**
threaten a woman!   But the law will **protect**
me from you, and I shall claim **my rights!'**

Pale as death, he blocked her **passage.**

'Let me pass!' she **cried.**

'Not yet.   Before you go, you shall **tell**
me what you mean to do!'

'Never mind,' she answered, setting **her**
lips together.

'I *will* know.   Do you mean to **proclaim**
my infamy to the world?'

'I mean,' she replied, ' to prevent you **from**
passing yourself off as a free man, whe**n you**
are bound to *me*.   Our marriage has **never**

been dissolved ; you can never marry another woman, till you are divorced from me.'

He threw his arms up into the air, and uttered a sharp despairing cry :

' O God, my God ! '

Then, changing his tone to one of wild entreaty, he proceeded :

' Woman, have pity ! I will do anything that you wish, if you will only keep our secret. It is not for my own sake that I ask this, but for the sake of one who is innocent, and who loves me. I have never injured you ; I tried to do my duty by you ; our union has been annulled over and over again by your infidelities. Have pity, for God's sake, have pity ! '

She saw that he was at her mercy, and, woman-like, proceeded to encroach.

'Why did you preach at me from the pulpit?' she demanded. 'I am not a saint, but I am as good as most women. They say that, though you are a clergyman, you don't even believe in God at all. Everyone is saying you are an atheist, and this church of yours, which you call sacred, is a wicked place. Yet you set yourself up as my superior. Why should you? I am as good as you; perhaps better. You pass yourself off as a free man, because you are running after a rich woman; and you have taken money from her, everyone knows that. I think she ought to know the truth concerning you, to know that she can never be anything more than your mistress—never your wife. You say I am infamous. I think *you* are more infamous, to deceive a lady you pretend to love.'

She paused, and looked at him. He stood trembling like a leaf, white as death. Every word that she uttered went like a knife into his heart.

'You are right,' he murmured. 'I should not have reproached you ; for I have behaved like a villain. I should have told Miss Craik the whole truth.'

'Just so ; but you have left that disagreeable task to me!'

'You will not tell her! No, no! It will break her heart.'

Mrs. Montmorency shrugged her shoulders.

'Promise me at least one thing,' he cried. 'Give me time to think how to act. Keep our secret until I see you again.'

And as he spoke, he stretched out his arms imploringly, touching her with his trembling hands.   After a moment's hesitation, she replied :

'I think I can promise that!'

'You do? you will?'

'Well, yes; only let me warn you to treat me civilly.   I won't be insulted, or preached at; remember that.'

So saying, she left the vestry, leaving the miserable clergyman plunged in desolation, and more dead than alive.

CHAPTER XVII.

COUNTERPLOT.

Master L. Good morrow, Mistress Light-o'-Love.
Mistress L. Good morrow, Master Lackland. What's the news?
Master L. News enow, I warrant. One Greatheart hath stolen my sweetling away to a green nook i' the forest, where an old hermit hath made them one. Canst thou give me a philtre to poison the well wherein they drink—or a charm to steal upon them while they sleep i' the bower, and slay them ? Do so, good dame, and by Hecate's crows I will make thee rich, when I come unto mine own.—*The Game at Chess : a Comedy.*

MRS. MONTMORENCY passed out into the sunshine, and speedily found herself on the quiet carriage-way which encircles Regent's Park. Living not far away, she had come without her victoria, in which she generally took the air ; and as she strolled along, her dress and general style were sufficiently peculiar to attract considerable attention among the passers-by. For her dress, as usual, was re-splendent.

> She carried on her back and round her neck
> A poor man's revenue.

Amorous shop-walkers, emancipated for the day, stared impudently into her face, and wheeled round on their heels to look at her. Shop-girls in their Sunday finery giggled as they passed her. Quite unconscious of and indifferent to the attention she attracted, she walked lightly on, holding up a black parasol lavishly ornamented with valuable lace.

As she walked, she reflected. In reality, she was rather sorry for Bradley than otherwise, though she still resented the indignant and scornful terms in which he had described her class to his congregation. But she was not malicious for the mere sake of malice ; and she was altogether too indifferent to Bradley personally to feel the slightest interest in his affairs. She knew she had used him ill, that he and she were altogether unfit persons ever to have come together, and no persuasion whatever would have made her resume her old position in relation to him. Thus, unless she could gain something substantial by molesting him and reminding society of her existence, she was quite content to let him alone.

As she reached the south side of the park, she heard a footstep behind her, and the next moment George Craik joined her, out of breath.

' Well ? ' he said questioningly.

' Well ! ' she repeated, smiling.

' Did you see him ? '

' Yes.   I found him in the vestry of his church, and reminded him that we had met before.'

' Just so,' said the young man ; ' but now I want you to tell me, as you promised to do, exactly what you know about him.   I've put this and that together, and I suppose there used to be something between you.   Is it anything which gives you a hold upon the scoundrel *now ?* '

' Perhaps,' she replied quietly.   ' However, I've made up my mind not to tell you anything more at present.'

'But you promised,' said the young man, scowling.

' I dare say I did, but ladies' promises are seldom kept, *mon cher*.   Besides, what do you want me to tell, and, above all, what am I to get by siding with you against him ? '

'If you can do or say anything to convince my cousin he is a rascal,' said George eagerly, ' if you can make her break off her friendship with him, my father would pay you any amount of money.'

' I'm not hard up, or likely to be. Money is of no consequence. Really, I think this is no affair of mine.'

' But what's the mystery ? ' demanded the other. ' I mean to find out, whether you tell me or not; and I have my suspicions, mind you ! Dottie Destrange tells me that you were once *married*. Is that true? and is this the man ? I'd give a thousand pounds to hear you answer, " yes." '

Mrs. Montmorency smiled, and then laughed aloud, while George Craik continued :

'Even if you could show that you and Bradley once lived together, I think it would serve the purpose. I know my cousin's temper. She thinks the fellow a saint, but if he were once degraded in her opinion, she would throw him over like a shot.'

'And take you in his place, you think?'

'Perhaps; I don't know.'

'What a fool you must think me!' said Mrs. Montmorency, sarcastically. 'I am to rake up all my past life, make myself the common talk of the world, all to oblige *you*. Can't do it, *mon cher*. It wouldn't be fair, either to myself or to the man.'

At that moment a hansom passed, and she beckoned to the driver with her parasol.

'*Au revoir*,' she cried, stepping into the vehicle. 'Come and see me in a few days, and I shall have had time to think it over.'

CHAPTER XVIII.

A SOLAR BIOLOGIST.

What's this? Heyday! Magic! Witchcraft!
Passing common hedge and ditch-craft!
You whose soul no magic troubles,
Crawling low among the stubbles,
Thing compact of clay, a body
Meant to perish,—think it odd, eh?
Raise your eyes, poor clod, and try to
See the tree-tops, and the sky too!
There's the sun with pulses splendid
Whirling onward, star attended!
Child of light am I, the wizard,
Fiery-form'd from brain to gizzard,
While for *you*, my sun-craft spurning,
Dust thou art, to dust returning!

Joke and Hysteria: a Medley.[1]

LIKE most men famously or infamously familiar in the mouths of the public, the Rev. Ambrose

---

[1] NOTE.—A joke, and a very poor one, which an honoured and great master must forgive, since the joker himself has laboured more than most living men to spread the fame of the master and to do him honour.—R. B.

Bradley was a good deal troubled with busy-bodies, who sometimes communicated with him through the medium of the penny post, and less frequently forced themselves upon his privacy in person. The majority demanded his autograph; many sought his advice on matters of a private and spiritual nature; a few requested his immediate attention to questions in the nature of conundrums on literature, art, sociology, and the musical glasses. He took a good deal of this pestering good-humouredly, regarding it as the natural homage to public success, or notoriety; but sometimes he lost his temper, when some more than common impertinence aroused his indignation.

Now, it so happened that on the very evening of his painful interview with Mrs.

Montmorency, he received a personal visit from one of the class to which we are alluding; and as the visit in question, though trivial enough in itself, was destined to lead to important consequences, we take leave to place it upon special record. He was seated alone in his study, darkly brooding over his own dangerous position, and miserably reviewing the experiences of his past life, when the housemaid brought in a card, on which were inscribed, or rather printed, these words :—

Professor Salem Mapleleafe,

Solar Biologist.

'What is this?' cried Bradley irritably. 'I can see nobody.'

As he spoke a voice outside the study door answered him, in a high-pitched American accent—

'I beg your pardon. I shan't detain you two minutes. I am Professor Mapleleafe, representing the Incorporated Society of Spiritual Brethren, New York.'

Simultaneously there appeared in the doorway a little, spare man with a very large head, a gnome-like forehead, and large blue eyes full of troubled 'wistfulness' so often to be found in the faces of educated Americans. Before the clergyman could utter any further remonstrance this person was in the room, holding out his hand, which was small and thin, like that of a woman.

'My dear sir, permit me to shake you by the hand. In all America, and I may add in all England, there is no warmer admirer than myself of the noble campaign you are leading against superstition. I have lines of introduction to you from our common friends and fellow-workers, Ellerton and Knowlesworth.'

And he mentioned the names of two of the leading transcendental thinkers of America, one an eccentric philosopher, the other a meditative poet, with whom Bradley had frequently corresponded.

There was really no other way out of the dilemma short of actual rudeness and incivility, than to take the letters, which the little Professor eagerly handed over. The first was brief and very characteristic of the writer, meaning as follows :—

'See Mapleleafe. He talks nonsense, but he is a man of ideas. I like him. His sister, who accompanies him, is a sibyl.'

The other was less abrupt and unusual, though nearly as brief.

' Let me introduce to your notice Professor Mapleleafe, who is on a visit to Europe with his charming sister. You may have heard of both in connection with the recent developments in American spiritualism. The Professor is a man of singular experience, and Miss Mapleleafe is an accredited clairvoyante. Such civility as you can show them will be fully appreciated in our circle here.'

Bradley glanced up, and took a further survey of the stranger. On closer scrutiny he perceived that the Professor's gnome-like head and wistful eyes were associated with a somewhat mean and ignoble type of features, an insignificant turn-up nose, and a receding chin ; that his hair, where it had not thinned away, was pale straw-coloured, and that his eyebrows and eyelashes were almost white.

His small, shrunken figure was clad in shabby black.

To complete the oddity of his appearance, he carried an eye-glass, dangling from his neck by a piece of black elastic; and as Bradley eyed him from head to foot, he fixed the glass into his right eye, thereby imparting to his curious physiognomy an appearance of jaunty audacity not at all in keeping with his general appearance.

' You come at a rather awkward time,' said Bradley. ' I seldom or never receive visits on Sunday evening, and to-night especially——'

He paused and coughed uneasily, looking very ill at ease.

' I understand, I quite understand,' returned the Professor, gazing up at him in real or assumed admiration. ' You devote your seventh-day evening to retirement and to meditation. Well, sir, I'm real grieved to disturb you; but sister and I heard you preach this morning, and I may at once tell you that for a good square sermon and elocution fit for the Senate, we never heard anyone to match you, though we've heard a few. After hearing you orate, I couldn't rest till I presented my lines of introduction, and that's a fact. Sister would have come to you, but a friendly spirit from the planet Mars dropt in just as she was fixing herself, and she *had* to stay.'

Bradley looked in surprise at the speaker, beginning to fancy that he was conversing with a lunatic; but the Professor's manner was quite commonplace and matter-of-fact.

'Have you been long in Europe?' he asked, hardly knowing what to say.

'Two months, sir. We have just come from Paris, where we were uncommon well entertained by the American circle. You are aware, of course, that my sister has transcendental gifts ? '

' That she is clairvoyante ? So Knowlesworth says in his letter. I may tell you at once that I am a total disbeliever in such matters. I believe spiritualism, even clairvoyance, to be mere imposture.'

' Indeed, sir ? ' said the Professor, without the slightest sign of astonishment or irritation. ' You don't believe in solar biology ? '

' I don't even know what that means,' answered Bradley with a smile.

' May I explain, sir ? Solar biology is the science which demonstrates our connection with radiant existences of the central luminary of this universe; our dependence and inter-dependence as spiritual beings on the ebb and flow of consciousness from that shining centre ; our life hitherto, now, and hereafter, as solar elements. We are sunbeams, sir, materialised ; thought is psychic sunlight. On the basis of that great principle is established the reality of our correspondence with spiritual substances, alien to us, existing in the other solar worlds.'

Bradley shrugged his shoulders. His mood of mind at that moment was the very reverse of conciliatory towards any form of transcendentalism, and this seemed arrant non-sense.

' Let me tell you frankly,' he said, ' that in all such matters as these I am a pure mate-rialist.'

'Exactly,' cried the Professor. 'So are we, sir.'

'Materialists?'

'Why, certainly. Spiritualism *is* materialism; in other words, everything is spirit matter. All bodies, as the great Swedenborg demonstrated long ago, are spirit; thought is spirit—that is to say, sir, sunlight. The same great principle of which I have spoken is the destruction of all religion save the religion of solar science. It demolishes Theism, which has been the will-o'-the-wisp of the world, abolishes Christianity, which has been its bane. The God of the universe is solar Force, which is universal and pantheistic.'

'Pray sit down,' said Bradley, now for the first time becoming interested. 'If I understand you, there is no personal God?'

'Of course not,' returned the little man, sidling into a chair and dropping his eyeglass. 'A personal God is, as the scientists call it, merely an anthropomorphic Boom. As the great cosmic Bard of solar biology expresses it in his sublime epic :

> The radiant flux and reflux, the serene
> Atomic ebb and flow of force divine,
> This, this alone, is God, the Demiurgus;
> By this alone we are, and still shall be.
> O joy! the Phantom of the Uncondition'd
> Fades into nothingness before the breath
> Of that eternal ever-effluent Life
> Whose centre is the shining solar Heart
> Of countless throbbing pulses, each a world!

The quotation was delivered with extraordinary rapidity, and in the off hand matter-of-fact manner characteristic of the speaker. Then, after pausing a moment, and fixing his glass again, the Professor demanded eagerly :

'What do you think of that, sir?'

' I think,' answered Bradley, laughing contemptuously, ' that it is very poor science, and
still poorer poetry.'

' You think so, really ? ' cried the Professor,
not in the least disconcerted. ' I think I could
convince you by a few ordinary manifestations,
that it's at any rate common sense.'

It was now quite clear to Bradley that the
man was a charlatan, and he was in no mood
to listen to spiritualistic jargon. What both
amused and puzzled him was that two such
men as his American correspondents should
have franked the Professor to decent society
by letters of introduction. He reflected, however, that from time immemorial men of genius,
eager for glimpses of a better life and a serener
state of things, had been led ' by the nose,' like
Faust, by charlatans. Now, Bradley, though

an amiable man, had a very ominous frown
when he was displeased ; and just now his
brow came down, and his eyes looked out of
positive caverns, as he said :

'I have already told you what I think of
spiritualism and spiritualistic manifestations.   I
believe my opinion is that of all educated
men.'

'Spiritualism, as commonly understood, is
one thing, sir,' returned the Professor quietly ;
'spiritualistic materialism, or solar science, is
another.   Our creed, sir, like your own, is the
destruction of supernaturalism.   If you will
permit me once more to quote our sublime
Bard, he sings as follows :—

> All things abide in Nature ; Form and Soul,
> Matter and Thought, Function, Desire, and Dream,
> Evolve within her ever-heaving breast ;
> Within her, we subsist ; beyond and o'er her
> Is naught but Chaos and primæval Night.

The Shadow of that Night for centuries
Projected Man's phantasmic Deity,
Formless, fantastic, hideous, and unreal;
God is Existence, and as parts of God
Men ebb and flow, for evermore divine.

'If you abolish supernaturalism,' asked the clergyman impatiently, 'what do you mean by manifestations?'

'Just this,' returned the little man glibly, 'the interchange of communications between beings of this sphere and beings otherwise conditioned. This world is one of many, all of which have a two-fold existence—in the sphere of matter, and in the sphere of ideas. Death, which vulgar materialists consider the end of consciousness, is merely one of the many phenomena of change; and spiritualistic realities being indestructible——'

Bradley rose impatiently.

'I am afraid,' he exclaimed, 'that I cannot

discuss the matter any longer. Our opinions on the subject are hopelessly antagonistic, and to speak frankly, I have an invincible repugnance to the subject itself.'

'Shared, I am sorry to say, by many of your English men of science.'

'Shared, I am glad to say, by most thinking men.'

'Well, well, sir, I won't detain you at present,' returned the Professor, not in the least ruffled. 'Perhaps you will permit me to call upon you at a more suitable time, and to introduce my sister?'

'Really, I——' began Bradley with some embarrassment.

'Eustasia Mapleleafe is a most remarkable woman, sir. She is a medium of the first degree; she possesses the power of prophecy, of clairvoyance, and of thought-reading. The book of the Soul is open to her, and you would wonder at her remarkable divinations.'

'I must still plead my entire scepticism,' said Bradley coldly.

'I guess Eustasia Mapleleafe would convert you. She was one of your congregation to-day, and between ourselves is greatly concerned on your account.'

'Concerned on my account!' echoed the clergyman.

'Yes, sir. She believes you to be under the sway of malign influences, possibly lunar or stellar. She perceived a dark spectrum on the radiant orb of your mind, troubling the solar effluence which all cerebral matter emits, and which is more particularly emitted by the phosphorescent cells of the human brain.'

Bradley would by this time have considered that he was talking to a raving madman, had not the Professor been self-contained and matter-of-fact. As it was, he could hardly conceive him to be quite sane. At any other time, perhaps, he might have listened with patience and even amusement to the fluent little American; but that day, as the reader is aware, his spirit was far too pre-occupied.

His face darkened unpleasantly as the Professor touched on his state of mind during the sermon, and he glanced almost angrily towards the door.

'May I bring my sister?' persisted the Professor. 'Or stay—with your leave, sir, I'll write our address upon that card, and perhaps you will favour her with a call.'

As he spoke, he took up his own card

from the table, and wrote upon it with a pencil.

'That's it, sir——care of Mrs. Piozzi Baker, 17 Monmouth Crescent, Bayswater.'

So saying, he held out his hand, which Bradley took mechanically, and then, with a polite bow, passed from the room and out of the house.

Bradley resumed his seat, and the meditations which his pertinacious visitor had interrupted ; but the interruption, irritating as it was, had done him good. Absurd as the Professor's talk had been, it was suggestive of that kind of speculation which has invariably a fascination for imaginative men, and from time to time, amidst his gloomy musings over his own condition, amidst his despair, his dread, and his self-reproach, the clergyman found

himself reminded of the odd propositions of the
so-called biologist.

After all, there was something in the little
man's creed, absurd as it was, which brought a
thinker face to face with the great phenomena
of life and being.   How wretched and ignoble
seemed his position, in face of the eternal
Problem, which even spiritualism was an
attempt to solve !   He was afraid now to look
in the mirror of Nature, lest he should behold
only his own lineament, distorted by miserable
fears.   He felt, for the time being, infamous.
A degrading falsehood, like an iron ring, held
him chained and bound.

Even the strange charlatan had discovered
the secret of his misery.   He would soon be a
laughing-stock to all the world ; he, who had
aspired to be the world's teacher and prophet,

who would have flown like an eagle into the very central radiance of the sun of Truth !

He rose impatiently, and paced up and down the room. As he did so, his eye fell upon something white, lying at the feet of the chair where his visitor had been sitting.

He stooped and picked it up. He found it to be a large envelope, open, and containing two photographs. Hardly knowing what he did, he took out the pictures, and examined them.

The first rather puzzled him, though he soon realised its character. It represented the little Professor, seated in an armchair, reading a book open upon his knee ; behind him was a shadowy something in white floating drapery, which, on close scrutiny, disclosed the outline of a human face and form, white and vague

M

like the filmy likeness seen in a smouldering fire. Beneath this picture was written in a small clear hand,—' Professor Mapleleafe and Azaleus, a Spirit of the Third Magnitude, from the Evening Star.'

It was simply a curious specimen of what is known as ' Spirit-Photography.' The clergy-man returned it to its envelope with a smile of contempt.

The second photograph was different; it was the likeness of a woman, clad in white muslin, and reclining upon a sofa.

The figure was *petite*, almost fairy-like in its fragility; the hair, which fell in masses over the naked shoulders, very fair; the face, elfin-like, but exceedingly pretty; the eyes, which looked right out from the picture into those of the spectator, were wonderfully large, lustrous and wild. So luminous and searching were these eyes, so rapt and eager the pale face, that Bradley was startled, as if he were looking into the countenance of a living person.

Beneath this picture were written the words—' Eustasia Mapleleafe.'

The clergyman looked at this picture again and again, with a curious fascination. As he did so, holding it close to the lamplight, a peculiar thrill ran through his frame, and his hand tingled as if it touched the warm hand of some living being. At last, with an effort, he returned it also to the envelope, which he threw carelessly upon his desk.

It was quite clear that the Professor had dropt the pictures, and Bradley determined to send them by that night's post. So he sat down, and addressed the envelope according to the address on the card ; but before sealing it up, he took out the photographs and inspected them again.

A new surprise awaited him.

The photograph of the Professor and his ghostly familiar remained as it had been ; but the photograph of the woman, or girl, was mysteriously changed—that is to say, it had become so faint and vague as to be almost unrecognisable. The dress and figure were dim as a wreath of vapour, the face was blank and featureless, the eyes were faded and indistinct.

The entire effect was that of some ghostly presence, fading slowly away before the vision.

Bradley was amazed, in spite of himself, and his whole frame shook with agitation.

He held the sun-picture again to the lamp-light, inspecting it closely, and every instant it seemed to grow fainter and fainter, till nothing remained on the paper but a formless outline, like the spirit-presence permanent on the other photograph.

By instinct a superstitious or rather a nervous man, Bradley now felt as if he were under the influence of some extraordinary spell. Already unstrung by the events of the day, he trembled from head to foot. At last, with an effort, he conquered his agitation, sealed up the photographs, and rang for the servant to put the letter in the post.

Although he suspected some trick, he was greatly troubled and perplexed ; nor would his trouble and perplexity have been much lessened, if at all, had he been acquainted with the truth—that the little Professor had left the photographs in the room not by accident, but intentionally, and for a purpose which will be better understood at a later period of the present story.

CHAPTER XIX.

EUSTASIA MAPLELEAFE.

O eyes of pale forget-me-not blue,
Wash'd more pale by a dreamy dew!
O red red lips, O dainty tresses,
O heart the breath of the world distresses!
O little lady, do they divine
That they have *fathomed* thee and thine?
Fools! let them fathom fire, and beat
Light in a mortar; ay, and heat
Soul in a crucible! Let them try
To conquer the light, and the wind, and the sky!
Darkly the secret faces lurk,
We know them least where most they work;
And here they meet to mix in thee,
For a strange and mystic entity,
Making of thy pale soul, in truth,
A life half trickery and half truth!

Ballads of St. Abe.

MONMOUTH CRESCENT, Bayswater, is one of
those forlorn yet thickly populated streets

which lie under the immediate dominion of the great Whiteley, of Westbourne Grove. The houses are adapted to limited means and large families ; and in front of them is an arid piece of railed-in ground, where crude vegetable substances crawl up in the likeness of trees and grass. The crescent is chiefly inhabited by lodging-house and boarding-house keepers, City clerks, and widows who advertise for persons ' to share the comforts of a cheerful home,' with late dinners and carpet balls in the evening. It is shabby-genteel, impecunious, and generally depressing.

To one of the dingiest houses in this dingy crescent, Professor Mapleleafe, after his interview with our hero, cheerfully made his way.

He took the 'bus which runs along Marylebone Road to the Royal Oak, and thence made his way on foot to the house door. In answer to his knock the door was opened by a tall red-haired matron wearing a kitchen apron over her black stuff dress. Her complexion was sandy and very pale, her eyes were bold and almost fierce, her whole manner was self-assertive and almost aggressive; but she greeted the Professor with a familiar smile, as with a friendly nod he passed her by, hastening upstairs to the first floor.

He opened a door and entered a large room furnished in faded crimson velvet, with a dining-room sideboard at one end, cheap lithographs on the walls, and mantelpiece ornamented with huge shells and figures in common china.

The room was quite dark, save for the

light of a small paraffin lamp with pink shade;
and on a sofa near the window the figure of a
young woman was reclining, drest in white
muslin, and with one arm, naked almost to the
shoulder, dabbling in a small glass water tank,
placed upon a low seat, and containing several
small water-lilies in full bloom.

Anyone who had seen the photograph
which the Professor had left behind him in the
clergyman's house, would have recognised the
original at a glance. There was the same
petite almost child-like figure, the same loose
flowing golden hair, the same elfin-like but
pretty face, the same large, wild, lustrous eyes.
But the face of the original was older, sharper,
and more care-worn than might have been
guessed from the picture. It was the face of
a woman of about four- or five-and-twenty,

and though the lips were red and full-coloured, and the eyes full of life and lightness, the complexion had the dulness of chronic ill-health.

The hand which hung in the water, playing with the lily-leaves, was thin and transparent, but the arm was white as snow and beautifully rounded.

The effect would have been perfectly poetic and ethereal, but it was spoiled to some extent by the remains of a meal which stood on the table close by—a tray covered with a soiled cloth, some greasy earthenware plates, the remains of a mutton chop, potatoes and bread.

As the Professor entered, his sister looked up and greeted him by name.

'You are late, Salem,' she said with an

unmistakeable American accent. 'I was wondering what kept you.'

'I'll tell you,' returned the Professor. 'I've been having a talk with Mr. Ambrose Bradley, at his own house. I gave him our lines of introduction. I'm real sorry to find that he's as ignorant as a redskin of the great science of solar biology, and the way he received me was not reassuring—indeed, he almost showed me the door.'

'You're used to that, Salem,' said Eustasia with a curious smile.

'Guess I am,' returned the Professor dryly; 'only I did calculate on something different from a man of Bradley's acquirements, I did indeed. However, he's just one of those men who believe in nothing by halves or quarters, and if we can once win him over

to an approval of our fundamental propositions, he'll be the most valuable of all recruits
to new causes—a hot convert.'

The woman sighed—a sigh so long, so
weary, that it seemed to come from the very
depths of her being, and her expression grew
more and more sad and *ennuyée*, as she drew
her slender fingers softly through the waters
of the tank.

' Ain't you well to-night, Eustasia ? ' inquired the Professor, looking at her with some
concern.

' As well as usual,' was the reply. ' Suppose European air don't suit me ; I've never
been quite myself since I came across to this
country.'

Her voice was soft and musical enough,
and just then, when a peculiar wistful light

filled the faces of both, it was quite possible to believe them to be brother and sister. But in all other outward respects, they were utterly unlike.

'Tell me more about this young clergyman,' she continued after a pause. 'I am interested in him. The moment I saw him I said to myself he is the very image of—— of'——

She paused without finishing the sentence, and looked meaningly at her brother.

'Of Ulysses E. Stedman, you mean?' cried the Professor, holding up his forefinger. 'Eustasia, take care! You promised me never to think of him any more, and I expect you to keep your word.'

'But don't you see the resemblance?'

'Well, I dare say I do, for Ulysses was

well-looking enough when he wasn't in liquor.
Don't talk about him, and don't think about
him! He's buried somewhere down Florida
way, and I ain't sorry on your account
neither.'

'Killed! murdered! and so young!' cried
the girl, with a cry so startling, and so full of
pain, that her brother looked aghast. As he
spoke, she drew her dripping right hand from
the tank and placed it wildly upon her forehead. The water-drops streamed down her
face like tears, while her whole countenance
looked livid with pain.

'Eustasia!'

'I loved him, Salem! I loved him with all
my soul!'

'Well, I know you did,' said the little man
soothingly. 'I warned you against him, but

you wouldn't listen. Now that's all over ; and as for Ulysses being murdered, he was killed in a free fight, he was, and he only got what he'd given to many another. Don't you take on, Eustasia ! If ever you marry, it will be a better man than he was.'

' Marry ? ' cried the girl with a bitter laugh. ' Who'd marry *me?* Who'd ever look at such a thing as I am ? Even he despised me, Salem, and thought me a cheat and an impostor. Wherever we go, it's the old story. I hate the life ; I hate myself. I'd rather be a beggar in the street than what I am.'

' Don't underreckon yourself, Eustasia ! Don't underreckon your wonderful gifts ! '

' What are my gifts worth ? ' said Eustasia. ' Can they bring *him* back to me? Can they bring back those happy, happy days we spent together? Haven't I tried, and tried, and tried, to get a glimpse of his face, to feel again the touch of his hand; and he never comes — he will never come—never, never! I wish I was with him in the grave, I do.'

Her grief was truly pitiable, yet there was something querulous and ignoble in it too, which prevented it from catching the tone of true sorrow. For the rest, the man whose memory awakened so much emotion had been pretty much what the Professor described him to be—a handsome scoundrel, with the manners of a gentleman and the tastes of a rowdy. A professional gambler, he had been known as one of the most dangerous adventurers in the Southern States, having betrayed more women, and killed more men, than any person in his district. A random shot had at last laid him low, to the great relief of the respectable portion of the community.

The Professor eyed his sister thoughtfully, waiting till her emotion had subsided. He had not long to wait. Either the emotion was shallow itself, or Eustasia had extraordinary power of self-control. Her face became comparatively untroubled, though it retained its peculiar pallor; and reaching out her hand, she again touched the water and the lilies swimming therein.

'Salem!' she said presently.

'Yes, Eustasia.'

'Tell me more about this Mr. Bradley. Is he married?'

'Certainly not.'

'Engaged to be married?'

'I believe so. They say he is to marry

Miss Craik, the heiress, whom we saw in church to-day.'

Eustasia put no more questions; but curiously enough, began crooning to herself, in a low voice, some wild air. Her eyes flashed and her face became illuminated; and as she sang, she drew her limp hand to and fro in the water, among the flowers, keeping time to the measure. All her sorrow seemed to leave her, giving place to a dreamy pleasure. There was something feline and almost forbidding in her manner. She looked like a pythoness intoning oracles :—

> Dark eyes aswim with sibylline desire,
> And vagrant locks of amber!

Her voice was clear though subdued, resembling, to some extent, the purring of a cat.

'What are you singing, Eustasia?'

'"In lilac time when blue birds sing," Salem.'

'What a queer girl you are!' cried the Professor, not without a certain wondering admiration. 'I declare I sometimes feel afraid of you. Anyone could see with half an eye that we were brother and sister only on one side of the family. Your mother was a remarkable woman, like yourself. Father used to say sometimes he'd married a ghost-seer; and it might have been, for she hailed from the Highlands of Scotland. At any rate, you inherit her gift.'

Eustasia ceased her singing, and laughed again—this time with a low, self-satisfied gladness.

'It's all I do inherit, brother Salem,' she

said; adding, in a low voice, as if to herself, 'But it's something, after all.'

'Something!' cried the Professor. 'It's a Divine privilege, that's what it is! To think that when you like you can close your eyes, see the mystical coming and going of cosmic forces, and, as the sublime Bard expresses it,

> Penetrate where no human foot hath trod
> Into the ever-quickening glories of God,
> See star with star conjoin'd as soul with soul,
> Swim onward to the dim mysterious goal,
> Hear rapturous breathings of the Force which flows
> From founts wherein the eternal godhead glows!

I envy you, Eustasia; I do, indeed.'

Eustasia laughed again, less pleasantly.

'Guess you don't believe all that. Sometimes I think myself that it's all nervous delusion.'

'Nervous force you mean. Well, and what is nervous force but solar being? What

you see and hear is as real as—as real as—
spiritual photography. Talking of that, I gave
Mr. Bradley one of your pictures, taken under
test conditions.'

'You gave it him?'

'Dropt it in his room, where he's certain to
find it.'

'Why did you do that?' demanded the
girl almost sharply.

'Why? Because, as I told you, I want to
win him over. Such a man as he is will be
invaluable to us, here in England. He has the
gift of tongues, to begin with; and then he
knows any number of influential and wealthy
people. What we want now, Eustasia, is
money.'

'We always have wanted it, as long as I
ean remember.'

'I don't mean what you mean,' cried the Professor indignantly. 'I mean money to push the great cause, to propagate the new religion, to open up more and more the arcanum of mystic biology. We want money, and we want converts. If we can win Bradley over to our side, it won't be a bad beginning.'

'Who is to win him over? I?'

'Why, of course. You must see him, and when you do, I think it is as good as done. Only mind this, Eustasia! Keep your head cool, and don't go spooning. You're too susceptible, you are! If I hadn't been by to look after you, you'd have thrown yourself away a dozen times.'

Eustasia smiled and shook her head. Then, with a weary sigh, she arose.

'I'll go to bed now, Salem.'

'Do—and get your beauty-sleep. You'll want all your strength to-morrow. We have a séance at seven, at the house of Mrs. Uptcn. Tyndall is invited, and I calculate you'll want to have all your wits about you.'

'Good night!'

'Good night,' said the Professor, kissing her on the forehead ; then, with a quiet change from his glib, matter-of-fact manner to one of real tenderness, he added, looking wistfully into her eyes, 'Keep up your spirits, Eustasia ! We shan't stay here long, and then we'll go back to America and take a long spell of rest.'

Eustasia sighed again, and then glided from the room. She was so light and fragile that her feet seemed to make no sound, and in her white floating drapery she seemed almost like a ghost.

Left alone, the Professor sat down to the table, drew out a pencil and number of letters, and began making notes in a large pocket-book.

Presently he paused thoughtfully, and looked at the door by which Eustasia had retreated.

'Poor girl!' he muttered. 'Her soul's too big for her body, and that's a fact. I'm afraid she'll decline like her mother, and die young.'

CHAPTER XX.

THE THUNDERCLAP.

The Mighty and the Merciful are one;
The morning dew that scarcely bends the flowers,
Exhal'd to heaven, becomes the thunderbolt
That strikes the tree at noon.

Judas Iscariot : a Drama.

THERE are moments in a man's life when all the forces of life and society seem to conspire for his destruction ; when, look which way he will, he sees no loophole for escape ; when every step he takes forward seems a step downward towards some pitiless Inferno, and when to make even one step backward is impossible, because the precipice down which he has been thrust seems steep as a wall. Yet there is still hope for such a man, if his own conscience is not in revolt against him ; for that conscience, like a very angel, may uplift him by the hair and hold him miraculously from despair and death. Woe to him, however, if he has no such living help ! Beyond that, there is surely no succour for him, beyond the infinite mercy, the cruel kindness, of his avenging God.

The moment of which I speak had come to Ambrose Bradley.

Even in the very heyday of his pride, when he thought himself strong enough to walk alone, without faith, almost without vital belief, his sins had found him out, and he saw the Inferno waiting at his feet. He knew that there was no escape. He saw the powers of evil arrayed on every side against him. And cruellest of all the enemies leagued for his destruction, was the conscience which might have been his sweetest and surest friend.

It was too late now for regrets, it was too late now to reshape his course. Had he only exhibited a man's courage, and, instead of snatching an ignoble happiness, confided the whole truth to the woman he loved, she might have pitied and forgiven him ; but he had accepted her love under a lie, and to confide the truth to her now would simply be to make a confession of his moral baseness. He dared not, could not, tell her ; yet he knew that detection was inevitable. Madly, despairingly, he wrestled with his agony. and soon lay prostrate before it, a strong man self-stripped of his spiritual and moral strength.

Not that he was tamely acquiescent; not that he accepted his fate as just.

On the contrary, his whole spirit rose in revolt and indignation. He had tried to serve God—so at least he assured himself; he had tried to become a living lesson and example to a hard and unbelieving world ; he had tried to upbuild again a Temple where men might worship in all honesty and freedom ; and what was the result ? For a slight fault, a venial blunder, of his own youth, he was betrayed to a punishment which threatened to be everlasting.

His intellect rebelled at the idea.

With failing strength he tried to balance himself on the satanic foothold of revolt. His doubts thickened around him like a cloud. If there was a just God, if there was a God at all, why had he made such a world ?

In simple truth, the man's fatal position was

entirely the consequence of his once lack of moral courage.

He had missed the supreme moment, he had lacked the supreme sanction, which would have saved him, even had his danger been twenty-fold more desperate than it had been. Instead of standing erect in his own strength, and defying the Evil One, who threatened to hurl him down and destroy him, he had taken the Evil One's hand and accepted its support. Yes, the devil had helped him, but at what a cost!

'Get thee behind me, Satan!' he should have said. It was the sheerest folly to say it now.

He cowered in terror at the thought of Alma's holy indignation. He dreaded not her anger, which he could have borne, but her dis-enchantment, which he could not bear.

Her trust in him had been so absolute, her self-surrender so supreme ; but its motive had been his goodness, her faith in his unsullied truth. She had been his handmaid, as she had called herself, and had trusted herself to him, body and soul. So complete had been his intellectual authority over her, that even had he told her his secret and thereupon assured her that he was morally a free man, though legally fettered, she would have accepted his genial pleading and still have given him her love. He was quite sure of that. But he had chosen a course of mere deception, he had refused to make her his confidant, and she had married him in all faith and fervour, believing there was no corner in all his heart where he had anything to conceal.

It was just possible that she might still

forgive him ; it was simply impossible that she could ever revere and respect him, as she hitherto had done.

Does he who reads these lines quite realise what it is to fall from the pure estate of a loving woman's worship? Has he ever been so throned in a loving heart as to understand how kingly is the condition—how terrible the fall from that sweet power? So honoured and enthroned, he is still a king, though he is a beggar of all men's charity, though he has not a roof to cover his head; so dethroned and fallen, he is still a beggar, though all the world proclaims him king.

Mephistopheles Minor, in the shape of gay George Craik, junior, scarcely slept on his discovery, or rather on his suspicions. He was now perfectly convinced that there was some mysterious connection between the clergyman and Mrs. Montmorency; and as the actress refused for the time being to lend herself to any sort of open persecution, he determined to act on his own responsibility. So he again canvassed Miss Destrange and the other light ladies of his acquaintance, and receiving from them further corroboration of the statement that Mrs. Montmorency had been previously married, he had no doubt whatever that Ambrose Bradley was the man who had once stood to her in the relation of a husband.

Armed with this information, he sought out his father on the Monday morning, found him at his club, told him of all he knew, and asked his advice.

'My only wish, you know,' he explained, 'is to save Alma from that man, who is evidently a scoundrel. So I thought I would come to you at once. The question is, what is to be done?'

'It's a horrible complication,' said the baronet, honestly shocked. 'Do you actually mean to tell me that you suspect an improper relationship between Alma and this infernal infidel?'

'I shouldn't like to go as far as that; but they were seen travelling together, like man and wife, in France.'

'Good heavens! It is incredible.'

'I should like to shoot the fellow,' cried George furiously. 'And I would, too, if this was a duelling country. Shooting's too good for him. He ought to be hung!'

The upshot of the conversation was that father and son determined to visit Alma at once together, and to make one last attempt to bring her to reason. At a little after midday they were at her door. The baronet stalked in past the servant, with an expression of the loftiest moral indignation.

' Tell Miss Craik that I wish to see her at once,' he said.

It was some minutes before Alma appeared. When she did so, attired in a pink morning *peignoir* of the most becoming fashion, her face was bright as sunshine ; but it became clouded directly she met her uncle's eyes. She saw at a glance that he had come on an unpleasant errand.

George Craik sulked in a corner, waiting for his father to conduct the attack.

'What has brought you over so early, uncle?' she demanded. 'I hope George has not been talking nonsense to you about me. He has been here before on the same errand, and I had to show him the door.'

'George has your interest at heart,' returned the baronet, fuming; 'and if you doubt his disinterestedness, perhaps you will do me the justice to believe that *I* am your true friend, as well as your relation. Now my brother is gone, I am your nearest protector. It is enough to make your father rise in his grave to hear what I have heard.'

'What have you heard?' cried Alma, turning pale with indignation. 'Don't go too far, uncle, or I shall quarrel with you as well as George; and I should be sorry for that.'

'Will you give me an explanation of your

conduct—yes or no?—or do you refuse my right to question you? Remember, Alma, the honour of our family—your father's honour— is in question.'

'How absurd you are!' cried Alma, with a forced laugh. 'But there, I will try to keep my temper. What is it that you want to know?'

And she sat down quietly, with folded hands, as if waiting to be interrogated.

'Is it the fact, as I am informed, that you and Mr. Bradley were seen travelling alone together, some weeks ago, in Normandy?'

Alma hesitated before speaking; then, smiling to herself, she said,

'Suppose it is true, uncle—what then?'

The baronet's face went red as crimson, and he paced furiously up and down the room.

'What then? Good heavens, can you ask that question? Do you know that your character is at stake? Then you do not deny it?'

'No; for it is true.'

Father and son looked at one another; then the baronet proceeded :

'Then all the rest is true. You are that man's mistress!'

The shot struck home, but Alma was prepared for it, and without changing her attitude in the least, she quietly replied :

'No, uncle ; I am *that man's wife!*'

'His wife!' ejaculated father and son in the same breath.

'Yes. We were married some weeks ago, and after the wedding, went for a few days to France. There! I intended to keep the secret, till I was free to tell it ; but gross, cruel importunity has wrung it from me. Do not think, however,' she continued, rising to her feet and exchanging her self-possessed manner for one of angry wrath, ' that I shall ever forgive you, either of you, for your shameful suspicions concerning me. You might have spared me so many insults. You might have known me better. However, now you know the truth, perhaps you will relieve me from any further persecution.'

Father and son exchanged another look.

' Do you actually affirm that you are married ? ' exclaimed the baronet.

' Actually,' returned the young lady with a sarcastic bow.

Thereupon George Craik sprang to his feet, prepared to deliver the *coup de grâce*.

'Tell her the truth, father!' he exclaimed. 'Tell her that she is no more married than I am!'

'What does he mean?' cried Alma, looking at her uncle. 'Is he mad?'

'He means simply this, Alma,' said Sir George, after a prompting glance from his son. 'If you have gone through the marriage ceremony with this man, this infidel, you have been shamefully betrayed. The scoundrel was unable to marry again, if, as we have reason to believe, his first wife is still living!'

The two men, father and son, had struck their blow boldly but very cruelly, and it came with full force on the devoted woman's head. At first Alma could scarcely believe her ears; she started in her chair, put out her hands quickly as if to ward off another savage attack, and then shrank in terror, while every vestige of colour in her cheeks faded away.

Sir George stood gazing down at her, also greatly agitated, for he was well-bred enough to feel that the part he was playing was unmanly, almost cowardly. He had spoken and acted on a mere surmise, and even at that moment, amidst the storm of his nervous indignation, the horrible thought flashed upon him that he might be wrong after all.

' " His first wife is still living ! " ' repeated Alma with a quick involuntary shudder, scarcely able to realise the words. ' Uncle, what do you mean ? Have *you* gone mad, as well as George ? Of whom are you speaking ? Of—of Mr. Bradley ? '

' Of that abominable man,' cried the baronet, ' who, if my information is correct, and if there is law in the land, shall certainly pay the penalty of his atrocious crime! Do not think that we blame *you*,' he added more gently; ' no, for you are not to blame. You have been the dupe, the victim of a villain!'

Like a prisoner sick with terror, yet gathering all his strength about him to protest against the death-sentence for a crime of which he is innocent, Alma rose, and trembling violently, still clutching the chair for support, looked at her uncle.

' I do not believe one word of what you say! I believe it is an infamous falsehood. But whether it is true or false, I shall never forgive you in this world for the words you have spoken to me to-night.'

' I have only done my duty, Alma!' returned Sir George, uneasily, moving as he spoke towards her and reaching out his arms to support her. 'My poor child—courage! George and I will protect and save you.'

Hereupon Mephistopheles junior uttered a sullen half-audible murmur, which was understood to be a solemn promise to punch the fellow's head—yes, smash him—on the very earliest opportunity!

'Don't touch me!' exclaimed Alma. 'Don't approach me! What is your authority for this cruel libel on Mr. Bradley? You talk of punishment. It is you that will be punished, be sure of that, if you cannot justify so shameful an accusation.'

The two men looked at each other. If, after all, the ground should give way beneath them! But it was too late to draw back or temporise.

'Tell her, father,' said George, with a prompting look.

'You ask our authority for the statement,' replied the baronet.   'My dear Alma, the thing is past a doubt. We have seen the— the *person.*'

'The person ?   What person ? '

'Bradley's *wife !* '

'He has no wife but me,' cried Alma.   'I love him—he is my husband ! '

Then, as Sir George shrugged his shoulders pityingly, she leant forward eagerly, and de- manded in quick, spasmodic gasps :—

'Who is the woman who wrongs my rights? Who is the creature who has filled you with this falsehood ?   Who is she ?   Tell me ! '

'She is at present passing under the name of Montmorency, and is, I believe, an actress.'

As he spoke, there came suddenly in Alma's remembrance the vivid picture of the woman whom she had seen talking with the clergyman in the vestry, and simultaneously she was conscious of the sickly odour of scent which had surrounded her like a fume of poison. Alma grew faint. Some terrible and foreboding presence seemed overpowering her. She thought of the painted face, the shameless dress and bearing of the strange woman, of Bradley's peculiar air of nervous uneasiness, of the thrill of dislike and repulsion which had run momentarily through her own frame as she left them together. Overcome by an indescribable and sickening horror, she put her hand to her forehead, tottered, and seemed about to fall.

Solicitous and alarmed, the baronet once

more approached her as if to support her. But before he could touch her she had shrunk shuddering away.

Weak and terrified now, she uttered a despairing moan.

'Oh! why did you come here to tell me this?' she cried. 'Why did you come here to break my heart and wreck my life? If you had had any pity or care for me, you would have spared me; you would have left me to discover my misery for myself, Go now, go; you have done all you can. I shall soon know for myself whether your cruel tale is false or true.'

'It is true,' said Sir George. 'Do not be unjust, my child. We could not, knowing what we did, suffer you to remain at the mercy of that man. Now, be advised. Leave the affair to us, who are devoted to you ; we will see that you are justified, and that the true culprit is punished as he deserves.'

And the two men made a movement towards the door.

' Stop ! ' cried Alma. ' What do you intend to do ? '

' Apply for a warrant, and have the scoundrel apprehended without delay.'

' You will do so at your peril,' exclaimed Alma, with sudden energy. ' I forbid you to interfere between him and me. Yes, I forbid you ! Even if things are as you say—and I will never believe it till I receive the assurance from his own lips, never!—even if things are as you say, the wrong is mine, not yours, and I need no one to come between me and the man I love.'

'The man you love!' echoed Sir George in amazement. 'Alma, this is infatuation!'

'I love him, uncle, and love such as mine is not a light thing to be destroyed by the first breath of calumny or misfortune. What has taken place is between him and me alone.'

'I beg your pardon,' returned her uncle, with a recurrence to his old anger. 'Our good name—the honour of the house—is at stake ; and if you are too far lost to consider these, it is my duty, as the head of the family, to act on your behalf.'

'Certainly,' echoed young George between his set teeth.

'And how would you vindicate them?' asked Alma, passionately. 'By outraging and degrading *me?* Yes; for if you utter to any other soul one syllable of this story, you drag my good name in the mire, and make me the martyr. I need no protection, I ask no justification. If necessary I can bear my misery, as I have borne my happiness, in silence and alone.'

'But,' persisted Sir George, 'you will surely let us take some steps to——'

'Whatever I do will be done on my own responsibility. I am my own mistress. Uncle, you must promise me—you must swear to me —to do nothing without my will and consent. You can serve me yet; you can show that you are still capable of kindliness and compassion, by saving me from proceedings which you would regret, and which I should certainly not survive.'

Sir George looked at his son in fresh perplexity. In the whirlwind of his excitement he had hardly taken into calculation the unpleasantness of a public exposure. True, it would destroy and punish the man, but, on the other hand, it would certainly bring disgrace on the family. Alma's eccentricities, both of opinion and of conduct, which he had held in very holy horror, would become the theme of the paragraph-maker and the leader-writer, and the immediate consequence would be to make the name of Craik ridiculous. So he stammered and hesitated.

George Craik, the younger, however, had none of his father's scruples. He cared little or nothing now for his cousin's reputation. All he wanted was to expose, smash, pulverise, and destroy Bradley, the man whom he had always cordially detested, and who had subjected him to innumerable indignities on the part of his cousin. So, seeing Alma's helplessness, and no longer dreading her indignation, he plucked up heart of grace and took his full part in the discussion.

'The fellow deserves penal servitude for life,' he said, 'and in my opinion, Alma, it's your *duty* to prosecute him. It is the only course you can take in justice to yourself and your friends. I know it will be deucedly unpleasant; but not more unpleasant than going through the Divorce Court, which respectable people do every day.'

'Silence!' exclaimed his cousin, turning upon him with tremulous indignation.

'Eh? what?' ejaculated George.

'I will not discuss Mr. Bradley with *you*. To my uncle I will listen, because I know he has a good heart, and because he is my dear father's brother; but I forbid *you* to speak to me on the subject. I owe all this misery and humiliation to you, and you only.'

'That's all humbug!' George began furiously, but his father interposed and waved him to silence.

'Alma is excited, naturally excited; in her cooler senses she will acknowledge that she does you an injustice. Hush, George!—My dear child,' he continued, addressing Alma, 'all my son and I desire to do is to save you pain. You have been disgracefully misled, and I repeat, I pity rather than blame you. To be sure you have been a little headstrong, a little opinionated, and I am afraid the doctrines promulgated by your evil genius have led you to take too rash a view of—hum—moral sanctions. Depend upon it, loose ideas in matters of religion lead, directly and indirectly, to the destruction of morality. Not that I accuse you of wilful misconduct—Heaven forbid ! But you have erred from want of caution, from, if I may so express it, a lack of discretion ; for you should have been aware that the man that believes in neither Our Maker nor Our Saviour—an—in short, an infidel—would not be deterred by any moral consideration from acts of vice and crime.'

This was a long speech, but Alma paid little or no attention to it. She stood against the mantelpiece, leaning her forehead against it, and trembling with agony ; but she did not cry—the tears would not come yet—she was still too lost in amazement, pain, and dread.

Suddenly, as Sir George ended, she looked up and said :—

'The name of this woman, this actress? Where is she to be found?'

'Her name—as I told you, her assumed name—is Montmorency. George can give you her address; but I think, on the whole, you had better not see her.'

'I *must*,' replied Alma, firmly.

Sir George glanced at his son, who thereupon took out a notebook and wrote on one of the leaves, which he tore out and handed to his father.

'Here is the address,' said the baronet, passing the paper on to Alma.

She took it without looking at it, and threw it on the mantelpiece.

'Now pray leave me. But, before you go, promise to do nothing—to keep this matter secret—until you hear from me. I must first ascertain that what you say is true.'

'We will do as you desire, Alma,' returned Sir George ; 'only I think it would be better— much better—to let *us* act for you.'

'No ; I only am concerned. I am not a child, and am able to protect myself.'

'Very well,' said her uncle. 'But try, my child, to remember that you have friends who are waiting to serve you. I am heart-broken— George is heart-broken—at this sad affair. Do nothing rash, I beseech you ; and do not forget, in this hour of humiliation, that there is One above Who can give you comfort, if you will turn humbly and reverently to *Him !* '

With this parting homily the worthy baro- net approached his niece, drew her to him, and kissed her benignantly on the forehead. But she shrank away quickly, with a low cry of distress.

'Do not touch me ! Do not speak to me ! Leave me now, for God's sake ! '

After a long-drawn sigh, expressive of supreme sympathy and commiseration, and a prolonged look full of quasi-paternal emotion, Sir George left the room. George followed, with a muttered ' Good-night ! ' to which his cousin paid no attention.

Father and son passed. out into the street, where the manner of both underwent a decided change.

' Well, that's over ! ' exclaimed the baronet. ' The poor girl bears it far better than I expected ; for it is a horrible situation.'

' Then you mean to do as she tells you,' said George, ' and let the scoundrel alone ? '

' For the time being, yes. After all, Alma is right, and we must endeavour to avoid a public exposure.'

' It's sure to come out. It's *bigamy*, you

know—*Bigamy* !' he added, with more emphasis and a capital letter.

'So it is—if it is true. At present, you know, we have no proofs whatever—only suspicions. God bless me ! how ridiculous we should look if the whole thing turns out a mare's nest after all ! Alma will never forgive us ! You really feel convinced that there was a previous marriage ?'

'I'm sure of it,' returned George. 'And, whether or not——'

He did not finish the sentence ; but what he added to himself, spitefully enough, was to the effect that, ' whether or not,' he had paid out his cousin for all her contumelious and persistent snubbing.

CHAPTER XXI.

THE CONFESSION.

' Dieu, qui, dès le commencement de la création, avez en
tirant la femme d'une côte de l'homme établi le grand sacrement
du mariage, vous qui l'avez honorée et relevée si haut soit en vous,
incarnant dans le sein d'une femme, soit en commençant vos
miracles par celui des noces de Cana, vous qui avez jadis accordé
ce remède, suivant vos vues, à mon incontinente faiblesse, ne
repoussez pas les prières de votre servante : je les verse humble-
ment aux pieds de votre divine majesté pour mes péchés et pour
ceux de mon bien-aimé. O Dieu qui êtes la bonté même,
pardonnez à nos crimes si grands, et que l'immensité de votre
miséricorde se mesure à la multitude de nos fautes. Prenez
contre vos serviteurs la verge de la correction, non le glaive de
la fureur. Frappez la chair pour conserver les âmes. Venez
en pacificateur, non en vengeur ; avec bonté plûtot qu'avec
justice ; en père miséricordieux, non en maître sévère.'

THE PRAYER OF HÉLOISE (*written for her by* ABELARD).

ALMA remained as her uncle and cousin had
left her, leaning against the mantelpiece, with

her eyes fixed, her frame convulsively trembling. Yet her look and manner still would have confirmed Sir George in his opinion that she bore the shock 'better than might have been expected.' She did not cry or moan. Once or twice her hand was pressed upon her heart, as if to still its beating, that was all.

Nevertheless, she was already aware that the supreme sorrow, the fatal dishallucination, of her life had come. She saw all her cherished hopes and dreams, her fairy castles of hope and love, falling to pieces like houses of cards ; the idol of her life falling with them, changing to clay and dust ; the whole world darkening, all beauty withering, in a chilly wind from the eternity of shadows. If Ambrose Bradley was base, if the one true man she had ever known and loved was false, what remained? Nothing but disgrace and death.

He had been in her eyes next to God, without speck or flaw, perfectly noble and supreme; one by one he had absorbed all her childish faiths, while in idolatry of passion she had knelt at his feet adoring him—

He for God only, she for God in *him*.

And that godhead had sufficed.

She had given up to him, together with her faith, her hope, her understanding, her entire spiritual life.

Passionate by nature, she had never loved any other human creature; even such slight thrills of sympathy as most maidens feel, and which by some are christened ' experiences,' having been almost or quite unknown to her. She had been a studious, reserved girl, with a

manner which repelled the approaches of beard-
less young men of her own age; her beauty
attracted them, but her steadfast intellectual
eyes frightened and cowed the most impudent
among them. Not till she came into collision
with Bradley did she understand what personal
passion meant; and even the first overtures
were intellectual, leading only by very slow
degrees to a more tender relationship.

Alma Craik, in fact, was of the same fine
clay of which enthusiasts have been made in
all ages. Born in the age of Pericles, she would
doubtless have belonged to the class of which
Aspasia was an immortal type; in the early
days of Christianity, she would have perhaps
figured as a Saint; in its mediæval days as a
proselytising abbess; and now, in the days of
Christian decadence, she opened her dreamy

eyes on the troublous lights of spiritual Science, found in them her inspiration and her heavenly hope. But men cannot live by bread alone, and women cannot exist without love. Her large impulsive nature was barren and incomplete till she had discovered what the Greek *hetairai* found in Pericles, what the feminine martyrs found in Jesus, what Eloisa found in Abelard ; that is to say, the realisation of a masculine ideal. She waited, almost without anticipation, till the hour was ripe.

> Love comes not as a slave
> To any beckoning finger; but, some day,
> When least expected, cometh as a King,
> And takes his throne.

So at last it was with the one love of Alma's life. Without doubt, without fear or question, she suffered her lover to take full sovereignty, and to remain thenceforth throned and crowned.

And now, she asked herself shudderingly, was it all over? Had the end of her dream come, when she had scarcely realised its beginning? If this was so, the beautiful world was destroyed. If Bradley was unworthy, there was no goodness in man; and if the divine type in humanity was broken like a cast of clay, there was no comfort in religion, no certainty of God.

She looked at her watch; it was not far from midnight. She moved from her support, and walked nervously up and down the room.

At last her mind was made up. She put on her hat and mantle, and left the house.

In her hand she clutched the piece of paper which George Craik had given her, and which contained the name and address of Mrs. Montmorency.

The place was close at hand, not far indeed from Bradley's residence and her own. She hastened thither without hesitation. Her way lay along the borders of the park, past the very Church which she had spared no expense to build, so that she came into its shadow almost before she knew.

It was a still and windless night; the skies were blue and clear, with scarcely a cloud, and the air was full of the vitreous pour of the summer moon, which glimmered on the church windows with ghostly silvern light. From the ground there exhaled a sickly heavy odour— the scent of the heated dew-charged earth.

Alma stood for some time looking at the building with the fortunes of which her own seemed so closely and mysteriously blent. Its shadow fell upon her with ominous darkness.

Black and sepulchral it seemed now, instead of bright and full of joy. As she gazed upon it, and remembered how she had laboured to upbuild it, how she had watched it grow stone by stone, and felt the joy a child might feel in marking the growth of some radiant flower, it seemed the very embodiment of her own despair.

Now, for the first time, her tears began to flow, but slowly, as if from sources in an arid heart. If she had heard the truth that day, the labour of her life was done; the place she looked upon was curst, and the sooner some thunderbolt of God struck it, or the hand of man razed it to the ground, the better for all the world.

There was a light in the house close by—in the room where she knew her lover was sit-

ting. She crept close to the rails of the
garden, and looked at the light through her
tears.   As she gazed, she prayed ; prayed that
God might spare her yet, rebuke the satanic
calumny, and restore her lord and master to
her, pure and perfect as he had been.

Then, in her pity for him and for herself,
she thought how base he might think her if
she sought from any lips but his own the confirmation of her horrible fear. She would be
faithful till the last. Instead of seeking out
the shameless woman, she would go in and ask
Bradley himself to confess the truth.

Swift action followed the thought. She
opened the gate, crossed the small garden, and
rang the bell.

The hollow sound, breaking on the solemn
stillness, startled her, and she shrank trembling

in the doorway; then she heard the sound of bolts being drawn, and the next moment the house door opened, and the clergyman appeared on the threshold, holding a light.

He looked wild and haggard enough, for indeed he had been having his dark hour alone. He wore a black dressing jacket with no waistcoat, and the collar of his shirt was open and tieless, falling open to show his powerful muscular throat.

'Alma!' he exclaimed in astonishment. '*You* here, and so late!'

'Yes, it is I,' she answered in a low voice. 'I wish to speak to you. May I come in?'

He could not see her face, but the tones of her voice startled him, as he drew back to let her enter. She passed by him without a word, and hastened along the lobby to the study.

He closed the door softly, and followed her.

The moment he came into the bright lamp-light of the room he saw her standing and facing him, her face white as death, her eyes dilated.

'My darling, what is it? Are you ill?' he cried.

But he had no need to ask any question. He saw in a moment that she knew his secret.

'Close the door,' she said in a low voice; and after he had obeyed her she continued, 'Ambrose, I have come here to-night because I could not rest at home till I had spoken to you. I have heard something terrible—so terrible that, had I believed it utterly, I think I should not be living now. It is something that concerns us both—me, most of all. Do you know what I mean? Tell me, for God's sake, if you know! Spare me the pain of an explanation if you can. Ah, God help me! I see you know!'

Their eyes met. He could not lie to her now.

'Yes, I know,' he replied.

'But it is not true? Tell me it is not true?'

As she gazed at him, and stretched out her arms in wild entreaty, his grief was pitiful beyond measure. He turned his eyes away with a groan of agony.

She came close to him, and, taking his head in her trembling hands, turned his face again to hers. He collected all his strength to meet her reproachful gaze, while he replied, in a deep tremulous voice :—

' You have heard that I have deceived you, that I am the most miserable wretch beneath the sun. You have heard—God help me !—that there is a woman living, other than yourself, who claims to be my wife.'

' Yes ! that is what I have heard. But I do not believe—I will not believe it. I have come to have from your own lips the assurance that it is a falsehood. Dear Ambrose, tell me so. I will believe *you.* Whatever *you* tell me, I will believe with all my soul.'

She clung to him tenderly as she spoke, with the tears streaming fast down her face.

Disengaging himself gently, he crossed the room to his desk, and placed his hand upon some papers scattered there, with the ink fresh upon them.

' When I heard you knock,' he said, ' I was

trying to write down, for your eyes to read, what my lips refused to tell, what I could not speak for utter, overpowering shame. I knew the secret must soon be known; I wished to be first to reveal it to you, that you might know the whole unvarnished truth. I was too late, I find. My enemies have been before me, and you have come to reproach me—as I deserve.'

' I have *not* come for that,' answered Alma, sobbing. ' It is too late for reproaches. I only wish to know my fate.'

' Then try and listen, while I tell you everything,' said Bradley, in the same tone of utter misery and despair. ' I am speaking my own death-warrant, I know; for with every word I utter I shall be tearing away another living link that binds you to my already broken heart. I have nothing to say in my own justification;

no, not one word.   If you cou'd strike me
dead at your feet, in your just and holy anger,
it would be dealing with me as I deserve.   I
should have been strong ; I was weak, a coward!
I deserve neither mercy nor pity.'

It was strange how calm they both seemed ;
he as he addressed her in his low deep voice,
she as she stood and listened.   Both were
deathly pale, but Alma's tears were checked, as
she looked in despair upon the man who had
wrecked her life.

Then he told her the whole story : of how,
in his youthful infatuation, he had married
Mary Goodwin, how they had lived a wretched
life together, how she had fled from him, and
how for many a year he had thought her dead.
His face trembled and his cheek flushed as he
spoke of the new life that had dawned upon

him, when long afterwards he became acquainted with herself; while she listened in
agony, thinking of the pollution of that other
woman's embraces from which he had passed.

But presently she hearkened more peace-
fully, and a faint dim hope began to quicken in
her soul—for as yet she but dimly apprehended
Bradley's situation. So far as she had heard,
the man was comparatively blameless. The
episode of his youth was a repulsive one, but
the record of his manhood was clear. He had
believed the woman dead, he had had every
reason to believe it, and he had been, to all
intents and purposes, free.

As he ceased, he heaved a sigh of deep
relief, and her tears flowed more freely. She
moved across the room, and took his hand.

' I understand now,' she said. ' O Ambrose,

why did you not confide in me from the first?
There should have been no secrets between us.
I would freely have forgiven you. . . . . And
I forgive you now! When you married me,
you believed the woman dead and in her grave.
If she has arisen to part us so cruelly, the blame
is not yours—thank God for that!'

But he shrank from her touch, and uttering
a cry of agony sank into a chair, and hid his
face in his hands.

'Ambrose!' she murmured, bending over
him.

'Do not touch me,' he cried; 'I have more
to tell you yet—something that must break the
last bond uniting us together, and degrade me
for ever in your eyes. Alma, do not pity me;
your pity tortures and destroys me, for I do
not deserve it—I am a villain! Listen, then!

I betrayed you wilfully, diabolically ; for when I went through the marriage ceremony with you I *knew* that Mary Goodwin was still alive ! '

' You knew it !—and, knowing it, you——'

She paused in horror, unable to complete the sentence.

' I knew it, for I had seen her with my own eyes—so long ago as when I was vicar of Fensea. You remember my visit to London ; you remember my trouble then, and you attributed it to my struggle with the Church authorities. That was the beginning of my fall; I was a coward and a liar from that hour ; for I had met and spoken with my first wife.'

She shrank away from him now, indeed. The last remnant of his old nobility had fallen from him, leaving him utterly contemptible and ignoble.

'Afterwards,' he continued, 'I was like a man for whose soul the angels of light and darkness struggle. You saw my anguish, but little guessed its cause. I had tried to fly from temptation. I went abroad; even there, your heavenly kindness reached me, and I was drawn back to your side. Then for a time I forgot everything, in the pride of intellect and newly acquired success. By accident, I heard the woman had gone abroad; and I knew well, or at least I believed, that she would never cross my path again. My love for you grew hourly; and I saw that you were unhappy, so long as our lives were passed asunder. Then in an evil moment I turned to my creed for inspiration. I did not turn to God, for I had almost ceased to believe in Him; but I sought justification from my conscience, which the spirit of evil had already warped. I reasoned with myself; I persuaded myself that I had been a martyr, that I owed the woman no faith, that I was still morally free. I examined the laws of marriage, and, the wish being father to the thought, found in them only folly, injustice, and superstition. I said to myself, "She and I are already divorced by her own innumerable acts of infamy;" I asked myself, "Shall I live on a perpetual bondslave to a form which I despise, to a creature who is utterly unworthy?" Coward that I was, I yielded, forgetting that no happiness can be upbuilt upon a lie. And see how I am punished! I have lost you for ever; I have lost my soul alive! I, who should have been your instructor in all things holy, have been your guide in all things evil. I have brought the curse of heaven upon myself. I have put out my last strength in wickedness, and brought the roof of the temple down upon my head.'

In this manner his words flowed on, in a wild stream of sorrowful self-reproach. It seemed, indeed, that he found a relief in denouncing himself as infamous, and in prostrating himself, as it were, under the heel of the woman he had wronged.

But the more he reproached himself, the greater her compassion grew; till at last, in an agony of sympathy and pain, she knelt down by his side, and, sobbing passionately, put her arms around him.

'Ambrose,' she murmured, 'Ambrose, do not speak so! do not break my heart! That woman shall *not* come between us. I do not care for the world, I do not care for the judgment of men. Bid me to remain with you to the end, and I will obey you.'

And she hid her face, blinded with weeping, upon his breast.

For a time there was silence ; then the clergyman, conquering his emotion, gathered strength to speak again.

' Alma ! my darling ! Do not tempt me with your divine goodness. Do not think me quite so lost as to spare myself and to destroy *you.* I have been weak hitherto ; henceforth I will be cruel and inexorable. Do not waste a thought upon me ; I am not worth it. To-morrow I shall leave London. If I live, I will try, in penitence and suffering, to atone ; but whether I live or die, you must forget that I ever lived to darken your young life.'

As he spoke, he endeavoured gently to

disengage himself, but her arms were wound about him, and he could not stir.

'No,' she answered, 'you must not leave me. I will still be your companion, your handmaid. Grant me that last mercy. Let me be your loving sister still, if I may not be your wife.'

' Alma, it is impossible. We must part ! '

' If you go, I will follow you. Ambrose, *you* will not leave me behind you, to die of a broken heart. To see you, to be near you, will be enough ; it is all I ask. You will continue the great work you have begun, and I—I will look on, and pray for you as before.'

It was more than the man could bear ; he too began to sob convulsively, as if utterly broken.

' O God! God ! ' he cried, ' I forgot Thee

in mine own vain-glory, in my wicked lust of happiness and power! I wandered farther and farther away from Thy altars, from my childish faith, and at every step I took, my pride and folly grew! But now, at last, I know that it was a brazen image that I worship—nay, worse, the Phantom of my own miserable sinful self. Punish me, but let me come back to Thee! Destroy, but save me! I know now there is no God but One—the living, bleeding Christ whom I endeavoured to dethrone!'

She drew her face from his breast, and looked at him in terror. It seemed to her that he was raving.

'Ambrose! my poor Ambrose! God has forgiven you, as I forgive you. You have been His faithful servant, His apostle!'

'I have been a villain! I have fallen, as

Satan fell, from intellectual vanity and pride. You talk to me of the great work that I have done; Alma, that work has been wholly evil, my creed a rotten reed. A materialist at heart, I thought that I could reject all certitude of faith, all fixity of form. My God became a shadow, my Christ a figment, my morality a platitude and a lie. Believing and accepting everything in the sphere of ideas, I believed nothing, accepted nothing, in the sphere of living facts. Descending by slow degrees to a creed of shallow materialism, I justified falseness to myself, and treachery to *you.* I walked in my blind self-idolatry, till the solid ground was rent open beneath me, as you have seen. In that final hour of temptation, of which I have spoken, a Christian would have turned to the Cross and found salvation. What was that Cross to me? A dream of the poet's brain, a symbol which could not help me. I turned from it, and have to face, as my eternal punishment, all the horror and infamy of the old Hell.'

Every word that he uttered was true, even truer than he yet realised.

He had refined away his faith till it had become a mere figment. Christ the Divine Ideal had been powerless to keep him to the narrow path, whereas Christ the living Lawgiver might have enabled him to walk on a path thrice as narrow, yea, on the very edge of the great gulf, where there is scarcely foothold for a fly. I who write these lines, though perchance far away as Bradley himself from the acceptance of a Christian terminology, can at least say this for the Christian scheme—that it is complete as a law for life. Once accept its facts and theories, and it becomes as strong as an angel's arm to hold us up in hours of weariness, weakness, and vacillation. The difficulty lies in that acceptance. But for common workaday use and practical human needs, transcendentalism, however Christian in its ideas, is utterly infirm. It will do when there is fair weather, when the beauty of Art will do, and when even the feeble glimmer of æstheticism looks like sunlight and pure air. But when sorrow comes, when temptation beckons, when what is wanted is a staff to lean upon and a Divine finger to point and guide, woe to him who puts his trust in any transcendental creed, however fair!

It is the tendency of modern agnosticism to slacken the moral fibre of men, even more than to weaken their intellectual grasp. The laws of human life are written in letters of brass on the rock of Science, and it is the task of true Religion to read them and translate them for the common use. But the agnostic is as shortsighted as an owl, while the atheist is as blind as a bat ; the one will not, and the other cannot, read the colossal cypher, interpret the simple speech, of God.

Ambrose Bradley was a man of keen intellect and remarkable intuitions, but he had broadened his faith to so great an extent that it became like one of many ways in a wilderness, leading anywhere, or nowhere. He had been able to accept ideals, never to cope with practicalities. His creed was beautiful as a rainbow, as many-coloured, as capable of stretching from heaven to earth and earth to heaven, but it faded, rainbow-like, when the sun sank and the darkness came. So must it be with all creeds which are not solid as the ground we walk on, strength-giving as the air we breath, simple as the thoughts of childhood, and inexorable as the solemn verity of death.

Such has been, throughout all success or failure, and such is, practical Christianity. Blessed is he who, in days of backsliding and unbelief, can become as a little child and lean all his hope upon it. Its earthly penance and its heavenly promise are interchangeable terms. The Christian dies that he may live ; suffers that he may enjoy ; relinquishes that he may gain ; sacrifices his life that he may save it. He knows the beatitude of suffering, which no merely happy man can know. We who are worlds removed from the simple faith of the early world may at least admit all this, and then, with a sigh for the lost illusion, go dismally upon our way.

That night Ambrose Bradley found, to his astonishment, that Alma was still at his mercy, that at a word from him she would defy the world. Therein came his last temptation, his last chance of moral redemption. The Devil was at hand busily conjuring, but a holier presence was also there. The man's soul was worth saving, and there was still a stake.

The game was decided for the time being when the clergyman spoke as follows :—

' My darling, I am not so utterly lost as to let you share my degradation. I do not deserve your pity any more than I have deserved your love. Your goodness only makes me feel my own baseness twenty-fold. I should have told you the whole truth; I failed to do so, and I grossly deceived you; therefore it is just that I should be punished and driven forth. I have broken the laws of my country as well as the precepts of my creed. I shall leave England to-morrow, never to return.'

'You must not go,' answered Alma. 'I know that we must separate, I see that it is sin to remain together, but over and above our miserable selves is the holy labour to which you have set your hand. Do not, I conjure you, abandon that! The last boon I shall ask you is to labour on in the church I upbuilt for you, and to keep your vow of faithful service.'

'Alma, it is impossible! In a few days,

possibly in a few hours, our secret will be known, and then——'

' Your secret is safe with me,' she replied, ' and I will answer for my uncle and my cousin—that they shall leave you in peace. It is I that must leave England, not you. Your flight would cause a scandal and would destroy the great work for ever ; my departure will be unnoticed and unheeded. Promise me, promise me to remain.'

' I cannot, Alma !— God forbid !— and allow you, who are blameless, to be driven forth from your country and your home ! '

'I have no home, no country now,' she said, and as she spoke her voice was full of the pathos of infinite despair. ' I lost these, I lost everything, when I lost *you.* Dearest Ambrose, there is but one atonement possible for both of us! We must forget our vain happiness, and work for God.'

Her face became Madonna-like in its beautiful resignation. Bradley looked at her in wonder, and never before had he hated himself so much for what he had done. Had she heaped reproaches upon him, had she turned from him in the pride of passionate disdain, he could have borne it far better. But in so much as she assumed the sweetness of an angel, did he feel the misery and self-scorn of a devil.

And, if the truth must be spoken, Alma wondered at herself. She had thought at first, when the quick of her pain was first touched, that she must madden and die of agony; but her nature seemed flooded now with a piteous calm, and her mind hushed itself to the dead stillness of resignation. Alas! she had yet to discover how deep and incurable was the wound that she had received; how it was to fester and refuse all healing, even from the sacred unguents of religion.

'Promise me,' she continued after a pause, 'to remain and labour in your vocation.'

'Alma, I cannot!'

'You *must*. You say you owe me reparation; let your reparation be this—to grant my last request.'

'But it is a mockery!' he pleaded. 'Alma, if you knew how hollow, how empty of all living faith, my soul had become!'

'Your faith is not dead,' she replied. 'Even if it be, He who works miracles will restore it to life. Promise to do as I beseech you, and be sure *then* of my forgiveness. Promise!'

'I promise,' he said at last, unable to resist her.

'Good-bye!' she said, holding out her hand, which he took sobbing and covered with kisses. 'I shall go away to some still place abroad where I may try to find peace. I may write to you sometimes, may I not? Surely there will be no sin in that! Yes, I will write to you; and you—you will let me know that you are well and happy.'

'O Alma!' he sobbed, falling on his knees before her, 'my love! my better angel! I have destroyed you, I have trampled on the undriven snow!'

'God is good,' she answered. 'Perhaps even this great sorrow is sent upon us in mercy, not in wrath. I will try to think so! Once more, good-bye!'

He rose to his feet, and, taking her tear-drenched face softly between his hands, kissed her upon the brow.

'God bless and protect you!' he cried. 'Pray for me, my darling! I shall need all your prayers! Pray for me and forgive me!'

A minute later, and he was left alone. He would have followed her out into the night, as far as her own door, but she begged him not to do so. He stood at the gate, watching her as she flitted away. Then, with a cry of anguish, he looked towards his empty church standing shadowy in the cold moonlight, and re-entered his desolate home.

END OF THE SECOND VOLUME

Spottiswoode & Co., Printers, New-street Square, London.

THE NEW ABELARD

VOL. III.

THE NEW ABELARD

A Romance

BY

ROBERT BUCHANAN

AUTHOR OF 'THE SHADOW OF THE SWORD' 'GOD AND THE MAN' ETC

IN THREE VOLUMES—VOL. III.

London

CHATTO & WINDUS, PICCADILLY

1884

LONDON : PRINTED BY
SPOTTISWOODE AND CO., NEW-STREET SQUARE
AND PARLIAMENT STREET

CONTENTS

OF

THE THIRD VOLUME.

THE NEW ABELARD.

CHAPTER XXII.

FROM THE POST-BAG.

I.

Sir George Craik, Bart., to Alma Craik.

MY DEAR NIECE,—The receipt of your letter, dated 'Lucerne,' but bearing the post-mark of Geneva, has at last relieved my mind from the weight of anxiety which was oppressing it. Thank Heaven you are safe and well, and bear your suffering with Christian resignation. In a little time, I trust, you will have left this dark passage of your experience quite behind

you, and return to us looking and feeling like
your old self.   George, who now, as always,
shares my affectionate solicitude for you, joins
me in expressing that wish.   The poor boy is
still sadly troubled at the remembrance of
your misconception, and I sometimes think
that his health is affected.   Do, if you can, try
to send him a line or a message, assuring him
that your unhappy misunderstanding is over.
Believe me, his one thought in life is to secure
your good esteem.

There is no news—none, that is to say, of
any importance.   We have kept our promise
to you, and your secret is still quite safe in our
custody.   The man to whom you owe all this
misery is still here, and still, I am informed,
prostituting the pulpit to his vicious heresies.
If report is to be believed, his utterances have

of late been more extraordinary than ever, and he is rapidly losing influence over his own congregation. Sometimes I can scarcely conquer my indignation, knowing as I do that with one word I could effectually silence his blasphemy, and drive him beyond the pale of society. But in crushing him I should disgrace you, and bring contempt upon our name ; and these considerations, as well as my pledge to keep silence, make any kind of public action impossible. I must therefore wait patiently till the inevitable course of events, accelerated by an indignant Providence, destroys the destroyer of your peace.

In the mean time, my dear Alma, let me express my concern and regret that you should be wandering from place to place without a protector. I know your strength of mind, of course ; but you are young and handsome, and the world is censorious. Only say the word, and although business of a rather important nature occupies me in London, I will put it aside at any cost, and join you. In the absence of my dear brother, I am your natural guardian. While legally your own mistress, you are morally under my care, and I would make any sacrifice to be with you, especially at this critical moment of your life.

I send this letter to the address you have given me at Lucerne. I hope it will reach you soon and safely, and that you will, on seeing it, fall in with my suggestion that I should come to you without delay.

With warmest love and sympathy, in which your cousin joins, believe me as ever,—Your affectionate uncle,

GEORGE CRAIK.

II.

From Alma Craik to Sir George Craik, Bart.

MY DEAR UNCLE,—I have just received your letter. Thank you for attending to my request. With regard to your suggestion that you should come to me, I know it is meant in all kindness, but as I told you before leaving London, I prefer at present to be quite alone, with the exception of my maid Hortense. I will let you know of my movements from time to time,—Your affectionate niece,

ALMA CRAIK.

III.

Alma Craik to the Rev. Ambrose Bradley.

Your letter, together with one from my uncle, found me at Lucerne, and brought me at once grief and comfort : grief, that you still

reproach yourself over what was inevitable ;
comfort, that you are, as you assure me, still
endeavouring to pursue your religious work.
Pray, pray, do not write to me in such a strain
again. You have neither wrecked my life nor
broken my heart, as you blame yourself for
doing ; I learned long ago from our Divine
Example that the world is one of sorrow, and
I am realising the truth in my own experience,
that is all.

You ask me how and where I have spent
my days, and whether I have at present any
fixed destination. I have been wandering, so
to speak, among the gravestones of the Catholic
Church, visiting not only the great shrines and
cathedrals, but lingering in every obscure
roadside chapel, and halting at every Calvary,
in southern and western France. Thence I

have come on to Switzerland, where religion grows drearier, and life grows dismaller, in the shadow of the mountains. In a few days I shall follow in your own footsteps, and go on to Italy—to Rome.

Write to me when you feel impelled to write. You shall be apprised of my whereabouts from time to time.—Yours now as ever,

ALMA.

P.S.—When I sat down to write the above, I thought I had so much to say to you; and I have said nothing! Something numbs expression, though my thoughts seem full to overflowing. I am like one who longs to speak, yet fears to utter a syllable, lest her voice should be clothed with tears and sobs. God help me! All the world is changed, and I can hardly realise it, yet!

IV.

Ambrose Bradley to Alma Craik.

DEAREST ALMA,—You tell me in your letter that you have said nothing of the thoughts that struggle within you for utterance; alas! your words are only too eloquent, less in what they say than in what they leave unsaid. If I required any reminder of the mischief I have wrought, of the beautiful dream that I have destroyed, it would come to me in the pathetic reticence of the letter I have just received. Would to God that you had never known me! Would to God that, having known me, you would have despised me as I deserved! I was unworthy even to touch the hem of your garment. I am like a wretch who has profaned the altar of a saint. Your patience and devotion are an eternal rebuke. I could bear your bitter blame ; I cannot bear your forgiveness.

I am here as you left me ; a guilty, conscience-stricken creature struggling in a world of nightmares. Nothing now seems substantial, permanent, or true. Every time that I stand up before my congregation I am like a shadow addressing shadows ; thought and language both fail me, and I know not what platitudes flow from my lips ; but when I am left alone again, I awaken as from a dream to the horrible reality of my guilt and my despair.

I have thought it all over again and again, trying to discover some course by which I might bring succour to myself and peace to her I love; and whichever way I look, I see but one path of escape, the rayless descent of death. For, so long as I live, I darken your sunshine. My very existence is a reminder to you of what I am, of what I might have been.

But there, I will not pain you with my penitence, and I will hush my self-reproaches in deference to your desire. Though the staff you placed in my hand has become a reed, and though I seem to have no longer any foothold on the solid ground of life, I will try to struggle on.

I dare not ask you to write to me—it seems an outrage to beg for such a blessing; yet I know that you *will* pity me, and write again.—Ever yours,

AMBROSE BRADLEY.

CHAPTER XXIII.

ALMA'S WANDERINGS.

Scoff not at Rome, or if thou scoff beware
Her vengeance waiting in the heaven and air ;
Her love is blessing, and her hate, despair.

Yet see ! how low the hoary mother lies,
Prone on her face beneath the lonely skies—
On her head ashes, dust upon her eyes.

Men smile and pass, but many pitying stand,
And some stoop down to kiss her withered hand,
Whose sceptre is a reed, whose crown is sand.

Think'st thou no pulse beats in that bounteous breast
Which once sent throbs of rapture east and west ?
Nay, but she liveth, mighty tho' opprest.

Her arm could reach as low as hell, as high
As the white mountains and the starry sky ;
She filled the empty heavens with her cry.

Wait but a space, and watch—her trance of pain
Shall dry away—her tears shall cease as rain—
Queen of the nations, she shall smile again!

THE LADDER OF ST. AUGUSTINE.

BRADLEY'S letter was fowarded from Lucerne

after some little delay, and reached Miss Craik at Brieg, just as she was preparing to proceed by private conveyance to Domo d'Ossola. She had taken the carriage and pair for herself and her maid, a young Frenchwoman; and as the vehicle rounded its zigzag course towards the Klenenhorn, she perused the epistle line by line, until she had learned almost every word by heart.

Then, with the letter lying in her lap, she gazed sadly, almost vacantly, around her on the gloomy forests and distant hills, the precipices spanned by aerial bridges, the quaint villages clinging like birds'-nests here and there, the dark vistas of mountain side gashed by torrents frozen by distance to dazzling white.

Dreary beyond measure, though the skies

were blue and the air full of golden sunlight, seemed the wonderful scene :—

> **We make** the world we look on, and create
> **The summer** or the winter with our seeing!

And cold and wintry indeed was all that Alma beheld that summer day.

Not even the glorious panorama unfolded beneath her gaze on passing the Second Refuge had any charms to please her saddened sight. Leaving the lovely valley of the Rhone, sparkling in sunlight, encircled by the snow-crowned Alps, with the Jungfrau towering paramount, crowned with glittering icy splendour and resting against a heaven of deep insufferable blue, she passed through avenues of larch and fir, over dizzy bridges, past the lovely glacier of the Kaltwasser, till she reached the high ascent of the Fifth Refuge.

Here the coarse spirit of the age arose before her, in the shape of a party of English and American tourists crowding the diligence and descending noisily for refreshment.

A little later she passed the barrier toll, and came in sight of the Cross of 'Vantage. She arrested the carriage, and descended for a few minutes, standing as it were suspended in mid air, in full view of glacier upon glacier, closed in by the mighty chain of the Bernese Alps.

Never had she felt so utterly solitary. The beautiful world, the empty sky, swam before her in all the loveliness of desolation, and turning her face towards Aletsch, she wept bitterly.

As she stood thus, she was suddenly conscious of another figure standing near to her, as if in rapt contemplation of the solemn scene. It was that of a middle-aged man, rather above the middle stature, who carried a small knapsack on his shoulders and leant upon an Alpine staff. She saw only his side face, and his eyes were turned away; yet, curiously enough, his form had an air of listening watchfulness, and the moment she was conscious of his presence he turned and smiled, and raised his hat. She noticed then that his sunburnt face was clean shaven, like that of a priest, and that his eyes were black and piercing, though remarkably good-humoured.

'Pardon, Madame,' he said in French, ' but I think we have met before.'

She had turned away her head to hide her tears from the stranger's gaze. Without waiting for her answer, he proceeded.

' In the hotel at Brieg. I was staying
there when Madame arrived, and I left at day-
break this morning to cross the Pass on foot.'

By this time she had mastered her agitation,
and could regard the stranger with a certain
self-possession. His face, though not handsome,
was mobile and expressive ; the eyebrows were
black and prominent, the forehead was high,
the mouth large and well cut, with glittering
white teeth. It was difficult to tell the man's
age ; for though his countenance was so fresh
that it looked quite young, his forehead and
cheeks, in repose, showed strongly-marked
lines ; and though his form seemed strong and
agile, he stooped greatly at the shoulders. To
complete the contradiction, his hair was as white
as snow.

What mark is it that Rome puts upon her

servants, that we seem to know them under almost any habit or disguise? One glance convinced Alma that the stranger either belonged to some of the holy orders, or was a lay priest of the Romish Church.

'I do not remember to have seen you before, Monsieur,' she replied, also in French, with a certain hauteur.

The stranger smiled again, and bowed apologetically.

'Perhaps I was wrong to address Madame without a more formal introduction. I know that in England it is not the custom. But here on the mountain, far away from the conventions of the world, it would be strange, would it not, to meet in silence? We are like two souls that encounter on pilgrimage, both looking wearily towards the Celestial Gate.'

' Are you a priest, Monsieur ? ' asked Alma abruptly.

The stranger bowed again.

' A poor member of the Church, the Abbé Brest. I am journeying on foot through the Simplon to the Lago Maggiore, and thence, with God's blessing, to Milan. But I shall rest yonder, at the New Hospice, to-night.'

And he pointed across the mountain towards the refuge of the monks of St. Bernard, close to the region of perpetual snow. The tall figure of an Augustine monk, shading his eyes and looking up the road was visible ; and from the refectory within came the faint tolling of a bel mingled from time to time with the deep barking of a dog.

' The monks receive travellers still ? ' asked Alma. ' I suppose the Hospice is rapidly becoming, like its compeers, nothing more or less than a big hotel ? '

' Madame——'

' Please do not call me Madame. I am unmarried.'

She spoke almost without reflection, and it was not until she had uttered the words that their significance dawned upon her. Her face became crimson with sudden shame.

It was characteristic of the stranger that he noticed the change in a moment, but that, immediately on doing so, he turned away his eyes and seemed deeply interested in the distant prospect, while he replied :—

' I have again to ask your pardon for my stupidity. Mademoiselle, of course, is English?'

' Yes.'

' And is therefore, perhaps, a little pre-

judiced against those who, like the good monks
of the Hospice, shut themselves from all human
companionship, save that of the wayfarers whom
they live to save and shelter? Yet, believe me,
it is a life of sacred service! Even here, among
the lonely snows, reaches the arm of the Holy
Mother, to plant this cross by the wayside, as a
symbol of her heavenly inspiration, and to build
that holy resting-place as a haven for those who
are weary and would rest.'

He spoke with the same soft insinuating
smile as before, but his eye kindled, and his
pale face flushed with enthusiasm. Alma, who
had turned towards the carriage which stood
awaiting her, looked at him with new interest.
Something in his words chimed in with a secret
longing of her heart.

' I have been taught to believe, Monsieur,

that your faith is practically dead. Everywhere we see, instead of its living temples, only the ruins of its old power. If its spirit exists still, it is only in places such as this, in company with loneliness and death.'

'Ah, but Mademoiselle is mistaken!' returned the other, following by her side as she walked slowly towards the carriage. 'Had you seen what I have seen, if you knew what I know, of the great Catholic reaction, you would think differently. Other creeds, gloomier and more ambitious, have displaced ours for a time in your England; but let me ask you—you, Mademoiselle, who have a truly religious spirit —you who have yourself suffered—what have those other creeds done for humanity? Believe me, little or nothing. In times of despair and doubt, the world will again turn to its first

Comforter, the ever-patient and ever-loving Church of Christ.'

They had by this time reached the carriage door. The stranger bowed again and assisted Alma to her seat. Then he raised his hat with profound respect in sign of farewell. The coachman was about to drive on when Alma signed for him to delay.

'I am on my way to Domo d'Ossola,' she said. 'A seat in my carriage is at your service if you would prefer going on to remaining at the Hospice for the night.'

'Mademoiselle, it is too much! I could not think of obtruding myself upon you! I, a stranger!'

Yet he seemed to look longingly at the comfortable seat in the vehicle, and to require little more pressing to accept the offer.

'Pray do not hesitate,' said Alma, smiling, 'unless you prefer the company of the monks of the mountain.'

'After that, I can hesitate no longer,' returned the Abbé, looking radiant with delight ; and he forthwith entered the vehicle and placed himself by Alma's side.

Thus it came to pass that my heroine descended the Pass of the Simplon in company with her new acquaintance, an avowed member of a Church for which she had felt very little sympathy until that hour. To do him justice, I must record the fact that she found him a most interesting companion. His knowledge of the world was extensive, his learning little short of profound, his manners were charming. He knew every inch of the way, and pointed out the objects of interest, digressing lightly into the topics they awakened. At every turn the prospect brightened. Leaving the wild and barren slopes behind them, the travellers passed through emerald pasturages, and through reaches of foliage broken by sounding torrents, and at last emerging from the great valley, and crossing the bridge of Crevola, they found themselves surrounded on every side by vineyards, orchards, and green meadows. When the carriage drew up before the door of the hotel at Domo d'Ossola, Alma felt that the time had passed as if under enchantment. Although she had spoken very little, she had quite unconsciously informed her new friend of three facts—that she was a wealthy young Englishwoman travelling through Europe at her own free will; that she had undergone an unhappy experience, involv-

ing, doubtless, some person of the opposite
sex ; and that, in despair of comfort from
creeds colder and less forgiving, she was just in
a fit state of mind to seek refuge in the bosom
of the Church of Rome.

The acquaintance, begun so curiously in
the Simplon Pass, was destined to continue.
At Domo d'Ossola, Alma parted from the Abbé
Brest, whose destination was some obscure
village on the banks of Lago Maggiore ; but a
few weeks later, when staying at Milan, she
encountered him again. She had ascended the
tower of the Duomo, and was gazing down on
the streets and marts of the beautiful city, when
she heard a voice behind her murmuring her
name, and turning somewhat nervously, she
encountered the bright black eyes of the
wandering Abbé.

He accosted her with his characteristic *bonhomie.*

' Ah, Mademoiselle, it *is* you ! ' he cried smiling. ' We are destined to meet in the high places—here on the tower of the cathedral, there on the heights of the Simplon ! '

There was something so unexpected, so mysterious in the man's reappearance, that Alma was startled in spite of herself, but she greeted him courteously, and they descended the tower steps together. The Abbé kept a solemn silence as they walked through the sacred building, with its mighty walls of white marble, its gorgeous decorations, its antique tombs, its works in bronze and in mosaic ; but when they passed from the porch into the open sunlight, he became as garrulous as ever.

They walked along together in the direction of the Grand Hotel, where Alma was staying.

' Have you driven out to the cathedral at Monza?' inquired the Abbé in the course of their conversation.

' No ; is it worth seeing?'

' Certainly. Besides, it contains the sacred crown of Lombardy, the iron band of which is made out of nails from the true cross.'

' Indeed !' exclaimed Alma with a smile that was incredulous, even contemptuous. She glanced at her companion, and saw that he was smiling too.

It was not until she had been some weeks away from England that Alma Craik quite realised her position in the world. In the first wild excitement of her flight her only feeling was one of bewildered agitation, mingled with a mad impulse to return upon her own footsteps, and, reckless of the world's opinion, take her place by Bradley's side. A word of encouragement from him at that period would have decided her fate. But after the first pang of grief was over, after she was capable of regretful retrospection, her spirit became numbed with utter despair. She found herself solitary, friendless, hopeless, afflicted with an incurable moral disease to which she was unable to give a name, but which made her long, like the old anchorites and penitents, to seek some desert place and yield her life to God.

In this mood of mind she turned for solace to religion, and found how useless for all practical purposes was her creed of beautiful ideas.

Her faith in Christian facts had been shaken
if not destroyed ; the Christian myth had the
vagueness and strangeness of a dream ; yet,
true to her old instincts, she haunted the
temples of the Church, and felt like one wandering through a great graveyard of the dead.

Travelling quite alone, for her maid was in
no sense of the words a confidante or a companion, she could not fail to awaken curious
interest in many with whom she was thrown
into passing contact. Her extraordinary personal beauty was heightened rather than ob-
scured by her singularity of dress ; for though
she wore no wedding-ring, she dressed in black
like a widow, and had the manners as well as
the attire of a person profoundly mourning.
At the hotels she invariably engaged private
apartments, seldom or never descending to the

public rooms, or joining in the tables-d'hôte. The general impression concerning her was that she was an eccentric young Englishwoman of great wealth, recently bereaved of some person very near and dear to her, possibly her husband.

Thus she lived in seclusion, resisting all friendly advances, whether on the part of foreigners or of her own countrymen ; and her acquaintance with the Abbé Brest would never have passed beyond a few casual courtesies had it not begun under circumstances so peculiar and in a place so solitary, or had the man himself been anything but a member of the mysterious Mother Church. But the woman's spirit was pining for some kind of guidance, and the magnetic name of Rome had already awakened in it a melancholy fascination. The strange priest attracted her, firstly, by his eloquent personality, secondly, by the authority he seemed to derive from a power still pretending to achieve miracles : and though in her heart she despised the pretensions and loathed the dogmas of his Church, she felt in his presence the sympathy of a prescient mind. For the rest, any companionship, if intellectual, was better than utter social isolation.

So the meeting on the tower of the Duomo led to other meetings. The Abbé became her constant companion, and her guide through all the many temples of the queenly city.

CHAPTER XXIV.

GLIMPSES OF THE UNSEEN.

The earth has bubbles as the water hath,
And these are of them !—*Macbeth.*

WHILE the woman he had so cruelly deceived and wronged was wandering from city to city, and trying in vain to find rest and consolation, Ambrose Bradley remained at the post where she had left him, the most melancholy soul beneath the sun.　All his happiness in his work being gone, his ministration lost the fervour and originality that had at first been its dominant attraction.

Sir George had not exaggerated when he

said that the clergyman's flock was rapidly falling away from him. New lights were arising; new religious whims and oddities were attracting the restless spirits of the metropolis. A thought-reading charlatan from the New World, a learned physiologist proving the oneness of the sympathetic system with polarised light, a maniacal non-jurist asserting the prerogative of affirmation at the bar of the House of Commons, became each a nine-days' wonder. The utterances of the new gospel were forgotten, or disregarded as flatulent and unprofitable; and Ambrose Bradley found his occupation gone.

For all this he cared little or nothing. He was too lost in contemplation of his own moral misery. All his thought and prayer being to escape from this, he tried various distractions—

the theatre, for example, with its provincial theory of edification grafted on the dry stem of what had once been a tree of literature. He was utterly objectless and miserable, when, one morning, he received the following letter:—

'Monmouth Crescent, Bayswater.

'MY DEAR SIR,—Will you permit me to remind you, by means of this letter, of the notes of introduction presented recently by me to you, and written by our friends, —— and ——, in America? My sister gives a *séance* to-morrow evening, and several notabilities of the scientific and literary world have promised to be present. If you will honour us with your company, I think you will be able to form a disinterested opinion on the importance of the new biology, as manifestations of an extraordinary kind are confidently expected.

—With kind regards, in which my sister joins, I am, most faithfully yours,

> ' SALEM MAPLELEAFE,
>
> ' *Solar Biologist.*'

' P.S.—The *séance* commences at five o'clock, in this domicile.'

Bradley's first impulse was to throw the letter aside, and to write a curt but polite refusal. On reflection, however, he saw in the proposed séance a means of temporary distraction. Besides, the affair of the mysterious photograph had left him not a little curious as to the machinery used by the brother and sister—*arcades ambo*, or impostors both, he was certain—to gull an undiscerning public.

At a little before five on the following evening, therefore, he presented himself at

the door of the house in Monmouth Crescent,
sent up his card, and was almost immediately
shown into the drawing-room.   To his surprise
he found no one there, but he had scarcely
glanced round the apartment when the door
opened, and a slight sylph-like figure, clad in
white, appeared before him.

At a glance he recognised the face he had
seen on the fading photograph.

'How do you do, Mr. Bradley?' said
Eustasia, holding out a thin transparent hand,
and fixing her light eyes upon his face.

'I received your brother's invitation,' he
replied rather awkwardly.   'I am afraid I
am a little before my time.'

'Well, you're the first to arrive.   Salem's
upstairs washing, and will be down directly.
He's real pleased to know you've come.'

She flitted lightly across the room, and sat down close to the window. She looked white and worn, and all the life of her frame seemed concentrated in her extraordinary eyes, which she fixed upon the visitor with a steadiness calculated to discompose a timid man.

'Won't you sit down, Mr. Bradley?' she said, repeating the name with a curious familiarity.

'You seem to know me well,' he replied, seating himself, 'though I do not think we have ever met.'

'Oh, yes, we have; leastways, I've often heard you preach. I knew a man once in the States, who was the very image of *you*. He's dead now, he is.'

Her voice, with its strong foreign inflexion, rang so strangely and plaintively on the last

words, that Bradley was startled. He looked
at the girl more closely, and was struck by her
unearthly beauty, contrasting so oddly with
her matter-of-fact, offhand manner.

'Your brother tells me that you are a
sibyl,' he said, drawing his chair nearer. 'I
am afraid, Miss Mapleleafe, you will find me
a disturbing influence. I have about as much
faith in solar biology, spiritualism, spirit-
agency, or whatever you like to call it, as I
have in—well, Mumbo-Jumbo.'

Her eyes still looked brightly into his, and
her wan face was lit up with a curious
smile.

'That's what they all say at first! Guess
you think, then, that I'm an impostor? Don't
be 'afraid to speak your mind; I'm used to it;
I've had worse than hard names thrown at

me ; stones and all that. I was stabbed once down South, and I've the mark still ! '

As she spoke, she bared her white arm to the elbow, and showed, just in the fleshy part of the arm, the mark of an old scar.

' The man that did that drew his knife in the dark, and pinioned my arm to the table. The very man that was like *you*.'

And lifting her arm to her lips she kissed the scar, and murmured, or crooned, to herself as she had done on the former occasion in the presence of her brother. Bradley looked on in amazement. So far as he could perceive at present, the woman was a half-mad creature, scarcely responsible for what she said or did.

His embarrassment was not lessened when Eustasia, still holding the arm to her lips, looked at him through thickly gathering tears, and then, as if starting from a trance, gave vent to a wild yet musical laugh.

Scarcely knowing what to say, he continued the former topic of conversation.

' I presume you are what is called a clairvoyante. That, of course, I can understand. But, do you really believe in supernatural manifestations ? '

Here the voice of the little Professor, who had quietly entered the room, supplied an answer.

' Certainly not, sir. The office of solar biology is not to vindicate, but to destroy, supernaturalism. *You* mean superhuman, which is quite another thing.

> All things abide in Nature, nought subsists
> Beyond the infinite celestial scheme.
> Motes in the sunbeam are the lives of men,

But in the moonlight and the stellar ray,
In every burning flame of every sphere,
Exist intelligible agencies
Akin to thine and mine.

That's how the great Bard puts it in a nutshell. Other lives in other worlds, sir, but no life out or beyond Nature, which embraces the solid universe to the remotest point in space.'

Concluding with this flourish, Professor Mapleleafe dropped down into commonplace, wrung the visitor's hand, and wished him a very good-day.

' How do you feel, Eustasia ? ' he continued with some anxiety, addressing his sister. ' Do you feel as if the atmosphere this afternoon was properly conditioned ? '

' Yes, Salem, I think so.'

The Professor looked at his watch, and simultaneously there came a loud rapping at the door. Presently three persons entered, a tall, powerful-looking man, who was introduced as Doctor Kendall, and two elderly gentlemen ; then a minute later, a little gray-haired man, the well-known Sir James Beaton, a famous physician of Edinburgh. The party was completed by the landlady of the house, who came up dressed in black silk, and wearing a widow's cap.

'Now, then, ladies and gentlemen,' said the little Professor glibly, 'we shall, with your permission, begin in the usual manner, by darkening the chamber and forming an ordinary circle. I warn you, however, that this is trivial, and in the manner of professional mediums. As the séance advances and the power deepens, we shall doubtless be lifted to higher ground.'

So saying he drew the heavy curtains of the

window, leaving the room in semi-darkness. Then the party sat down around a small circular table, and touched hands ; Bradley sitting opposite Eustasia, who had Dr. Kendall on her right and Sir James Beaton on her left. The usual manifestations followed. The table rose bodily into the air, bells were rung, tiny sparkles of light flashed about the room.

This lasted about a quarter of an hour, at the end of which time Mapleleafe broke the circle, and drawing back a curtain, admitted some light into the room. It was then discovered that Eustasia, sitting in her place, with her hands resting upon the table, was in a state of mesmeric trance ; and ghastly and sibylline indeed she looked, with her great eyes wide open, her golden hair fallen on her shoulders, her face shining as if mysteriously anointed.

' Eustasia ! ' said the Professor softly.

The girl remained motionless, and did not seem to hear.

' Eustasia ! ' he repeated.

This time her lips moved, and a voice, that seemed shriller and clearer than her own, replied :—

' Eustasia is not here.   I am Sira.'

' Who is Sira ? '

' A spirit of the third magnitude, from the region of the moon.'

A titter ran round the company, and Sir James Beaton essayed a feeble joke.

' A lunar spirit—we shall not, I hope, be *de lunatico inquirendo.*'

' Hush, sir ! ' cried the Professor ; then he continued, addressing the medium his sister,

' See ! see ! '

' What is it, Sira ? ' demanded the Professor.

' Shapes like angels, carrying one that looks like a corpse. They are singing—do you not hear them ? Now they are touching me—they are passing their hands over my hair. I see my mother ; she is weeping and bending over me. Mother ! mother ! '

Simultaneously, Bradley himself appeared conscious of glimpses like human faces flashing and fading. In spite of his scepticism, a deep dread, which was shared more or less by all present, fell upon him. Then all at once he became aware of something like a living form, clad in robes of dazzling whiteness, passing by him. An icy cold hand was pressed to his forehead, leaving a clammy damp like dew.

'I see a shape of some kind,' he cried. 'Does anyone else perceive it?'

'Yes! yes! yes!' came from several voices.

'It is the spirit of a woman,' murmured the medium.

'Do you know her?' added the Professor.

'No; she belongs to the living world, not to the dead. I see far away, somewhere on this planet, a beautiful lady lying asleep; she seems full of sorrow, her pillow is wet with tears. This is the lady's spirit, brought hither by the magnetic influence of one she loves.'

'Can you describe her to us more closely?'

'Yes. She has dark hair, and splendid dark eyes; she is tall and lovely. The lady and the spirit are alike, the counterpart of each other.'

Once more Bradley was conscious of the white form standing near him ; he reached out his hands to touch it, but it immediately vanished.

At the same moment he felt a touch like breath upon his face, and heard a soft musical voice murmuring in his ear—

' Ambrose ! beloved ! '

He started in wonder, for the voice seemed that of Alma Craik.

' Be good enough not to break the chain ! ' said the landlady, who occupied the chair at his side.

Trembling violently, he returned his hands to their place, touching those of his immediate neighbours on either side. The instant he did so, he heard the voice again, and felt the touch like breath.

'Ambrose, do you know me?'

'Who is speaking?' he demanded.

A hand soft as velvet and cold as ice was passed over his hair.

'It is I, dearest!' said the voice. 'It is *Alma!*'

'What brings you here?' he murmured, almost inaudibly.

'I knew you were in sorrow;—I came to bring you comfort, and to assure you of my affection.'

The words were spoken in a low, just audible voice, close to his ear, and it is doubtful if they were heard by any other member of the company. In the meantime the more commonplace manifestations still continued; the room was full of strange sounds, bells ringing, knocking, shuffling of invisible feet.

Bradley was startled beyond measure. Either her supernatural presence was close by him, or he was the victim of some cruel trick. Before he could speak again, he felt the pressure of cold lips on his forehead, and the same strange voice murmuring farewell.

Wild with excitement, not unmingled with suspicion, he again broke the chain and sprang to his feet. There was a sharp cry from the medium, as he sprang to the window and drew back the curtain, letting in the daylight. But the act discovered nothing. All the members of the circle, save himself, were sitting in their places. Eustasia, the medium, was calmly leaning back in her chair. In a moment, however, she started, put her hand quickly to her forehead as if in pain, and seemed to emerge from her trance.

'Salem,' she cried in her own natural voice, 'has anything happened?'

'Mr. Bradley has broken the conditions, that's all,' returned the Professor, with an air of offended dignity. 'I do protest, ladies and gentlemen, against that interruption. It has brought a most interesting séance to a violent close.'

There was a general murmur from the company, and dissatisfied glances were cast at the offender.

'I am very sorry,' said the clergyman. 'I yielded to an irresistible influence.'

'The spirits won't be trifled with, sir,' cried Mapleleafe.

'Certainly not,' said one of the elderly gentlemen. 'Solemn mysteries like these should be approached in a fair and a—hum—

a respectful spirit. For my own part, I am quite satisfied with what I have seen. Iᴜ convinces me of—hum—the reality of these phenomena.'

The other elderly gentleman concurred. Dr. Kendall and Sir James, who had been comparing notes, said that they would reserve their final judgment until they had been present at another séance. In the mean time they would go so far as to say that what they had witnessed was very extraordinary indeed.

' How are you now, Eustasia?' said the Professor, addressing his sister.

' My head aches. I feel as if I had been standing for hours in a burning sun. When you called me back I was dreaming so strangely. I thought I was in some celestial place, walking hand in hand with the Lord Jesus.'

Bradley looked at the speaker's face. It looked full of elfin or witch-like rather than angelic light. Their eyes met, and Eustasia gave a curious smile.

'Will you come again, Mr. Bradley?'

'I don't know. Perhaps; that is to say, if you will permit me.'

'I do think, sir,' interrupted the Professor, 'that you have given offence to the celestial intelligences, and I am not inclined to admit you to our circle again.'

Several voices murmured approval.

'You are wrong, brother,' cried Eustasia, 'you are quite wrong.'

'What do you mean, Eustasia?'

'I mean that Mr. Bradley is a medium himself, and a particular favourite with spirits of the first order.'

The Professor seemed to reflect.

'Well, if that's so (and *you* ought to know), it's another matter. But he'll have to promise not to break the conditions. It ain't fair to the spirits; it ain't fair to his fellow-inquirers.'

One by one the company departed, but Bradley still lingered, as if he had something still to hear or say. At last, when the last visitor had gone, and the landlady had grimly stalked away to continue her duties in the basement of the house, he found himself alone with the brother and sister.

He stood hesitating, hat in hand.

'May I ask you a few questions?' he said, addressing Eustasia.

'Why, certainly,' she replied.

'While you were in the state of trance did

you see or hear anything that took place in this room ? '

Eustasia shook her head.

' Do you know anything whatever of my private life ? '

' I guess not, except what I've read in the papers.'

' Do you know a lady named Craik, who is one of the members of my congregation ? '

The answer came in another shake of the head, and a blank look expressing entire ignorance. Either Eustasia knew nothing whatever, or she was a most accomplished actress. Puzzled and amazed, yet still suspecting fraud of some kind, Bradley took his leave.

CHAPTER XXV.

A CATASTROPHE.

'After life's fitful fever, she sleeps well!'

THE few days following the one on which the spiritualistic *séance* was held were passed by Bradley in a sort of dream. The more he thought of what he had heard and seen, the more puzzled he became. At times he seemed half inclined to believe in supernatural collaboration, then he flouted his belief and laughed contemptuously at himself. Of course it was all imposture, and he had been a dupe.

Then he thought of Eustasia, and the

interest which she had at first aroused in him rapidly changed to indignation and contempt.

Very soon these people ceased to occupy his thoughts at all; so self-absorbed was he, indeed, in his own trouble that he forgot them as completely as if they had never been. After all they were but shadows which had flitted across his path and faded. Had he been left to himself he would assuredly never have summoned them up again.

But he was evidently too valuable a convert to be let go in that way. One morning he received the following note, written on delicate paper in the most fairylike of fragile hands:

'My dear Mr. Bradley,—We hold a *séance* to-morrow night at six, and hope you'll come; at least, *I* do! Salem don't particularly

want you, since you broke the conditions, and
he regards you as a disturbing influence. *I
know better* : the spirits like you, and I feel that
with you I could do great things ; so I hope
you'll be here.

'EUSTASIA MAPLELEAFE.'

Bradley read the letter through twice, then
he gazed at it for a time in trembling hesitation. Should he go? Why not? Suppose
the people were humbugs, were they worse
than dozens of others he had met? and they
had at least the merit of bringing back to him
the presence of the one being who was all in
all to him. His hesitation lasted only for a
moment—the repulsion came. He threw the
letter aside.

A few days later a much more significant
incident occurred. As Bradley was leaving

his house one morning he came face to face
with a veiled woman who stood before his
door. He was about to pass : the lady laid a
retaining hand upon his arm and raised her
veil.

It was Eustasia.

'Guess you're surprised to see me,' she
said, noticing his start; 'suppose I may come
in, though, now I'm here ? '

Bradley pushed open the door, and led the
way to his study. Eustasia followed him ;
having reached the room, she sat down and
eyed him wistfully.

'Did you get my letter ? ' she asked.

'Yes.'

'You didn't answer it ? '

'No.'

'Why not ? '

Bradley hesitated.

'Do you want me to tell you?' he said.

'Why, certainly—else why do I ask you? but I see you don't wish to tell me. Why?'

'Because I dislike giving unnecessary pain.'

'Ah! in other words you believe me to be a humbug, but you haven't the cruelty to say so. Well, that don't trouble me. *Prove* me to be one, and you may call me one, but give me a fair trial first.'

'What do you mean?'

'Come to some more of our *séances*, will you? *do* say you'll come!'

She laid her hand gently upon his arm, and fixed her eyes almost entreatingly upon him. He stared at her like one fascinated, then shrank before her glance.

'Why do you wish me to come?' he said.
'You know my thoughts and feelings on this
subject.   You and I are cast in different
moulds ; we must go different ways.'

She smiled sadly.

'The spirits will it otherwise,' she said ;
while under her breath she added, 'and so
do I.'

But he was in no mood to yield that day.
As soon as Eustasia saw this she rose to go.
When her thin hand lay in his, she said softly :

'Mr. Bradley, if ever you are in trouble
come to *us* ; you will find it is not all humbug
then ! '

Eustasia returned home full of hope.   'He
will come,' she said ; 'yes, he will assuredly
come.'   But days passed, and he neither came
nor sent ; at last, growing impatient, she called

again at his house ; then she learned that he had left London.

' He has flown from me,' she thought ; ' he feels my influence, and fears it.'

But in this Eustasia was quite wrong. He was flying not from her but from himself. The wretched life of self-reproach and misery which he was compelled to lead was crushing him down so utterly that unless he made some effort he would sink and sicken. Die ? Well, after all, that would not have been so hard ; but the thought of leaving Alma was more than he could bear. He must live for the sake of the days which might yet be in store for them both.

He needed change, however, and he sought it for a few days on foreign soil. He went over one morning to Boulogne, took rooms in the Hôtel de Paris, and became one of the swarm of tourists which was there filling the place.

The bathing season was then at its height, and people were all too busy to notice him ; he walked about like one in a dream, watching the pleasure-seekers, but pondering for ever on the old theme.

After all it was well for him that he had left England, he thought—the busy garrulous life of this place came as a relief after the dreary monotony of town. In the evenings he strolled out to the concerts or open-air dances, and observed the fisher girls with their lovers moving about in the gaslight ; while in the mornings he strolled about the sand watching with listless amusement the bathers who crowded down to the water's edge like bees in swarming time.

One morning, feeling more sick at heart than usual, he issued from the hotel and bent his steps towards the strand. On that day the scene was unusually animated. Flocks of fantastically-dressed children amused themselves by making houses in the sand, while their *bonnes* watched over them, and their mammas, clad in equally fantastic costumes, besieged the bathing-machines. Bradley walked for a time on the sands watching the variegated crowd ; it was amusing and distracting, and he was about to look around for a quiet spot in which he could spend an hour or so, when he was suddenly startled by an apparition.

A party of three were making their way towards the bathing-machines, and were even then within a few yards of him. One was a child dressed in a showy costume of serge, with long curls falling upon his shoulders; on one side of him was a French *bonne*, on the other a lady extravagantly attired in the most gorgeous of sea-side costumes. Her cheeks and lips were painted a bright red, but her skin was white as alabaster. She was laughing heartily at something which the little boy had said, when suddenly her eyes fell upon Bradley, who stood now within two yards of her.

It was his wife.

She did not pause nor shrink, but she ceased laughing, and a peculiar look of thinly veiled contempt passed over her face as she walked on.

'*Maman*,' said the child in French, ' who is that man, and why did he stare so at you ? '

The lady shrugged her shoulders, and laughed again.

' He stared because he had nothing better to look at, I suppose, *chéri ;* but come, I shall miss my bath ; you had best stay here with Augustine, and make sand-hills till I rejoin you. *Au revoir*, Bébé.'

She left the child with the nurse, hastened on and entered one of the bathing-machines, which was immediately drawn down into the sea.

Bradley still stood where she had left him, and his eyes remained fixed upon the machine which held the woman whose very presence poisoned the air he breathed. All his old feelings of repulsion returned tenfold ; the very sight of the woman seemed to degrade and drag him down.

As he stood there the door of the machine opened, and she came forth again. This time she was the wonder of all. Her shapely limbs were partly naked, and her body was covered with a quaintly cut bathing-dress of red. She called out some instructions to her nurse; then she walked down and entered the sea.

Bradley turned and walked away. He passed up the strand and sat down listlessly on one of the seats on the terrace facing the water. He took out Alma's last letter, and read it through, and the bitterness of his soul increased tenfold.

When would his misery end? he thought. Why did not death come and claim his own, and leave him free? Wherever he went his existence was poisoned by this miserable woman.

'So it must ever be,' he said bitterly. 'I

must leave this place, for the very sight of her almost drives me mad.'

He rose and was about to move away, when he became conscious, for the first time, that something unusual was taking place. He heard sounds of crying and moaning, and everybody seemed to be rushing excitedly towards the sand. What it was all about Bradley could not understand, for he could see nothing. He stood and watched ; every moment the cries grew louder, and the crowd upon the sands increased. He seized upon a passing Frenchman, and asked what the commotion meant.

' *Ras de marée, monsieur!*' rapidly explained the man as he rushed onward.

Thoroughly mystified now, Bradley resolved to discover by personal inspection what it all meant. Leaving the terrace he leapt upon the shore, and gained the waiting crowd upon the sand. To get an explanation from anyone here seemed to be impossible, for every individual member of the crowd seemed to have gone crazy. The women threw up their hands and moaned, the children screamed, while the men rushed half wildly about the sands.

Bradley touched the arm of a passing Englishman.

' What is all this panic about ? ' he said.

' The *ras de marée !* '

' Yes, but what is the *ras de marée ?* '

' Don't you know ? It is a sudden rising of the tide ; it comes only once in three years. It has surprised the bathers, many of whom are drowning. See, several machines have gone to pieces, and the others are floating like drift-wood ! Yonder are two boats out picking up the people, but if the waves continue to rise like this they will never save them all. One woman from that boat has fainted ; no, good heavens, she is dead.'

The scene now became one of intense excitement. The water, rising higher and higher, was breaking now into waves of foam ; most of the machines were dashed about like corks upon the ocean, their frightened occupants giving forth the most fearful shrieks and cries. Suddenly there was a cry for the lifeboat ; immediately after it dashed down the sand, drawn by two horses, and was launched out upon the sea; while Bradley and others occupied themselves in attending to those who were laid fainting upon the shore.

But the boats, rapidly as they went to work, proved insufficient to save the mass of frightened humanity still struggling with the waves. The screams and cries became heartrending as one after another sank to rise no more. Suddenly there was another rush.

'Leave the women to attend to the rescued,' cried several voices. 'Let the men swim out to the rescue of those who are exhausted in the sea.'

There was a rush to the water; among the first was Bradley, who, throwing off his coat, plunged boldly into the water. Many of those who followed him were soon overcome by the force of the waves and driven back to shore; but Bradley was a powerful swimmer, and went on.

He made straight for a figure which, seemingly overlooked by everyone else, was drifting rapidly out to sea. On coming nearer he saw, by the long black hair, which floated around her on the water, that the figure was that of a woman. How she supported herself Bradley could not see ; she was neither swimming nor floating ; her back was towards him, and she might have fainted, for she made no sound.

On coming nearer he saw that she was supporting herself by means of a plank, part of the *débris* which had drifted from the broken machines. By this time he was quite near to her ;—she turned her face towards him, and he almost cried out in pain.

He recognised his wife !

Yes, there she was, helpless and almost fainting—her eyes were heavy, her lips blue ; and he seemed to be looking straight into the face of death. Bradley paused, and the two gazed into each other's eyes. He saw that her strength was going, but he made no attempt to put out a hand to save her. He thought of the past, of the curse this woman had been to him ; and he knew that by merely doing nothing she would be taken from him.

Should he let her die? Why not? If he had not swum out she most assuredly would have sunk and been heard of no more. Again he looked at her and she looked at him : her eyes were almost closed now : having once looked into his face she seemed to have resigned all hopes of rescue.

No, he could not save her—the temptation was too great. He turned and swam in the direction of another figure which was floating helplessly upon the waves. He had only taken three strokes when a violent revulsion of feeling came ; with a terrible cry he turned again to the spot where he had left the fainting and drowning woman. But she was not there —the plank was floating upon the water—that was all.

Bradley dived, and reappeared holding the woman in his arms. Then he struck out with her to the shore.

It was a matter of some difficulty to get there, for she lay like lead in his hold. Having reached the shore, he carried her up the beach, and placed her upon the sand.

Then he looked to see if she was conscious.

Yes, she still breathed ;—he gave her some brandy, and did all in his power to restore her to life. After a while she opened her eyes, and looked into Bradley's face.

'Ah, it is *you!*' she murmured faintly, then, with a long-drawn sigh, she sank back, dead !

Still dripping from his encounter with the sea, his face as white as the dead face before him, Bradley stood like one turned to stone. Suddenly he was aroused by a heartrending shriek. The little boy whom he had seen with the dead woman broke from the hands of his nurse, and sobbing violently threw himself upon the dead body.

'*Maman! maman!*' he moaned.

The helpless cries of the child forced upon Bradley the necessity for immediate action. Having learned from the nurse the address of the house where 'Mrs. Montmorency' was staying, he had the body put upon a stretcher and conveyed there. He himself walked beside it, and the child followed, screaming and crying, in his nurse's arms.

Having reached the house, the body was taken into a room to be properly dressed, while Bradley tried every means in his power to console the child! After a while he was told that all was done, and he went into the chamber of death.

CHAPTER XXVI.

THE LAST LOOK.

Dead woman, shrouded white as snow
  While Death the shade broods darkly nigh,
Place thy cold hand in mine, and so—
  'Good-bye.'

No prayer or blessing born of breath
  Came from thy lips as thou didst die ;
I loath'd thee living, but in death—
  'Good-bye ! '

So close together after all,
  After long strife, stand thou and I,
I bless thee, while I faintly call—
  'Good-bye ! '

Good-bye the past and all its pain,
  Kissing thy poor dead hand, I cry—
Again, again, and yet again—
  'Good-bye!'—*The Exile : a Poem.*

IT would have been difficult to analyse
accurately the emotions which filled the bosom

of Ambrose Bradley, as he stood and looked
upon the dead face of the woman who, according to the law of the land and the sacrament
of the Church, had justly claimed to be his
wife.   He could not conceal from himself that
the knowledge of her death brought relief
to him and even joy ; but mingled with that
relief were other feelings less reassuring—pity,
remorse even, and a strange sense of humiliation.   He had never really loved the woman,
and her conduct, previous to their long separa-
tion, had been such as to kill all sympathy in
the heart of a less sensitive man, while what
might be termed her unexpected resurrection
had roused in him a bitterness and a loathing
beyond expression.   Yet now that the last
word was said, the last atonement made, now
that he beheld the eyes that would never open

again, and the lips that would never again
utter speech or sound, his soul was stirred to
infinite compassion.

After all, he thought, the blame had not
been hers that they had been so ill-suited to
each other, and afterwards, when they met in
after years, she had not wilfully sought to
destroy his peace. It had all been a cruel
fatality, from the first: another proof of the
pitiless laws which govern human nature, and
make men and women suffer as sorely for
errors of ignorance and inexperience as for
crimes of knowledge.

He knelt by the bedside, and taking her
cold hand kissed it solemnly. Peace was
between them, he thought, then and for ever.
She too, with all her faults and all her follies,
had been a fellow-pilgrim by his side towards

the great bourne whence no pilgrim returns, and she had reached it first. He remembered now, not the woman who had flaunted her shamelessness before his eyes, but the pretty girl, almost a child, whom he had first known and fancied that he loved. In the intensity of his compassion and self-reproach he even exaggerated the tenderness he had once felt for her ; the ignoble episode of their first intercouse catching a sad brightness reflected from the heavens of death. And in this mood, penitent and pitying, he prayed that God might forgive them both.

When he descended from the room, his eyes were red with tears. He found the little boy sobbing wildly in the room below, attended by the kindly Frenchwoman who kept the house. He tried to soothe him, but found it impossible, his grief being most painful to witness, and violent in the extreme.

'Ah, monsieur, it is indeed a calamity!' cried the woman. 'Madame was so good a mother, devoted to her child. But God is good—the little one has a father still!'

Bradley understood the meaning of her words, but did not attempt to undeceive her. His heart was welling over with tenderness towards the pretty orphan, and he was thinking too of his own harsh judgments on the dead, who, it was clear, had possessed many redeeming virtues, not the least of them being her attachment to her boy.

'You are right, madame,' he replied, sadly, 'and the little one shall not lack fatherly love and care. Will you come with me for a few moments? I wish to speak to you alone.'

He placed his hand tenderly on the child's head, and again tried to soothe him, but he shrank away with petulant screams and cries. Walking to the front entrance he waited till he was joined there by the landlady, and they stood talking in the open air.

'How long had she been here, madame?' he asked.

'For a month, monsieur,' was the reply. 'She came late in the season for the baths, with her *bonne* and the little boy, and took my rooms. Pardon, but I did not know madame had a husband living, and so near.'

'We have been separated for many years. I came to Boulogne yesterday quite by accident, not dreaming the lady was here. Can you tell me if she has friends in Boulogne?'

'I do not think so, monsieur. She lived quite alone, seeing no one, and her only thought and care was for the little boy. She was a proud lady, very rich and proud; nothing was too good for her, or for the child; she lived, as the saying is, *en princesse.* But no, she had no friends! Doubtless, being an English lady, though she spoke and looked like a *compatriote,* all her friends were in her own land.'

'Just so,' returned Bradley, turning his head away to hide his tears; for he thought to himself, 'Poor Mary! After all, she was desolate like myself! How pitiful that I, of all men, should close her eyes and follow her to her last repose!'

'Pardon, monsieur,' said the woman, 'but madame, perhaps, was not of our Church? She was, no doubt, Protestant?'

It was a simple question, but simple as it was Bradley was startled by it. He knew about as much of his dead wife's professed belief as of the source whence she had drawn her subsistence. But he replied :

' Yes, certainly. Protestant, of course.'

' Then monsieur will speak to the English clergyman, who dwells there on the hill ' (here she pointed townward), ' close to the English church. He is a good man, Monsieur Robertson, and monsieur will find——'

' I will speak to him,' interrupted Bradley. ' But I myself am an English clergyman, and shall doubtless perform the last offices, when the time comes.'

The woman looked at him in some astonishment, for his presence was the reverse of clerical, and his struggle in and with the sea had left his attire in most admired disorder :

but she remembered the eccentricities of the nation to which he belonged, and her wonder abated. After giving the woman a few more general instructions, Bradley walked slowly and thoughtfully to his hotel.

More than once already his thoughts had turned towards Alma, but he had checked such thoughts and crushed them down in the presence of death; left to himself, however, he could not conquer them, nor restrain a certain feeling of satisfaction in his newly-found freedom. He would write to Alma, as in duty bound, at once, and tell her of all that had happened. And then? It was too late, perhaps, to make full amends, to expect full forgiveness; but it was his duty to give to her in the sight of the world the name he had once given to her secretly and in vain.

But the man's troubled spirit, sensitive to a degree, shrank from the idea of building up any new happiness on the grave of the poor woman whose corpse he had just quitted. Although he was now a free man legally, he still felt morally bound and fettered. All his wish and prayer was to atone for the evil he had brought on the one being he reverenced and loved. He did not dare, at least as yet, to think of uniting his unworthy life with a life so infinitely more beautiful and pure.

Yes, he would write to her. The question was, where his letter would find her, and how soon?

When he had last heard from her she was at Milan, but that was several weeks ago; and since then, though he had written twice, there had been no response. She was possibly travelling farther southward; in all possibility, to Rome.

The next few days passed drearily enough. An examination of some letters recently received by the deceased discovered two facts —first, that she had a sister, living in Oxford, with whom she corresponded; and, second, that her means of subsistence came quarterly from a firm of solicitors in Bedford Row, London. Next day the sister arrived by steamboat, accompanied by her husband, a small tradesman. Bradley interviewed the pair, and found them decent people, well acquainted with their relative's real position. The same day he received a communication from the solicitors, notifying that the annuity enjoyed by 'Mrs. Montmorency' lapsed with her decease, but that a large sum of money had been settled by the late Lord Ombermere upon the child, the interest of the sum to be used for his maintenance and education, and the gross amount with additions and under certain reservations, to be at his disposal on attaining his majority.

On seeking an interview with the Rev. Mr. Robertson, the minister of the English Church, Bradley soon found that his reputation had preceded him.

'Do I address the famous Mr. Bradley, who some time ago seceded from the English Church?' asked the minister, a pale, elderly, clean-shaven man, bearing no little resemblance to a Roman Catholic priest.

Bradley nodded, and at once saw the not too cordial manner of the other sink to freezing point.

'The unfortunate lady was your wife?'

'Yes; but we had been separated for many years.'

'Ah, indeed!' sighed the clergyman with a long-drawn sigh, a furtive glance of repulsion, and an inward exclamation of 'no wonder!'

'Although we lived apart, and although, to be frank, there was great misunderstanding between us, all that is over for ever, you understand. It is in a spirit of the greatest tenderness and compassion that I wish to conduct the funeral service—to which I presume there is no objection.'

Mr. Robertson started in amazement, as if a bomb had exploded under his feet.

'To conduct the funeral service! But you have seceded from the Church of England.'

'In a sense, yes; but I have never done so formally. I am still an English clergyman.'

'I could never consent to such a thing,' cried the other, indignantly. 'I should look upon it as profanity. Your published opinions are known to me, sir; they have shocked me inexpressibly; and not only in my opinion, but in that of my spiritual superiors, they are utterly unworthy of one calling himself a Christian.'

'Then you refuse me permission to officiate?'

'Most emphatically. More than that, I shall require some assurance that the lady did not share your heresies, before I will suffer the interment to take place in the precincts of my church.'

'Is not my assurance sufficient?'

'No, sir, it is *not!*' exclaimed the clergyman with scornful dignity. 'I do not wish to say anything offensive, but, speaking as a Christian and a pastor of the English Church, I can attach no weight whatever to the assurances of one who is, in the public estimation, nothing better than an avowed infidel. Good morning!'

So saying, with a last withering look, the clergyman turned on his heel and walked away.

Seeing that remonstrance was useless, and might even cause public scandal, Bradley forthwith abandoned his design; but at his suggestion his wife's sister saw the incumbent, and succeeded in convincing him that Mrs. Montmorency had died in the true faith. The result of Mr. Robertson's pious indignation was soon apparent. The sister and her husband, who had hitherto treated Bradley with marked respect, now regarded him with sullen dislike and suspicion. They could not prevent him, however, from following as chief mourner, when the day of the funeral came.

That funeral was a dismal enough experience for Ambrose Bradley. Never before had he felt so keenly the vanity of his own creed and the isolation of his own opinions, as when he stood by the graveside and listened to the last solemn words of the English burial service. He seemed like a black shadow in the sacred place. The words of promise and resurrection had little meaning for one who had come to regard the promise as only beautiful 'poetry,' and the resurrection as only a poet's dream. And though the sense of his own sin lay on his heart like lead, he saw no benign Presence blessing the miserable woman who had departed, upraising her on wings of gladness; all he perceived was Death's infinite desolation, and the blackness of that open grave.

CHAPTER XXVII

THE SIREN.

Weave a circle round him thrice. . . .
For he on honey-dew hath fed,
And drunk the milk of Paradise.—*Kubla Khan.*

BRADLEY'S first impulse, on quitting Boulogne,
was to hasten at once on to Italy, seek out
Alma, and tell her all that had occurred; but
that impulse was no sooner felt than it was
conquered. The man had a quickening conscience left, and he could not have stood just
then before the woman he loved without the
bitterest pain and humiliation. No, he would
write to her, he would break the news gently

by letter, not by word of mouth ; and afterwards, perhaps, when his sense of spiritual agony had somewhat worn away, he would go to her and throw himself upon her tender mercy. So instead of flying on to Italy he returned by the mail to London, and thence wrote at length to Alma, giving her full details of his wife's death.

By this time the man was so broken in spirit and so changed in body, that even his worst enemies might have pitied him. The trouble of the last few months had stript him of all his intellectual pride, and left him supremely sad.

But now, as ever, the mind of the man, though its light was clouded, turned in the direction of celestial or supermundane things. Readers who are differently constituted, and

who regard such speculations as trivial or irrelevant, will doubtless have some difficulty in
comprehending an individual who, through
all vicissitudes of moral experience, invariably
returned to the one set purpose of spiritual
inquiry. To him one thing was paramount,
even over all his own sorrows—the solution of
the great problem of human life and immortality. This was his haunting idea, his mono-
mania, so to speak. Just as a physiologist
would examine his own blood under the
microscope, just as a scientific inquirer would
sacrifice his own life and happiness for the
verification of a theory, so would Bradley ask
himself, even when on the rack of moral torment, How far does this suffering help me to a
solution of the mystery of life ?

True, for a time he had been indifferent,

even callous, drifting, on the vague current of agnosticism, he knew not whither ; but that did not last for long : the very constitution of Bradley saved him from that indifferentness which is the chronic disease of so many modern men.

Infinitely tender of heart, he had been moved to the depths by his recent experience ; he had felt, as all of us at some time feel, the sanctifying and purifying power of Death. A mean man would have exulted in the new freedom Death had brought ; Bradley, on the other hand, stood stupefied and aghast at his own liberation. On a point of conscience he could have fought with, and perhaps conquered, all the prejudices of society ; but when his very conscience turned against him he was paralysed with doubt, wonder, and despair.

He returned to London, and there awaited Alma's answer. One day, urged by a sudden impulse, he bent his steps towards the mysterious house in Bayswater, and found Eustasia Mapleleafe sitting alone. Never had the little lady looked so strange and *spirituelle*. Her elfin-like face looked pale and worn, and her great wistful eyes were surrounded with dark melancholy rings. But she looked up as he entered, with her old smile.

'I knew you would come,' she cried. 'I was thinking of you, and I felt the celestial agencies were going to bring us together. And I'm real glad to see you before we go away.'

'You are leaving London?' asked Bradley, as he seated himself close to her.

'Yes. Salem talks of going back home

before winter sets in and the fogs begin. I don't seem able to breathe right in this air. If I stopped here long, I think I should die.'

As she spoke, she passed her thin transparent hand across her forehead, with a curious gesture of pain As Bradley looked at her steadfastly she averted his gaze, and a faint hectic flush came into her cheeks.

' Guess you think it don't matter much,' she continued with the sharp nervous laugh peculiar to her, ' whether I live or die. Well, Mr. Bradley, I suppose you're right, and I'm sure I don't care much how soon I go.'

' You are very young to talk like that,' said Bradley gently ; ' but perhaps I misunderstand you, and you mean that you would gladly exchange this life for freer activity and larger happiness in another ? '

Eustasia laughed again, but this time she looked full into her questioner's eyes.

'I don't know about that,' she replied. 'What I mean is that I am downright tired, and should just like a good long spell of sleep.'

'But surely, if your belief is true, you look for something more than that?'

'I don't think I do. You mean I want to join the spirits, and go wandering about from one planet to another, or coming down to earth and making people uncomfortable? That seems a *stupid* sort of life, doesn't it?— about as stupid as this one? I'd rather tuck my head under my wing, like a little bird, and go to sleep for ever!'

Bradley opened his eyes, amazed and a little disconcerted by the lady's candour. Before he could make any reply she continued, in a low voice:

'You see, I've got no one in the world to care for me, except Salem, my brother. He's good to me, he is, but that doesn't make up for everything. I don't feel like a girl, but like an old woman. I'd rather be one of those foolish creatures you meet everywhere, who think of nothing but millinery and flirtation, than what I am. That's all the good the spirits have done me, to spoil my good looks and make me old before my time. I hate them sometimes; I hate myself for listening to them, and I say what I said before—that if I'm to live on as *they* do, and go on in the same curious way, I'd sooner die!'

'I wish you would be quite honest with me,' said Bradley, after a brief pause. 'I see you are ill, and I am sure you are unhappy. Suppose much of your illness, and all your unhappiness, came from your acquiescence in a scheme of folly and self-deception? You already know my opinion on these matters to which you allude. If I may speak quite frankly, I have always suspected you and your brother—but your brother more than you—of a conspiracy to deceive the public; and if I were not otherwise interested in you, if I did not feel for you the utmost sympathy and compassion, I should pass the matter by without a word. As it is, I would give a great deal if I could penetrate into the true motives of your conduct, and ascertain how far you are self-deluded.'

'It's no use,' answered Eustasia, shaking her head sadly. 'I can't explain it all even to myself; impossible to explain to you.'

'But do you seriously and verily believe in

the truth of these so-called spiritual manifestations ? '

' Guess I do,' returned the lady, with a decided nod.

' You believe in them, even while you admit their stupidity, their absurdity ? '

' If you ask me, I think life is a foolish business altogether. That's why I'd like to be done with it ! '

' But surely if spiritualism were an accepted fact, it would offer a solution of all the mysterious phenomena of human existence? It would demonstrate, at all events, that our experience does not cease with the body, which limits its area so much.'

Eustasia sighed wearily, and folding her thin hands on her knee, looked wearily at the fire, which flickered faintly in the grate. With all her candour of speech, she still presented to her interlocutor an expression of mysterious evasiveness. Nor was there any depth in her complaining sorrow. It seemed rather petulant and shallow than really solemn and profound.

'I wish you wouldn't talk about it,' she said. 'Talk to me about yourself, Mr. Bradley. You've been in trouble, I know; *they* told me. I've liked you ever since I first saw you, and I wish I could give you some help.'

Had Bradley been a different kind of man, he would scarcely have misunderstood the look she gave him then, full as it was of passionate admiration which she took no care to veil. Bending towards him, and looking into his eyes, she placed her hand on his; and the warm touch of the tremulous fingers went through him with a curious thrill. Nor did she withdraw the hand as she continued :

'I've only seen one man in the world like *you.* He's dead, he is. But you're his image. I told Salem so the day I first saw you. Some folks say that souls pass from one body into another, and I almost believe it when I think of him and look at *you.*'

As she spoke, with tears in her eyes and a higher flush on her cheek, there was a footstep in the room, and looking up she saw her brother, who had entered unperceived. His appearance was fortunate, as it perhaps saved her from some further indiscretions. Bradley, who had been too absorbed in the thoughts awakened by her first question to notice the peculiarity of her manner, held out his hand to the new-comer.

THE SIREN. 107

'Glad to see you again,' said the Professor. 'I suppose Eustasia has told you that we're going back to the States? I calculate we haven't done much good by sailing over. The people of England are a whole age behind the Americans, and won't be ripe for our teaching till many a year has passed.'

'When do you leave London?'

'In eight days. We're going to take passage in the "Maria," which sails to-morrow week.'

'Then you will give no more *séances?* I am sorry, for I should have liked to come again.'

Eustasia started, and looked eagerly at her brother.

'Will you come *to-night?*' she asked suddenly.

'To-night!' echoed Bradley. 'Is a *séance* to be held?'

'No, no,' interrupted Mapleleafe.

'But yes,' added Eustasia. 'We shall be alone, but that will be all the better. I should not like to leave England without convincing Mr. Bradley that there is something in your solar biology after all.'

'You'll waste your time, Eustasia,' remarked the Professor drily. 'You know what the poet says?

> A man convinced against his will
> Is of the same opinion still.

And I guess you'll never convert Mr. Bradley.'

'I'll try, at any rate,' returned Eustasia, smiling; then turning to the clergyman with an eager wistful look, she added, 'You'll come, won't you? To-night at seven.'

Bradley promised, and immediately afterwards took his leave. He had not exaggerated in expressing his regret at the departure of the curious pair; for since his strange experience at Boulogne he was intellectually unstrung, and eager to receive spiritual impressions, even from a quarter which he distrusted. He unconsciously felt, too, the indescribable fascination which Eustasia, more than most women, knew how to exert on highly organised persons of the opposite sex.

Left alone, the brother and sister looked at each other for some moments in silence; then the Professor exclaimed half angrily:

'You'll kill yourself, Eustasia, that's what *you'll* do! I've foreseen it all along, just as I foresaw it when you first met Ulysses S. Stedman. You're clean gone on this man, and if I wasn't ready to protect you, Lord knows you'd make a fool of yourself again.'

Eustasia looked up in his face and laughed. It was curious to note her change of look and manner; her face was still pale and elfin-like, but her eyes were full of malicious light.

' Never mind, Salem,' she replied. ' You just leave Mr. Bradley to me.'

' He's not worth spooning over, said Mapleleafe indignantly ; ' and let me tell you, Eustasia, you're not strong enough to go on like this. Think of your state of health ! Doctor Quin says you'll break up if you don't take care ! '

He paused, and looked at her in consternation. She was lying back in the sofa with her thin arms joined behind her head, and ' crooning ' to herself, as was her frequent habit.

This time the words and tune were from a familiar play, which she had seen represented at San Francisco.

> Black spirits and white,
> Blue spirits and grey,
> Mingle, mingle, mingle,
> You that mingle may!

'I do believe you're downright *mad!*' exclaimed the little Professor. 'Tell me the truth, Eustasia—do you love this man Bradley?'

Eustasia ceased singing, but remained in the same attitude.

'I loved him who is dead,' she replied, 'and I love Mr. Bradley because he is so like the other. If you give me time I will win him over; I will make him love *me.*'

'What nonsense you're talking!'

'Nonsense? It's the truth!' cried Eustasia, springing up and facing her brother. 'Why should I not love him? Why should he not love me? Am I to spend all my life like a slave, with no one to care for me, no one to give me a kind word? I won't do it. I want to be free. I'm tired of sitting at home all day alone, and playing the sibyl to the fools you bring here at night. Lord knows I haven't long to live; before I die I want to draw in one good long breath of love and joy! Perhaps it will kill me as you say—so much the better—I should like to die like that!'

'Eustasia, will you listen to reason?' exclaimed the distracted Professor. 'You're following a will-o'-the-wisp, that's what you are! This man don't care about any woman in the world but one, and you're wasting your precious time.'

'I know my power, and you know it too, Salem. I'm going to bring him to my feet.'

' How, Eustasia ? '

' Wait, and you will see! ' answered the girl, with her low, nervous laugh.

' Think better of it ! ' persisted her brother. ' You promised me, after Ulysses S. Stedman died, to devote all your life, strength, and thought to the beautiful cause of scientific spiritualism. Nature has made you a living miracle, Eustasia ! I do admire to see one so gifted throwing herself away, just like a school-girl, on the first good-looking man she meets ! '

' I hate spiritualism,' was the reply. ' What has it done for me ? Broken my heart, Salem, and wasted my life. I've dwelt too long with ghosts ; I want to feel my life as other women do. And I tell you I *will !* '

' The poor Professor shook his head dubiously, but saw that there was no more to be said—at any rate just then.

At seven o'clock that evening Bradley returned to the house in Bayswater, and found the brother and sister waiting for him.

Eustasia wore a loose-fitting robe of black velvet, cut low round the bust, and without sleeves.   Her neck and arms were beautifully though delicately moulded, white and glistening as satin, and the small serpent-like head, with its wonderfully brilliant eyes, was surmounted by a circlet of pearls.

Bradley looked at her in surprise.   Never before had she seemed so weirdly pretty.

The Professor, on the other hand, despite his gnome-like brow, appeared unusually ignoble and commonplace. He was ill at ease, too, and cast distrustful glances from time to time at his sister, whose manner was as brilliant as her appearance, and who seemed to have cast aside the depression which she had shown during the early part of the day.

After some little desultory conversation, Bradley expressed his impatience for the *séance* to begin. The landlady of the house, herself (as the reader is aware) an adept, was therefore summoned to give the party, and due preparations made by drawing the window-blinds and extinguishing the gas. Before the lights were quite put out, however, the Professor addressed his sister.

'Eustasia, you're not well! Say the word, and I'm sure Mr. Bradley will excuse you for to-night.'

The appeal was in vain, Eustasia persisting. The *séance* began. The Professor and Mrs. Piozzi Smith were *vis-à-vis*, while Eustasia, her back towards the folding-doors communicating to the inner chamber, sat opposite to Bradley.

The clergyman was far less master of himself than on the former occasions. No sooner did he find himself in total darkness than his heart began to beat with great muffled throbs, and nervous thrills ran through his frame. Before there was the slightest intimation of any supernatural presence, he seemed to see before him the dead face of his wife, white and awful as he had beheld it in that darkened chamber at Boulogne. Then the usual manifestations began ; bells were rung, faint lights flashed hither and thither, the table round which they were seated rose in the air, mysterious hands were passed over Bradley's face. He tried to retain his self-possession, but found it impossible ; a sickening sense of horror and fearful anticipation overmastered him, so that the clammy sweat stood upon his brow, and his body trembled like a reed.

Presently the voice of the little Professor was heard saying :

' Who is present ? Will any of our dear friends make themselves known ? '

There was a momentary pause. Then an answer came in the voice of Eustasia, but deeper and less clear.

' I am here.'

' Who are you ? '

' Laura, a spirit of the winged planet Jupiter. I speak through the bodily mouth of our dear sister, who is far away, walking with my brethren by the lake of golden fire.'

' Are you alone ? '

' No! others are present—I see them passing to and fro.   One is bright and beautiful.   Her face is glorious, but she wears a raiment like a shroud.'

' What does that betoken ? '

' It betokens that she has only just died.'

A shiver ran through Bradley's frame. Could the dead indeed be present? and if so, what dead ?   His thoughts flew back once more to that miserable death-chamber by the sea. The next moment something like a cold hand touched him, and a low voice murmured in his ear:

' Ambrose! are you listening ?   It is I ! '

' Who speaks ? ' he murmured under breath.

' Alma !   Do you know me ? '

Was it possible? Doubtless his phantasy deceived him, but he seemed once more to hear the very tones of her he loved.

' Do not move!' continued the voice. ' Perhaps this is a last meeting for a long time, for I am called away. It is your Alma's spirit that speaks to you ; her body lies dead at Rome.'

A wild cry burst from Bradley's lips, and he sank back in his chair, paralysed and over-powered.

' It is a cheat!' he gasped. ' It is no spirit that is speaking to me, but a living woman.'

And he clutched in the direction of the voice, but touched only the empty air.

'If you break the conditions, I must depart!' cried the voice faintly, as if from a distant part of the room.

'Shall I break up the *séance?*' asked the Professor.

'No!' cried Bradley, again joining his hands with those of his neighbours to complete the circle. 'Go on! go on!'

'Are our dear friends still present?' demanded the Professor.

'I am here,' returned the voice of Eustasia. 'I see the spirit of a woman, weeping and wringing her hands; it is she that wears the shroud. She speaks to me. She tells us that her earthly name was a word which signifies holy.'

'In God's name,' cried Bradley, 'what does it mean? She of whom you speak is not dead?—no, no!'

Again he felt the touch of a clammy hand, and again he heard the mysterious voice.

'Death is nothing; it is only a mystery—
a change. The body is nothing; the spirit is
all-present and all-powerful. Keep quiet; and
I will try to materialise myself even more.'

He sat still in shivering expectation; then
he felt a touch like breath upon his forehead,
and two lips, warm with life, were pressed close
to his, while at the same moment he felt what
seemed a human bosom heaving against his
own. If this phenomenon was supernatural,
it was certainly very real; for the effect was
of warm and living flesh. Certain now that
he was being imposed upon, Bradley determined to make certain by seizing the
substance of the apparition. He had scarcely,
however, withdrawn his arms from the circle,
when the phenomenon ceased; there was a
loud cry from the others present; and on the

gas being lit, Eustasia and the rest were seen sitting quietly in their chairs, the former just recovering from a state of trance.

'I warned you, Eustasia,' cried the Professor indignantly. 'I knew Mr. Bradley was not a fair inquirer, and would be certain to break the conditions.'

'It is an outrage,' echoed the lady of the house. 'The heavenly intelligences will never forgive us.'

Without heeding these remonstrances, Bradley, deathly pale, was gazing intently at Eustasia. She met his gaze quietly enough, but her heightened colour and sparkling eyes betokened that she was labouring under great excitement.

'It is infamous!' he cried. 'I am certain *now* that this is a vile conspiracy.'

'Take care, sir, take care!' exclaimed the Professor. 'There's law in the land, and——'

'Hush, Salem!' said Eustasia gently. 'Mr. Bradley does not mean what he says. He is too honourable to make charges which he cannot substantiate, even against a helpless girl. He is agitated by what he has seen to-night, but he will do us justice when he has thought it over.'

Without replying, Bradley took up his hat and moved to the door; but, turning suddenly, he again addressed the medium:

'I cannot guess by what means you have obtained your knowledge of my private life, but you are trading upon it to destroy the happiness of a fellow-creature. God forgive you! Your own self-reproach and self-contempt will avenge me; I cannot wish you any sorer punishment than the infamy and degradation of the life you lead.'

With these words he would have departed, but, swift as lightning, Eustasia flitted across the room and blocked his way.

'Don't go yet!' she cried. 'Of what do you accuse me? Why do you blame me for what the spirits have done?'

'The spirits!' he repeated bitterly. 'I'm not a child, to be so easily befooled. In one sense, indeed, you have conjured up devils, who some day or another will compass your own destruction.'

'That's true enough—they *may* be devils,' said Eustasia. 'Salem knows—we all know—that we can't prevent the powers of evil from controlling the powers of good, and coming in their places. Guess some of them have been at

work to-night. Mr. Bradley, perhaps it's our
last meeting on earth. Won't you shake hands?'

As she spoke her wild eyes were full of
tears, which streamed down her face. Acting
under a sudden impulse, Bradley took her outstretched hand, held it firmly, and looked her
in the face.

'Confess the cheat, and I will freely forgive you. It was *you* personated one who is
dear to me, and whom you pretended to be a
spirit risen from the grave.'

'Don't answer him, Eustasia!' exclaimed
the Professor. 'He ought to know that's
impossible, for you never left your seat.'

'Certainly not,' said Mrs. Piozzi Smith.

But Bradley, not heeding the interruption,
still watched the girl and grasped her passive
hand.

' Answer me !   Tell me the truth ! '

' How can I tell you ? ' answered Eustasia.
' I was tranced, and my spirit was far away.
I don't even know what happened.'

With a contemptuous gesture, Bradley released her, and walked from the room.   All
his soul revolted at the recent experience ; yet
mingled with his angry scepticism was a certain
vague sense of dread.   If, after all, he had not
been deceived, and something had happened
to Alma ; if, as the *séance* seemed to suggest,
she was no longer living !   The very thought
almost turned his brain.   Dazed and terrified,
he made his way down the dark passage and
left the house.

No sooner had he gone than Eustasia
uttered a low cry, threw her arms into the air,
and sank swooning upon the floor.

Her brother raised her in a moment, and placed her upon the sofa. It was some minutes before she recovered. When she did so, and gazed wildly around, there was a tiny fleck of red upon her lips, like blood.

She looked up in her brother's face, and began laughing hysterically.

' Eustasia ! For God's sake, control yourself ! You'll make yourself downright ill ! '

Presently the hysterical fit passed away.

' Leave us together, please ! ' she said to the grim woman of the house. ' I—I wish to speak to my brother.'

Directly the woman had retired, she took her brother by the hand.

' Don't be angry with me, Salem ! ' she said softly. ' I'm not long for this world now, and I want you to grant me one request.'

'What is it, Eustasia?' asked the Professor, touched by her strangely tender manner.

'Don't take me away from England just yet. Wait a little while longer.'

'Eustasia, let me repeat, you're following a will-o'-the-wisp, you are indeed! Take my advice, and never see that man again!'

'I must—I will!' she cried. 'O Salem, I've used him cruelly, but I love him! I shall die now if you take me away!'

CHAPTER XXVIII.

THE ETERNAL CITY.

In the night of the seven-hill'd city, disrobed, and uncrown'd,
    and undone,
Thou moanest, O Rizpah, Madonna, and countest the bones of
    thy son.

The bier is vacant above thee, His corpse is no longer thereon,
A wind came out of the dark, and he fell as a leaf, and is gone!

They have taken thy crown, O Rizpah, and driven thee forth
    with the swine,
But the bones of thy Son they have left thee—yea, wash them
    with tears—they are thine!

Thou moanest an old incantation, thou troublest earth with thy
    cries. . . .
Ah, God, if the bones should hear thee, and join once again,
    and arise!—*Rome: a Poem.*

As the days passed, Bradley found his state of suspense and anxiety intolerable. Day after day he had hoped to hear from Alma, until at length disappointment culminated in despair.

He then determined he should know with
certainty what had become of her, and resolved to go to Milan.

What he had seen at the *séance* had im-
pressed him more than he would admit to
himself.   He could not believe that any evil
had happened—he would not believe it without the most positive evidence of the fact.   So
he said to himself one hour, and the next his
heart grew sick with an uncontrollable dread;
and he refused to hope that the revelation of
the *séance* was a delusion.

He left his home and proceeded to the
station in the former mood, but the train had
hardly moved from the platform when his
despair seized him, and if he could he would
have relinquished the journey.   Alternating
thus between hope and despair, he travelled

without a break, and in due course he reached Milan.

His inquiries about Alma were promptly answered.

The beautiful and wealthy English lady was well known. She had, until quite recently, been the occupant of a splendid suite of apartments in the best quarter of the city ; but she had gone.

Bradley heard all this, and almost savagely he repeated after his informant, an old Italian waiter who spoke English well, the word 'Gone !'

' Gone where?' he demanded. ' You must know where she has gone to ? '

' Yes, Signor ; she has gone to Rome!'

' To Rome! And her address there is —— ? '

' That I do not know, Signor.'

'Have me taken to the house she occupied when here,' Bradley ordered; and he was driven to the house Alma had dwelt in.

There also he failed to learn Alma's address. All that was known was that she had gone to Rome; that her departure had been sudden, and that she had said she would not return to Milan.

Dismissing the carriage that had brought him, he walked back to his hotel.

It was night; the cool breeze from the Alps was delightfully refreshing after the sultry heat of the day; the moon was full and the fair old city was looking its fairest, but these things Bradley heeded not. Outward beauty he could not see, for all his mind and soul was dark— the ancient palaces, the glorious Cathedral, the splendid Carrara marble statue of Leonardo, and the bronze one of Cavour, were passed unnoticed and uncared for. One thing only was in his mind—to get to Rome to find Alma. One thing was certain : she had left Milan in good health, and must surely be safe still

'Ah !' he said to himself, 'when did she leave Milan ? Fool that I am, not to have learned,' and, almost running, he returned to the house and inquired.

He was disappointed with the information he received. Alma had left Milan some time before the *séance* in London had been held.

Entering a restaurant, he found that he could get a train to Rome at midnight. He returned to his hotel, ate a morsel of food, drank some wine, and then went to the railway station.

It was early morning when he entered the

Eternal City, and the lack of stir upon the streets troubled and depressed him. It accentuated the difference between his present visit and the last he had made, and he cried in his heart most bitterly that the burden of his sorrow was too great.

He was about to tell the driver of the fiacre to take him to his old quarters on the Piazza di Spagna, when he changed his mind. If he went there he would be in the midst of his countrymen, and in his then mood the last being he wished to see was an Englishman. So he asked the driver to take him to any quiet and good boarding-house he knew, and was taken to one in the Piazza Sta. Maria in Monti.

In the course of the day he went out to learn what he could of Alma.

He met several acquaintances, but they had neither seen nor heard of her; indeed, they were not in her circle, and though they had seen or heard of her, they would hardly have remembered. Bradley well knew the families Alma would be likely to visit, but he shrank from inquiring at their houses; he went to the doors of several and turned away without asking to be admitted.

By-and-by he went into the Caffè Nuovo, and eagerly scanned the papers, but found no mention of Alma in them. A small knot of young Englishmen and Americans sat near to him, and he thought at last that he caught the name of Miss Craik mentioned in their conversation.

He listened with painful attention, and found that they were speaking of some one the Jesuits had ' hooked,' as they put it.

'And, by Jove, it was a haul!' one young fellow said. 'Any amount of cash, I am told.'

'That is so,' replied one of his comrades; 'and the girl is wonderfully beautiful, they say.'

Bradley started at this, and listened more intently than before.

'Yes,' the first speaker said, 'she is beautiful. I had her pointed out to me in Milan, and I thought her the best-looking woman I had ever seen.'

'Excuse me,' said Bradley, stepping up to the speakers. 'I—I would like to know the name of the lady you refer to.'

'Oh, certainly; her name is Miss Alma Craik.'

'Alma living!' Bradley shrieked, and staggered, like one in drink, out of the caffè.

Dazed and half maddened, he found his way to the lodging. He locked the door of his room and paced the floor, now clenching his hands together, then holding his forehead in them as if to still its bounding pain.

' Taken by the Jesuits ! ' he muttered. ' Then she is dead indeed—ay, worse than dead ! '

He paused at length at the window and looked out. The next instant he sprang back with a look of utter horror on his face.

' What if she is over *there* ! ' he gasped, and sank into a chair.

By over there he meant the convent of the Farnesiani nuns. From the window he could see down the *cul-de-sac* that led to the convent. He knew the place well ; he knew it to be well deserving of its name, the Living Tomb, and that of its inmates it was said ' they daily die and dig their own graves.'

If Alma was indeed in there, then she was lost.

Bradley shook off as far as he could his feeling of helplessness and hopelessness, and with frenzied haste he rose from the chair, left the house, and went over towards the convent.

He knew that the only way to communicate with the inmates was to mount to a platform above the walls of the houses, and to rap on a barrel projecting from the platform. He had once been there and had been admitted. He forgot that then he had proper credentials, and that now he had none.

He was soon on the platform, and not only rapped, but thundered on the barrel.

A muffled voice from the interior demanded his business.

His reply was whether an Englishwoman named Craik was within the convent. To that question he had no answer, and the voice within did not speak again.

He stayed long and repeated his question again and again in the hope of obtaining an answer, and only left when he had attracted attention, and was invited by the police to desist.

What was to be done? he asked himself as he stood in the street. Do something he must, but what?

' I have it ! ' he said. ' I will go to the Jesuit head-quarters and demand to be informed ; ' and putting his resolve into action he walked thither.

He was courteously received, and asked his business.

'My business is a painful one,' Bradley began. 'I wish to know if an English lady named Craik has joined your church?'

'She did return to the true faith,' replied the priest, raising his eyes to heaven, 'and for her return the Holy Virgin and the Saints be praised!'

'And *now*—where is she *now?*'

With painful expectancy he waited for the priest to answer.

'Now! now, Signor, she is *dead!*' was the reply.

Bradley heard, and fell prone upon the floor.

On recovering from his swoon, Bradley found himself surrounded by several priests,

one of whom was sprinkling his face with
water, while another was beating the palms of
his hands.   Pale and trembling, he struggled
to his feet, and gazed wildly around him,
until his eyes fell upon the face of the aged
official whom he had just accosted. He endeavoured to question him again, but the little
Italian at his command seemed to have for-
saken him, and he stammered and gasped in
a kind of stupefaction.

At this moment he heard a voice accost
him in excellent English ; a softly musical voice,
full of beautiful vibrations.

'I am sorry, sir, at your indisposition.   If
you will permit me, I will conduct you back to
your hotel.'

The speaker, like his companions, had the
clean-shaven face of a priest, but his expression

was bright and good-humoured. His eyebrows were black and prominent, but his hair was white as snow.

Bradley clutched him by the arm.

' What—what does it mean ? I must have been dreaming. I came here to inquire after a dear friend—a lady; and that man told me—told me——'

' Pray calm yourself,' said the stranger gently. ' First let me take you home, and then I myself will give you whatever information you desire.'

' No ! ' cried Bradley, ' I will have the truth *now !* '

And as he faced the group of priests his eyes flashed and his hands were clenched convulsively. To his distracted gaze they seemed like evil spirits congregated for his torture and torment.

' What is it you desire to know ? ' demanded
he who had spoken in English. As he spoke
he glanced quietly at his companions, with a
significant movement of the eyebrows ; and, as
if understanding the sign, they withdrew from
the apartment, leaving himself and Bradley
quite alone.

' Pray sit down,' he continued gently, before Bradley could answer his former question.

But the other paid no attention to the
request.

' Do not trifle with me,' he cried, ' but
tell me at once what I demand to know. I
have been to the convent, seeking one who is
said to have recently joined your church—
which God forbid ! When I mentioned her
name I received no answer ; but it is common
gossip that a lady bearing her name was re-

cently taken there. You can tell me if this is true.'

The priest looked at him steadfastly, and, as it seemed, very sadly.

' Will you tell me the lady's name ? '

' She is known as Miss Alma Craik, but she has a right to another name, which she shall bear.'

' Alas ! ' said the other, with a deep sigh and a look full of infinite compassion, ' I knew the poor lady well. Perhaps, if you have been in correspondence with her, she mentioned my name—the Abbé Brest ? '

' Never,' exclaimed Bradley.

' What is it you wish to know concerning her ? I will help you as well as I can.'

' First, I wish to be assured that that man lied (though of course I *know* he lied) when he said that evil had happened to her, that—that she had died. Next, I demand to know where she is, that I may speak to her. Do not attempt to keep her from me! I *will* see her!'

The face of the Abbé seemed to harden, while his eyes retained their sad, steadfast gaze.

'Pardon me,' he said after a moment's reflection, 'and do not think that I put the question in rudeness or with any want of brotherly sympathy—but by what right do you, a stranger, solicit this information? If I give it you, I must be able to justify myself before my superiors. The lady, or, as I should rather say, our poor Sister, is, as I understand, in no way related to you by blood?'

'She is my *wife!*' answered Bradley.

It was now the other's turn to express, or

VOL. III.   L at least assume, astonishment. Uttering an incredulous exclamation, he raised his eyes to heaven, and slightly elevated his hands.

'Do you think I lie?' cried Bradley sternly. 'Do you think I lie, like those of your church, whose trade it is to do so? I tell you I have come here to claim her who is my wife, by the laws of man and God!'

Again the Abbé repeated his pantomime expressive of pitiful incredulity.

'Surely you deceive yourself,' he said. 'Miss Craik was never married. She lived unmated, and in blessed virginity was baptised into our church.'

'Where is she? Let me speak to her!' cried Bradley, with a sudden access of his old passion.

The Abbé pointed upward.

' She is with the saints of heaven ! ' he said, and crossed himself.

Again the unfortunate clergyman's head went round, and again he seemed about to fall ; but recovering himself with a shuddering effort, he clutched the priest by the arm, ex-claiming—

' Torture me no more ! You are juggling with my life, as you have done with hers. But tell me it is all false, and I will forgive you. Though you are a priest, you have at least the heart of a man. Have pity ! If what you have said is true, I am destroyed body and soul— yes, body and soul ! Have mercy upon me ! Tell me my darling is not dead ! '

The Abbé's face went white as death, and at the same moment his lustrous eyes seemed to fill with tears. Trembling violently, he took Bradley's hand, and pressed it tenderly. Then releasing him, he glanced upward and turned towards the door of the chamber.

'Stay here till I return,' he said in a low voice, and disappeared.

Half swooning, Bradley sank into a chair, covering his face with his hands. A quarter of an hour passed, and he still remained in the same position. Tears streamed from his eyes, and from time to time he moaned aloud in complete despair. Suddenly he felt a touch upon his shoulder, and looking up he again encountered the compassionate eyes of the Abbé Brest.

'Come with me!' the Abbé said.

Bradley was too lost in his own wild fears and horrible conjectures to take any particular note of the manner of the priest. Had he done

so, he would have perceived that it betrayed
no little hesitation and agitation. But he rose
eagerly, though as it were mechanically, and
followed the Abbé to the door.

A minute afterwards they were walking
side by side in the open sunshine.

To the bewildered mind of Ambrose Bradley it all seemed like a dream. The sunlight dazzled his brain so that his eyes could
scarcely see, and he was only conscious
of hurrying along through a crowd of living
ghosts.

Suddenly he stopped, tottering.

'What is the matter?' cried the Abbé,
supporting him. 'You are ill again, I fear;
let me call a carriage.'

And, suiting the action to the word, he
beckoned up a carriage which was just then

passing. By this time Bradley had recovered from his momentary faintness.

' Where are you taking me ? ' he demanded.

' Get in, and I will tell you ! ' returned the other ; and when Bradley had seated himself, he leant over to the driver and said something in a low voice.

Bradley repeated his question, while the vehicle moved slowly away.

' I am going to make inquiries,' was the reply ; ' and as an assurance of my sympathy and good faith, I have obtained permission for you to accompany me. But let me now conjure you to summon all your strength to bear the inevitable ; and let it be your comfort if, as I believe and fear, something terrible has happened, to know that there is much in this world sadder far than death.'

' I ask you once more,' said Bradley in a broken voice, ' where are you taking me ? '

' To those who can set your mind at rest, once and for ever.'

' Who are they ? '

' The Farnesiani sisters,' returned the Abbé.

Bradley sank back on his seat stupefied, with a sickening sense of horror.

The mental strain and agony were growing almost too much for him to bear. Into that brief day he had concentrated the torture of a lifetime ; and never before had he known with what utterness of despairing passion he loved the woman whom he indeed held to be, in the sight of God, his wife. With frenzied self-reproach he blamed himself for all that had taken place. Had he never consented to an ignoble deception, never gone through the mockery of a marriage ceremony with Alma, they might still have been at peace together ; legally separated for the time being, but spiritually joined for ever ; pure and sacred for each other, and for all the world. But *now*— now it seemed that he had lost her, body and soul !

The carriage presently halted, and Bradley saw at a glance that they were at the corner of the *cul-de-sac* leading to the convent. They alighted, and the Abbé paid the driver. A couple of minutes later they were standing on the platform above the walls of the houses.

All around them the bright sunshine burnt golden over the quivering roofs of Rome, and the sleepy hum of the Eternal City rolled up to them like the murmur of a summer sea.

There they stood like two black spots on

the aërial brightness; and again Bradley fell into one of those waking trances which he had of late so frequently experienced, and which he had frequently compared, in his calmer moments, to the weird seizures of the young Prince, ' blue-eyed and fair of face,' in the ' Princess.'

He moved, looked, spoke as usual, showing no outward indication of his condition; but a mist was upon his mind, and nothing was real; he seemed rather a disembodied spirit than a man; the Abbé's voice strange and far off, though clear and distinct as a bell; and when the Abbé rapped on the barrel, as he himself had done so recently, the voice that answered the summons sounded like a voice from the very grave itself.

CHAPTER XXIX.

THE NAMELESS GRAVE.

The all-beholding sun shall see no more
In all his course ; nor yet in the cold ground
Where thy pale form was laid with many tears,
Nor in the embrace of Ocean shall exist
Thy image.   Earth, that nourished thee, shall claim
Thy growth, to be resolved to earth again ;
And, lost each human trace, surrend'ring up
Thine individual being, shalt thou go
To mix for ever with the elements,
To be a brother to th' insensible rock
And to the sluggish clod.— *Thanatopsis.*

IT seemed a dream still, but a horrible sunless
dream, all that followed ; and in after years
Ambrose Bradley never remembered it without
a thrill of horror, finding it ever impossible to
disentangle the reality from illusion, or   to

separate the darkness of the visible experience from that of his own mental condition. But this, as far as he could piece the ideas together, was what he remembered.

Accompanied by the mysterious Abbé, he seemed to descend into the bowels of the earth, and to follow the figure of a veiled and sibylline figure who held a lamp. Passing through dark subterranean passages, he came to a low corridor, the walls and ceiling of which were of solid stone, and at the further end of which was a door containing an iron grating.

The priest approached the door, and said something in a low voice to some one beyond.

There was a pause; then the door revolved on its hinges, and they entered,—to find themselves in a black and vault-like chamber, the darkness of which was literally 'made visible' by one thin, spectral stream of light, trickling through an orifice in the arched ceiling.

Here they found themselves in the presence of a tall figure stoled in black, which the Abbé saluted with profound reverence. It was to all intents and purposes the figure of a woman, but the voice which responded to the priest's salutation in Italian was deep—almost—as that of a man.

'What is your errand, brother?' demanded the woman after the first formal greeting was over. As she spoke she turned her eyes on Bradley, and they shone bright and piercing through her veil.

'I come direct from the Holy Office,' answered the Abbé, 'and am deputed to inquire of you concerning one who was until recently an inmate of this sacred place,—a poor suffering Sister, who came here to find peace, consolation, and blessed rest. This English signor, who accompanies me, is deeply interested in her of whom I speak, and the Holy Office permits that you should tell him all you know.

The woman again gazed fixedly at Bradley as she replied—

' She who enters here as an inmate leaves behind her at the gate her past life, her worldly goods, her kith and kin, her very name. Death itself could not strip her more bare of all that she has been. She becomes a ghost, a shadow, a cipher. How am I to follow the fate of one whose trace in the world has disappeared ? '

' You are trifling with me ! ' cried Bradley.

' Tell me at once, is she or is she not an inmate
of this living hell?'

'Do not blaspheme!' cried the Abbé in
English, while the veiled woman crossed herself with a shudder. 'It is only in compassion
for your great anguish of mind that our blessed
Sister will help you, and such words as you are
too prone to use will not serve your cause.
Sister,' he continued in Italian, addressing the
woman, 'the English signor would not willingly
offend, though he has spoken wildly, out of the
depth of his trouble. Now listen! It is on the
record of the Holy Office that on a certain day
some few months ago an English lady, under
sanction, entered these walls and voluntarily
said farewell to the world for ever, choosing
the blessed path of a divine death-in-life to the
sins and sorrows of an existence which was

surely life-in-death. The name she once bore,
and the date on which she entered the convent, are written down on this paper. Please
read them, and then perhaps you will be able
to guide us in our search.'

So saying, the Abbé handed to the woman
a folded piece of paper. She took it quietly,
and, stepping slowly to the part of the chamber
which was lit by the beam of chilly sunshine,
opened the paper and appeared to read the
writing upon it. As she did so, the dim and
doubtful radiance fell upon her, and showed
through the black but semi-transparent veil the
dim outline of a livid human face.

Leaving the chamber, she approached a
large vaulted archway at its inner end, and
beckoned to the two men. Without a word
they followed.

Still full of the wild sense of unreality, like a man walking or groping his way in a land of ghosts, Bradley walked on. Passing along a dismal stone corridor, where, at every step he took,

> **He dragged**
> **Foot-echoes after him !**

past passage after passage of vaulted stone, dimly conscious as he went of low doors opening into the gloomiest of cells, he hurried in the wake of his veiled guide. Was it only his distempered fancy, or did he indeed hear, from time to time, the sound of low wailings and dreary ululations proceeding from the darkness on every side of him ? Once, as they crossed an open space dimly lit by dreary shafts of daylight, he saw a figure in sable weeds, on hands and knees, with her lips pressed close against the stone pavement ; but at a word from his guide the figure rose with a feeble moan and fluttered away down a corridor into the surrounding darkness.

At last they seemed to pass from darkness into partial sunshine, and Bradley found himself standing in the open air. On every side, and high as the eye could reach, rose gloomy walls with overhanging caves and buttresses, leaving only one narrow space above where the blue of heaven was dimly seen. There was a flutter of wings, and the shadows of a flight of birds passed overhead—doves which made their home in the gloomy recesses of the roofs and walls.

Beneath was a sort of quadrangle, some twenty feet square, covered with grass, which for the most part grew knee-deep, interspersed

M

with nettles and gloomy weeds, and which was in other places stunted and decayed, as if withered by some hideous mildew or blight. Here and there there was a rude wooden cross stuck into the earth, and indicating what looked to the eye like a neglected grave.

The Sister led the way through the long undergrowth, till she reached the side of a mound on which the grass had scarcely grown at all, and on which was set one of those coarse crosses.

'You ask me what has become of the poor penitent you seek. She died in the holy faith, and her mortal body is buried *here*.'

With a wild shriek Bradley fell on his knees, and tearing the cross from the earth read the inscription rudely carved upon it :—

'SISTER ALMA.

Obiit 18—.'

That was all. Bradley gazed at the cross in utter agony and desolation; then shrieking again aloud, fell forward on his face. The faint light from the far-off blue crept down over him, and over the two black figures, who gazed in wonder upon him; and thus for a long time he lost the sense of life and time, and lay as if dead.

CHAPTER XXX.

IN PARIS.

Lay a garland on my hearse,
　Of the dismal yew ;
Maidens, willow gardens bear ;
　Say I dièd true.

My love was false, but I was firm
　From my hour of birth ;
Upon my buried body lie
　Lightly, gentle earth.—*The Maid's Tragedy.*

PROFESSOR MAPLELEAFE speedily saw that to oppose his sister would be inopportune—might perhaps even cause her decline and death. He determined therefore to humour her, and to delay for a short time their proposed return to America.

'Look here, Eustasia,' he said to her one day, ' I find I've got something to do in Paris; you shall come with me. Perhaps the change there may bring you back to your old self again. Anyhow we'll try it; for if this goes on much longer you'll die!'

' No, Salem, I shan't die till I've seen *him* again!' she answered, with a faint forced smile.

They set about making their preparations at once, and were soon on their way to Paris. The movement and change had given colour to Eustasia's cheeks, and brought a pleasurable light of excitement into her eyes, so that already her brother's spirits were raised.

'She'll forget him,' he said to himself, ' and we'll be what we were before he came !'

But in this Salem was mistaken. Eustasia

was not likely to forget Bradley. Indeed, it was the thought of seeing him again that seemed to give new life to her rapidly wasting frame. She knew that he had left England ; she thought that, like herself, he might be travelling to get rid of his own distracting thoughts ; so wherever she went she looked about her to try and catch a glimpse of his face.

They fixed themselves in Paris, and Salem soon dropped into the old life. He fell amongst some kindred spirits, and the *séances* began again ; Eustasia taking part in them to please her brother, but no more. She was utterly changed ; each day as it rolled away seemed to take with it a part of her life, until her wasted frame became almost as etherealised as those of the spirits with whom she had dealt so much.

With constant nursing and brooding upon, her fascination for the Englishman increased ; it seemed, indeed, to be the one thing which kept her thin thread of life from finally breaking.

' If I could see him again,' she murmured to herself, ' only once again, and then (as Salem says) die ! '

The wish of her heart was destined to be realised : she did at least see Bradley once again.

She was sitting at home one day alone, when the door of the room opened, and more like a spectre than a man he walked in.

At the first glimpse of his face Eustasia uttered a wild cry and staggered a few steps forward, as if about to throw herself into his arms ; but suddenly she controlled herself, and sank half swooning into a chair.

'You have come!' she said at length, raising her eyes wistfully to his; 'you have come at last!'

He did not answer, but kept his eyes fixed upon hers with a look which made her shudder.

'How—how did you find me?' she asked faintly.

'I came to Paris, and by accident I heard of you,' he answered in a hollow voice.

Again there was silence. Bradley kept his eyes fixed upon the sibyl with a look which thrilled her to the soul. There was something about him which she could not understand; something which made her fear him. Looking at him more closely, she saw that he was curiously changed; his eyes were sunken and hollow; and though they were fixed upon her they seemed to be looking at something far away; his hair, too, had turned quite grey.

She rose from her seat, approached him, and gently laid her hand upon his arm.

'Mr. Bradley,' she said, 'what is it?'

He passed his hand across his brow as if to dispel a dream, and looked at her curiously.

'Eustasia,' he said, using for the first time her Christian name, 'speak the truth to me to-day; tell me, is all this real?'

'Is what real?' she asked, trembling. His presence made her faint, and the sound of her name, as he had spoken it, rang continually in her ears.

'Is it not all a lie? Tell me that what you have done once you can do again; that you can bring me once more into the presence of the spirit of her I love!'

'Of her you love?' said the girl, fixing her large eyes wistfully upon his face. 'What —what do you want me to do?'

'Prove that it is not all a lie and a cheat: if you are a true woman, as I trust, I want you to bring back to me the spirit of my darling who is dead!'

She shrank for a moment from him, a sickening feeling of despair clouding all her senses; then she bowed her head.

'When will you come?' she said.

'To-night.'

Eustasia sank into her chair, and, without another word, Bradley departed.

At seven o'clock that night Bradley returned, and found the sibyl waiting for him.

She was quite alone. Since the morning her manner had completely changed; her hands were trembling, her cheek was flushed, but there was a look of strange determination about her lips and in her eyes. Bradley shook hands with her, then looked around as if expecting others.

She smiled curiously.

'We are to be alone!' she said—'quite alone. I thought it better for you!'

For some time she made no attempt to move; at length, noticing Bradley's impatience, she said quietly—

'We will begin.'

She rose and placed herself opposite Bradley, and fixed her eyes intently upon him. Then, at her request, he turned down the gas; they were in almost total darkness touching hands.

For some time after Bradley sat in a

strange dream, scarcely conscious of anything
that was taking place, and touching the outstretched hands of Eustasia with his own.

Suddenly a soft voice close to his ear murmured,—

'Ambrose, my love!'

He started from his chair, and gazed wildly
about him. He could see nothing, but he
could feel something stirring close to him.
Then he staggered back like a drunken man,
and fell back in his chair.

'Alma!' he cried piteously, still conscious
of the medium's trembling hands, 'Alma, my
darling, come to me!'

For a moment there was silence, and
Bradley could hear the beating of his heart.
Then he became conscious of a soft hand
upon his head; of lips that seemed to him like

warm human lips pressed against his fore-head.

Gasping and trembling he cried—

'Alma, speak; is it *you?*'

The same soft voice answered him—

'Yes, it is I!'

The hand passed again softly over his head and around his neck, and a pair of lips rich and warm were pressed passionately against his own. Half mad with excitement, Bradley threw one arm around the figure he felt to be near him, sprang to his feet while it struggled to disengage itself, turned up the light, and gazed full into the eyes of—Eustasia Maple-leafe.

Never till his dying day did Bradley forget the expression of the face which the sibyl now turned towards his own, while, half crouching, half struggling, she tried to free herself from the grip of his powerful arms; for though the cheeks were pale as death, the eyes wildly dilated, they expressed no terror—rather a mad and reckless desperation. The mask had quite fallen; any attempt at further disguise would have been sheer waste of force and time, and Eustasia stood revealed once and for all as a cunning and dangerous trickster, a serpent of miserable deceit.

Yet she did not quail. She looked at the man boldly, and presently, seeing he continued to regard her steadfastly, as if lost in horrified wonder, she gave vent to her characteristic, scarcely audible, crooning laugh.

A thrill of horror went through him, as if he were under the spell of something diabolic.

For a moment he felt impelled to seize her by the throat and strangle her, or to savagely dash her to the ground. Conquering the impulse, he held her still as in a vice, until at last he found a voice—

'Then you have lied to me? It has all been a lie from the beginning?'

'Let me go,' she panted, 'and I will answer you!'

'Answer me *now*,' he said between his set teeth.

But the sibyl was not made of the sort of stuff to be conquered by intimidation. A fierce look came into her wonderful eyes, and her lips were closely compressed together.

'Speak—or I may kill you!' he cried.

'Kill me, then!' she answered. 'Guess I don't care!'

There was something in the wild face
which mastered him in spite of himself. His
hands relaxed, his arms sank useless at his
side, and he uttered a deep despairing groan.
Simultaneously she sprang to her feet, and
stood looking down at him.

' Why did you break the conditions? ' she
asked in a low voice. ' The spirits won't be
trifled with in that way, and they'll never forgive you, or me ; never.'

He made no sign that he heard her, but
stood moveless, his head sunk between his
shoulders, his eyes fixed upon the ground.
Struck by the sudden change in him, she
moved towards him, and was about to touch
him on the shoulder, when he rose, still white
as death, and faced her once more.

' Do not touch me ! ' he cried.   ' Do not

touch me, and do not, if you have a vestige of goodness left within you, try to torture me again. But look me in the face, and answer me, if you can, truly, remembering it is the last time we shall ever meet. When you have told me the truth, I shall leave this place, never to return; shall leave *you*, never to look upon your face again. Tell me the truth, woman, and I will try to forgive you; it will be very hard, but I will try. I know I have been your dupe from the beginning, and that what I have seen and heard has been only a treacherous mirage called up by an adventuress and her accomplices. Is it not so? Speak! Let me have the truth from your own lips.'

'I can't tell,' answered Eustasia coldly. 'If you mean that my brother and I have conspired to deceive you, it is a falsehood.

We are simply agents in the hands of higher agencies than ours.'

'Once more, cease that jargon,' cried Bradley; 'the time has long past for its use. Will you confess, before we part for ever? You will not? Then good-bye, and God forgive you.'

So saying he moved towards the door; but with a sharp, bird-like cry she called him back.

'Stay! you must not go!'

He turned again towards her.

'Then will you be honest with me? It is the last and only thing I shall ask of you.'

'I—I will try,' she answered in a broken voice.

'You will!'

'Yes; if you will listen to me patiently.'

She sank into a chair, and covered her face with her hands. He stood watching her, and saw that her thin, white, trembling fingers were wet with tears.

' Promise,' she said, ' that what I am about to say to you shall never be told to any other living soul.'

' I promise.'

' Not even to my brother.'

' Not even to *him.*'

There was a long pause, during which he waited impatiently for her to continue. At last, conquering her agitation, she uncovered her face, and motioned to a chair opposite to her ; he obeyed her almost mechanically, and sat down. She looked long and wistfully at him, and sighed several times as if in pain.

' Salem says I shan't live long,' she mur-

mured thoughtfully.   ' To-night, more than
ever, I felt like dying.'

She paused and waited as if expecting him
to speak, but he was silent.

' Guess *you* don't care if I live or die?' she
added piteously, more like a sick child than a
grown woman—and waited again.

' I think I do care,' he answered sadly, ' for
in spite of all the anguish you have caused me,
I am sorry for you.   But I am not myself, not
the man you once knew.   All my soul is set
upon one quest, and I care for nothing more in
all the world.   I used to believe there was a
God ; that there was a life after death ; that
if those who loved each other parted here,
they might meet again elsewhere.   In my
despair and doubt, I thought that you could
give me assurance and heavenly hope ; and I

clutched at the shadows you summoned up before me. I know now how unreal they were; I know now that you were playing tricks upon my miserable soul.'

She listened to him, and when he ceased began to cry again.

'I never meant any harm to *you*,' she sobbed! 'I—I loved you too well.'

'You loved me!' he echoed in amaze.

She nodded quickly, glancing at him with her keen wild eyes.

'Yes, Mr. Bradley. When Salem first took me to hear you preach, you seemed like the spirit of a man I once loved, and who once loved me. He's dead now, he is; died over there in the States, years ago. Well, afterwards, when I saw you again, I began to make believe to myself that you were that very man,

and that he was living again in you. You
think me crazy, don't you? Ah well, you'll
think me crazier when you hear all the rest.
I soon found out all about you ; it wasn't very
hard, and our people have ways of learning
things you'd never guess. I didn't look far till
I found out your secret ; that you loved another
woman, I mean. That made me care for you
all the more.'

Her manner now was quite simple and
matter-of-fact. Her face was quite tearless,
and, with hands folded in her lap, she sat
quietly looking into his face. He listened in
sheer stupefaction. Until that moment no
suspicion of the truth had ever flashed upon
his mind. As Eustasia spoke, her features
seemed to become elfin-like and old, with a
set expression of dreary and incurable pain ;

but she made her avowal without the slightest indication of shame or self-reproach, though her manner, from time to time, was that of one pleading for sympathy and pity.

She continued—

'You don't understand me yet, and I guess you never will. I'm not a European, and I haven't been brought up like other girls. I don't seem ever to have been quite young. I grew friends with the spirits when I wasn't old enough to understand, and they seem to have stolen my right heart away, and put another in its place.'

'Why do you speak of such things as if they were real? You know the whole thing is a trick and a lie.'

'No, I don't,' she answered quickly. 'I'm not denying that I've played tricks with *them*,

just as they've played tricks with *me;* but
they're downright real—they are indeed.
First mother used to come to me, when I was
very little; then others, and in after-days I
saw *him;* yes, after he was dead. Then sometimes, when they wouldn't come, Salem helped
out the manifestations, that's all.'

'For God's sake, be honest with me!' cried
Bradley. 'Confess that all these things are
simple imposture. That photograph of yourself, for example—do you remember?—the
picture your brother left in my room, and
which faded away when I breathed upon it?'

She nodded her head again, and laughed
strangely.

'It was a man out West that taught Salem
how to do that,' she replied naïvely.

'Then it was a trick, as I suspected?'

'Yes, I guess that was a trick. It was something they used in fixing the likeness, which made it grow invisible after it had been a certain time in contact with the atmospheric air.'

Bradley uttered an impatient exclamation.

'And all the rest was of a piece with that! Well, I could have forgiven you everything but having personified one who is now lost to me for ever.'

'I never did. I suppose you *wished* to see her, and she came to you out of the spirit-land.'

'*Now* you are lying to me again.'

'Don't you think I'm lying,' was the answer; 'for its gospel-truth I'm telling you. I'm not so bad as you think me, not half so bad.'

Again shrinking from her, he looked at her with anger and loathing.

' The device was exposed to-day,' he said sternly. ' You spoke to me with her voice, and when I turned up the light I found that I was holding in my arms no spirit, but yourself.'

' Well, I'm not denying that's true,' she answered with another laugh. ' Something came over me—I don't know how it happened —and then, all at one, I was kissing you, and I had broken the conditions.'

By this time Bradley's brain had cleared, and he was better able to grasp the horrible reality of the situation. It was quite clear to him that the sibyl was either an utter impostor, or a person whose mental faculties were darkened by fitful clouds of insanity. What

startled and horrified him most of all was the
utter want of maidenly shame, the curious and
weird sang-froid, with which she made her
extraordinary confession. Her frankness, so
far as it went, was something terrible—or, as
the Scotch express it, ' uncanny.' Across his
recollection, as he looked and listened, came
the thought of one of these mysterious sibyls,
familiar to mediæval superstition, who come
into the world with all the outward form and
beauty of women, but without a Soul, but who
might gain a spiritual existence in some mysterious way by absorbing the souls of men.
The idea was a ghastly one, in harmony with
his distempered fancy, and he could not shake
it away.

' Tell me,' said Eustasia gently, ' tell me
one thing, now I have told you so much. Is

that poor lady dead indeed—I mean the lady you used to love?'

The question went into his heart like a knife, and with livid face he rose to his feet.

'Do not speak of her!' he cried. 'I cannot bear it—it is blasphemy! Miserable woman, do you think that you will ever be forgiven for tampering, as you have done, with the terrible truth of death? I came to you in the last despairing hope that among all the phantoms you have conjured up before me there might be some reality; for I was blind and mad, and scarcely knew what I did. If it is any satisfaction to you, know that you have turned the world into a tomb for me, and destroyed my last faint ray of faith in a living God. In my misery, I clung to the thought of your spirit world; and I came to you for some fresh assurance that such a world might be. All that is over now. It is a cheat and a fraud like all the rest.'

With these words he left her, passing quickly from the room. Directly afterwards she heard the street door close behind him. Tottering to the window, she looked down in the street, and saw him stalk rapidly by, his white face set hard as granite, his eyes looking steadily before him, fixed on vacancy. As he disappeared, she uttered a low cry of pain, and placed her hand upon her heart.

CHAPTER XXXI.

AMONG THE MOUNTAINS.

Give me thy hand, terrestrial; so! Give me thy hand,
celestial; so !—*Merry Wives of Windsor.*

IT was the close of a bright sunshiny day in
the spring of 18—. The sun was setting
crimson on the lonely peak of the Zugspitz
in the heart of the Bavarian Highlands, and
the shadows of the pine woods which fringed
the melancholy gorges beneath were lengthen-
ing towards the valleys.

Through one of these mountain gorges,
following a rocky footpath, a man was rapidly

walking. He was roughly, almost rudely, dressed in a sort of tourist suit. On his head he wore a broadbrimmed felt hat of the shape frequently worn by clergymen, and in his hand he carried a staff like a shepherd's crook.

Scarcely looking to left or right, but hastening with impatient paces he hurried onward, less like a man hastening to some eagerly-sought shelter, than like one flying from some hated thing behind his back. His cheeks were pale and sunken, his eyes wild and sad. From time to time he slackened his speed, and looked wearily around him—up to the desolate sunlit peaks, down the darkening valley with its green pastures, belts of woodland, and fields of growing corn.

But whichever way he looked, he seemed

to find no joy in the prospect, indeed hardly
to behold the thing he looked on, but to gaze
through it and beyond it on some sorrowful
portent.

Sometimes where the path became unusually
steep and dangerous, he sprang from rock to
rock with reckless haste, or when its thread
was broken, as frequently happened by some
brawling mountain stream, he entered the
torrent without hesitation, and passed reck-
lessly across.   Indeed, the man seemed utterly
indifferent to physical conditions, but labouring
rather under some spiritual possession, completely and literally realising in his person the
words of the poet:

> His own mind did like a tempest strong
> Come to him thus, and drave the weary wight along.

The wild scene was in complete harmony

with his condition. It was still and desolate, no sound seeming to break its solemn silence; but pausing and listening intently, one would in reality have become conscious of many sounds—the deep under-murmur of the mountain streams, the 'sough' of the wind in the pine woods, the faint tinkling of goat-bells from the distant valleys, the solitary cry of rock doves from the mountain caves.

The man was Ambrose Bradley.

Nearly a year had elapsed since his sad experience in Rome. Since that time he had wandered hither and thither like another Ahasuerus; wishing for death, yet unable to die; burthened with the terrible weight of his own sin and self-reproach, and finding no resting-place in all the world.

Long before, as the reader well knows, the

man's faith in the supernatural had faded. He had refined away his creed till it had wasted away of its own inanition, and when the hour of trial came and he could have called upon it for consolation, he was horrified to find that it was a corpse, instead of a living thing. Then, in his horror and despair, he had clutched at the straw of spiritualism, only to sink lower and lower in the bitter waters of Marah. He found no hope for his soul, no foothold for his feet. He had, to use his own expression, lost the world.

It was now close upon night-time, and every moment the gorges along which he was passing grew darker and darker.

Through the red smokes of sunset one lustrous star was just becoming visible on the extremest peak of the mountain chain. But instead of walking faster, Bradley began to linger, and presently, coming to a gloomy chasm which seemed to make further progress dangerous, impossible, he halted and looked down. The trunk of an uprooted pine-tree lay close to the chasm's brink. After looking quietly round him, he sat down, pulled out a common wooden pipe, and began to smoke.

Presently he pulled out a letter bearing the Munich post-mark, and with a face as dark as night began to look it through. It was dated from London, and ran as follows:

' Reform Club, *March 5,* 18——.

'My dear Bradley,—Your brief note duly reached me, and I have duly carried out your wishes with regard to the affairs of the new church. I have also seen Sir George Craik, and found him more amenable to reason than

I expected. Though he still regards you with the intensest animosity, he has sense enough to perceive that you are not directly responsible for the unhappy affair at Rome. His thoughts seem now chiefly bent on recovering his niece's property from the clutches of the Italian Jesuits, and in exposing the method by which they acquired such dominion over the unhappy lady's mind.

'But I will not speak of this further at present, knowing the anguish it must bring you. I will turn rather to the mere abstract matter of your letter, and frankly open my mind to you on the subject.

'What you say is very brief, but, from the manner in which it recurs in your correspondence, I am sure it represents the absorbing topic of your thoughts. Summed up in a few words, it affirms your conclusion that all human effort is impossible to a man in your position, where the belief in personal immortality is gone.

'Now I need not go over the old ground, with which you are quite as familiar as myself. I will not remind you of the folly and the selfishness (from one point of view) of formulating a moral creed out of what, in reality, is merely the hereditary instinct of self-preservation. I will not repeat to you that it is nobler, after all, to live impersonally in the beautiful future of Humanity than to exist personally in a heaven of introspective dreams. But I should like, if you will permit me, to point out that this Death, this cessation of consciousness, which you dread so much, is not in itself an unmixed evil. True, just at present, in the sharpness of your bereavement, you see nothing but the shadow, and would eagerly follow into its oblivion the shape of her you mourn. But as every day passes, this desire to die will grow less keen; and ten years hence, perhaps, or twenty years, you will look back upon to-day's anguish with a calm, sweet sense of spiritual gain, and with a peaceful sense of the sufficiency of life. Then, perhaps, embracing a creed akin to ours, and having reached a period when the physical frame begins slowly, and without pain, to melt away, you will be quite content to accept—what shall I say?—Nirwâna.

'What I mean, my dear friend, is this, simply: that Death is only evil when it comes painfully or prematurely; coming in the natural order of things, in the inevitable decay of Nature, it is by no means evil. And so much is this the case that, if you were to discover the consensus of opinion among the old, who are on the threshold of the grave, you would find the majority quite content that life should end for ever. Tired out with eighty or a hundred years of living, they gladly welcome sleep. It is otherwise, of course, with the victims of accidental disease or premature decay. But in the happy world to which we Positivists look forward, these victims would not exist.

'Day by day Science, which you despise too much, is enlarging the area of human health. Think what has been done, even within the last decade, to abolish both physical and social disease! Think what has yet to be done to make life freer, purer, safer, happier!

I grant you the millennium of the Grand Être is still far off; but it is most surely coming, and we can all aid, more or less, that blessed consummation—not by idle wailing, by useless dreams, or by selfish striving after an impossible personal reward, but by duty punctually performed, by self-sacrifice cheerfully undergone, by daily and nightly endeavours to ameliorate the condition of Man.

' Men perish ; Man is imperishable. Personal forms change ; the great living personality abides. And the time must come at last when Man shall be as God, certain of his destiny, and knowing good and evil.

' " A Job's comforter ! " I seem to hear you cry. Well, after all, you must be your own physician.

> No man can save another's soul,
> Or pay another's debt !

But I wish that you, in your distracted wandering after certainty, would turn your thoughts *our* way, and try to understand what the great Founder of our system has done, and will do, for the human race. I am sure that the study would bring you comfort, late or soon.

  ' I am, as ever, my dear Bradley,

   ' Your friend and well-wisher,

    ' JOHN CHOLMONDELEY.

 ' P.S.—What are you doing in Munich ? I hear of curious doings this year at Ober-Ammergau, where that ghastly business, the Passion Play, is once more in course of preparation.'

 Bradley read this characteristic epistle with a gloomy frown, which changed before he had finished to a look of bitter contempt ; and, as he read, he seemed once more conscious of the babble of literary club-land, and the affected jargon of the new creeds of the future. Returning the letter to his pocket, he continued to smoke till it was almost too dark to see the wreaths of fume from his own pipe.

The night had completely fallen before he rose and proceeded on his way.

CHAPTER XXXII.

ANOTHER OLD LETTER.

Love! if thy destined sacrifice am I,
　Come, slay thy victim, and prepare thy fires;
Plunged in thy depths of mercy let me die
　The death which every soul that lives desires.
Madame Guyon.

'I AM writing these lines in my bedroom in the house of the Widow Gran, in the village of Ober-Ammergau. They are the last you will receive from me for a long time; perhaps the last I shall ever send you, for more and more, as each day advances, I feel that my business with the world is done.

'What brought me hither I know not. I

am sure it was with no direct intention of witnessing what so many deem a mere mummery or outrage on religion; but after many wanderings hither and thither, I found myself in the neighbourhood, and whether instinctively or of set purpose, approaching this lonely place.

'As I have more than once told you, I have of late, ever since my past trouble, been subject to a kind of waking nightmare, in which all natural appearances have assumed a strange unreality, as of shapes seen in dreams; and one characteristic of these seizures has been a curious sense within my own mind that, vivid as such appearances seemed, I should *remember* nothing of them on actually *awaking*. A wise physician would shake his head and murmur " diseased cerebration;" nor would his diagnosis of my condition be less gloomy, on learning that my physical powers remain unimpaired, and seem absolutely incapable of fatigue. I eat and drink little ; sleep less ; yet I have the strength of an athlete still, or so it seems.

'I walked hither across the mountains, having no other shelter for several nights than the boughs of the pine-woods where I slept. The weather was far from warm, yet I felt no cold ; the paths were dangerous, yet no evil befell me. If I must speak the truth, I would gladly have perished—by cold, by accident, by any swift and sudden means.

'But when a man thirsts and hungers for death, Death, in its dull perversity, generally spares him. More than once, among these dizzy precipices and black ravines, I thought of suicide ; one step would have done it, one quick downward leap; but I was spared that last degradation—indeed, I know not how.

'It was night time when I left the mountains, and came out upon the public road. The moon rose, pale and ghostly, dimly lighting my way.

'Full of my own miserable phantasy, I walked on for hours and descended at last to the outlying houses of a silent village, lying at the foot of a low chain of melancholy hills. All was still; a thin white mist filled the air, floating upward from the valley, and forming thick vaporous clouds around the moon. Dimly I discerned the shadows of the houses, but in none of the windows was there any light.

'I stood hesitating, not knowing which way to direct my footsteps or at which cottage door to knock and seek shelter, and never, at any moment of my recent experience, was the sense of phantasy and unreality so full upon me. While I was thus hesitating I suddenly became conscious of the sound of voices coming from a small cottage situated on the roadside, and hitherto scarcely discernible in the darkness. Without hesitation I approached the door and knocked.

'Immediately the voices ceased, and the moment afterwards the door opened and a figure appeared on the threshold.

' If the sense of unreality had been strong before it now became paramount, for the figure I beheld wore a white priestly robe quaintly embroidered with gold, and a golden head-dress or coronet upon his head. Nor was this all. The large apartment behind him—a kind

of kitchen, with rude benches around the ingle
—was lit by several lamps, and within it were
clustered a fantastic group of figures in white
tunics, plumed head-dresses of Eastern device,
and mantles of azure, crimson, and blue, which
swept the ground.

' " Who is there ? " said the form on the
threshold in a deep voice, and speaking German
in a strong Bavarian patois.

' I answered that I was an Englishman, and
sought a night's shelter.

' " Come in ! " said the man, and thus invited I crossed the threshold.

' As the door closed behind me, I found
myself in the large raftered chamber, surrounded on every side by curious faces.
Scattered here and there about the room were
rudely-carved figures, for the most part repre-

senting the Crucifixion, many of them un-
finished, and on a table near the window was a
set of carver's tools. Rudely coloured pictures,
all of biblical subjects, were placed here and
there upon the walls, and over the fireplace
hung a large Christ in ebony, coarsely carven.

'Courteously enough the fantastic group
parted and made way for me, while one of the
number, a woman, invited me to a seat beside
the hearth.

'I sat down like one in a dream, and
accosted the man who had invited me to enter.

' " What place is this ? " I asked. " I have
been walking all night and am doubtful where
I am."

' " You are at Ober-Ammergau ! " was the
reply.

'I could have laughed had my spirit been

less oppressed. For now, my brain clearing, I began to understand what had befallen me. I remembered the Passion Play and all that I had read concerning it. The fantastic figures I beheld were those of some of the actors still attired in the tinsel robes they wore upon the stage.

'I asked if this was so, and was answered in the affirmative.

' "We begin the play to-morrow," said the man who had first spoken. "I am Johann Diener the *Chorführer*, and these are some of the members of our chorus. We are up late, you see, preparing for to-morrow, and trying on the new robes that have just been sent to us from Annheim. The pastor of the village was here till a few minutes ago, seeing all things justly ordered amongst us, and he would gladly have welcomed you, for he loves the English."

'The man's speech was gentle, his manner kindly in the extreme, but I scarcely heeded him, although I knew now what the figures around me were—the merest supernumeraries and chorus-singers of a tawdry show. They seemed to me none the less ghostly and un- real, shadows acting in some grim farce of death.

'"Doubtless the gentleman is fatigued," said a woman, addressing Johann Diener, "and would wish to go to rest."

'I nodded wearily. Diener, however, seemed in some perplexity.

'"It is not so easy," he returned, "to find the gentleman a shelter. As you all know, the village is overcrowded with strangers. However, if he will follow me, I will take him to Joseph Mair, and see what can be done."

'I thanked him, and without staying to alter his dress, he led the way to the door.

'We were soon out in the open street. Passing several châlets, Diener at last reached one standing a little way from the roadside, and knocked.

'"Come in," cried a clear kind voice.

'He opened the door and I followed him into an interior much resembling the one we had just quitted, but smaller, and more full of tokens of the woodcutter's trade. The room was dimly lit by an oil lamp swinging from the ceiling. Seated close to the fireplace, with his back towards us, engaged in some nandy work, was a man.

'As we entered the man rose and stood

looking towards us. I started in wonder, and uttered an involuntary cry.

'It was Jesus Christ, Jesus the son of Joseph, in his habit as he lived !

'I had no time, and indeed I lacked the power, to separate the true from the false in this singular manifestation. I saw before me, scarce believing what I saw, the Christ of History, clad as the shape is clad in the famous fresco of Leonardo, but looking at me with a face mobile, gentle, beautiful, benign. At the same moment I perceived, scarcely understanding its significance, the very crown of thorns, of which so many a martyr since has dreamed. It was lying on the coarse table close to a number of wood-carving tools, and close to it was a plate of some red pigment, with which it had recently been stained.

'Johann Diener advanced.

' " I am glad to find you up, Joseph. This English gentleman seeks shelter for the night, and I scarcely knew whither to take him."

' " You will not find a bed in the place," returned the other; and he continued addressing me. " Since this morning our little village has been overrun, and many strangers have to camp out in the open air. Never has Ober-Ammergau been so thronged."

' I scarcely listened to him; I was so lost in contemplation of the awful personality he represented.

' " Who are you ? " I asked, gazing at him in amaze.

' He smiled, and glanced down at his dress.

' " I am Joseph Mair," he replied. " To-morrow I play the Christus, and as you came

I was repairing some portion of the attire, which I have not worn for ten years past."

'Jesus of Nazareth! Joseph Mair! I understood all clearly now, but none the less did I tremble with a sickening sense of awe.

'That night I remained in the house of Joseph Mair, sitting on a bench in the ingle, half dying, half dreaming, till daylight came. Mair himself soon left me, after having set before me some simple refreshment, of which I did not care to partake. Alone in that chamber, I sat like a haunted man, almost credulous that I had seen the Christ indeed.

'I *have* seen him! I understand now all the piteous humble pageant! I have beheld the Master as He lived and died; not the creature of a poet's dream, not the Divine Ideal I pictured in my blind and shadowy creed; but Jesus who perished on Calvary, Jesus the Martyr of the World.

' All day long, from dawn to sunset, I sat in my place, watching the mysterious show. Words might faintly foreshadow to you what I beheld, but all words would fail to tell you what I felt; for never before, till these simple children of the mountains pictured it before me, had I realised the full sadness and rapture of that celestial Life. How faint, miserable, and unprofitable seemed my former creed, seen in the light of the tremendous Reality foreshadowed on that stage, with the mountains closing behind it, the blue heaven bending tranquilly above it, the birds singing on the branches round about, the wind and sunshine shining over it and bringing thither all the gentle motion of the world. Now for the first time I conceived that the Divine Story was not a poet's dream, but a simple tale of sooth, a living experience which even the lowliest could understand and before which the highest and wisest must reverently bow.

'I seem to see your look of wonder, and hear your cry of pitying pain. Is the man mad? you ask. Is it possible that sorrow has so weakened his brain that he can be overcome by such a summer cloud as the *Passionspiel* of a few rude peasants—a piece of mummery only worthy of a smile! Well, so it is, or seems. I tell you this " poor show " has done for me what all intellectual and moral effort has failed to do—it has brought me face to face with the living God.

'This at least I know, that there is no *via media* between the full acceptance of Christ's miraculous life and death, and acquiescence in the stark materialism of the new creed of scientific experience, whose most potent word is the godless Nirwâna of Schopenhauer.

'Man cannot live by the shadowy gods of men—by the poetic spectre of a Divine Ideal, by the Christ of Fancy and of Poesy, by the Jesus of the dilettante, by the Messiah of a fairy tale. Such gods may do for happy hours; their ghostliness becomes apparent in times of spiritual despair and gloom.

' " Except a man be born again, he shall not enter the kingdom of Heaven ! " I have heard these divine words from the lips of one who seemed the Lord himself; nay, who perchance *was* that very Lord, putting on again the likeness of a poor peasant's humanity, and clothing himself with flesh as with a garment. I have seen and heard with a child's eyes, a child's ears ; and even as a child, I question no longer but believe.

'*Mea culpa ! mea culpa !* In the light of that piteous martyrdom I review the great sin of my life ; but out of sin and its penalty has come transfiguration. I know now that my beloved one was taken from me in mercy, that I might follow in penitence and love. Patience, my darling, for I shall come ;—God grant that it may be soon ! '

CONCLUSION.

THE following letter, written in the summer of 18—, by John Cholmondeley to Sir George Craik, contains all that remains to be told concerning the fate of Ambrose Bradley, some-time minister of Fensea, and a seceder from the Church of England :—

' My dear Sir,—You will remember our conversation, when we last met in London, concerning that friend of mine with whose fortunes those of your lamented niece have been unhappily interwoven. Your language was then sufficiently bitter and unforgiving. Perhaps you will think more gently on the subject when you hear the news I have now to convey to you. The Rev. Ambrose Bradley died a fortnight ago, at Ober-Ammergau, in the Bavarian highlands.

'From time to time, during his wanderings in the course of the past year, we had been in correspondence; for, indeed, I was about the only friend in the world with whom he was on terms of close intimacy. Ever since the disappearance of Miss Craik his sufferings had been most acute ; and my own impression is that his intellect was permanently weakened. But that, perhaps, is neither here nor there.

'Some ten days ago, I received a com munication from the village priest of Ober-Ammergau, informing me that an Englishman had died very suddenly and mysteriously in the village, and that the only clue to his friends and connexions was a long letter found upon his person, addressed to me, at my residence in the Temple. I immediately hastened over to Germany, and found, as I had anticipated, that the corpse was that of my poor friend. It was lying ready for interment in the cottage of Joseph Mair, a wood-carver, and a leading actor in the Passion Play.

'I found, on inquiry, that Mr. Bradley had been in the village for several weeks, lodging at Mair's cottage, and dividing his time between constant attendance at the theatre, whenever the Passion Play was re-presented, and long pedestrian excursions among the mountains. He was strangely taciturn, indifferent to ordinary comforts, eating little or nothing, and scarcely sleeping. So at least the man Mair informed me, adding that he was very gentle and harmless, and to all intents and purposes in perfect health.

' Last Sunday week he attended the theatre as usual. That night he did not return to the cottage of his host. Early next morning, Joseph Mair, on going down to the theatre with his tools, to do some carpenter's work upon the stage, found the dead body of a man there, lying on his face, with his arms clasped around the mimic Cross; and turning the dead face up to the morning light, he recognised my poor friend.

' That is all I have to tell you. His death, like his life, was a sad affair. I followed him to his grave in the little burial-place of Ober-Ammergau—where he rests in peace. I am, &c.,

'JOHN CHOLMONDELEY.

' Judging from some talk I had before leaving with the village priest, a worthy old fellow who knew him well, I believe poor Bradley died in full belief of the Christian faith ; but as I have already hinted to you, his intellect, for a long time before his death, was greatly weakened. Take him for all in all, he was one of the best men I ever knew, and might have been happy but for the unfortunate " set " of his mind towards retrograde superstitions.'

THE END.

LONDON : PRINTED BY
SPOTTISWOODE AND CO., NEW-STREET SQUARE
AND PARLIAMENT STREET